TRAVEL
LIGHT

Jilly Chadwick

**BLUE
ORMER**

2021

*For my daughter Emily, a strong, brave,
woman who inspires me to be the best version
of myself and for Joyce who taught us both
the meaning of being strong.*

Storms make trees take deeper roots.

Dolly Parton

Jesse Bailey had sought the warm sunshine, turquoise seas and solitude of Antigua when her heart was broken and her life fell to pieces. Her solution was to head off to a beachside mansion at Jolly Beach with three strangers who, like herself, needed some time out.

Now in the quiet backwater of Jolly Harbour with its laidback lifestyle and beach front mansions, trendy bars, millionaires and bored spouses, Jesse Bailey has created a haven for them to get their lives on track. But life is not all that it seems in this blissful community, where having it all seems to come as standard.

The Lady Magazine, personal column

Girl Power Caribbean Style!
Join me for a month or two at Jolly Harbour and rediscover the real you!
Are you stuck in a career rut? Has someone in your life let you down or do you simply need to run away to the Caribbean for a reset and some much-needed time out?
I am looking for some adventurous spirits to join me on a holiday with a difference, to share the cost of a luxury villa right on the beach, have some fun, and perhaps find the strength and will to get their lives back on track. If any of the above sounds like you, then please email me and sign up for a trip of a lifetime!
Jesse Bailey

Two weeks later Jesse had her posse organised and she was amazed at how many women out there were keen to take up the invitation.

The group of four she had finally selected were meeting at Gatwick for the mid-morning Virgin Atlantic Flight to Antigua. Strangers with a variety of reasons for wanting an escape route for a few weeks. Three emails, and she had received many of them, had touched her and had stood out from the rest. It was clear the group would be an interesting one and she was certain there would be fun along the way.

Re: I need time out! It feels weird being so open with a stranger, but your ad somehow called to me. I feel it important to be honest about why I need to escape for a while. A month ago, my husband came home and while he has been violent to me in the past, I knew that this time he really wanted to hurt me. I just need some head space and time to breathe! I have no idea of my next move, but I do know I need some time away to decide what to do next. Above all I just feel so diminished and embarrassed to admit to putting up with the life I have for so long.

I have finally found the strength to leave this man and the idea of going back to him is unthinkable. I need to get strong and find me again so a few weeks away in the sun is absolutely what I need. I promise I am usually upbeat and easy going. I used to be fun, I know I will be again and I love to cook. I also make a mean mojito. Fingers crossed you feel able to count me in!
Regards, Gina Davies.

Re ...
Dear Jesse,
'My mother spotted your ad and called me yesterday to beg me to reply. I am in a bit of a mess as I recently discovered that my husband was having an affair. The worst part is that the woman he was seeing was my so-called best friend.
It's felt like such a double betrayal. I am left feeling worthless and so stupid for not realising what was going on. I desperately need some time out to hide away for a while and get my head together. I would be so grateful if you would let me come. I will enjoy cooking for everyone, though of late I have been eating so much I feel like a beached whale! But enjoying the sunshine and peace and meeting a few new people may be just what I need to give me some perspective to be able to move forward. I know you would prefer an eight-week commitment, but I am happy to pay for the two-month rental and only stay for a month. I have an eight-year-old daughter, so I am not sure about leaving her for that long. Why is it that you can reach out to complete strangers and just blurt out your deepest most painful secrets? Even my best friends don't know as much as you do right now!
I look forward to hearing from you and I will start looking for a swimsuit just in case.
Claire Ryder

Hi Jesse

I am not going to pretend; women groups are not normally my thing, but I need some time out and feel that the Caribbean hideaway and some space with people who don't know me is the answer. I am researching a book about women and relationships so joining a girly group would be great. I have forgotten how important it is to have some female support. I have also experienced a few drastic life-changing incidents that I am struggling with and a far-flung hideaway may be just what I need. They tell me that life in Antigua is chilled out so all in all, it seems like the place for me. It could be fun. I warn you that I enjoy my privacy so don't expect me to pour my heart out, but I have a great ear for a problem and am detached enough to be able to give good advice. I don't judge, I love cleaning and tidying up! Am I in?

best

Anna Smith

Jesse had countless emails from women keen to join her Antiguan jaunt, but those three emails stood out and her choice was made. Each of them seemed to be in a bad place and they had been so upfront and honest.

She suspected it was going to be an interesting trip and it was anyone's guess if the group would gel, but from what she had read what did any of them have to lose?

One by one Jesse emailed the women and confirmed that yes, they were indeed in! Let the adventures begin.

THE BEGINNING

THE SIMPLE ADVERTISEMENT PLACED in a discreet but very tasteful semi display box in the personal column of *The Lady* magazine was really meant as a bit of an experiment.

Jesse Bailey had booked her waterfront villa on a whim. It was a two-month rental, a luxurious five bedroom des res with an infinity pool overlooking the sweep of the bay, and a five-minute walk to the nearest cocktail bar. One of her clients owned the place and only rented it out to people she knew and trusted. When Jesse discovered the man she had fallen so in love with was about to marry someone else, she knew it was the place she needed to run to.

Jesse knew she should hate him, but she couldn't. Worse still she was sure that if she did not get far enough away, if he called her, she would cave in and go back for more.

In any event the wedding was about to happen, and she could not bear the idea of it. So she hit on the idea of advertising for a few kindred spirits to join her in the luxury rental she had drooled over so many times.

They could share the cost of the villa, drink lots of cocktails and maybe she could get her head straight. She had never done anything so spontaneous and downright crazy before, but maybe she would meet some new much-needed girl mates to help take the pain away.

The group she assembled was a mixed bunch, but life was about to get very interesting for them all as fate stepped in to help them find new lives – and perhaps love in a Caribbean paradise.

GINA

GINA DAVIES SAT AT her kitchen table quietly examining the welts around her wrists. The angry red bands were still painful but she simply pulled down the sleeves of her pale blue cashmere sweater and shivered. She recalled the fight which had ended with her husband grabbing her arms and twisting the flesh on her wrists until they were burning hot and sore. It was a warm sunny day and she was worried that once again she would have to wear a long-sleeved shirt to the office. A couple of times lately she had gone in with a bruise on her face and a cut under her eye and she knew that people were becoming suspicious about what was going on at home.

'I am so clumsy, James is always telling me off for it. I bump into cupboards and trip on steps. He is convinced that one day I will break my neck if I am not more careful!' she would say, laughing off her latest mishap. Once he had punched her in the face and had broken a front tooth. That day she had phoned in sick. Her lip was cut and swollen and she didn't have the heart to lie her way through it. That incident seemed to make him a bit more discerning about where he landed his blows. Bruises on her back and arms could be covered up, he knew that. But no matter how traumatic the beatings and verbal onslaughts were, it was the emotional damage he caused that left the deepest scars. She was continually left feeling worthless and in despair. Gina felt powerless to stop him and incapable of finding a way out. He always made her feel responsible for his violent outbursts and he would insist she was the reason he felt so angry.

Countless times he would tell her she was pathetic and stupid. Most days she agreed with him.

Tears sprung in her eyes as she remembered the night before when he had mocked her and grabbed at her until hot tears fell over her cheeks. As usual there was no warning before his outburst. She had not said or done anything to justify his terrible anger and as usual, he had made her believe that she had brought it upon herself.

She looked at the man she had loved so deeply and found it hard to recognise the kind, handsome, charmer who had seemed to want her and need her. He had wooed and won her quickly, then over a matter of months he had taken control of her life. Within a year he had cut her off from all her friends and most of her family.

'We don't need anyone, we have each other, you are all I need,' he would whisper to her softly. Slowly she changed her whole life to please him. She no longer met friends and rarely went home to see her family. At the beginning of their relationship, it was because she was so giddily in love with James and would rush home every day to be with him. Weekends were spent walking, talking, or staying in bed all day making love. He would cook her favourite foods and woo her with champagne and candlelit baths.

She counted herself the luckiest girl in the world and would look at her dark-haired husband and almost had to pinch herself to believe she had found her soul mate. The fact that he was so attractive and exuded a sexy brooding presence at times made her tummy turn over. How lucky was she?

Later as they approached their second wedding anniversary, he became withdrawn and she became aware of a moody controlling side to his character. She was no longer allowed to meet friends and family visits at weekends were frowned upon. If he knew she was planning to go to her parents for Sunday lunch he would sulk and not speak to her. It became easier to simply make lame excuses and not go. Afterwork drinks, nights out with the girls or family barbeques were also a no-no. It was not worth enduring his black moods and angry silences. Once she had relented and cancelled her arrangements, he would reward her with affectionate cuddles and smiles. But it began to grate on her. She realised she was being controlled.

She knew her family were aware that something was wrong, but she tried hard to convince them that all was well between her and James. But her pathetic efforts to look happy did not always work and she felt powerless to talk about how miserable she really was.

She would often think back to the time she had met James and wondered if there had been signs she had missed that would have warned her to keep clear of this violent and troubled man.

She had not even liked him when she met him. She was hosting a charity dinner for some out-of-town clients and he was playing in the band at the hotel. The other musicians were larger than life, outgoing and loud; he seemed quiet and a bit shy.

While he made it clear that he did not want to get involved in the event and had brushed off her attempts to get him to join them all for drinks, by the end of the party James was smitten with her. Though she had not known that then.

Gina felt drawn to him as she watched him pack up his gear and make a point of steering clear of the other band members. They were in a rush to start chatting up the women who had made a beeline for them at the bar. He was clearly not interested.

James disappeared and Gina felt a strange sadness that she had missed out on talking to him. However as she headed out of the ballroom, she had found him playing an old upright piano in an adjoining room, away from the ears and eyes of the crowds. He had looked so sad that she wanted to wrap her arms around him.

Suddenly noticing her behind him, he beckoned her over. 'This one is for you,' he said simply. It was a corny Elton John classic from way back, but it became their song. He fixed her with sad haunted eyes and she was lost.

Tall and rangy, strangely detached and awkward around other people, he was not her usual type. Gina's boyfriends were usually strapping rugby lads who were fun and noisy and filled her parents' home with banter and laughter. James was withdrawn and quiet and from the start he made her family feel slightly ill at ease. He felt uncomfortable around strangers he would say, and he hated and avoided talking about himself or his past. She was drawn to him and gradually stopped including friends in their plans. He was not a party animal, he hated crowds and he was far happier simply being with Gina. She became increasingly distant from her friends and family and while at times she missed the easy-going life she had enjoyed, being with James more than made up for this. He would change, she knew she could help him and they could become part of the gang again. They would one day see him as she did, a wonderful warm man who just needed time and a lot of love to heal his past. He was so attentive and kind when they were alone, but when they met her friends he refused to engage with anyone and was offish and dismissive.

Everyone was silently a bit worried about Gina and her new man and as the months went by fewer and fewer of her friends bothered to include them in their regular parties and Sunday brunches.

'Give him a chance Mum, he's just different, he's not cold or unkind and he loves me,' she would say when her mother questioned his preference in keeping Gina to himself.

She had changed from the happy-go-lucky girl who was the first to join in picnics in the park and Sunday lunchtime pub sessions, to a quiet shadowy figure who had vanished from their social lives.

The family stayed silent about their concerns but they all noticed how Gina was becoming increasingly withdrawn and anxious on the rare occasions she dropped by to see them.

In the early days James had almost broken Gina's heart as he gently confided in her about his disrupted childhood with a mother and father constantly at war. He spoke of fights, tantrums, terrible tense silences and awful mealtimes where his mother would sit white faced and stressed with bruised eyes and cut lips.

One day his mother simply walked out on them. He had been put into care for a while, and Gina's heart ached as he told her of his feelings of loss and sadness at losing his mum. Two years later, again with no explanations, his mother returned home so the family was brought together again.

Nothing was ever mentioned about her having left or where she had gone, but the family unit was never the same and the household was not a happy one.

James had briefly mentioned that he had a younger sister but that he had lost touch with her. He refused to be drawn on any details of why they were estranged.

After talking about those painful times, he never spoke of his mother or father again. Gina had no idea if they were dead or alive, and all he would say was that he had no feelings either way. That part of his life was over. He would insist he was perfectly happy with his life and Gina was all the family he needed. He wanted nobody else in their lives and that sadly seemed to include Gina's parents. He never said so directly but his intentions were made very clear.

She suspected he had never forgiven his mother for abandoning him and, in some warped way, he envied Gina's close-knit unit where she was obviously adored. He would be dismissive about family life and any mention of his past would cause a black angry shadow to cross his face. It was easier to say nothing. Some days he would sit in silence, refusing to eat or talk. It made her heart melt, but she felt that given time, she could help him heal his wounds and show him the love he had never been shown as a child. She truly believed he could be different and despite her family's insistence that she should wait to know him a bit better, they were living together within months.

As time went on, he made no effort to make friends or let her family into his life. While Gina was worried about how her life was changing, she was at a loss to do anything about it.

When they were married with a simple civil ceremony attended only by her parents, Gina thought her new husband would finally relax and loosen what was becoming a worrying grip on her. But he demanded even more of her time and attention. Wordlessly he managed to convince her that it was his right to treat her as his possession.

Gina still felt she could make him change and decided the best way to do this was to make him the centre of her world. Her friends, she rationalised, would one day come back into their circle. But James gradually became more withdrawn, with frequent and quite sudden angry outbursts. He seemed to despise the attention she now gave him. She was at a loss to know what was going on in his head.

Gina was now constantly anxious around him, dreading going home to face him, never knowing what she could say or do to please him. She had ignored the awful truth for so long but finally she had realised that she was in an abusive relationship.

Scared and ashamed, and blaming herself for letting this happen to her, she didn't have the energy to get away, Gina would wake up in the middle of the night in a blind panic. She wanted out and knew she couldn't save him. It was time to save herself, but how to even begin that process?

Her best friend Ruth had finally spoken out when she called around and found Gina crying after yet another angry scene.

'Men like him never change, you have to face up to the fact that he wants to rule your life and keep you away from us.' She implored her to rethink the relationship and to leave, if only to get some perspective. But Gina felt powerless. She had always thought of herself as strong, but that Gina seemed a million miles away.

James made ridiculous rules about what she did, how she dressed and where she went but she had no energy to challenge him on any of it. James would flip at the smallest thing.

His tastes were minimal and cold and she had not been allowed to fill their home with warm throws, candles or lamps. He berated her for having bad taste. He liked things glossy and modern, there was to be no clutter and bit by bit she lost her will to even try to make the home the warm haven she so craved.

The house had to be clean, calm and organised and she also knew never to give him the smallest reason to get angry with her. He came home one day to find their laundry folded and airing on their heated Aga rail and it sent him into a terrible rage. 'You can't even manage to launder my shirts properly so please don't bother in future.' He left the house for hours and he hardly spoke to her for the next two days.

She would look in the mirror and not recognise the woman staring back at her. Gone was the shiny, swinging highlighted hair. Her sexy wrap dresses and sharp tailored suits were also a thing of the past. She took the term dressing down to an all-time low. Her wardrobe now looked as bleak as her life, black and grey and very dull.

He would berate her for what she wore and on rare nights out she would agonise over what outfit to choose. If she dared put on a dress he hated she knew that their night out would be spoiled. He would be distant and scathing. More than once he had ignored her throughout a whole evening because he had not approved of what she was wearing.

So, she played it safe, never stood out from the crowd or dressed up too much. Her hair was also under constant scrutiny and one day when she arrived home excited to show off her new hairstyle, a blunt bob that sat just beneath her chin, he slammed out of the house saying it made her look ancient.

All the joy of the new style, which everyone in the salon had raved over, was gone. How could she live her life like this?

She hated herself for being so weak and needy. Everything about their relationship was wrong on so many levels.

Time had shown her that Ruth had been so right. James was a control freak, a classic narcissist, but how was she to fight that? She had to live life on his terms and put up with his constant put downs. He needed her on the down low so that he could feel good about himself. She knew it but she had lost sight of the strong woman she had been and had no idea how to break free.

Gina had little if any self-respect and her self-esteem was almost non-existent. All she felt was shame. The emotional abuse was bad enough but she had never feared that he would physically hurt her.

Then one day, not long after they had moved into their new home, James flew into a violent rage and slammed out of the house. There was no reason for his ill temper, she had prepared his favourite meal and had looked forward to a quiet evening. But he'd had a row with his boss, something he seemed to do regularly, and was stressed and refused to eat anything. He said he hated her dress and was furious that she would dare to go to her office wearing something so revealing. She looked at her plain grey shift dress and for once stood up for herself and told him he was being stupid. He threw a plate across the room and slammed out shouting that she was a whore, and he would make her pay later.

By the time he came back Gina had cleared up the kitchen and was calm, quietly suggested that they should talk things through. James fixed her with a look that she had never seen before, grabbed her by the hair and threw her to the floor. He kicked her and calmly helped himself to a sandwich as if nothing had happened.

She heard the door slam followed by the sound of him driving out onto the road. She felt as though she was in some weird dreamlike state. Could this have just happened?

Shocked, she made her way up to bed and lay there for hours, afraid to move.

Gina would often look back to that day and realise that this was the moment she should have walked away. James had crossed a line and she should have gone home and told her family what had happened. She felt ashamed that she had allowed herself to get into this state and she had hoped it would never happen again. She just couldn't bring herself to say the words. 'My husband is violent and abusive.'

One evening as she served his dinner, he threw down his napkin and aimed the plate at her head.

Food splattered all over the floor and as she bent to clear it, he aimed a punch at her head.

'You are pathetic and ugly. Just looking at you brings me down, it's no wonder I hate coming home. What happened to the intelligent woman I married?'

There was no reason for his outburst. Tearfully she stared at the man she loved so much and didn't recognise him.

The spittle caught at the corners of his mouth as he spat his words at her and she felt the bile rise in her throat as he forced her to the floor, his hands holding her wrists while he kicked her feet from under her causing her to fall onto her back.

He aimed kicks at her abdomen and legs and all she could do was cry out in pain and beg him to stop as he slapped her face repeatedly.

Her cheeks were on fire and she felt a sticky trail of blood fall from a gash across her right eye.

As suddenly as his temper had flared, it ended. He left the room and stormed out of the house. As she heard his car speed out of the driveway, she put a shaking hand up to her face and tried to stand up. A wave of nausea hit and she had to lay back down on the floor where she rolled into a ball of misery.

'This time is the last time, it has to be,' she chanted in her head. But this was the same hollow promise she always made. After laying on the kitchen floor for what seemed like hours, she finally managed to stand up and stagger to the bedroom where she pulled out a canvas holdall, she had packed days ago. It was small but it contained the few things she would need to get away fast. A change of clothes, her passport and a few toiletries. After double checking her passport was there, she zipped it up and headed for the door.

Catching a glance of her bruised and bloodied face she knew finally it was time to leave him. Today she would tell her family what was happening, and they would help her.

Going back to get her coat and keys she saw his car headlights through the glass door.

Terrified she ran back up to the bedroom and threw off her clothes, her heart pounding out of her chest. She felt weak and pathetic and powerless to do anything but lay in her bed and wonder if he was right, perhaps she had brought this upon herself. The signs were there, why had she not woken up sooner and walked away.

Sliding under the duvet she waited for him to climb the stairs. She just prayed that he would sleep in the guest room as he usually did after one of his freak-outs. Next time she would leave, she had to.

CLAIRE

CLAIRE COULD REMEMBER THE exact moment that she had fallen in lust with Richard Ryder.

She had been driving to pick up her daughter Harriet from school and as usual she was running late because she had left work a bit too late. A mile down the road the car veered onto the hard shoulder and her heart sank as she got out of the car to discover she had a puncture. Groaning and reaching for her mobile telephone, Claire steeled herself to ring the snooty school secretary. She dreaded having to ask her to keep hold of Harriet for a little while until she could sort out a lift, the woman was always so rude and dismissive. A minute later Richard had tapped on her side window and offered to help.

He had the most amazing blue eyes and the kind of wide smile which left you breathless. He heard her garbled story, realised how urgent the school run was and insisted on driving Claire to school right away. He then deposited her at home and headed back to fix her tyre.

'Let me pinch you to make sure you are for real!' she teased. But he simply flashed another boyish grin which made her stomach do back flips.

'You can buy the ice cream when we go on a picnic with Harriet,' he said; an invitation which set her pulse racing.

He had seemed too good to be true, and now, looking back, that was exactly what he had been. He drove off to complete his rescue mission and Claire watched, smiling to herself and thinking that perhaps life could be happy again.

Men like Richard never crossed her path and at that moment she thought he was everything she looked for in a man. He was tall with an athletic build and he carried himself in a way that showed he was comfortable in his skin. He was easy going and kind and Claire could tell that something exciting had happened from the first moment he gave her that mega-watt smile.

Claire had been widowed, leaving her with a toddler when she was just 30. Stevie, the soulmate whom she had married when she was just 20, had died at the wheel of his car in a motorway pile up. She had never expected to get over the loss and pain of his death. But six years down the line this handsome stranger had literally walked into her life and won her heart and made her his own. Yes, she had reasoned, it had all happened so fast but then when something is right, why not?

Some of her friends had cautioned her to take it slowly. She had only ever had one boyfriend, that being Stevie, so her experience of men was limited. She was such a trusting soul that her friends were a bit concerned at the speed at which this man had become her partner. Quietly her closest friends and her parents had been a bit worried. Claire was a lovely girl, but they simply didn't see her and Richard as a couple. Stevie had been so quiet and gentle and adored his young wife who shared his love of the simple things in life. They spent hours in their garden, enjoyed walking and simply being together. Richard was a brash go-getter who drove fast cars and liked the high life. They wondered how the two would manage to come to a compromise. But Claire was starry eyed and was certain that her new partner was just perfect for her. She had grieved her husband and now she decided the time had come to live again. She didn't seem to worry about Richard's love of going out to pubs and clubs and his need to be constantly spending money on fancy restaurants and trips away. At first, she tried to keep up with his racy lifestyle and he would often surprise her with trips to the theatre or exciting weekends away. But Harriet was fretting about Claire's frequent absences, and she began to feel under pressure to always fall in with his last-minute plans.

Richard never consulted her about these trips or appreciated the fact that she had a young child to look after. She would make half-hearted attempts to get him to realise that she had to put Harriet first but he wasn't having any of it.

'That's what grandparents are for,' he would say and turn that smile on full blast and she would melt. Of course, she reasoned, he was right, they were in love and they deserved some time away. He would settle down eventually and as he said, Harriet did enjoy spending time with her grandparents.

Within weeks of meeting, they were inseparable and a year later they were married and Richard had moved into Claire's beautiful cottage. It was a dream property that she and Stevie had worked so hard to renovate. While Claire could hardly believe her luck that such a handsome, vibrant man wanted her as his wife, her family remained worried about how different he was.

Claire was so in love she could not see anything but the rosy future he had promised her. She wanted to share every part of his life and was delighted that he was so happy and relaxed about simply slotting into her home. She loved him for this and decided that finally her luck had changed. He appeared to be content to be a stepfather to Harriet though he was far from a hands-on parent.

From the start of their relationship Richard would not be drawn to talk about his own family.

'You never talk about your past.' she would tell him, but Richard was adamant that he had no significant past.

'I have always been a lone wolf but that ends with you and I am so lucky to have found you,' he would tell her, and that was enough.

'You are my future and that's what counts,' he assured her. She was more than happy to hear this and didn't bother to dig any deeper. They were blissfully happy, a great match and that was all that mattered. She was in love with a vibrant, handsome man who admittedly was a bit wild and unpredictable, but that made him even more exciting in her book.

What really counted was they loved each other with a passion, and she just felt so very lucky to have found him.

OK, so at times Richard was a bit closed about his finances, and he didn't seem very keen on contributing to the household bills, but she let that slip. He more than made up for this with wonderful nights out and thoughtful gifts.

But as they were preparing for their second anniversary Claire detected a few slight changes in the way her husband treated her. Small things that one day simply added up to the fact that the honeymoon period seemed to be well and truly over.

They had always enjoyed a great sex life but lately he would say he was too tired or too stressed to make love. He ridiculed her if she tried to make the first move in the bedroom and he would often make excuses to sleep in the spare room.

'I'm restless and I don't want to disturb you,' was his latest excuse for leaving her to sleep alone. She knew that their physical connection had gone, even though he would get angry and deny it when she tried to bring the subject up. 'Will you just get off my case, you drive me mad when you get all needy. I am not like a bloody machine, sometimes I just want a break. Leave it won't you.'

Those conversations, or variations of them, become more and more frequent and Claire realised that the more she broached the subject of their non-existent sex life, the more she drove him away.

He was right, she was too clingy and of course he needed his space.

Her solace became the cookie jar and dipping into Harriet's treats which were kept in the large Neptune pantry that Claire used to store all her special jars of preserves and spices. It used to be a joke between her and Stevie that when she had the blues, he would always find her rummaging around in that cupboard looking for chocolate. The thought of her life with Stevie, who could make her feel safe and loved with a single smile, caused her eyes to fill and big, sad tears slid slowly down her face.

She was not a woman who indulged in self-pity and she was angry that she allowed these silly thoughts to invade her head space. It was hard not to compare her easy-going first husband to her second, who lately made her feel like a thorn in his side.

When she and Richard had first married, she was so contented and felt very secure with her new husband. Every day she would clean the house and arranged the flowers she had grown in her cottage garden in jugs and glass vases. She cooked amazing meals for him to enjoy when he came home. She knew it was all a bit old fashioned, but she and Richard enjoyed sitting at the large, scrubbed farmhouse table in the massive kitchen with the wood burner ablaze talking about their days.

Before Stevie died, they had added a huge wooden framed garden room extension to the kitchen and the mix of warm stone walls and grey painted timbers was a stunning combination. They installed a beautiful hand painted kitchen and Stevie insisted on buying her a pale blue Aga which she had admired for years and had dreamed of owning. When he died her love for the house had seemed to die with him. When Richard came into her life it reignited and she went once again to her favourite auction houses to seek out treasures to be taken home and loved.

On one of these trips, she had found an enormous wooden sleigh bed and she could hardly believe her luck when she bid for it and got it at a ridiculously low price.

She spent weeks in the garage, sanding it down and lovingly painting it in her favourite shade of dove grey. It became the centrepiece of her new bedroom and she bought crisp, white bedding and added piles of silk print cushions. She had to admit the effect was stunning. At night after dinner, Richard would lead her upstairs, lay her on the bed and they would enjoy making love for hours. Afterwards he would talk about the things he loved about her and they would make plans for the life they would have together.

There was an old granite barn at the bottom of the garden and they were thinking of converting it into a two-bedroom unit they could rent out. Their village was beautiful and quite near to the South coast and Claire dreamed of how she would paint the walls and furnish the rooms. She liked the idea of welcoming people to her home, playing host and making sure they were comfortable. She was a home maker and a nurturer; she couldn't help herself. Richard said it was one of the things he loved about her.

She had never felt so loved or desired and she could hardly believe how lucky she was to have found love for a second time. Her new husband was so kind and he couldn't get enough of her.

Those days were long gone and she couldn't fathom how they had come to this. At night she slept right at the very edge of the bed, afraid to even touch him, she wondered what had gone so wrong. She could not recall exactly when things changed but he had become increasingly distant and the silliest things irritated him. Just weeks ago, they had been out shopping in the supermarket and she had slipped a cheesecake into the trolley. He gave her a dark, angry look and made a snide comment about her no longer caring about her weight. She had been shocked and hurt and told him so. Richard just stormed out of the supermarket and made his own way home leaving her upset and mystified at what she had experienced.

She began to get odd phone calls late at night or sometimes very early in the morning. Nobody ever spoke to her, but she could swear that she could detect someone's presence. She suspected it was a woman, listening, but fear and pride kept her from asking any questions. She was too terrified of what she may hear.

Claire would often confide in Martha, her best friend, and ask her if she thought there was a possibility that Richard was having an affair. The classic signs were pointing that way.

'Why else would he stop wanting to have sex with me? And he never walks around the bedroom naked anymore. He even rushes to cover up when I walk into the shower room.'

To begin with Martha would sympathise and insist that Claire was overthinking things.

'You have it all wrong, he's probably just a bit stressed at work and it will pass. Look, he adores you, he has since he met you,' Martha reasoned. 'It can't always be a chapter out of Mills and Boon, cut the guy some slack. You have had a two-year honeymoon, don't be greedy. Marriage is like that, you know it is,' Martha consoled her.

But that was the problem, Claire did not know that! When Stevie was with her, they were always on the same page. He loved her and she felt secure with him. They had their differences, but he never made her feel bad about herself. They were lovers, but they were best friends too and she never remembered feeling ignored or lacking in any way. Richard did not seem to care about her anymore and she was struggling to ignore his silences and his indifference in the bedroom and out of it.

But Martha was insistent that Claire was overreacting. 'Face it Claire, Richard is a gorgeous love god, and you are so lucky to have him.'

She advised Claire to put up and shut up, whatever was wrong would blow over and she should ride out this bad patch. He was worth it.

Claire was a bit put out to say the least. Previously she could have relied upon Martha to be in her team, but she let it pass. It was clear that Richard had Martha in his thrall too, he had that effect on women, so maybe she should stop whingeing, take Martha's advice, and just let things blow over.

What else could she do? She could not comprehend a life without Richard. Claire felt a chill pass through her when she thought about losing him. No, she would join a slimming club, lose some weight, and maybe look at joining the Zumba fitness group in the village hall. She knew she needed to feel better about herself and maybe this cloud of suspicion would lift. Maybe she had simply fallen into the trap of becoming a bit dull. That extra stone or two was not helping her morale and she felt listless, drab and overweight. It was no wonder Richard had lost interest in her. She had lost interest in herself. Martha was right. It was all in her head, she had to sort herself out and the rest would follow. Richard loved her, of course he did.

But things did not improve, far from it. As the weeks went on Richard seemed to shut her out even more and he avoided being alone with Claire whenever he could. He would criticise her cooking, the way she looked and bit by bit Claire felt her confidence simply disappear.

She would wake up every day feeling sad and weighed down. If it hadn't been for Harriet needing to be taken to school and cared for, there were days when she would have simply stayed in bed.

What was wrong with her? She began to think that she had never been good enough for him. She knew he hated it that she was a little curvier of late. She had always been curvy, and she embraced that, but she had become listless and could not be bothered to move out of the house. She had become a bit complacent and their marriage seemed to be in a rut, but she could change things. She would start that exercise regime, get fitter, start feeling happier in her skin and maybe buy new clothes. There must be a way to get Richard to notice her. She would do it!

But despite her best efforts over the next few months, Claire could not stick to a healthy eating plan or manage to make the Zumba classes in the village hall. She had tried to go once, but when she looked at her reflection, as she stood in front of the floor to ceiling mirrors, the sight of herself in skin-tight leggings and a grey baggy vest made her wince. Her legs looked like thick shapeless sausages and the unforgiving Lycra clung to every roll of fat around her waist.

She rushed home and broke into a sweat simply pulling off the hated exercise garb. She stood under the shower feeling increasingly miserable and resigned to being trapped in this heavy dumpy body. She put on a loose kimono, pulled her hair into a ponytail and took a pot of tea and a packet of digestives out into the garden.

She resolved to become even more of an earth mother. She would cook all Richard's favourite meals, keep the house compulsively clean and tidy and make sure she had his drink at the ready when he walked through the door.

She spent hours looking through Delia Smith's finest comfort food favourites and Jamie Oliver's trendy new recipes which took about two minutes to rustle up but looked incredible. However, Richard's response was to complain that she was trying to make him fat. If she made a move on him in the bedroom, he would get mad and accuse her of being demanding and not appreciating how tired he was. She felt diminished but was still determined to get their marriage on track, so she took another route.

She had thought about asking Martha for some advice, but she realised that was out of the question. She would think she was being ridiculous.

After Googling tips on how to revive a flagging sex life she had invested in a red lace body suit and killer black heels. The article that caught her eye suggested buying sexy underwear and stockings could make all the difference in the bedroom. She had to admit that her Bridget Jones style stretch briefs were hardly a turn on and she was desperate to do something!

She struggled into the outfit when it arrived, looking decidedly dodgy in a discreet brown parcel. Even the postman had seemed to give her a wry grin as he waited for her to sign for the package. Later, standing in the mirror, she looked at her reflection and once again she felt appalled and ridiculous. She felt like one of those women you see standing in windows in the Red-Light district of Amsterdam. Fat, slutty and utterly hideous! Richard would just laugh at her, or worse still, feel pity at her pathetic attempt at looking seductive.

Sweating and berating herself, she threw the outfit and shoes into the bin. She thought of the amount of money she had wasted but the bin was the only place she could rid herself of this evidence. Blushing and giggling to herself she imagined what the reaction would have been if she had popped into the Red Cross charity shop and donated the outfit to them!

Most nights Claire had to contend with Richard's insistence that there was no need to wait up for him. She got into the habit of going upstairs hours before he did. She tried to go to sleep and leave her misery behind, but his indifference in the bedroom was becoming unbearable.

On the odd occasion she did stay awake until he came to bed, he would stay far away from her and go to sleep within minutes. Sometimes she suspected that he was not asleep at all and she would inch toward him, just to feel close. But he would never respond and she would shrink back to her own side. She felt like a boring old hag. She retreated more and more into herself and felt so miserable it was becoming harder and harder to even find the energy to get Harriet to school.

Claire knew too that although she used to be described by her friends as a sexy Nigella Lawson lookalike, she was now a shapeless blob. She dressed to hide the added pounds, well stones, but she knew she looked drab. Her once long lustrous hair was lank, and her skin no longer had the luminous bloom she had been so proud of.

Claire toyed with the idea of seeing her doctor. Maybe she was going mad, or perhaps she was depressed and needed to go back on those pills they had given her when Stevie died. The anti-depressants had helped her and eventually she had begun to feel a bit better. With her doctor's help she gently came off the medication and felt pleased that she found natural ways of feeling more positive about life. She had learned to look at the good things she had to be grateful for and to seek simple pleasures to occupy her time. Friends helped her find new interests to bring her out of her gloom and she loved creating a fabulous home and a newly replanted garden. But this time it was different, there did not seem to be a way out of her gloom and the man who was causing it was oblivious of the pain he was causing her. Or worse still he did not care.

There would be no happy pills she decided, a deep-rooted strength screamed this was not the path to take this time. This man was not worth that. But she accepted that at some point she had to face whatever it was head on and deal with it.

She would get up in the morning and look in the bathroom mirror and see dark shadows under her eyes. Her sparkle had gone and she felt disgusted with herself as she smoothed her hands over her lumpy hips and bulging waistline. She looked and felt terrible and most days she didn't blame her husband for not fancying her or wanting to make love to her. She felt disgusting and ugly and a lot of the time she wished she were dead.

Then one day the fog that had threatened to engulf her cleared slightly and a few things started to make sense.

The text message came out of nowhere and while she felt afraid and her heart sank, there was a tiny part of her that felt vaguely relieved. The misery and confusion clouding her head began to clear a little, and certain things began to fall into place. Maybe she was not wholly to blame for what was going on at home after all. If what the text said was true this realisation was a bittersweet one as it meant accepting the ultimate betrayal involving two people she loved dearly.

Ask Richard about Martha

was all it said but her heart plummeted, and she felt sick. She didn't recognise the number and felt too afraid to call up to see who the message was from. It did not change the fact that someone was pushing her to maybe address what she should have seen a long time ago. When she looked back at recent months and the times the three of them had spent time together, she should have heard warning shots.

Was something going on between Richard and Martha? Had she been so blind and stupid that her best friend and her husband had been betraying her, right under her nose? She cringed as she thought of all the times she had confided in Martha, sharing very intimate details about their lack of a love life.

She tried to picture the pair of them together and she groaned out loud and banged the steering wheel. Had he really been having an affair with the one person she most trusted? Was this the reason why Richard was no longer interested in her? It was unthinkable and yet, she had to admit there had been a lot of strange changes in the relationship between her and Martha of late and an affair suddenly made sense of it all.

Martha had not been so open with Claire, and at times had seemed strangely dismissive. Claire now felt angry that she had almost done backflips to get their friendship back to where it had been. In recent weeks she had helped her clear out her wardrobe. When she had failed to get a promotion, Claire had taken her for lunch to cheer her up and treated her to a Jo Malone candle and body oil. Surely Martha, her best friend of more than 10 years, would never betray her by seeing Richard behind her back? Or would she?

Claire pulled over and put her head onto the steering wheel and mentally processed their last conversation.

Martha had just headed off to a workshop event in Cornwall and Claire had agreed to feed her cat while she was away. Only yesterday she had set off early to help Martha to pack. Claire had salivated over the new clothes Martha had bought but her friend had seemed a bit embarrassed when Claire had admired a slinky black satin nightgown studded with crystals. It was slashed seductively to reveal her long tanned thighs and the mesh panels left nothing to the imagination. Claire had raised her eyebrows and teased her friend that this did not seem like something you would take to a conference if you were not expecting company.

'Expecting company?' she had laughed, but Martha had snatched the sexy sheath of satin from her and told her not to be so stupid. As Claire headed home to iron Richard's shirts for him to take to the conference he was attending up in Edinburgh later that day, she wondered if she had touched a nerve.

Perhaps Martha had planned on seeing a married lover in Cornwall she wondered, then dismissed the idea. No, Martha would have told her if she was. Now, she wondered, would she be showing off her underwear to Claire knowing that she had invested in the lingerie to seduce her husband! Claire had even joked about how hard it would be to cope with both Martha and Richard being away at the same time. Usually when Richard went away on one of his frequent business trips, she and Martha arranged some girly outings. She felt a cold sweat running down her back as she recalled how lately Martha had avoided being on her own with Claire, almost as much as Richard had. There had been few get togethers lately.

Martha had seemed distracted and not as keen as she used to be to share the gossip about her chaotic love life either. Perhaps even more significantly, Martha, who had always had a string of boyfriends on the go, had not had a date in months, claiming that she felt she needed a break from the dating scene. Now Claire felt her stomach churn as she began to wonder if she had been fooled by both of them. She tried to shake off the images of Martha parading her slim body in front of Richard in that beautiful satin nightgown and thought that yes, maybe she was going mad. It was unthinkable.

She arrived home, showered, gave Harriet a bath and read her a bedtime story, before settling down in the kitchen with a large glass of wine.

Had she built this up into something it wasn't? Feeling guilty and paranoid she tried but failed to ignore a growing gnawing feeling that she had been blind to a few things of late that had seemed odd and out of sorts.

She thought about how Richard had let her down so many times and strangely, Martha had always been around to see it happen.

A fortnight ago she and Richard had been going to a ball and Martha had been babysitting for Harriet, but at the last moment Richard called up to say that she should go ahead without him and he would join her later. Something had come up at the office.

She was upset that once again Richard was not making any effort for her, but she went ahead and tried to enjoy herself as the hours ticked by and he had still not shown up. At 10pm Claire finally conceded that he was not going to make it, so she got a taxi home alone; making a few lame excuses to her friends about a family emergency that Richard had had to deal with. She felt angry at Richard and humiliated by his failure to join her as she arrived home to find Richard's car in the driveway. When she went into the lounge the fire was ablaze and he and Martha were all cosied up on the sofa watching a movie, sharing a bottle of his favourite red wine.

Claire had walked in wearing her new full-length satin dress, a shade of red Richard had always said suited her. Claire felt invisible as Richard barely acknowledged her presence. She had the distinct feeling that she was the third wheel as the pair of them were so engrossed in their film and their wine to even be bothered to include her. Richard seemed more intent on pouring Martha another glass of wine than apologising to his wife for standing her up.

Claire had gone to a lot of trouble having her glossy mane sculpted into a fashionable French pleat and the beauty salon had given her a professional make over. She could see was the way Martha's eyes were shining and suddenly she realised with a jolt how amazing her friend looked these days. She was slim and pretty and had always been attractive, but she seemed to have an inner glow about her. Richard had seemed to notice too but Claire had berated herself for feeling so envious.

Martha was her best friend so surely it was a good thing that her husband enjoyed her company. Arriving home and finding them looking so happy together she decided that she was being childish and jealous.

'I am sorry Claire,' he finally conceded, 'my meetings ran over and there seemed no point in trying to get there for just an hour.'

She wanted him to acknowledge that he could have at least messaged her. She felt rejected and unworthy because it was clear her husband didn't have the least bit of interest in her.

Quelling her feelings of anger and disappointment, she gamely went upstairs to put on a pair of jogging pants and a sweatshirt and attempted to join in their banter. She tried but failed to watch the film and get involved in their chatter so decided to leave them to it. As she left the room, she noted with a feeling of growing resentment that it was a new release she had begged Richard to watch with her. Looking at how engrossed in it he seemed on the sofa with Martha she wondered once again just where she had gone so wrong. Her handsome husband looked so relaxed and happy lying alongside Martha and with a jolt she realised what a beautiful couple they made. They looked a good match, his dark good looks and her sexy figure stretched out so seductively alongside him.

The next day Claire could not shake off the feeling that she should voice her concerns. She had tried to talk to Richard about his friendship with Martha, but he had brushed her off and told her that as usual, she was being paranoid and stupid. Once again, she felt pathetic and unworthy. Her best friend would never make a play for her husband, it was unthinkable! Now, staring at the text, she felt such a fool; surely this could not be true. Her friend Martha would not do this to her, she would *not* betray her like this.

She dialled Richard's mobile and left a voicemail. 'Is Martha there?' she asked, her voice shaking with pain.

An hour later he texted back saying no, Martha was certainly not with him, adding that Claire was being ridiculous and suggested she see someone about her insecurities. 'You are driving me mad,' he texted back. A few minutes later she received a second text saying, 'I am worried about you, I think you need help!'

Claire sat at the kitchen table crying and trying to compose herself and wondered if she was going a little crazy. But she could not help but dwell on the growing suspicions racing around in her brain and a small voice that insisted that she had to find out more. Maybe he was right, she was being ridiculous and irrational. But she would not let it rest.

'Why not call me and at least talk to me?' she asked him silently. She had tried to call Richard several times, but he did not pick up the calls and they went instantly to voicemail. Nothing felt right about this, and she knew she had to find out if there was any truth in the text message.

A long weekend lay ahead of her, and Claire knew she would go mad if she didn't at least try to find out the truth.

Finally, after much soul searching, she took Harriet to stay with her parents and booked herself on a late evening flight to Edinburgh. Sitting on the aircraft she realised the enormity of what she was doing and felt suddenly afraid. Maybe Richard was right, had she lost a grip on her senses? Perhaps she did need some professional help. Either way, she knew she had to do this. The two days stretching ahead of her would have been intolerable. She decided she could simply explain that she had felt sorry and guilty about the messages and had wanted to surprise him by way of an apology. They were long overdue for some quality time alone as a couple and maybe this was what they needed. Surely if he was annoyed, he would eventually forgive her and realise it was a gesture that had come from her love for him?

A few hours later Claire walked into his hotel and found Richard hand in hand with Martha as they sipped cocktails in the restaurant bar. The shocked look on his face was something Claire would never forget.

She walked up to where Martha was perched on a bar stool, one beautifully manicured hand resting proprietorially on Richard's thigh. Claire felt she was living in a nightmare. Martha was looking into his eyes, sensually biting down on her lower lip which was coated with a rich scarlet gloss. It took all Claire's resolve not to slap her.

She glared at them and it was a few moments before they even seemed to register her presence. They looked like lovers, and it was clear that was exactly what they were; totally wrapped up with one another in a cocoon of passion and lust.

'So, I am mad am I? Making it all up? Richard, how could you do this and with her my so called best friend? And what about you?' she almost spat at her friend. 'This must have been going on for so long behind my back, how could you be so two faced and cruel?'

There was a long silence and Martha leaned back ever so slightly and folded her arms. She wore an expression of complete boredom and it struck Claire that she had never really known this woman at all. How could she ever have thought Martha was her best friend?

She felt almost paralysed by shock and she waited for Richard to at least get off his bar stool and do or say something.

Neither of them spoke a word and after what seemed like an eternity, Claire turned on her heel, looked at Martha who was still holding Richard's hand and told her sarcastically, 'You had better get someone else to feed your cat.'

It sounded pathetic and she knew she should have said something more to show her pain and anger, but she felt an overwhelming need to just get out of the bar. She ran from the hotel and out into the street.

Much later she would recall that throughout the whole humiliating episode Richard and Martha had continued to hold hands and he had stroked Martha's thigh as if to reassure her.

She also remembered with a jolt that Martha had almost looked jubilant when Claire had walked into the bar. In fact, thinking about it, Martha looked as though she had been half expecting to be found out.

Maybe that had been her plan all along.

As she sat broken hearted at the airport waiting for her flight home to face an empty future without the man she loved, Claire broke off a piece from a huge slab of chocolate and mindlessly ate her way through it.

'It doesn't matter what I eat or how I look, so why not?' she consoled herself as tears coursed down her cheeks.

She was fat, gullible, and stupid and worst of all, she had never felt so lonely or miserable. She had been so totally blind to it all but she realised, at least, she had not been wrong about them. The only positive thing to come out of this was that she was not mad, demented or delusional. Richard had tried to make her take the blame for his cruel betrayal and for an instant she felt something that tasted a little like relief. She would get through this; she would have to. She had thought her life had ended when she lost Stevie and if she could get through that, then she could and would get through this.

Being free to be herself was the only way forward. She owed it to herself and to Harriet not to crumble. She also knew she had to be the sort of mother who could dig deep and find the strength to rid herself of this toxic man.

As she flew home, she felt as though she never wanted to land and face up to a life that suddenly had no meaning. She felt as worthless as Richard told her she was. How could she go on? Momentarily she couldn't imagine a time when this pain would stop but she had been here before and in time she knew it would fade.

When she arrived home Claire did not call her mother and arrange to collect Harriet. She could not face the questions they were going to ask – or the humiliation of having to admit that all their misgivings about her hasty marriage had been right.

She decided she would just get under the duvet and try to get some sleep. She needed to find a way to be strong and get through this. The worst thing was in the past Martha would have been there for her. It struck her that she could not decide what hurt most, being betrayed by Richard or by her best friend.

ANNA

ANNA WAS USED TO getting her own way, be it in the newsroom where she ruled the team and made their lives hell, or in the bedroom where Piers, her long-suffering live-in partner, lived in fear of her regular outbursts.

'I love stress and deadlines and thrive on them,' she would announce to anyone who would listen, and for years the double lie had worked.

She had joined a lowly regional title as a junior reporter, rising through the ranks and becoming the youngest features editor the newspaper had ever had, before realising that to get any higher up the ladder she would have to move to London and try her luck on the nationals.

After working as a day shift news hound on a particularly low rent red top, she had managed to secure a job on a glossy woman's magazine. Ten years later she was the editor of *Glitz* magazine, the must-have monthly for young professionals fighting their way to the top. She had created the persona of a celebrity style media bitch who looked and sounded the part, barking her orders in the newsroom. She had dyed her mousey brown hair a vibrant russet red and gone for a pixie crop way before the supermodels had made the gamine look fashionable. Her figure was toned to perfection and she had a wardrobe of designer clothes, a capsule collection which took her effortlessly from the office to a night out on the town. Her wardrobe contained racks of shoes and bags and countless pairs of designer sunglasses which she wore rain or shine. Looking good was part of her day job and while secretly she would much rather have thrown on a pair of jeans and a battered leather jacket, she always looked beautiful and elegantly turned out. Clothes and makeup were part of her armoury and she knew how to use them. She had perfect porcelain skin and amazing clear green eyes which she made up to perfection. Heavy signature pearl bangles completed her look. She was classy, groomed and envied by every woman she knew.

But this persona did however prevent her from having many woman friends. Women were in awe of her, but they also kept their distance. Her junior staff admired and feared her but none ever engaged in small talk or invited her to join them in after-work activities. While they all headed off to the pub or went on weekend shopping trips, Anna would busy herself with final mark ups and discussions about what image would make next month's magazine cover. Anna did not seek out friendships at work. She wanted respect but had little time for anything else. If that kept people at bay then so be it.

Anna did not care for small talk or have time for friendships. She was ambitious and eager to get to the top of her tree and stay there. However, life as a magazine editor bored her at times. Articles on how to wear red lipstick or how to look for tell-tale signs of your man having an affair were not exactly life changing. Though she had a knack of being able to package up fluffy, psychobabble issues and make them work for her titles, she missed the buzz and banter of the news boys. She also realised that magazine deadlines were a bit boring and predictable, and it was no fun doing Christmas shoots in June. Even the annual fashion weeks in Paris and Milan had begun to get a bit tiresome.

After a while, plush hotel suites had lost their appeal. She was bored by the posturing and bitch fest atmosphere of the post fashion show parties. She would much rather curl up in her jogging pants listening to music while Piers created her favourite steak and kidney pie supper.

She was tired of working in the world of magazines and quietly she missed being in the thick of a newsroom. She enjoyed the way men blustered through the sort of petty stuff women media moguls got so hung up on. They seldom had huge egos or engaged in feuds with better looking or more successful colleagues the way her magazine tribe did.

Then out of the blue, one of the big nationals wanted a news editor and the word was they wanted Anna. While she had loved the glossy world of magazines, she was tired of the long feature lead times; she was a news girl at heart. She jumped at the chance of being in the cut and thrust of a newsroom again and after a long boozy lunch with the big-name newspaper boss she had the job.

Long-suffering Piers simply shook his head and accepted that once again he was going to be a poor second to her new title. Anna was going to be off radar even more. He reasoned that he was used to this, and as long as she was happy and fulfilled, he could cope. Anna was a great journalist and a respected boss. She deserved her success and he was happy for her. Anna was good at calling the shots and he was happy, most of the time, to sit back and let her.

With his blessing she took the job and wasted no time in choosing her team. Her second in command, Frank Solano, was a burly, roughly spoken Irish-Italian guy who took no nonsense from anyone. However, he was a man who backed his team to the hilt. Everyone feared him and loved him equally as he had a heart of gold under all that gruff talk. He started work at 6am, had three-hour lunches at the pub behind the newspaper offices and never left the office before 10pm. He had no family. The office was his life and the pub was his second home – where he got his tip offs and did his deals. He left the glamour stuff to Anna. They were a good team. She did the barking, the hiring and firing and could terrify a reporter at five paces. Frank was Mr Nice Guy who calmed down the younger hacks when they had been chewed up by Anna. He also brought home the exclusives. Anna relied upon him and in turn he was grateful that she overlooked his shortcomings and his drinking. Frank was loyal and had her back. As a duo they were an unlikely pairing, but they stayed ahead of the game and got the job done.

She quietly enjoyed being the alpha female in such a male dominated arena. When the paper was put to bed she and Frank simply went out and had a few beers in the grungy local pub. It was called The Stab (real name – The Stag) for good reason and woe betide the guy who went home early to an angry wife. He would be pilloried and ridiculed, which is why many of the team stayed late and got way more inebriated than was good for them. Anna held her own and they respected her for it. Piers had tried to join in but he had to admit, he did not have the stomach for it. The last time he had joined Anna's mob he had spent the whole night on the bathroom floor groaning in misery as he was violently ill. He decided not to try to keep up with their endless drinking sessions so often he would go home and make supper in the hope that Anna would make it back in time. She rarely did and he would leave her a meal and a note to advise her how long to give it in the microwave. Anne did not cook or have a clue about any kitchen equipment. She left that part of their domestic life to Piers.

Anna had stopped remembering when the persona she had built up for herself took over her real life. She used to be fun and down to earth. She had grown up with brothers so she was always one of the boys and felt more comfortable in male company. But along the way she had lost touch with all her friends and the only people she mixed with were the staff she worked with – and they were all terrified of her. She realised that she didn't have any real friends, only work colleagues, and she was astute enough to know that they only paid lip service to liking her because they were afraid not to. Sometimes she enjoyed the feeling that they lived in fear of her, it gave her a feeling of power and security. But lately she had to admit to herself that she was just plain lonely. A best friend would have been a life saver at times, if nothing else to keep her feet on the ground and tell her when to reel her neck in. Nobody had done that in a very long time. Even Piers felt unable to pull her up short these days. He was in awe of her but the relationship was becoming increasingly one-sided and Piers had to admit that he had begun to feel lonely.

Along the way Anna had bought a fabulous flat in Wimbledon village. She had (somehow) found time to meet gorgeous PR guru Piers to share it with and she had a time share in Spain which she rarely, if ever, had time to visit.

She never saw her family. Way down the line she had chosen to bury her past in a forgotten hick town that nobody had heard of, and apart from the round of corporate first nights and film screenings and after work pub sessions she rarely socialised. She had plenty of money, a beautiful black Audi was parked in her parking space at the office and life was good, albeit a bit plastic.

'Are you ever going to just sit back and enjoy all you have achieved?' Piers would ask her. 'You don't need to prove yourself to anyone Anna; you were the queen of the magazine world, Britain's Anna Wintour, and now you are riding high as the most famous and youngest newspaper boss in Britain. Time to kick back a bit?'

But she didn't know how to kick back or didn't want to for that matter!

Piers was good looking and fun and he put up with her constant mood swings. Secretly she knew he enjoyed the lifestyle and the fact she didn't make too many demands upon him. Now in her mid-thirties she had waited for her body clock to kick in and announce the need to be a mother, but she decided, either the clock had stopped, or she didn't have one. Babies didn't feature on her radar, and Piers certainly didn't seem too bothered. It was a set up that suited them both, and if at weekends they sometimes seemed a bit bored of the constant round of dinners for two or ten; or coffee and newspapers with some very long silences, she figured they had fallen into a comfortable lifestyle that suited them both. Who needed all that walking in the park, feeding ducks and sticky-fingered mess in her shiny new Mark Wilkinson Cook's kitchen? No, children were not for them and it was not even a subject she wished to discuss.

Looking back, she realised that there were a few tell-tale signs that she should have noticed. One Sunday morning while they were heading off to a jazz brunch in Covent Garden, Piers had mentioned a picnic his friends were holding in Richmond Park.

'Fancy a change? Have a barbeque with some of my friends and play a few games with their children in the park?' he asked her.

She was appalled: who played bloody rounders on a beautiful sunny Sunday morning? She had a new Mulberry handbag to show off and she had bought some beautiful Jimmy Choo's that needed an airing. Running around a muddy park was not on the agenda, what was he thinking of! As for a lunch that included children, she could think of nothing worse!

They had never discussed having a family or getting married for that matter. She had just assumed that, like her, he enjoyed things the way they were.

Giving up her career was unthinkable. Their lives were ordered and fun, they had no childcare worries, sleepless nights, or tussles over holidays and school runs; all they had to consider were themselves. She knew it was a selfish way of life, but she decided, that was how they both liked it. Children would ruin things for them both so why bother? They were perfectly happy and, if in doubt, do nothing; it was one of her life mantras. She was in no doubt that children would come between them and wreck their idyllic, well-ordered and very expensive lifestyle.

But she had been shocked when one Saturday instead of heading for their usual coffee and croissant date in the village, Piers had headed off to a garden centre to buy flowerpots and trailing geraniums. 'What the hell are you on? Since when did you want to be a bloody gardener?'

Looking put out and slightly pink-faced, Piers explained that he had fancied creating pots for their terrace and made the point that maybe it was time that they shared a few interests outside of her work. She had sulked and had gone home and not talked much for the rest of the day. They never got to the garden centre. Later that night Piers had walked out of the flat, just as she was about to host six corporate contacts for supper, saying he was not in the mood for another of her dinner parties with people he didn't know and did not want to get to know.

Anna was shocked. Piers had always simply gone along with whatever she wanted to do at weekends. He never shouted or sulked or wanted a say in what they did usually. She made a mental note to maybe be a bit more easy-going and thoughtful. Maybe she would buy him a subscription to *Gardening Monthly* and would suggest a day out at Chelsea Flower Show next year. Uncharacteristically he did not come back in time to help her host the dinner and when he did come home, he was strangely morose and refused to talk to her. They had a rule never to go to bed without making up after a row but that night she went to bed to find Piers asleep. When she tried to wake him up to clear the air, he was either fast asleep or not willing to talk to her.

The following weekend they were still very ill at ease with one another and Anna wondered if maybe she should compromise and suggest they drop into one of his friend's Richmond Park barbeques. She had a pair of designer high top Nikes that a company had asked her to endorse. Teaming them with some rather snazzy crop jeans and her new Armani tee-shirt might be fun. Yes, he would like that.

Two weeks later Piers arrived home looking white, stricken and strangely guilty. Those classic four words haunted her still. 'We have to talk,' he said quietly.

Piers it seems *did* have a biological clock ticking away. Not only was it ticking but the sodding alarm had gone off and it had bloody exploded! 'There is no easy way to say this Ans, I think I am pregnant, I mean, we, we think we are, hell I am making a hash of this …'.

She felt as though her life was suddenly imploding in slow motion, a bit like a motorway pile up that you see up ahead; you know what is going to happen but your life simply slows right down as you wait for the impact to hit.

Using her pet name Ans had made it all the more terrible. He only called her that when there was a crisis, and this she decided, was *definitely* a crisis.

'What are you talking about?' she asked him through lips which suddenly didn't seem to be able to form words too well. Her throat and mouth felt as though they were filled with sand and her heart was heading down into her stomach.

She slumped onto their huge, dove grey leather sofa and waited for Piers to hopefully make this all go away. She wanted her life to be where it had been an hour ago when all she was concerned about was whether she could get away with putting Madonna on her front page yet again.

'I am so sorry, but it just happened, we didn't mean it to, but it has and now it has I realise how happy I am. I want children, we both do. I always thought you and I would one day be a family but lately all we do is bicker and you are just not interested in having the sort of life I want; the sort of life I think I need.'

He sat down and put his head in his hands and started to cry softly. Anna thought her heart would break, she had never seen him so crushed. She had never seen him cry either. But a hot anger was now surging through her, and she was desperate to find out what this madness was all about. So far nothing was making too much sense apart from the fact that somewhere out there, someone appeared to be having a baby with Piers, her Piers!

'What are you talking about? Who is this "we" person? Don't tell me you are having some stupid affair, we agreed we would never do that to each other,' she whispered.

She hadn't even begun to process the news that this so-called other woman was pregnant.

How could he have gotten another woman pregnant? She had no idea he had even been seeing another woman; that was never Piers' style. He hated infidelity; it was one of the things they had agreed on when they first got together. Somehow someone had changed all that. It was clear suddenly that this had not been some stupid fling, it must have been going on for a while and Anna was angry and sick with herself for being so blind.

Piers looked up miserably and faced her for the first time, his eyes still pink and brimming with unshed tears.

'I know I said I would never betray you and I meant it. But lately, well, we just seemed to drift and to be honest I didn't think you were too bothered about being with me forever. I never meant for this to happen, I have never been unfaithful to you before, or wanted to be, and I do still love you but I don't think I am in love with you anymore. We want different things, different lives ... Jane is different. She isn't that focused on a career anymore because she says she has been there and done that, and she needs me, life has been ...'.

Anna didn't give him the time to finish his sentence before aiming one of her new Jimmy Choos at his head.

'Jane? Do you mean Jane as in my assistant Jane? You have to be kidding me! Could you not have at least looked outside of my office for your bit on the side, you asshole! She is a mess, she is ... well she's just Jane. She's not even pretty or particularly bright for God's sake. Don't you realise that she is probably just seeing you as a challenge to get at me! You are an idiot! Jane has never had a career. Why else is a woman her age still a lowly editorial assistant?'

She knew she was being a bitch and coming across as the classic wronged woman, but the image of Piers with scruffy, moody Jane with her terrible acne was just too much to take in.

Anna was incensed that he had betrayed her with a woman who, though very organised when it came to her working diary, was a bit of an office joke. She chain smoked, wore awful clothes that always looked stained and her bitten fingernails were never clean. She never arrived on time and Anna had struggled to justify why she kept her on the payroll. It was Frank who had spoken up to keep her and now Anna was furious that she hadn't followed her instincts to just get rid! She had been swayed because though she was sometimes offhand and scruffy, she did get the job done and held her own in a predominantly male world. She was one of the boys and seamlessly managed to deflate any aggression and therefore earned her place on the team. She had also played a very clever game at making Anna believe she was loyal to her! What a joke.

How could he have preferred the mess that was Jane to her? She felt betrayed and humiliated and suddenly very tearful. She never cried about anything, but here she was blubbing away like a baby.

Piers reddened and looked down at his shoes, then sitting up straight, he shook his head and, looking directly at her simply told her it was over between them.

'Look we may as well get it all out there now while it's so painful and raw. The truth is we are having a baby. I know that Jane loves me very much and I think I have fallen in love with her too. The baby has cemented things for me.'

'She may not be as pretty or driven or clever as you, but she loves me; she puts me first and she makes me laugh. She cares what I do, what I want and we have fun. She talks to me Anna, not at me. Do you remember what having fun is Anna? When is the last time we actually had fun together? You treat Jane like a doormat and when she and I first met we often joked that we had that in common. I am sorry but over the months Jane became a friend, and lately, well, I fell for her. She is not you, but I think that is what I love about her the most.'

'I am sorry Anna, but you are too much for me. I am not who you want and you know it. I am not the one for you. You will look back and realise I have done us both a big favour; it was always going to end. Let's face it, the only thing bothering you is that I am walking away.'

His words came out in a torrent and for once Anna could only sit and listen in shock.

'You love her? Are you mad? You hardly know the woman! And I have never ever wanted us to end. This is us you are talking about Piers, you and me, I might not have given you the attention you deserved, but I always loved you. This is not making any sense to me.'

But Piers held firm and fixing Anna with a stern stare he said he planned to leave that night.

Anna had never heard Piers sound so sad or so strong and her heart lurched. All the clichés hit her at full force, the ones about not knowing what you have until it is gone, about being blind, pride coming before a fall ... For one split second she wondered if she should beg him to stay or plead that they could work things through.

But she knew it was pointless. There was not just Jane to consider, there was now a baby too. A baby! She could hardly comprehend it.

Being weak did not figure in her life; Anna had a reputation for being tough and she had to ride this one out as best she could. But all she wanted to do right this second was to crumple on the floor and cry. She realised with a huge jolt that Piers had been her world, the reason why she could be so strong and hard faced at work. He was her rock and she had never ever told him so. Now it seemed, it was too late to tell him anything ever again.

She sat stunned and silent in the living room while he went up to their bedroom and collected a few things. She watched sadly as he walked out of the house after throwing his house keys into the pottery bowl in the hallway, slammed the door shut and without a backward glance drove away. She knew that he would never walk back in again and for the first time in years Anna had no idea what she was going to do. She felt sick, sinking onto the sofa she stared at nothing for what seemed like hours.

His words had been cruel and had washed over her like iced water, but she had to admit there were grains of truth in what he had said. She hadn't really looked at Piers or what he had wanted from their relationship in quite a while. They enjoyed a casual, fun existence, sex was on the agenda at least once a week. Or was it? She couldn't recall the last time they had made love now she came to think about it. He had never blown her mind in the bedroom, but that was fine, she was often too tired anyway. She got her thrills from her career, the cut and thrust of beating the other titles for those headline grabbing stories and celebrity kiss and tells. Then she thought back to when they had first met and remembered how sexy she had found him. Often they had spent whole days in bed, making love, eating brunch, watching movies and laughing. He could make her laugh like no other man had in the past and she had felt so warm and secure with him.

When had she stopped bothering to make him realise how much she loved him? When she thought about it, she could not remember when they had laughed together lately, not really laughed. No wonder he had looked at another woman. She had begun to treat him almost as a brother of late. How stupid had she been and now it was too late. He loved someone else and that someone else was having his baby. To make matters worse, the someone was Jane.

She didn't allow herself to cry, she was suddenly too mad to cry. That would come later. For the next few hours, she packed up all his clothes and the few possessions he had left in the flat, and had a courier take them to his office. There was no note, there was nothing to say. Piers was history, but what she did realise, ironically, was that replacing Jane was going to be hard. How was she to explain her sudden departure, because she was indeed going to be fired! Tomorrow was not going to be an easy day.

JESSE

JESSE CHECKED HER MOBILE phone for what seemed like the 50th time that morning, hoping against hope that there would be a message from Sam. It didn't have to be sweet or loving, or in any way significant, she would have settled for a simple 'hi, how r u?'. But quietly she accepted that there would be no more texts or calls. It was over and she just had to come to terms with it. Though she realised that she couldn't really say she had lost someone who had never really been hers in the first place.

She walked to the front of her tiny florist shop and idly adjusted a display of beautiful Avranche roses she had placed in an antique jug. The effect was simple and stunning. She looked around her and usually the sight of the tall, metal vases crammed with blooms lifted her heart. She loved her work as a florist and for years she had dreamed of owning her own business. Four years ago she had realised her dream, starting off with a battered van painted with a colourful collection of flowers emblazed with the words '*Jesse's Bloomers*'. She had found a pretty corner store just off the high street in Putney and filled it with shabby chic dressers painted in soft Farrow and Ball shades that acted as a backdrop for her stunning, country style floral arrangements. She sold a huge selection of scented candles and beautiful and unusual pottery and glass vases and jugs. Customers would drive up from north of the river just to see what she had in stock from month to month. She would browse around the weekend markets and car boot sales and came up with all sorts of antique treasures to tempt people through the door. Her reputation grew bit by bit and she secured a few high-profile clients along the way. The old van was replaced by a splendid shiny white one with professional sign writing and a profusion of massive pink orchids painted on the side, though she stuck to her original name. The van had proved to be a very effective marketing tool.

However, the business had really taken off after she had agreed to help another florist out at a minor celebrity wedding. Jesse had gone along out of curiosity and had agreed to transport some of the bouquets and help with the finishing touches.

Jesse had arrived at the venue, a massive marquee set up in the grounds of a country mansion, to find that her florist friend had nowhere near enough flowers to create the 30 table arrangements needed. One of the vans had come off the road in a lane nearby and the flowers and glass containers they were meant to stand in were broken and ruined. Luckily Jesse had brought the exquisite, trailing bridal bouquet and the posies for the bridesmaids in her own car. Sadly, there were only a few boxes of white roses that could be rescued from the crash to fill the vast empty tent. The florist had dissolved in tears and was having a hissy fit as the father of the bride tried to get her to drink a shot of brandy to calm her down. Nobody seemed to want to take control and there were fears that the flowers were going to be a huge let down.

Jesse had decided there was nothing to be done but be creative and make the best of a bad job. She had nothing to lose so she calmly took control and headed out into the huge garden with her secateurs returning with arms full of honeysuckle, ivy, bold blue hydrangea heads and masses of arum lilies she had found in a bank near the duck pond. She had set to work and engaged the help of a few early guests who gamely agreed to go into the garden and keep the flowers coming. With just an hour to go before the ceremony, she had to work fast.

She got the waitresses to scour the grand house for every glass jar and vase they could find, while she set about creating tied bunches finished with simple raffia. A couple of the catering staff who were keen amateur florists offered to help Jesse, and between them they worked a minor miracle.

Jesse had a pile of brown paper carrier bags in her van so she mixed and matched. Some tables had a selection of tall, coloured glass jugs and vases, and others had metal vases hidden in the brown bags with lots of rustic raffia bows. On the top table she had used tall pewter milk churns that looked incredibly effective with their displays of garden blooms. With little time to admire her work, she could tell that the theme was coming together and she was happy to have rescued the wedding from a complete floral disaster to a triumph.

The slightly weathered containers added to the rustic theme and there was a warm feeling of camaraderie as both families set to help.

Jesse even found time to do some last-minute highly effective finishing floral touches to a bower that led the couple to the ceremony.

Luckily, the bride was fashionably late!

With help from a few of the catering team, Jesse created small, tied bunches of mixed herbs and lavender wrapped with fine strands of potato sack string. The wine waiters, who worked like a production line, attached the tiny posies to all the women's chairs. Jesse was thankful that a bottle of Coco Mademoiselle, her favourite Chanel perfume, had been used as a table gift for the girls, so it was easy to see how many of the small posies she needed. One of the guests had also found an old candelabra in an adjoining barn so Jesse had quickly polished it up and made it the centrepiece using oversized white hydrangeas, bunches of lavender and mixed herbs. When she added six huge church candles, the centre piece looked amazing and brought the whole theme together.

The four-tier wedding cake was also adorned with a circlet of white rosebuds and lavender. It looked spectacular.

The original florist, who had sat weeping in the tent, dried her eyes and could not stop hugging Jesse; thanking her for saving her life and her professional reputation.

The effect was stylish, funky and simply incredible. She had pulled a disaster around to a floral triumph and a few weeks later she was shocked to see the wedding spread over 15 pages in *Hello*. Her flowers looked amazing and the editorial had waxed lyrical about how the up-and-coming celebrity florist, Jesse Bailey, had been working to a close brief with her co-worker to achieve a vintage floral extravaganza.

If only they knew she had simply gone along for the ride and had planned to simply drop off the bouquets before heading off to an antiques fair ... right place right time! She hugged herself and rushed out to buy a few more copies; her mum would be over the moon.

Within hours of the magazine hitting the stands her phone did not stop ringing with brides demanding that she meet up to discuss a floral theme for their country/retro/vintage affair. The word was out there and *Jesse's Bloomers* went into orbit on the celebrity flower front.

The icing on the cake was a call from the Palace no less to consult her about a royal affair but only on condition she told nobody prior to the ceremony. Jesse made the solemn promise, despite being desperate to share the amazing news with her mum. A month later she had been catapulted into celebrity mode with offers for huge events just falling out of the sky!

Suddenly she was being asked to do interviews for *Good Housekeeping*, *Woman and Home*, *Red* and *Homes and Gardens*. Then *Glamour* magazine had asked if she wanted to get involved in a fashion shoot. 'It's gone a bit mad, but I love it,' she told her best friend Alice who up until now had accused her of being a bit out of touch when it came to marketing and advertising. Suddenly she didn't need to spend money on advertising, and due to her increased workload she was doing so well she had to take on a couple of extra staff to cope with the growing list of high profile corporate and celebrity clients all demanding her attention.

Jesse was happily single, though at 35 she did wonder if she had missed the boat on the love front. Yes, there had been a succession of boyfriends along the way but nobody who had made her pulses race. Her latest man, Simon, was a nice bloke but he was dull. He liked football and cycling and fitted her around his training schedule. A few weeks ago, she decided it had to end and fortunately it had with no drama or tears. She had busied herself with taking on more weddings and corporate bookings and had even turned down an offer from one of her clients to enjoy a luxury two-week break in Antigua.

'It will do you good, all work and no play,' her assistant Viv teased her when Jesse told her the story.

'It did sound fabulous, right on the beach, but for now I am just too busy,' argued Jesse.

Then a few weeks later an Adonis had walked into her shop to buy a bunch of roses for his mum and she had felt the attraction hit her like a thunderbolt. He was not your run-of-the-mill tall, dark and handsome love god, but he had the most incredible green eyes. He gave her the sexiest smile ever and she loved the way his dark hair curled around his head like a wild halo. She felt a jolt hit her stomach and go right down to her feet. She knew she was blushing, but she didn't care. She had read about this love at first sight stuff in books and magazines, but she had never thought it existed. Suddenly all she could think of was how it would feel for his hands to be holding her and his lips to be kissing hers!

'These roses are beautiful – and so are you,' he said as he handed her a £20 note. Delivering another killer white smile, he walked out of the door.

She felt dazed and a bit daft for reacting so strongly to this stranger. For the whole day though she had a smile on her face as she remembered how it had sounded when he called her beautiful.

SAM

IN A SMALL FLAT the other side of the river, as Sam presented his soon to be wife with a beautiful bunch of roses, a peace offering for yet another of their rows, he found it hard to get the dark-haired flower shop girl out of his head. She had the most amazing brown eyes and a beautiful mouth. In the shop he had struggled not to stare at her. He felt terrible that he had kept wondering how it would feel to take the girl in his arms and kiss those amazing pink lips!

'What am I thinking of? I am getting married to Zoe, and soon; this is not the time to start fancying other women,' he told himself silently.

But later, as Zoe started nagging at him to look yet again at the guest list for their wedding dance, he wondered if the girl with the brown eyes was married. If she was, had she bothered with a wedding dance for 400 people she hardly knew? Somehow, she did not look like the high maintenance type. Sighing he took the list from Zoe's grasp and under her glare of disapproval he studied it and attempted to make a few changes. Zoe gave him a hard look and, not for the first time, Sam wondered if he was doing the right thing. Life with Zoe used to be fun, but he could not remember the last time they had laughed or made love or simply enjoyed being together. Pre-wedding jitters he told himself. Things would go back to normal once this awful wedding was out of the way. Somehow Sam had imagined that getting married to the woman you love should not feel like such a chore. He was dreading the day and was beginning to wonder if he was making a big mistake. They had been together for two years now and according to Zoe, getting married was the next step. Sam felt it had all happened too fast; he was being carried away on a tidal wave of bridal magazines, swatches of fabric and endless lists of people he did not know. She had changed so much he hardly recognised her.

In the beginning when she was still starry-eyed and breathless over the whole thing, Zoe had promised him that all he needed to do was to buy a suit, choose a best man and turn up – she would do the rest. And true to her word she had certainly done that. He realised sadly that he had not even proposed properly. He simply went along with it all and right now he was not sure he should have. He had often thought about how he would propose to a woman he wanted to spend the rest of his life with. He had visions of a walk in the countryside or on the beach. After he proposed they would cry and rush off to a pub for lunch to phone all their friends with the news. He had never got down on one knee, all he could vaguely remember was Zoe suggesting a wedding date. He had also had a vision of the sort of wedding he would like. It would be small and meaningful. He and his bride and their closest friends and family would gather somewhere amazing, preferably outdoors. They would have a bonfire and fireworks and he and his bride would dance and laugh and would have a ball.

It would not be about what they were wearing or how much it cost, it would be about the two of them and how much they wanted to share a future. The thought made him feel incredibly sad.

He certainly did not share Zoe's vision of a formal sit-down wedding for 200 people in a country manor he had never heard of followed by a dance for a further 200 guests, most of whom he hardly knew. Many were Zoe's work colleagues and she insisted she had to invite them as to snub anyone would kill her career prospects. She had allowed him to invite 50 of his family and friends but the rest were all people chosen by Zoe and he felt powerless to step in. His family had quietly felt he had made a bad choice but they knew better than to say anything to him.

He looked sadly at the flowers he had bought earlier that day that had been thrust into an old glass jar and he pulled a white petal from a large bloom and brushed it across his cheek. It felt like satin and once again he thought of the flower lady. This had to stop but he couldn't help but think about how the flower girl would probably cry if someone asked her to be their bride. Some lucky man would do that one day if by some miracle she was still single. Surely a beautiful girl like her had been snapped up by now. The thought made him feel strangely sad.

But despite his promises to himself to keep away from the shop and the girl, the next week Sam found himself standing outside the Putney premises. He stood nervously biting his lip and wondering why he was there and what he was going to do or say when he walked into the store. He was just about to open the door when the beautiful young florist bustled past him with her arms full of huge pink lilies. She seemed to blush slightly when she saw him. Time seemed to stand still as she looked up at him and smiled.

He pushed open the door to let her past him and stepped into the shop. He was once again impressed by the incredible stands of beautiful blooms, candles and arrangements. 'Nice to see you again,' she said, and he simply stared at her with no words forming in his mouth.

'Did your mum like her roses? '

'Yes, she thought they were amazing,' Sam blushed a little as the lie slipped out so easily.

'I just had to come back for more. But here's the thing, I thought you might have time for a coffee and to tell me about why your flowers are so incredible. Surely this flower arranging stuff must make you thirsty?'

Sam was amazed to hear the words pop out of his mouth. He certainly had not planned to ask her out, but right then he knew that he had to find out if this was a stupid crush to take his mind off the impending wedding, or had he fallen for this stunning young woman. Since the first moment he had set eyes on her she had taken up residence in his head.

She seemed to hesitate, then lifted her eyes to meet his. 'Yes, OK why not.' He caught his breath and felt the universe shift a little. Something very important had just happened. He would work out quite what it was and where it would lead later. The tiny, dark vision fixed him with a look he couldn't quite fathom then shyly she picked up her small canvas bag and nodded toward the door.

They fell in step naturally as they made their way to the Costa Coffee outlet nearby and two hours and four coffees later, they were still talking.

He was not sure what he had started, but somehow it felt safe and very right, even though going home later he did ask himself if all this talking and lingering over coffee counted as cheating. He supposed it did but right now he could not bear to think of not seeing Jesse again and he made a date for the following week. This was not going to end well he decided. He felt strangely unrepentant as he drove to see her for their next coffee date.

'I loved seeing you today,' she said smiling up at him afterwards. 'Me too,' he replied, adding, 'too much'. That was the beginning of a great friendship, although both secretly wanted more. Jesse held back because she was not sure where she stood; and for obvious reasons, Sam did the same. He felt badly about continuing with the madness of falling for Jesse but he couldn't help himself. When he was with her, he felt so different; a much better man.

They met often however Sam realised that he could not keep up the pretence forever. Their meetings were bittersweet and although he longed to kiss her, he was terrified of crossing that line. It was obvious to them both that the attraction was growing. He knew the time would come when Jesse would wonder why he was holding back and he didn't have a clue about what he would say. Then one dreadful day Sam decided it was time to come clean about Zoe. Jesse had been hinting about spending a day together at the coast and while he longed to spend time with her out of the city, he knew it was a step too far. He had to be honest about being in a relationship, he owed her that much, though he did chicken out of telling her about the impending wedding.

Jesse seemed shocked but she didn't berate him or react as he feared she might. She simply stated that as they had not taken anything further than a coffee, then she saw no reason for ending a friendship that had come to mean so much to them both.

He was absolutely stunned at her reaction, or rather lack of it. While Jesse had always had a golden rule about dating men who were not free, she decided as they were not actually dating, they were doing no harm. But in her heart of hearts, she knew she was kidding herself. She had fallen for Sam and stupidly she had decided that any time she could spend with him was worth the angst of knowing he was going home to someone else.

Every fibre of her being knew she should tell him this had to stop now, to admit she was getting in too deep, but part of her knew that she couldn't. It was madness, the sort of madness you read about in novels. The realist in Jesse had always dismissed women who walked wide-eyed into this sort of emotional turmoil as weak. The truth was she could not stop what was happening. It felt so right when they were together. She tried not to imagine what happened when Sam left her and went back home to his girlfriend. She started to hate that word. But she continued to meet Sam whenever he was free, and increasingly regularly he would turn up in the shop and whisk her off for lunch or a coffee or just a walk. She loved the way he walked, slowly yet purposefully. How when he talked, his eyes danced and he made wild gestures with his hands. He always made her laugh and she found him fascinating and sexy. He said he did not like aftershave, but he always had a lovely clean smell; a mix of freshly laundered clothes and the sea. She beat herself up with the image of the hated Zoe washing his clothes and she felt stupidly jealous that she was not the one doing his laundry! This has to stop she told herself over and over. But she could never find the words to tell him that he should leave her alone, and even if she had uttered them, she knew that she would not mean them. Two months later she was now totally in love and she suspected he was too. They had never spoken the words but it seemed so obvious. 'This is so wrong, and I try to keep away, but I can't even think about not seeing you. I am in a right mess and it's all my own doing,' he admitted to her one day as they were ambling at the nearby park. It was a cold blustery day and she longed for him to wrap her in his arms.

He went on to say that something had to change, they could not carry on as they were. She simply nodded and her eyes spilled over in a stream of tears that he brushed softly from her face. This was the first time he had taken her in his arms and he felt an overwhelming need to kiss her.

Many times Jesse tried to cancel their meetings but she was addicted to him. She lived for their chats and their lovely walks on the common nearby at Wimbledon. They even managed a lunch or two in the village pub. It was here, in a dark corner with a log fire burning, that Sam finally dropped the bombshell that he was about to get married. Any chance of them becoming a couple simply vanished and Jesse felt sick as the realisation of his words sunk in. 'I can't believe that I have not told you this before, I am the worst sort of bloke, in fact I hate myself. But I couldn't stay away from you and as time went on it got harder to be honest with you. I knew I would lose you, us, whatever us is…'. In that moment her world collapsed. She stared at her drink and struggled to think of a single thing to say. She had known she was heading for a fall, but nothing had prepared her for the terrible feeling of desolation she felt as he tried to explain why he hadn't told her sooner.

She knew she had to take some responsibility because she had known he wasn't free and she had allowed things to get totally out of hand. She finished her drink and without looking at him, said she had to go.

Her legs felt like lead. It was a term she had only read about in books, but she really was struggling to put one foot in front of the other. She felt like she had a huge stone in her stomach and she almost fell out of the pub door devastated that this was probably the last time she would see him.

She allowed herself a final look back at him. His face was awash with pain and regret and she felt her stomach flip with sheer longing as he stared back at her.

He ran after her a few moments later and pulled her back to make her face him and she looked at him with a mix of misery and disbelief.

Surely this could not be the end of them? His getting married seemed to be final in her book. She had walked into this relationship knowing there couldn't be a future for them but holding out in the vain hope that there might be. She knew there was another woman in his life, but the fact that she was about to become his wife changed everything. Finally, she found her voice and looked sadly up into that face for what she realized might be the last time.

'I don't want you to only blame yourself, I think I always knew this was all too good to be true.' She turned from him this time resolute that she would not turn back. She felt sick at heart and wondered what to do and where to go and struggled to imagine a life without him in it.

Jesse watched him walk back to the pub and a minute later she had followed him. 'Look, I suppose I just want to know if any of this has been real. Was this all just in my head? Did you come looking for me or just anyone because you were about to commit to someone – a last fling?'

But they both knew the answer was far from that. Jesse was in love and she knew Sam felt the same. She only had to look into those soulful eyes to see he was as miserable as she was. But she would not ask him to cancel the wedding. That didn't even seem an option.

He didn't try to stop her when she finally left. He had no words that could fix this and they both knew that.

Later after he had drunk himself into a deep pit of misery, he texted her and begged for a chance to try to explain. She ignored him but he continued to message her through the night. Every hour or so he crept into the bathroom to text hoping that at some point he would get a response. He felt disloyal to Zoe but he realised that what he had with Jesse was real. He knew he loved her and he had to see her again, if nothing else to try to make their last meeting a better one. The way she had looked at him the pub haunted him. He could not leave things that way.

Finally in the morning he called her at work, and she agreed to talk to him.

'I have to see you again. I will understand if you won't but please don't shut me out. I am in such a mess. My head is all over the place I can't think straight.'

Jesse didn't answer him; the lump in her throat making it difficult to speak. Silently she knew it was inevitable that she would agree to meet a final time.

The following day he came to her flat for the chat he had begged for.

They had never met in her flat before or even been totally alone for that matter. Without ever voicing it, they both knew they couldn't be trusted.

This was the first time she had ever allowed him into her home and as he walked in the door he felt so at ease there.

The flat reflected her warm personality. It was flooded with light and he felt so calm there in a way he never felt in his flat when Zoe spent the night. Jesse let him through the door suddenly feeling very shy. It felt bittersweet and the air was charged. As she followed him into the hallway he turned, swept her up and finally kissed her. He had not meant to touch her but in that moment, he knew it was now or never.

It seemed to be the most natural thing in the world when they ended up making love. Slowly and sensually, he stroked and kissed her, taking an excruciatingly long time to undress her and then himself. She finally realised why this was called making love. It had been a saying she had heard many times but had never really experienced. Yes, she had enjoyed some very satisfying sex but this was something much more than that. For the first time she got how it felt to connect with someone, not just physically but emotionally.

He pulled her on top of him and stroked her face before gently rolling her softly over. He took what seemed like forever kissing and stroking every inch of her body before taking her with such gentleness she wanted to cry with happiness. She was in heaven; her senses reeling as he touched her in a way no other man had done before. Their eyes locked as they rocked together and gained momentum until they both climaxed. They held on to each other as if their lives depended upon it.

She felt so loved and sated and giddy with happiness until the moment she saw him get up from the bed and look at her sadly. Suddenly the spell was broken and she realised this was all she would ever have of him. She simply lay back and crawled beneath the duvet.

He left the room to get dressed then came back to pick up his watch which he had left on the bedside table. With a guilty backwards look he walked out of the bedroom and went to sit at her kitchen table.

For the first time he took his surroundings and he felt sick to his core to think that he might never return here because one thing was certain, he was in deep and didn't see how it could end well.

The flat was just as he imagined it would be. The walls were a soft white linen colour and the painted furniture was in muted shades of grey. Her sofas were a neutral striped fabric and cashmere throws lured you to sink into them. There were bowls of tulips and roses everywhere and the air was filled with tuberose and sandalwood fragrances. The scene was such a beautiful one he felt strangely overcome.

Jesse appeared with a pale pink satin wrap around her tanned shoulders and Sam had to stop himself from launching himself at her again.

'I am possessed,' he told himself.

'Sam please stay away, I really can't be with you again. This hurts too much, this has to be the end of the madness.'

In the short time since he had left her bed, she had realised that although the lovemaking had been incredible it was something that could not be repeated, no matter how much they both wanted it.

Her words left him no choice but to sadly nod his head and leave, feeling every inch the coward he knew himself to be.

Jesse heard him slam the front door. She went back to the bed and hugged the pillow that still had a faint smell of him. Pulling the duvet over her head. she didn't know if she was able to get up and get on with her life again. How had she allowed this to happen? She was not usually such an idiot. Who falls in love with someone who is about to get married? She was the sort of woman she had always despised. She had just made love to a man who was about to become someone else's husband. How could she have acted so recklessly?

He belonged to someone else, a faceless girl called Zoe who deserved better. Stupidly she had made love to Sam and let him leave his imprint on her soul. Things were now ten times worse than they had been when he had left her in the pub the day before.

Sam felt powerless as he left the flat. He knew they had crossed a line and he also knew he could never go back to see her again. He felt like the worst shit in the world – to both women. But he felt far more cut up about leaving Jesse. He had taken advantage of her beautiful nature and now he was as devastated as he knew she was. He would have to somehow stay away and try to get over her in time for the wedding. It suddenly seemed like a prison sentence.

Not for the first time he tried to remember exactly how he had gotten into this situation. He was in love with one woman and yet, somehow, he was marrying another. The only thing left for him to do was to keep away from Jesse and try to get on with a life with Zoe, a woman who he realised he no longer loved. Should he take a step back, try and talk to Zoe; not about Jesse, but about the roller coaster ride he felt he was on? Maybe the Jesse thing had got out of hand because he felt so trapped and disengaged by this whole wedding fiasco.

He had loved Zoe, hadn't he? So why did the thought of becoming her husband made him feel queasy? He had never been able to talk to Zoe about pulling back or changing plans. Once she was on a mission, he had no say. He was the worst sort of coward and Jesse deserved better. Maybe Zoe did too but the thought of asking her to call a halt to their wedding filled him with dread. He was not brave or strong enough to do it. With a sinking heart he felt resigned to his fate.

Two weeks went by with no word from Sam. Jesse knew she had asked him to leave her be but part of her had hoped he would come to her and make things right. How could they have had such a connection and yet he was able to simply switch off and give up on her?

She missed him and her life seemed so empty without him in it. She had no interest in her work and even the sight of all her beautiful flowers did not help lift her spirits. The days seemed long and meaningless and every time someone walked into her shop, she hoped against hope that it would be Sam.

A few days later Jesse's world finally imploded when Sam called her out of the blue. Her heart lurched and she felt stupidly hopeful that he was going to end her misery. She had been about to launch into a breathy speech about being so happy to hear his voice, when he cut her short and said he had something important to tell her and she would not like it. His voice sounded cold and almost distant. Bluntly he explained he had been forced to call to warn her that Zoe intended to ring her up and try to book her for their wedding.

He explained that Zoe had a friend lined up to do her flowers but someone had shown her an article about Jesse and her vintage triumph in *Hello* and she was like a woman possessed. She was told Jesse was the best and she wanted her to come up with a rustic meadow theme at her manor house reception. She was not going to take no for an answer.

'You don't know what's she like when she wants something Jesse, she will bulldoze you into agreeing to do it and I don't think I could cope. She realises that it's all very last minute, but she says she is more than willing to pay anything to secure you for the wedding. I am afraid she has a habit of getting what she wants so be warned.'

She exploded with fury at his words.

'Thankfully for both our sakes I am not weak and won't be bullied into doing your bloody wedding. I hear nothing from you for weeks then you ring me and ask me to cover for you? Have you any idea how that makes me feel? And believe me, I will have no problem in telling your fiancée that I won't be doing her flowers so you can stop worrying. Your dirty little secret is safe with me. You have done me a favour because now I see that this has meant nothing to you. All you are afraid of is being found out and seen as the shit you really are!'

Jesse held her breath after her outburst. She felt strangely faint as he went on to say how sorry he felt but he didn't know what else to do but forewarn her and make sure the call didn't come out of the blue.

'Zoe found one of your cards in my wallet. I am so, so, sorry, I meant to throw it out but I couldn't bring myself to. When she found it, I had to make up a story about a friend recommending you as the best wedding florist – well you are! Now Zoe is insistent she meets you. She had a friend lined up to do her bouquet and the table arrangements and now it has to be you. I am sorry but she must not know what has happened. I hate myself for asking you to lie, but you must. You did, still do, mean the world to me, I just messed up that's all.'

Jesse was horrified at his cold attitude. She felt strangely remote about a man she thought had loved her. However, she also felt a curious desire to meet the woman he was going to marry. She realised that could never happen though, she didn't trust herself to do that.

'Don't worry I will just tell her my diary is full, you are in the clear. Go ahead and enjoy your wedding Sam. Goodbye.'

Jesse realised she had to abandon the faint hope she had not even realised she had been secretly holding onto. Deep down she had dreamt he would realise what he was giving up, wise up and come clean to Zoe before taking that walk down the aisle. In this fantasy he would ask Jesse to forgive him and beg her to let him make it up to her and begin again.

She had not bargained for him ringing her up and whingeing to her about his fear of being found out! When she realised how delusional she had been her heart broke all over again.

Jesse cut the call short and within minutes she had put the closed sign on the door.

On the other end of the line Sam was sad and felt sick to his stomach. He knew how cold and detached he had sounded but that had been the only way he could handle the call. The sound of her voice had been enough to make him want to go to her and look at that beautiful face.

Every fibre of his being wanted to beg her to meet him, but what could he say? Jesse was right he *was* a lying cheat. Zoe had no idea about his change of heart, and he had nothing to offer Jesse, at least not yet. He didn't deserve her and he also knew that Zoe deserved the truth too. But he was a coward, it was all moving too fast. He realised how cold and calculating he had sounded but how could he tell Jesse he still loved her?

The truth was, he really did. It was all a big mess and he had nobody to blame but himself.

Jesse found herself sobbing into a bouquet of pink rosebuds. She knew now it was finally all over between them. She had been kidding herself their relationship was something special and that he would fight for her. She had to try to move on and get on with her life, but right now she had no wish to do anything but crumple into a heap and cry this pain away.

In his flat Sam looked at the phone and longed to call Jesse back and beg for her forgiveness. He knew Jesse was the woman he wanted to be with but he had no idea how he was going to get out of the wedding. He had tried so many times, but the words just would not come. The thought of turning up at the church and making solemn vows to anyone other than Jesse filled him with dread. He was ashamed to admit that Zoe scared the life out of him.

In her Putney shop Jesse felt no joy in her work and when Zoe did eventually call, she felt sick and miserable and simply recommended another florist friend. Zoe sounded happy and excited about her wedding day and Jesse felt her heart break all over again. She blamed herself for having let the relationship go so far. Zoe had always seemed a shadowy figure but when she heard the excitement in her voice about the forthcoming wedding, Jesse realised she had been kidding herself. Sam may have feelings for her but he belonged to someone else. He had never been hers to love, and she was a fool to have let herself fall for him. She felt deflated and angry with herself, but worst still, she felt let down. She also felt furious with the man who had caused her all this pain.

Jesse limped through the next few weeks, miserable and snappy. Finally, she decided that she was not going to get her head straight if she stayed at the shop. She needed a change of scene and some time and space to sort herself out. She no longer recognised herself and passed the days in a sort of daze. She didn't feel in the least bit creative and felt guilty she had no heart to get excited about forthcoming weddings and events. She tended to avoid meeting brides one-to-one; it was all too painful. Although she knew it was a bad time to walk away from her business, she also sensed that she was not doing herself any favours by staying on when her heart was not in it. She had always put her heart and soul into her work and now she could barely be bothered to make up simple hand tied bouquets in her shop.

She needed to take time out.

She wanted to tell Sam she was going but she couldn't face calling him. She was afraid she would unravel and ask to meet him which was ridiculous.

She calculated that as it was several weeks from that fateful phone call the wedding must be looming. He would be married soon, and with a sudden realisation Jesse knew she had no intention of being in the same country as Sam when that happened. She needed to get away, a long way away.

On a whim she called the client who had offered the villa in Antigua all that time ago and asked if there was a chance that she could still take up her offer. Yes, she was told, the villa was available and the client was willing to let her rent it at a lower rate if she would commit to two months. After doing some quick sums in her head, Jesse worked out that she needed three companions to split the cost if she wanted to take it on for two months.

Surely there were women out there who like her, might need an escape route for a while?

Without thinking too much about it she placed an advertisement in *The Lady*. She often leafed through copies of it whilst she was at her dentist and it never failed to impress her and intrigue her with the weird and wonderful ads that cropped up.

She tried to make the trip sound like a once in a lifetime opportunity, and in many ways, she planned that it would be. She needed some fun and she was keen to see who might be out there hoping to share her adventure.

Jesse only had to wait for a few days before the letters and emails poured in. She had no idea that the invite would prompt so much interest. However, three of the women had stood out from the rest and it had proved an easy task to choose her crew. She had also received a few very entertaining emails from men but hadn't wanted a man in the mix. This was a girly trip and she couldn't wait for it to begin.

She didn't know all the details about why they were all so keen to run away, but she decided it would be fun to find out and they had plenty of time to do so. The women she had chosen were a diverse bunch, and she reckoned they would be an interesting mix. Two of the girls were up for the two-month option. The third, a single mum with a little girl, said she could only manage a four week stay but hoped that would be OK. She had offered to pay her share of the second month if it sealed the deal, which it did! She had sounded so lovely and so desperate to join the group. So Jesse had made her travel plans, booked the villa and also managed to avoid getting hold of Sam one last time to say goodbye.

She would leave him alone and get away to her Caribbean hideaway and try to somehow get through the day he was due to marry another girl. She felt so desolate but even by taking back a bit of control in her life she felt happier than she had in months. At least she had made a stand, and while she couldn't see the way forward yet she knew that this empty feeling would pass in time. She just wanted that time to come sooner rather than later.

She had never looked upon herself as an ardent feminist, but she did wonder why women allowed men to have this effect on them and let them bring them down so low?

Nobody had ever made her feel like this before and she vowed nobody ever would again. She had always prided herself on being a strong, self-sufficient character. This stupid affair had caused her life to unravel and she had become the sort of woman she despised, a weak, needy female who lacked the backbone to get on with her life. She went to sleep missing Sam and thinking of all she had lost. She awoke to those same bleak, awful emotions. It was like living in a grief bubble and she despised herself for it. She would go to Antigua and become whole again. Life did not end because a man left you. She had to do some healing before she would be ready to start again. There was no other way forward.

GINA

THIS WAS THE DAY she knew she was finally going to escape. Gina had no idea how she would find the strength to walk away from a toxic life with a man who she now feared and detested, but she knew she had to.

The day started like any other; in fact, James had been in a calm and cheerful frame of mind when he went off to work. She had smiled and promised to have supper on the go when he got in.

She waited until James drove off and cleared away the breakfast things. She loaded the dishwasher and took out a frozen lasagne for his supper. She realised it was madness, but this was the last wifely thing she would ever do for this man. Her marriage was over. She was going to leave him today!

She had been programmed to behave in a certain way but as she walked out of the door Gina smiled to herself feeling her self-confidence flow back into her soul. She was never going back. All she had taken with her was her small overnight bag containing a few basic outfits, some treasured photographs, and her passport. This was the most important thing as she planned to travel far away and very soon.

There was nothing else in the house she wanted or needed. Maybe in time she would feel differently and eventually the house sale would have to be sorted, but for now she was free. She almost skipped to her car. She felt afraid but also lighter in spirit than she had in months. She had fantasised about this moment many times but previously she had been too weak and afraid. She finally felt a steely resolve she had never experienced before, and she almost felt sorry for James. He was a coward and a bully but without her, he would be lost. He thrived because he controlled her. But she knew there was a new life out there. At last, she was brave enough to go and find it.

Gina had called into the estate agent's office where she worked and explained she needed to take some extended leave.

She was due lots of holiday time and the office was far from busy. She did admit that she had some domestic problems that might mean her staying away for some time.

Her office manager was kind and said she should take as long as she needed. There would always be a place for her in the team. She also hinted that she realised Gina may need this space and they understood why.

As she drove away from the small, suburban street Gina realised that she could go anywhere she wished. She might go back to work, but she might not, and that was what was so exciting about it all. She could do exactly as she pleased. She had managed to save up a little nest egg of cash which would keep her going until she decided what to do with the rest of her life. She grinned and put her foot down on the accelerator, keen to put as much distance between her and their house as possible. Goodbye James and good riddance!

A couple of hours later she was at her parents' house and as she had suspected, her family were only too happy to take her in. They clucked around her like hens. Her mother had opened the door and for a split second had looked surprised. Once the story was told her mother simply said, 'it's about time you left that bastard we never liked him you know.'

For a few weeks life was easy, even though James called her incessantly. He would plague her with late night calls, sometimes weeping and apologising, and at other times screaming abuse and threatening her with what he would do to her when she finally came to her senses and came home.

'Because you will come home; you are nothing without me. You are pathetic and you are stupid and you won't cope without me,' he told her.

She knew the reverse was true and she suspected he did too but for too long she had let this damaged man undermine her and make her his victim. She felt strangely calm and strong. It was as if she had come out of a long trance, and suddenly everything seemed very clear and simple. She had married an abusive man and she had left him. She had not recognised his controlling ways until she was trapped, ashamed and powerless. But now the scales had fallen from her eyes and all she could feel was relief for it to be over.

She had written him a long letter telling him their marriage was over, asking what he wanted to do about the practicalities of the separation. She suggested that in future they communicate through their lawyers. She did not want a bitter divorce and had no wish to make his physical abuse public. That part of her life was over.

He did not reply and she was not surprised. Gina knew that sadly, at some point, there would be another woman who would fall for his troubled charm and fall into the same trap she had. But that was no longer her concern. She had a new life to plan, and it was time to put herself first.

'What are you going to do now?' her mother asked. 'There is no rush, stay as long as you like but maybe it's time for a change of scene?' And with that she handed her a magazine that had a big black circle around a display advertisement.

The idea of a month or two in Antigua was like a dream come true. Could she really do this? Gina had a lot of life to catch up on. Stepping out of her comfort zone was exactly what she needed.

Within the hour Gina had emailed someone called Jesse about making up the numbers and hoped that she would make it into the group. She wondered if her story had made her sound too troubled, but from now on she intended to be honest about who she was and what had happened. A day later an email popped into her inbox ...

Hi Gina, you are in!
We all aim to fly on the Virgin Atlantic flight out of Gatwick next Thursday morning at 11am if you can make it, but don't worry if not. Just let me know what day you can fly out and I will come to collect you from the airport. This is an adventure for all of us

and it's clear we all need to relax, have some sun and leave our problems behind us. I am really looking forward to meeting you and I am sure you will get on with everyone.

I do expect you all to put the cost of at least a month's rental in my account up front please and hope that's OK. I will contact you again in a day or so with the details of my account and share the names of our travelling companions. I think we are going to be a fun group and it seems we all really need this break. Sometimes the only thing to do is to run away for a while, and I for one can't wait to do that – and meet you all.

Best regards Jesse x

Gina squealed with excitement and went racing into the kitchen to announce to her parents that she was off to the Caribbean.

When reality kicked in, she went online and managed to book a flight; economy was full but she shelled out on a business class seat. What the hell, she intended to have champagne all the way! The next few days were spent putting together a basic wardrobe of swimsuits, a sarong, shorts and sun dresses. She finally added sun creams and moisturisers. 'It is going to be so hot and so lovely,' said her mum who was just as excited as Gina was.

The night before the trip Gina had set out her clothes on the bed and realised that her wardrobe did not seem to cater for two months in the sun. Once she had finished packing her bag it looked a bit empty and lacked any glamorous outfits which she hoped she might need. But she had always envied the women doing their last-minute shopping at those tempting outlets at the airport and Gina decided that was exactly what she would do. She had a bit of a pang when she wondered what her travelling companions would be like. What if they were all model types with amazing clothes? However Jesse had sounded very chilled and she guessed that the women she would choose would not be divas.

She quickly dismissed her concerns and decided this was something she could worry about when they all met up.

'I have faced worse so how hard can it be to live with a few strangers for two months?' she asked herself. An exciting adventure awaited her and she was going to enjoy every moment of it. She had had her fill of putting up with a half-life. This was time for her to find out who she was and what she needed to give her a better and happier future.

Her father drove her to Gatwick, but she refused a long goodbye. 'Please just drop me off Dad, I have shopping to do. I will be fine, and I will ring you both when I get there.' He smiled at her as she ran into the crowd to begin an adventure like no other. Gina had never felt so alive or excited and while she had found meeting new people a bit of a trial when she was with James, she couldn't wait to meet her new house mates. It was obvious that they all had reasons why they needed to get away and she believed it would all work out just fine.

But for now the shops beckoned and she queued up to check in and get through security. She had some very important last-minute shopping to do. In the departure lounge she took a deep breath and headed for Accessorize where she treated herself to some jewelled flip flops, a gauzy white beach dress and some outrageous dangly earrings which somehow summed up her new life. She also bought a beach bag in vibrant colours with lots of beads and seashells embellishing it, a purchase she would not have dared make when she was with James. It was silly and frivolous and was everything he hated. Now it summed up how she was feeling about today.

Mango was her next port of call where she found two sexy chiffon evening tops and a pair of silk crop trousers in a pale pink satin which fitted her like a dream. A long, white cotton sweater and a tiny pink checked bikini also found its way into her basket alongside a tribal maxi dress which looked like something a super model would have packed. Gina felt strangely giddy as she looked back at the reflection of a young woman she barely recognised. She had always had a slender figure and long silky blonde hair. But her life with James had meant she had learned to blend in and never dress provocatively or stand out from the crowd. She wore basic work skirts in greys, classic cardigans from M&S and sensible court shoes or flats. Her hair was kept in a loose ponytail or scraped back into a bun and she rarely wore more than a slick of lip-gloss. James hated her to wear makeup, although when she had first met him, she had enjoyed looking glamorous on their nights out. Once they were married, he would mock her and she simply stopped bothering. For this trip she aimed to change all that. Her new purchases were the first step to becoming the new Gina, and, with a new-found confidence she gathered up her shiny carrier bags and headed out to look at the cosmetics area with their promise of exotic perfumes and shiny lipsticks.

When she had packed for her trip, she had realised that her make up bag was a sorry affair. It only contained a pair of tweezers, Body Shop lip balm and mascara which had long lost its ability to add volume to her lashes. She knew they used to be one of her best features.

Her mother had treated her to a morning at the local beauty salon and she had been amazed at her enhanced lashes thanks to a clever girl called Olivia. She was the queen of lash extensions and she assured Gina that they looked natural and lush. 'This is the thing everyone opts for when they are going on holiday, you won't need mascara and your eyes will look amazing,' she promised. Sure enough, Gina's blue eyes did look incredible looking out from under what felt like black curtains. Olivia had also shown her how to highlight her eyes with a smoky grey shadow. Gina finally splashed out on a creamy sun protection which doubled as a foundation and a bright coral lipstick.

Now at the duty-free shopping mall she felt the need to go a little bit crazy. She treated herself to the new summer

Prada fragrance and the nice lady at Mac assured her that a golden tinted moisturiser, waterproof eyeliner and a fabulous lip gloss with built in SPF 15 would complete her holiday make up. At Sunglass Hut she tried on a pair of outrageously expensive Ralph Lauren sunglasses which made her look a lot like Samantha out of *Sex and the City*, another must have!

Clutching her purchases like trophies she strode off to Gate 31 where she hoped there were three potentially new best friends waiting for her.

CLAIRE

CLAIRE HAD BEEN IN a spin ever since she got the email inviting her to join Jesse and the girls on the trip. Jesse's latest email had included a few photographs of the harbour-side villa and Claire had instantly fallen in love with the white-washed mansion covered in bright pink bougainvillea and hibiscus. The massive wooden deck overlooked a long stretch of powdery white sand backed by a bright turquoise sea.

> We seem to have different reasons for heading out to Antigua but it's going to be chilled out and fun... here are a few shots of the villa to give you an idea of where you are heading. Look forward to finally meeting you at Gatwick next week. I have suggested that we all carry a copy of The Lady Magazine at the Gate ... but I have forwarded the profiles you each sent me so we should be able to recognise each other. Best regards Jesse

Claire had felt a few pangs of guilt at the thought of leaving Harriet.

'She will be fine with us. We are taking her over to Aunty Connie's caravan for a few weeks so all her cousins will be there, and she'll have a ball. Then we are off to Spain for a week or so and after that you will be home, so just enjoy yourself,' her mother reassured.

Claire allowed herself to get caught up in the preparation for the trip as an antidote to the abject misery she felt following Richard's betrayal.

Previously she would have gone to Martha and over lots of wine and pizza they would have thrashed it out, called Richard a bastard and dredged up all the bad things he had said and done over the years. But Martha was a huge part of the pain itself and her affair with Richard meant that Claire had not only lost her husband, but her oldest friend. At times the hurt was so deep that Claire felt an awful tug around her heart. Is this what they call heartbreak? she would ask herself. She used to think it was just a phrase, now she realised it was a living thing. Her heart did feel broken and every day she struggled.

Following the awful scene in the hotel Claire had jumped into a taxi and returned to the airport. There was no commuter flight back to London until the following morning so she sat in a fog of misery drinking coffee and mulling over and over about what she had seen and what signs she had missed. Why had Richard betrayed her and how had her best friend allowed herself to fall for him? How had that happened? She went through all the times they had spent as a trio, trying to pin down the moment that things had changed. How long had they been having this affair; how many lies had they told her? She thought back to the countless times she had left them alone and felt sick at the thought of what they may have been doing behind her back. What a fool she had been and now she was paying the price with this pain and heartache. It seemed so unfair, given all the misery and heartache she had already lived through when her precious Stevie had been killed.

At times she felt physically sick and the misery would overwhelm her. Life seemed pointless. All she had done wrong was to love Richard almost from the moment she met him. Now she doubted that he had ever really cared for her. She felt as though he had died and in truth, the man she had thought he was had disappeared almost as if he had died.

It had seemed like an endless night sitting in that airport lounge but she was glad she had managed to work through a lot of the pain and anger.

If he came back after this, could she ever forgive him? Once she arrived home she was not completely over her husband's betrayal, but she had resolved never to forgive him and to cut him out of their lives. She owed it to herself, to Harriet and to her beloved Stevie to be strong and to see Richard for what he was. The old Claire would have tried to justify the affair and find a way to forgive him, but the Claire who got off that commuter flight was stronger and resolved to put herself and her daughter first. She knew that she deserved far better.

Richard had made her think that she was going mad; that she was dull and boring. Worst of all, she had lost all sense of self-worth. He had her thinking that she was the one who should be grateful to have him in her life. She thought of all the times she had bailed him out financially. Guiltily, she thought of the times Harriet had been pushed aside because Richard wanted her to do something that did not involve her child.

She could not have him back home. She just needed to find a way to carry on living without him. Take it a day at a time she told herself. Nobody has died … though at this moment in time she could have happily strangled both Richard and Martha. 'I will get through this, in time I will be happy again,' she told herself silently.

Strangely this betrayal had brought back all her painful memories of when Stevie had been killed.

That had been far worse, she told herself, but had it? At least Stevie had truly loved her, he hadn't wanted to leave or hurt her. This pain was a different pain but it was just as sharp as once again she had to accept that a part of her life was over. She consoled herself with the fact that at least she could recover her peace of mind. There would be no more nights crying herself to sleep endlessly wondering how to make her husband notice her and show her affection.

She thought back to the days when if it had not been for Harriet, she would have pulled the duvet over her head and stayed in bed.

At least she was thinking more clearly and she resolved to be kinder to herself and create a safe and happy home again; a home that did not include Richard. She had to find a way to make sure he was out of their lives forever.

A visit to the dentist proved to be the first step in her recovery.

'Please take a seat, the hygienist will be with you shortly,' the receptionist was pleasant but brisk and scooping a couple of magazines Claire settled herself into a corner seat to await her scale and polish appointment.

The Lady magazine was something she remembered from her youth and she marvelled that it was still going strong. There were lots of interesting ads including flat shares and requests for travelling companions; a bit reminiscent of days gone by. But there was something comforting and wholesome about the ads offering positions for housekeepers and nannies and requests for house sitters in remote places like the Shetlands! But it was a small advert giving the opportunity to head off to Antigua that had caught Claire's eye, and within a matter of days she had made email contact and found herself booking a flight. She was so grateful that Jesse had picked her out from the many replies she must have received.

This is not like me, but then right now nothing is like me, she rationalised. This trip was the start of a new phase for Claire, and she intended to make the most of every moment.

With Jesse's confirmation email safely in her inbox Claire hooked out her summer wardrobe and found it very lacking. She had wished more than once that she was tall and slim but Richard had insisted he loved her womanly figure. Now she realised he had probably been lying about that too. Martha was an elf-like woman with a tiny build. Claire looked at her size 16 reflection and felt mumsy and dull. She did however like her tumbling chocolate coloured hair. It was thick and glossy and suited her glowing skin and deep brown eyes. Her friends had always insisted that she had a look of Nigella Lawson, and she did enjoy cooking! It seemed as though she had also shared Nigella's ability to pick the wrong man too.

'Nigella, I am going to Antigua and bugger the men. I am going to have fun and try to lose some of this weight!' As food was her best friend right now, dieting was not really on her radar. She decided that she would start going for early morning walks and get in lots of swimming as they would be literally perched on a beach. Now to solve the wardrobe dilemma!

Her friend Maddie came to the rescue. She had a time share in Portugal and was always packing for impromptu summer breaks.

'I have lots of clothes to fit you,' she announced one day, arriving with a bundle of gaudy cotton garments that would not have looked out of place at the Notting Hill Carnival.

Claire did pick out a beautifully cut one-piece black swimsuit with a stylish buckle and body contouring bands which promised to suck in a spare tyre or three.

She also snapped up a couple of pairs of wide leg palazzo pants – a plain black pair and a printed pair together with a gauzy chiffon beach cover up. She owned some comfy Reef flip flops that would go with everything and some stretchy crop jeans. She decided they would be fine to travel in with her smartest navy cashmere cardigan. Her mother also kindly bought her a couple of cheap but pretty maxi dresses from a market stall at home.

She decided she would probably buy a few items at Gatwick Airport. She loved the shops there and always enjoyed treating herself to a pair of shoes and a bag. She would also invest in a pair of sunglasses, the Ray-Ban style she had seen Nigella wear in a recent shoot for a glossy magazine.

On departure day Claire felt like a child going to school for the first time. What would the other girls be like? Would they all get on, would they all be slim and beautiful, would they think her stupid and overweight?

She arrived at the airport by taxi and started to relax.

In departures she wandered into Mango and fell in love with a tribal maxi dress but stopped and put it back on the rail when she saw a beautiful blonde woman holding it across her slim body smiling at her reflection.

The woman had a few gorgeous tops slung over her arm as she headed for the changing room. Claire wandered over to the rails and picked up two similar styles. Yes, she could carry those off, she had always been complimented on her shapely shoulders, however she realised the dress would never look that good on her. She decided instead upon a blue chiffon beach dress and a bright red strapless maxi dress which made the most of those shoulders. Richard had always complimented her about her shoulders. Bloody Richard!

When she saw the boarding notice for flight VS 34 Claire strode purposefully to Gate 31. She couldn't wait to see who her travelling companions were. She had forgotten her copy of *The Lady* but she was sure Jesse would recognise her. She was on her way to Antigua and she would work out the rest of her life when she got back. Today was all about her, as were the next few weeks.

Looking around at the gate she couldn't see anyone who resembled Jesse so decided she would catch up with her at the other end. She planned to treat herself to a glass or two of champagne and put on a romantic movie. You never know what this holiday might bring.

ANNA

Anna woke up as her alarm sounded at 6am and for the first time in years she had no desire to jump out of bed and begin her day. Her hand drifted over to Piers' side of the bed and she allowed a tear to slide down her cheek as she saw the space that was usually filled by his cheery face. Why had she never fully appreciated that Piers had kept her grounded and happy? He had always been the one to head down to the kitchen and put the coffee on. Then on the way back he would hit the shower switch so it was all hot and steamy for her to jump in. She tried not to think of him all snuggled up with pregnant Jane in her Putney love nest.

Rolling over Anna decided she would do something she had not done in years. She would phone in sick. She could not face the sight of Jane, or the rest of the office. She realised her staff must have known what was going on throughout the affair between Jane and Piers.

She stayed home and didn't answer the phone or her emails for two days. She didn't bother to get dressed or showered and watched a succession of mindless day time TV.

'What a load of rubbish, no wonder people get depressed!' she stated out loud as she surfed the channels in search of anything to take her mind off her growing misery. She felt as though a large stone had taken up residence in her stomach and for the first time ever, she realised what heartache actually meant.

'It really does feel like a physical pain,' she told the empty flat. She made endless cups of tea and ate her way through two packets of chocolate Hob Nobs which Piers loved and kept in a big old vintage tin in the kitchen. For some reason the sight of this old tin with its images of faded roses made her cry loudly and properly for the first time. It evoked wonderful memories of a life when he had obviously loved her. They had been wandering through Wimbledon Village one Sunday morning and Piers had seen the tin in an antique shop.

'It's classic and beautiful, just like you,' he told her, and quickly nipped into the shop to buy her the gift. It became the tin they hid their goodies in, forbidden treats that Anna seldom indulged in, but Piers had a sweet tooth and loved to fill it with his favourite biscuits.

Tucking the tin under her arm Anna went back to bed and watched the lives of a family from Streatham crumble in front of the nation while the presenter shouted at a man who admitted he was sleeping with his mother-in-law and two of his sisters-in-law!

Miserably Anna kept checking her iPhone to see if Piers had left a message, though deep down she knew he would not be back in touch. Finally, she called Frank Solana and gave him the basic details. She found herself sobbing and once she started, she found it impossible to stop.

As she knew he would, Frank turned up with two bottles of red wine and a bottle of brandy and they drank it all as she poured out her sorry story.

It appeared Jane had done the decent thing and resigned. Anna groaned and realised that she would have to go back to work to sort out the mess. Jane was 'Mrs Organised' and without her things would not be getting done.

'Look, you are going to be fine; you are strong, great looking and there will be other men,' was all Frank could manage. But she didn't want another man; she wanted Piers. Safe, handsome, funny Piers who knew how to make her laugh, mix her favourite cocktail and choose the perfect outfit for a night out. She missed seeing his things around the flat and his warmth in bed. With a sinking heart she knew she had taken him totally for granted and now it was too late. She had had the perfect man, and now he was gone forever. Piers was with boring old Jane and worst of all they were expecting a baby.

And then, completely unexpectedly, her biological alarm clock went off. Big time. She knew in that instant that the strange longing and restlessness of late had not been her falling out of love with her job or with Piers; it was her need for a baby. She wanted to be a mother and sadly the only available man to help with that had gone out of her life forever. He had left her to have a child with messy Jane because he believed Anna would never want a baby.

The reality of her situation hit her like a hurricane and she slumped onto the sofa and wept. 'Frank, I feel so lost and alone. I don't know what to do, what should I do?'

Frank moved over to his young friend and taking her in his arms he rocked her like a child. She felt small and diminished and he found it hard to recognise the ball breaker who ran the office like a tyrant.

'Time is what you need, and a bit of distance. I really think you need to get away my love. Go somewhere different, go abroad for a while with a friend. You need a break.'

But Anna didn't really have any close friends. Again, she wished she had a bestie who would know what to say and who would head around with wine and sympathy to help her through.

'What has happened to me?' she wondered.

They talked for hours and although Anna felt better, she knew Frank was right. She needed to get away and get her head straight and work out this baby thing. Was the reason for this sudden need because of Jane's pregnancy?

Sadly, at the worst possible time she had finally known that she was ready to be a mother. The newspaper had been her 'baby' but now she was desperate for a real one. Endless sleepless nights, stretch marks and cracked nipples aside. Anna Smith wanted to be pregnant and be a mum but how the hell was that going to happen now? She desperately wanted to call Piers and pour all this out to him, but it was far too late and he would never believe her anyway.

It all happened very quickly. Anna went to the office and amazed everyone by announcing she was taking a three-month sabbatical and had appointed one of the up-and-coming news boys as acting editor. Rory O'Reardon had been a favourite of Anna for two years now and she admired his calm and no-nonsense approach. He knew how to make a good story into a great one; he was able to run the team and most of all he was loyal to Anna. She suspected that he had a bit of a crush on her and he was certainly very attractive and had a great body but Anna had kept their relationship very business-like. Nursing a broken heart may have softened her edges and made her seem ever so slightly vulnerable but she did not plan rebound sex any time soon. She had some important life decisions to make and she could not do that in London where at any moment, Piers or even bloody Jane could pop into view.

Anna had chosen Rory as her stand in for many reasons, but most of all because she trusted him. She had no idea when she would feel ready to return and get back in harness, but she knew that right now she was not able to carry on editing *The Globe*. She knew Rory would keep things on a level and would not stitch her up. Anna had witnessed so many cruel betrayals in her industry and had found herself on a redundancy list more than once as editors fought to get to the top. You could get fired for being too good or too ambitious. Many good writers had fallen foul of their bosses; women being the worst, especially those who felt threatened by a talented newcomer. While Anna was tough, she was also fair, and prided herself on promoting the people who showed skills and abilities. She believed that a good team reflected well on her and produced the best product – which was the reason her newspaper was one of the top titles and why she knew she could afford to take this much needed time out.

But where to go? Anna sat on the train idly looking out over little suburban houses lining the railway track as she travelled back to her flat. Many of the houses had small conservatories at the rear which were lit up and looked ready to welcome home husbands and families. She was in no rush to get home. There was nobody waiting for her there, only a ready meal and the prospect of a solitary movie night. How had her life suddenly fallen to pieces?

The young woman sitting opposite her got out of the train at Clapham Junction and left behind a copy of *The Lady* magazine. Anna was surprised to see that the title was still going strong after so many years. She picked it up and flicked through a few features on up-and-coming young things, charitable achievements, horsey events and the usual round of advertisements for flat shares and nannies.

One ad caught Anna's eye and she began to wonder if fate had thrown her a lifeline.

A woman was offering a house share in Antigua for two months and Anna wondered if this could be the answer to her problem, at least for a few weeks.

Antigua had been one of the places she and Piers had wanted to visit but had never got around to actually organising a trip. Anna was always too busy. She felt wistful and sad and, on a whim, she fired off an email on her iPhone asking if she could make up the Caribbean foursome.

She reasoned that the woman would be inundated and she had no wish to share the real reason she needed to get away, but what the hell. As her mother was so fond of saying, if you don't ask you don't get! She had come up with some cock and bull story about researching for a book and a girly trip to Antigua sounded perfect. Space and peace to relax and do a bit of work along the way.

Anna had almost forgotten about the email when two days later she found a reply informing her that she was welcome to join Jesse and her gang, Best of all, there in black and white was the date to fly out, escape the pain for a while and let the fun begin.

Dear Anna

You sound like the perfect addition to make up our foursome and
I would love you to join us. Hopefully you can find some fodder for

your research. I can certainly vouch for the villa being peaceful
and it's right on the beach so I would imagine it would be a great
place to chill out and write. I am booked on the Virgin Atlantic
flight out of Gatwick next Thursday morning. I am inviting you all
to join me but don't worry if you can't make that particular flight.
Simply let me know when you aim to head out and I will come to
pick you up. It's going to be fun and I am sure we will all get along
fine. I am attaching a few images of the villa so you can see where
you are heading. It looks fabulous, doesn't it?

We will sort the money situation out when we arrive. Nobody
seems precious about who gets the two master suites; so I have
suggested we do a draw ... but all the rooms look incredible.

Hopefully, we will all arrive on the same day, but I am very relaxed
about what room I get and the other two women sound as though
they are too so I am sure we can sort things out so that everyone
is happy.

Let me know if you can make the flight – the other two aim to
travel out on the same day as me so it would make sense if you
were able to join us too. My account details will follow, and I ask
for the rental sum upfront please.

I can't wait to meet you.

Best regards Jesse

Now she was making plans to join the group and for the
first time in weeks Anna felt light-hearted and excited at the
prospect of an adventure.

Rory had taken control of the office and had assured her
that she had no need to worry.

'Just go away and chill out, you deserve to,' he told her
in a soft, lilting voice. Had he always sounded that sexy,
she wondered? She popped on her out of office message
announcing she was off on sabbatical to do some research and
headed home to book a flight and pack a bag.

Anna went into her dressing room and slid open the door
of her walk-in wardrobe. She had always been very organised.

Spring and summer clothes were arranged colour wise to the right; autumn and winter to the left. There were rails of jeans and cropped trousers, cotton shirts and cardigans in every colour imaginable, jackets, tops and rows upon rows of pretty day and evening dresses. A huge antique pine chest housed her underwear and swimwear and she carefully selected a couple of basic bikinis, a black DKNY one piece that she had owned for years together with a skimpy, pale pink print Chanel set that always looked great and set off a tan to perfection. She threw in a red one piece then set about creating the perfect capsule holiday wardrobe.

She carefully chose a pair of espadrilles, a pair of flip flops and some sparkly low-heeled sandals which would go with everything. An aqua silk kimono would double as a beach cover up and dressing gown and she folded three soft jersey beach dresses which could be worn short or pulled down to calf length. It was a fabulous dress design which looked just as great on a night out as it did on the beach. She added a few pieces of bold jewellery, some huge gold bangles and a selection of earrings and belts. She packed a small evening bag; aiming to travel with her butter-soft leather tote mulberry bag. A pair of denim shorts and three halter tops completed her look.

Piers had bought her some Gucci sunglasses during their last weekend away in Paris but she decided that she would buy a cheapie pair at the airport.

She assembled a few basic jars of face and body lotions, some sunscreen and a lip gloss. She intended to be a lot more laid back on this trip so she would buy just a few essential cosmetics at the Mac counter. She loved to browse the make-up stands at the airport, it wasted a bit of time, and she needed a sun hat too. She had forgotten how much she enjoyed packing and planning a holiday wardrobe for in truth she had not had a holiday in a long while. This trip was going to be fun and she managed to keep dark thoughts of why she was heading off at bay. There would be plenty of time to miss Piers while she was away, right now she just had to get herself organised, packed and off to the airport.

Back at the office Frank Solano chewed on his pen while he read and re-read the email on his office screen.

How the hell was he going to break this news to Anna? She was flying off tomorrow and the timing could not be worse. Some conniving bastard was claiming that Anna had paid him to tap into a host of celebrity personal email accounts. In the US, stories were circulating and a scandal was soon to blow itself all the way across the Atlantic.

The sleaze bag wanted money, big money, to keep quiet and keep Anna out of the frame and Frank knew that the old Anna would want to stay and slug it out. But he also knew that right now Anna was in no state to fight. In any event, Frank needed to tap up his sources, make a few calls and find out what was behind this mess. The timing could not be worse and his young friend was in a dark enough place already without having to stress out about something which could potentially kill her career stone dead. The accusations were lies, but in this game, mud had a nasty habit of sticking.

Newspapers thrived on scandals. However, when something as big as this threatened, with lawsuits being discussed involving huge sums of money heads could roll and this situation had the potential to take Anna down.

With the media under ever increasing scrutiny and accusations of phone tapping and the like threatening to put top Fleet Street journalists behind bars; Frank knew that this story could blow up in Anna's beautiful face.

But this was a problem that he might be able to deal with and he was determined that Anna should leave for her trip before it hit the fan. He decided against telling her anything, after all, what was there to tell?

Teddy O'Sullivan was a Liverpudlian who had lived in London for 30 years but he had certainly not lost any of his thick Scouse accent. He had been a chauffeur for *The Globe* for 10 years and he enjoyed ferrying around all the top executives. Today he had a Gatwick run. Anna Smith was heading off to Antigua and he was booked to pick her up at 8am. He was under strict instructions not to reveal her travel plans and one thing he had learned was how to keep his mouth tightly shut.

Over the past couple of years Teddy had grown to like and respect Anna. When they first met, he thought she was a right stuck-up madam, but he had realised she was, actually a down-to-earth young woman. She treated him with respect and that he liked.

Anna ran to the car smiling and he was shocked to see how young she looked. Without all that make up and the posh clothes she looked a lot like his daughter Grace. Thinking about it, she was probably not much older. With her short, cropped hair and her face without its usual designer mask or signature red lipstick she looked different – fresher and prettier. He quickly stowed her luggage in the boot and pulled away from the kerb, assuring her that the traffic was light and she would be in good time for her flight.

Teddy hummed along to Radio 2 laughing at the jokes and banter provided by Chris Evans on his early show, while Anna talked to him about the trip. She was obviously happy and relaxed and Teddy was pleased that she was in such high spirits.

As they arrived at departures Teddy was shocked to see a crowd of photographers lined up on the kerbside. He heard a shout and suddenly the car was surrounded by lenses and flash bulbs popping off. They aimed their cameras into the car and a shocked Anna seemed to freeze as she stared out at the growing crush.

'Drive on, please drive on,' she shouted to Teddy who didn't need telling twice.

What the hell just happened back there?' she said, still shaken by the experience. A call to the office told her all she needed to know.

As a First-Class passenger she had entry into the Virgin Business Lounge. Anna was also privy to a private walkway where celebrities were able to avoid queuing with the masses. But first she had to get inside the terminal. Teddy drove her to a side entrance at the far side of the building and unloaded her bag.

'Just get away and have a break, your lot will sort this,' he said kindly. He had an old, battered trilby and he handed it to her. He also produced a navy pullover that swamped her but also made her feel strangely comforted.

'Here, have my baseball cap and pull it over your eyes, that will work better than that old trilby nobody will recognise you if you walk smartish.'

Anna flashed him a smile and did as instructed. She was swamped by the oversized sweater but the cap did hide her flame red hair and shielded her face. He dropped her off and she made her way quickly to the VIP entrance where she knew she would be safe.

Anna thought it was just as well that she was flying through the night. She would be thousands of miles away from home when the first editions went to press showing front page photos of her looking stricken and hiding her face in the back of a car under the banner headline 'Anna flees as US scandal breaks'.

Frank shook his head as Rory flung the paper onto his desk.

'It doesn't look good, does it? Nobody is buying the story that she is just off on holiday. They think that the board has given her the sack. Do you think any of the opposition will follow her out there? We have done our own piece and not said exactly where in the Caribbean she is going, but it won't take them long to find out.'

'You had better believe it. Someone tipped them off that she was going, I am not sure who, but once they know where she is they will be on it. Antigua is not such a big place, and she does have a habit of standing out in the crowd!'

Now safely inside the airport Anna kept her head down as she got to the gate. She had not wasted too much time in

Departures, simply dived into the Sunglass Hut to buy a pair of Ted Baker's, grabbed a neutral Maybelline lipstick, the first she had seen and a Rimmel bronzer. God, who would believe it? No chance to take her time at her favourite Chanel outlet. There was no way she could have browsed through the designer make up stands, but right now she could not have cared less. She just wanted to get away as soon as she could. She kept the black baseball cap over her face and slipped on her oversized glasses, hoping that none of the photographers had followed her through to departures.

She looked up to see that the flight was boarding at Gate 31. Grabbing a bottle of water from the Virgin lounge, she headed down as fast as she could. She just hoped that there were no bloody photographers on the flight. Bloody press!

The flight attendants were beautifully groomed and had slickly got everyone seated and ready for take-off. In First-Class Anna sipped a cold glass of champagne and tried not to think about the mess she had left behind her. The Piers situation had been bad enough but now she had a potential scandal blowing up in her face too. She had seen many talented and respected journalists fall on their swords following press witch hunts and she was not sure she had the strength or the will, to ride this one out. She knew there was no truth in what was being said about her, but the media preferred juice to truth and for the first time in many years Anna wondered if maybe she should walk away from her career. It was getting too stressful, and she wasn't sure she had the stomach for it any more. It had already cost her Piers. Accepting another glass of champagne, she resolved not to think about her job or her ex. This trip was all about giving herself space and time out. She intended to do just that. She looked around her wondering if any of her travelling companions were in First Class. She had not noticed anyone carrying copies of *The Lady* but then she had dashed on board with her head down not wanting to see or be seen. No doubt they would all meet at the other end. She reclined her seat a little and played with the movie selection. She chose a newly released rom-com and waited for dinner to arrive. She might have just one more glass of champagne – she was on holiday after all.

She would not have felt quite so calm and relaxed had she known that on board was a leader writer from one of the red tops together with one of their most notorious and utterly despicable photographers. He had a reputation for getting salacious and damaging images, no matter what.

Anna temporarily lost herself in the movie which portrayed Sandra Bullock finally getting her man and a baby. Anna hoped with all her heart that she would find a similar happy ending. Somehow, she doubted it. However, she was soon going to be relaxing on the sands in Antigua where, she was told, everything was possible.

CLAIRE

SITTING AT THE REAR of the aircraft Claire marvelled at the efficiency of the flight attendants as they swiftly served drinks prior to the meal service. She envied their beautifully cut red suits and immaculately made-up faces. They all looked like the ones on that iconic television ad where they strode through the airport in killer red stilettos. She looked down at her sensible sketchers and wished she had changed into her new jewelled flip flops.

She had escaped but she had still not morphed into the new Claire who was going to take chances, open herself up to new experiences and let the past go.

Accepting a glass of wine Claire settled down to read her book for a while but found it hard to concentrate. She had looked around for the other women at the departure gate, but it was a bit of a crush and she had decided to simply wait to meet up when they landed. Jesse had said there was a taxi booked and the driver would have their names on a board. She had a whole month to spend with them so a few hours were not going to make much of a difference. In any event, she was enjoying this time hovering in the air between her old life and her new one. She loved flying and found it exciting and strangely liberating. You were suspended in the clouds where nobody could reach you and for a few hours, nothing really mattered. The new Claire would be braver and more upbeat. She deserved a better life and she was going to find it in Antigua. She felt happier than she had in a long time.

'Things are going to be fine, I just know it,' she whispered to nobody. She decided that she would watch a movie, the sci fi that everyone had been talking about which had notched up a whole clutch of Oscar nominations. Later she would try to have a nap so that she would be fresh and rested when they landed. She intended to enjoy every single moment of this trip. She hoped the other women were going to be fun and easy to get along with. Jesse had sounded down-to-earth and funny and she felt she knew her already. Antigua here I come.

GINA

As the aircraft took off Gina felt strangely free and liberated. Two whole months away from all her problems was just what the doctor had ordered. No work, no James, and eight weeks to work out what to do with the rest of her life. She had no expectations – and a huge weight seemed to fall off her slim shoulders.

She accepted a cold glass of wine and polished off the vegetarian meal option, a tasty rice and bean concoction served with chilli and lime sauce, followed by a delicious raspberry mousse.

Gina had bought a new book in departures, the new Anita Shreve about a woman who is wronged and who wreaks vengeance on the man who has abused both her and her sister. But the story suddenly didn't appeal. Gina fancied a feel-good film so she selected a rom-com where Cameron Diaz got the man – didn't she always! Then browsing further through the movie offerings, she saw another fun sounding movie where Sandra Bullock gets a happy ending and a baby. Gina felt it may be a sign of better things to come. She had barely looked at her travelling companions but as the drinks trolley approached the man beside her asked for a gin and tonic and she suddenly realised how good looking he was. She watched as he raised his glass to his lips and found his mouth strangely compelling. He was tall, and well-built with a square jaw and the early signs of five o'clock shadow. On any other man this could have looked scruffy, but this guy wore his stubble with style. He did not seem to register her, but Gina kept a discreet eye on him as he ate his meal and plugged himself into his movie – a thriller she had rejected.

As the hours ticked by Gina got stuck into her book as sleep refused to claim her. She hated sleeping on planes anyway. She decided that the man beside her was probably happily married with beautiful children. It was only as they landed and she

100

prepared to gather her belongings from the overhead locker that she locked eyes with the handsome stranger and felt a searing hot flush race right through her.

'Hello and goodbye,' he said, shaking her hand and guiding her off the aircraft. She almost floated down the steps and watched wistfully as he made his way into the arrivals hall and joined the passport control queue. He didn't look back and didn't stop to collect any baggage. He seemed to have travelled with a small canvas backpack which suggested he was coming home. Either that or he was a man who travelled light and didn't need many possessions. He carried himself well and seemed confident and carefree. She wondered if he was a bit of a closed book who chose to keep himself to himself.

She wished that she had made the effort to at least engage the man in conversation. However she reminded herself she was not in the market for finding a man; even one as good looking as Mr Mystery.

She had to process what had happened with James and heal before she could even begin to think about getting involved with another man. But as she headed for the baggage claim area, she couldn't shake off the feeling she had missed an opportunity. Just what sort of opportunity was unclear. But those eyes and that rugged jaw complete with stubble were indelibly etched onto her brain. Maybe their paths would cross in Antigua. After all, it was not such a big place and he was certainly someone she would recognise if she ever came across him again. She did a double take. Was she really thinking about meeting a man on the heels of such a bad break up? Maybe she was in a better place than she had realised. Holding that thought headed out to arrivals eager to meet the others who she hoped would be there already.

JESSE

As SHE WAITED TO board the flight Jesse waited at Gate 31 with a home-made board spelling out the names of the three women who were to join her.

She had not bargained on the ground crew calling out her seat number almost as soon as she got to the gate, so she abandoned her plan for a group sign in. She reasoned they could all catch up at the end of the flight. In any event she was too excited to worry about it as she boarded the aircraft and found herself in Business Class. It turned out that her family had upgraded her as a treat. She had intended to find her travelling companions but as she luxuriated in the comfort of the huge leather reclining seat and had the sound and movie systems explained to her, she decided the introductions could wait.

Clutching a comprehensive menu and a clutch of gift-wrapped goodies, she decided that the women were probably enjoying their last few hours of peace and quiet. Group activities could come later. Selecting a great movie and snuggling down with a glass of Prosecco she decided that life was not so bad after all. As the aircraft climbed into the sky Jesse felt her spirits soar for the first time in weeks and thought ahead to the wonderful villa that awaited them. She hoped it would be as great as it looked online. She sighed and, closing her eyes, could almost feel the sunshine on her face and the blue sea lapping at her toes. For one fleeting moment she imagined how amazing it would have been to have had Sam sitting by her, but Sam had to be left in the past. He was not hers he never had been and now he was about to belong to someone else. She selected a movie, put in her ear plugs and ordered another glass of prosecco. For now, she was cocooned in a wonderful bubble and it felt great. She could worry about her future later. For the next few hours she was happy to be suspended in mid-air in the lap of luxury and enjoy a movie where the girl got her man. Because in films, they always do, don't they?

ANNA

ANNA WAS THE FIRST to get through passport control and into baggage reclaim. She was amazed at how small the airport was. Within 10 minutes she had been waved through and was now looking around for a sign with her name on. She walked to the entrance to arrivals and was relieved to see a dishy Antiguan guy holding a banner with all their names chalked in large red letters. With a huge smile on his face, he was talking to everyone around him and seemed in no rush to find his passengers.

Anna approached him with a smile and he matched it with a huge grin opening his arms wide like some long-lost uncle.

'Hi, I'm Denzil,' he told her.

He picked up her case and waved an arm towards a silver people carrier parked outside the terminal building. She had never given much thought to the airport or what it would be like. She was pleased that it was small with no real crowds to speak of; just a bustle of taxis being quickly snapped up by happy passengers.

'Just get inside and I will collect your friends,' Denzil told her as he gave her a respectful bow and headed back into the terminal.

She was grateful that her arrival had been seamless and she did not have to hang around and risk being seen by anyone. It crossed her mind that she may be overreacting wondering if rival papers had sent a hack out to find her to exposé any story about the scandal brewing back home. She tried to dismiss any doubts and sunk into the car to wait for her housemates.

Denzil had handed her a small travel guide and flicking through the pages she glanced at the ads for restaurants, hotels and bars and looked idly out of the window. She almost cried out loud when she saw Dan Bridges, one of the most hated Fleet Street news hacks, stride out of the terminal. There was no denying that he was handsome and incredibly sexy. But he had a terrible reputation as a womaniser with the ability to ruin a career with a few cruel paragraphs in a Sunday News Special. He was a rogue and a bit of a mystery man.

She suddenly felt cold fear grip her stomach. It seemed likely that he was on the island to do an expose on some poor soul. Herself? Surely, she didn't warrant sending that snake out here? The whole scene at Gatwick came back to her and she realised that, for the first time in her career, she could be the one being targeted. She just hoped the other women would show up soon. She was now in a hurry to get away from the airport and needed to get under cover fast. For one heart wrenching moment she wished she were back at home in Wimbledon with Piers in their cosy living room. He would have poured her a glass of wine, rustled up a dish of nibbles and made her feel safe, as only he could. Piers could always be relied upon to say the right thing to calm her down.

Bloody Piers. Bloody Jane.

JESSE

JESSE STRETCHED HER LEGS and began gathering her magazines and bag from the overhead locker. She had never had such enjoyed a flight so much and felt almost sorry that it was all over. The gloom of the past few weeks already seemed less raw, though she doubted she would ever really get over it.

Sam and the feelings she still felt for him were not going away any time soon.

'I am here and all I can think about is him, which is totally dumb, he is obviously not thinking of me,' she told herself out loud as she strode out of the aircraft to be met by a gentle blanket of afternoon heat. It felt beautifully warm but not in a clammy way. Jesse raised her face to the sun and decided that things were going to be fine. She would make them fine. She had two months of freedom ahead and three women to meet and maybe help with whatever had caused them to flee. They were going to have fun, she would make sure of it. She shaded her eyes as she made her way to the arrivals hall and felt another fleeting moment of sadness. She realised that she wished with all her heart that Sam was right beside her right now to share it all. Just bloody stop it, she told herself silently. Some girlie time was what she needed.

CLAIRE

CLAIRE FELT AS THOUGH she was in a dream as she queued up to go through passport control. She was behind a group of sailing types who were getting all fired up for a month at sea exploring the nearby islands. It was impossible not to feel light-hearted as they joked about their trip. One of the women started up a conversation with her and said how they were lacking a ship's cook. They jokily suggested she fill the post! Soon the others joined in and said that there was plenty of room for another stowaway. For one crazy moment she almost felt like heading off with them as they seemed fun, but she had other plans. Those plans began with a beautiful villa in Jolly Harbour and three potential best friends who she hoped would be waiting outside in arrivals. As she walked into the arrivals hall, she was met by a smiling man with a board listing all her housemates. Claire held out her hand and introduced herself. Denzil welcomed her to his island and guided her to a silver vehicle, inside of which a small, scowling red head angrily staring out at her.

'About bloody time, it is stifling in here,' the redhead said. Claire smiled weakly and offered her hand.

'Pleased to meet you, I am Claire, and I am sorry I missed you in London.'

The other woman, whom she realised must be Anna, simply nodded and continued to look out of the window. Claire could only hope that Anna was simply over tired and would loosen up a bit. This was not the sisterly welcome she had hoped for and just for a fleeting moment she wondered if she had made a mistake. What if the others were as standoffish as this woman was?

But her fears immediately vanished when within minutes Jesse arrived at the people carrier, wreathed in smiles, and staggering under the weight of a huge backpack. Claire breathed a huge sigh of relief, it was going to be fine. This

Anna woman obviously had a few issues. Jesse seemed lovely, and she hoped the others would be too.

'I can't seem to travel light,' said Jesse, as Denzil took her bag and loaded it into the boot. That just leaves Gina.'

And as if on cue the lovely Gina glided out of the Arrivals Hall dragging a small suitcase. Claire instantly recognised her as the beautiful woman she had seen buying clothes in Zara.

'Hi everyone, sorry if I kept you waiting. My bag was the last one to arrive and I was frantic. I treated myself to a whole new summer wardrobe at Gatwick and I would have cried if they had lost my case.'

The four women settled in the car and didn't talk as they allowed Denzil to give a running commentary about his island home all the way to Jolly Harbour.

Claire looked out at the ramshackle wooden houses and wondered what she had let herself in for. However, as they neared the resort the buildings looked more cared for. The houses got bigger and smarter the nearer they were to the bay. By the time they arrived at Jolly Harbour, the women were gaping in awe at the stunning beachside houses and the amazing views.

The vehicle finally stopped outside a very impressive white painted house. Beautiful shrubs surrounded a huge, square courtyard. The wooden double fronted door opened out onto a massive hallway. A glass wall looked out over one of the most stunning beaches the women had ever seen.

The floors were of a light oak and stretched to the outside space which they all longed to explore. The sun was shining and the sea looked impossibly blue. They were suddenly aware of how hot and sweaty they felt.

They oohed and aahhed and headed outside to a huge wooden deck which led directly onto the beach. There was a raised platform at the far end of the deck with an infinity pool. A glass and chrome staircase led up to a raised terrace, complete with a beautiful alfresco dining area. There was a collection of swish sofas piled with cream and blue striped cushions and the quartet could only gape and smile.

'It looks like something out of *Elle Decoration*,' exclaimed Anna, and the other women could only nod in awe. She seemed to have left her black mood behind and was openly smiling as she explored the villa.

They ran up another stairwell that took them to a mezzanine floor where two of the larger bedrooms looked out over the sweep of the bay. The two lower rooms were just as spacious. These led out onto the garden and pool areas so nobody minded which room they ended up with. They were all stunning suites, each had a lush en suite bathroom with a luxurious slipper bath and massive shower. Everyone seemed more than happy with their villa home for the next few weeks. Jesse made the introductions and said they should decide which room they wanted. Everyone was so chilled, they realised the group was going to get on and were just very happy to be there.

Claire and Jesse agreed to have the lower rooms while Anna and Gina opted for the first-floor suites. The rooms were all lavishly furnished with cream hand painted sleigh beds. The windows had stylish blinds made with pale, coastal striped cottons. The whole place was filled with light.

A pale grey, hand-painted kitchen fitted out with the very latest in high end appliances, with a feature island, also hit the mark.

A large, light oak refectory table was the perfect spot to sit and watch the sea and linger over lazy mealtimes. There were huge platters of cheeses, fruits and cold meats laid out for them to enjoy. Two bottles of iced champagne were in a massive silver wine cooler. The girls swooped on the feast and began to loosen up and chatter with the sheer joy of being in such a beautiful place.

The huge lounge overlooking the bay had a glass wall that could be pulled back so the tide appeared to be lapping at their toes.

'I am never going home,' announced Jesse and the other girls agreed they felt the same. This villa had surpassed their expectations. Whilst it was glamorous and luxurious, the owners had also added some homely touches such as a huge cream log burning stove and painted bookshelves filled with a variety of titles.

The house had simply enveloped them with its warmth and charm and Jesse could not wait to slip on a bathing suit and run into the sea.

Meanwhile Anna headed off to explore the rest of the house. She was delighted to find a cinema room which offered a 24-hour news service and a library of the latest movies.

'We can have some great nights in,' she thought, as she flicked through some of her favourite films.

She was also keen to get a grip on the latest news feeds to see if her worst nightmare was fact, but there was nothing to suggest she was in the news. For the time being, she felt she could keep her fears to herself.

Jesse and the others joined her, and Jesse finally felt able to relax after feeling under pressure to deliver a dream location. She let out a huge sigh of relief and satisfaction. She was so happy that the villa had exceeded everyone's expectations. This is going to be a place to heal us, she decided. Who could feel miserable in such a stunning beach house? The group had moved back to the kitchen and were sipping champagne and relaxing a little. They were gradually beginning to loosen up with one another.

As Denzil unloaded their luggage a tall, vibrant woman arrived laden with bags of groceries explaining that her services came with the property. She would be on hand to cook meals, do laundry and clean up every day. The rental also included a fully stocked fridge and larder, and a few bottles of complimentary champagne were chilling in the American-style fridge.

'Can this get any better?' enthused Claire who had never experienced such luxury.

Jesse said she was in her private heaven and Anna and Claire felt they were excited to be living the dream. Anna was secretly impressed with the set up but seeing Dan Bridges had unnerved her and put her in a defensive mood that she could not seem to shake off. She knew she was being cold and a bit unfriendly. The other women all seemed so upbeat and open but she was out of practice with being part of a girlie group. But she had warned Jesse that she was not a 'girlie' girl so she decided that she could afford to wait a while before she made an effort to fit in with the gang.

The housekeeper had been bustling around in the kitchen. She suddenly appeared with more provisions and another champagne cooler filled with a bottle of Cristal and four chilled glasses.

'This is how we welcome you all to Antigua,' she said, refilling the flutes with the chilled champagne.

The young women accepted their glasses and wandered out to the terrace, where for the next hour they sat and made small talk. They all secretly knew that the life stories would come later but for now everyone seemed content to sit and chill out as the sun started to lose its heat.

Jesse and Gina had given into temptation and raced down to the beach to slip into the warm, turquoise water. Claire had so wanted to join in, but she was keenly aware that the others all appeared to have model girl figures. She felt her own was sadly lacking and though she had comfy swimsuits and cover ups, she wasn't yet ready to put her body on show. She wandered to the water's edge to paddle her feet and drink in the views. She watched as the others splashed about laughing at the sheer freedom of being in warm seas in such a paradise location.

'I think I will unpack and have a nap and see you guys later,' Anna announced as she walked up the stairs to the upper floor suite she had chosen. The others simply smiled and headed out to the terrace where Eva, their beautiful housekeeper had prepared another feast of light snacks.

Later, after she had dried off and thrown on a chiffon kaftan, Jesse took control and felt it her role to encourage her new housemates to get to know each other a bit more.

'Why don't we give Eva a break tonight and cook dinner together? Maybe later we could head out to the Crow's Nest bar for a cocktail. Denzil tells me it's a great bar to head to for our first night and they have a two for one cocktail menu. It's karaoke on Tuesdays and he says it is a good chance to meet some of the locals.'

Gina and Claire nodded their approval and decided that going to bed early on their first night was a bit of a waste. Quietly they all hoped that Anna was going to get off her high horse and join in a bit, but it was too soon to start judging her. She seemed aloof but then she had warned Jesse that she enjoyed her space, and they needed to respect that.

Claire marinated some chicken while Gina made a salad. Jesse uncorked yet another bottle of champagne and poured each of them a glass.

'To us and our trip,' she said. 'I feel we are going to have to throttle back a bit on all this champagne but why not indulge on our first night.'

They told Eva they would look after themselves for the evening and feeling incredibly relaxed and ever so slightly tipsy, they headed for the pool.

An hour later Anna decided to join the group and happily accepted a glass of champagne. Gina and Claire had enjoyed their swim and were quietly confiding in one another about their man troubles. It seemed easy to talk to strangers about the nightmares they had left behind and the women agreed that the champagne had helped loosen their tongues!

The two women had bonded quickly as there were more than a few similarities in their sad stories of pain and deceit.

Claire had tears in her eyes as Gina attempted to play down the violence and abuse she had suffered.

She told them she had kept this side of her life a secret.

They all felt sad but offered their support and urged her to look upon them as allies.

Claire initially felt that her betrayal had not been so traumatic. Her man was weak and a cheat, but she had never been physically beaten. But as they all shared their stories, it began to dawn on Claire that what she had suffered was a form of abuse too.

The girls were both angry and appalled at Richard's cruel behaviour and for the first time Claire saw her life for what it had been.

Richard had systematically ground her down, made her feel worthless and unattractive and she had lost sight of the strong, beautiful Claire her family and friends loved so much. Her self-confidence and self-esteem were non-existent.

The group were so supportive and for the first time in a long time Claire felt she did have a contribution to make, she would get stronger and she would learn how to get her confidence back. 'I know I deserve more,' she said, and they all applauded her. The champagne and gin cocktails helped but she knew things were changing.

Jesse didn't feel ready yet to share her story, but she hinted that a love affair had gone wrong and she needed to get away for a while to lick her wounds and get a grip on life. Nobody pressured her to say more, but she felt part of a sisterhood. When she did feel ready to talk about Sam she knew they would understand.

Anna listened as they spoke about the pain and betrayals they had experienced and she felt her throat tighten with grief and regret. Once again she was reminded of how lovely Piers had been and how much she had taken him for granted. Had Piers ever criticised her? Had he ever tried to make her feel small or stupid? No, never. His only crime had been to refuse to put up with her obsession with her career and her stupid vanity and ego any more. She could not recall ever thanking him for all the kind things he did and all the moral support he had given her. She had become a selfish bitch; someone who was not interested in what anyone else wanted or thought. Now she was paying the price. Anna had never felt so alone or so stupid. How was she ever going to find a man as perfect as Piers? In fact how was she going to find any man who would be willing to put up with her again? She longed to tell the others her story, but she was not one to open up to strangers. She sipped her champagne and felt misery engulf her all over again. She thought of how Piers would have loved this villa and she wished with all her heart that he was sitting with her now, enjoying the view and holding her hand. Bloody Jane. She realised with a jolt that it was not Jane's fault that Piers had felt so beaten down. Only one person was responsible for making a hash of Anna's life, and she was standing right here.

The group enjoyed their supper and drifted off to their rooms to get changed for their trip to the cocktail bar, though they realised they did not really need any more alcohol.

They had noticed people driving around the resort on golf buggies and Eva had explained that was how a lot of the residents got around. The carts certainly came into their own when residents made trips to the marina and the North and South Finger properties.

She said the buggies were also handy to pop to the local supermarket for supplies and for heading off to the more secluded beach on North Finger. The girls thought it sounded fun and agreed that the next day they would hire a couple of buggies for the next few weeks. They realised they had drunk so much none of them could be trusted to drive anywhere now but Eva reassured them the bar was only a five-minute walk away. Could this trip get any better?

At just after 10pm, with a warm breeze to cool them off the women walked to the bar and ordered a round of cocktails. They had showered and changed into casual cotton tops and jeans and were glad that they had opted for a laid-back look.

Around them people of all ages were drinking, eating and having fun. A steel band was playing on stage and a huge billboard was offering half price cocktails.

By midnight they had consumed several rounds, having tried out most of the cocktail specials and had also met quite a lot of the people who lived nearby. Anna had loosened up considerably, aided by a few Long Island iced teas, and was finally opening up about the loss of Piers. Claire slipped her arm around Anna's slim shoulders as she shared her story. 'Maybe he is not gone forever. From what you say the two of you were great together; you just let your work get in the way.'

Anna had not told the whole truth. The fact that Jane was pregnant was not something she had mentioned.

'No, he won't be coming back. I think it's pretty clear that he is gone for good, I just have to get over him,' she said sadly.

Hearing herself say the words made Anna feel raw all over again and to her horror she felt tears fill her eyes and overflow and her throat tightened making it impossible for her to say anymore.

Instinctively Claire moved to her side and put a hand on her arm.

'I do know how you feel, I really do,' she said. An hour later the women had walked back to their beach villa. One by one they had given up and headed for bed. Only Anna had found it impossible to sleep. She lay on her bed thinking of the past few years. How she had worked so hard and how she had managed to lose the only man who had ever really understood her. Yes, he had betrayed her, but she felt she had pushed him away. She believed that she had played as big a part in their breakup as bloody Jane.

Anna lay awake for hours trying to stop grieving for Piers, and as the light began to filter through the blinds she finally succumbed to a troubled sleep.

Just before she lapsed into an exhausted doze, she felt strangely at peace with the fact she had found herself with a bunch of strangers on a Caribbean Island. For once she had no game plan. She had nowhere to be and nothing to do but relax and work out the next chapter of her life. She had to admit they were a fun group and they were all kind and easy going. She realised with a jolt they were probably the only women friends she had ever had. Tomorrow she decided, she would make the effort,

Jesse and Gina seemed like her type of women, and even the shy and under confident Claire had been easy company. She had to admit that previously she had never seen the benefit of making friends apart from with Piers. He had always wanted her to have girlfriends, he had felt sad at how isolated she was. What would Piers make of it all now? He would have got a kick out of seeing her enjoying herself with a gang of women friends. Sadness engulfed her as she fought the urge to call him and tell him, that yes, he was right, she had cut herself off from the simple things in life. The thought made her heart sink again. Finally she drifted off into a drunken and exhausted sleep.

Claire, Jesse and Gina were also lying in their beautiful rooms thinking about the events that had led them to this paradise and a group of relative strangers. One by one they finally fell asleep feeling hopeful of what the next few weeks would bring.

SAM

SAM WOKE UP WHEN his alarm sounded at 6am. This was the day he and Zoe were going to see the local vicar to choose hymns and readings for their wedding ceremony and he felt sick. How had he got himself into this ridiculous situation? He had never meant to hurt Zoe or be unfaithful to her, neither had he intended to meet and fall in love with another girl just months away from his wedding day. It had hit him like a train. He was in love with Jesse. He had also cared about Zoe but these days he was not so sure. But marriage? Surely he should not go ahead with it? He wanted to be with Jesse with her beautiful brown eyes and shy smile. He loved the way she always smelled of flowers and sunshine. He had asked her early on what her fragrance was. She had explained that her best friend had bought her a bottle of perfume called Happy which smelled of the sunflowers she loved.

Now he realised that he was not happy. Far from it. He had lost the woman who made him happy, she was somewhere else trying to forget him. She was probably with another man right this minute. Why wouldn't she be? He had lied to her, led her on and ignored her for weeks. He had picked up the telephone hundreds of times to call her, but what would he say? What had he done to change his situation? She must hate him. He hated him. The only time he had contacted her was to warn her that Zoe was about to get in touch. He had only warned her to save his skin; he was a coward and he didn't deserve someone like Jesse. But he knew that he wanted to be with her more than anything. He headed out of the door and into the car noting he had cut it a bit fine to meet Zoe. But he knew he could not let this pretence go on any longer. He had to find the guts to come clean and tell Zoe he couldn't go through with it. Even if he had missed his chance with Jesse, he could not imagine a life with Zoe and her snobby and controlling behaviour.

He could not go to the church and make any more plans for their wedding. It was all a sham. The final straw was when his wife-to-be insisted that he tell his mother she could not wear the teal coloured two piece she had bought to wear for the wedding. His mum was so proud of her outfit and she kept taking out the matching shoes and a ridiculously fussy feather hat so that he could admire the outfit.

'She has to wear blush or lilac,' insisted Zoe. 'She will clash with my colour scheme and the photos will look terrible. You have to tell her!'

Sam had no intention of telling his sweet-natured mum she would not be wearing the outfit she had spent months putting together. Zoe was not having any of it.

'You tell her, or I will,' was her last order when she called last night to moan about how the menu was not up to scratch and the hotel was being unreasonable about making yet more changes.

'Zoe, you have changed your mind so many times ...'. She screamed down the phone accusing him of being pathetic, and stating it was her prerogative to make as many changes as she wanted. She also added cruelly that she hoped once they were married, he would man up and stand up to his mother!

He didn't need this last spat to emphasise the huge mistake he was about to make. He didn't even like this woman anymore. The marriage thing had simply crept up on him and had taken over like a fast-moving locomotive. He wanted out. Although he had no way of knowing how he was going to achieve this, he had to. So, manning up was going to happen and not in the way his bride was expecting.

Zoe's insistence that he talk his mother out of wearing her much loved wedding outfit to suit her ridiculous whim about the wedding photos proved to be the final straw for him.

As he drove to Zoe he kept trying to conjure up the right words. Miserably he pressed the doorbell and felt his mouth go dry as he saw her outline through the glass door.

She looked flushed and angry and as he tried to walk into the hallway, she barged past him and shouted at him to get a move on. 'We are so late. I can't believe you. Can't you ever be on time, you are always letting me down!'

She continued to rage at him as she jumped into the passenger seat and fastened her seatbelt. She glared at him then casually got out a make-up mirror, applied a coat of lip gloss and fluffed up her hair. Exasperated she rolled her eyes at him and demanded he get into the car.

'Get in! We are so late, and we have so much to sort out.'

Sam looked at her as he had never looked at her before and thought how she looked vain and ugly. In that moment he knew it was all over. While he felt sick and lightheaded, he knew this was the time to be honest and say the words that had been circulating in his head for months. He turned away from the car, slumped down on her doorstep and put his head in his hands. Within seconds Zoe had jumped out of the car and was screaming at him to get a move on. 'What do you think you are doing? Are you mad? We are already late, and you just sit there looking idiotic on a doorstep? Have you lost the plot?'

Calmly Sam looked up at her and said simply 'Far from it, I have realised that there is no point going to the church. I can't marry you Zoe. We are done, our relationship is all wrong. It's over.'

As he said the words, he felt a huge weight lift though he knew the result of his outburst was going to create a huge row.

'What are you talking about? You arrive here looking like hell and start talking rubbish – just get in the car and let's go. We are late, and I don't have time for this nonsense.'

Zoe looked at him with a mixture of disgust and fury and it struck him that he had never really noticed how small and cruel her eyes were.

How could he have ever thought he loved her?

Sam raised his eyes to hers and simply shook his head.

'It's not nonsense. I don't love you Zoe, this has to end. I have felt like this for a while now and I have tried to tell you before. It has all gone too far and I should have spoken up, but I felt so pushed into it all. The wedding isn't about us, it's about who is coming to the wedding, colour schemes and impressing everyone. You never asked me what sort of wedding I wanted. Even my poor mum isn't allowed to wear what she wants! It's ridiculous. This is not how it should be.'

A moment later she lunged at him clawing at his face and screaming that she hated him and wasn't going to stand for him making a fool of her.

He remained sitting on the step powerless to say or do anything but feeling nevertheless a tremendous feeling of relief. Zoe continued to pound at him with her fists but Sam didn't care or even register the pain.

It might be too late to win back Jesse but he knew with conviction that he could never marry someone like Zoe. He had known for some time that she was vain and shallow and that she had no real feelings for him. She just wanted a wedding and a nice house. She was not in love with him, just the idea of him. As she pummelled his head with her fists, yelling abuse and kicking at him, he didn't feel anything other than the relief of knowing he was free of her.

He wished with all his heart that he had had the nerve to end things months before. Zoe continued to shout abuse at him, demanding to know what had happened and if someone had made him change his feelings toward her.

'There is someone else, I know there is, just tell me you bastard! I hate you! I bet it's those stupid friends of yours. They have never liked me, and you are so weak, you just listen to what they say, you are pathetic.'

Sam had no fight in him. She was right, he was pathetic and he hated himself He decided she deserved the truth. He stood up and faced her and he heard himself saying the words he had wanted to say for so long.

'It's nothing to do with my friends. But yes, I did meet someone. It didn't last long and it's over, but I still can't marry you, it wouldn't be fair to either of us.'

He didn't see the blow come, Zoe caught him full force and he fell to the ground. He lay there for some time simply because he could not think of a reason to try to stand up. He was free of Zoe but he had lost Jesse. A tiny flicker of hope ignited deep within his soul and he managed to sit upright. Zoe had flounced into her house and was still screaming at the top of her voice. He staggered to his car and sat inside feeling dazed.

Suddenly he realised what he had to do. He started the car and headed toward Putney and the pretty street with the beautiful flower shop on its corner.

He would drive to the shop and beg Jesse to take him back. He didn't care how long it took. He was going to get her back. He knew he looked a sight with a bruised, scratched face but he had left it far too long already. Part of him felt he should wait a while to get his head straight, but now he was on a mission. His head ached and he felt a cut throbbing above his eye, but he didn't seem to feel a thing.

He had deserved the blows she had metered out. He was happy to drive away knowing that he would never go back to Zoe again. He realised he had left behind an almighty mess. The wedding was planned, deposits paid, dresses bought and the honeymoon paid for. He didn't care. He was free and now he had to try to get Jesse to listen to him.

Once he had made the decision he couldn't wait to get there and see that beautiful face and stare into those soft, brown eyes. Sam felt bad about what he had done to Zoe but he had to see Jesse today. He had been stupid and had wasted so much time. How had he got it so wrong? He wondered if he had left it too long to put it right?

Sam pulled up outside the florist and was puzzled to see the door closed and the window devoid of any flowers. There was a white poster on the door and with mounting misery he read that Jesse had left for two months. She had left the number for another florist who was handling any future bookings on her behalf.

Deflated, Sam took a note of the number and tried to think where she may have gone. Surely there was nobody else in her life already? It had only been a few weeks. Although he had treated her so badly, she could be forgiven for thinking he had used her. He had been such a fool.

Dialling the number, he hoped against hope that Jesse was not too far away and that she would at least give him the chance to say how sorry he was. Above all he wanted her to know that he loved her and that he had left Zoe. The phone call was brief but told him all he needed to know. Jesse had flown off to Antigua. She had travelled alone as far as her friend knew, and she was not due back for two months. The friend was obviously aware that Jesse was running away from someone and while she had her address, she was not about to reveal that information to this stranger.

Antigua, why there? Who did she know in the Caribbean, and what was she doing there? Her friend said that Jesse had seemed down and had simply said she needed to get away and get her head straight. Sam reasoned that maybe all was not lost; she was not over him after all.

After a sleepless night with a few awful calls from Zoe, her father threatening to sue him, Sam reasoned that Jesse must be back at some point. She had a business to run, and when she returned, he would be waiting. He hoped that it was not too late.

PIERS

PIERS LOCKED THE DOOR of Jane's flat and strode toward his car. When he had first moved into her tiny studio flat it had seemed so romantic and fun. Jane had joked about how small it all was, how they would have to sleep and eat within a square metre. At first, he had been happy enough to do the dishes while she made up the sofa bed in the evenings.

He hated to admit it but he missed his spacious home with Anna; the lovely en suite bathroom, the huge wardrobes, and the sunny patio where they used to sit and share their news over breakfast. He loved their full-to-capacity American fridge, the arrival of the cleaner every Friday and the ironing lady every Saturday. His shirts were always laundered and ready for the week ahead.

He had not anticipated that Jane would be such an untidy housekeeper. She didn't care if dishes were left for a day or two or if the kitchen surfaces were sticky and scattered with breadcrumbs and butter. She left greasy pans in the sink, she was not fastidious about cleaning the shower or the basins either.

In fact, she was not bothered about cleaning full stop. He began to wonder how it would work once the baby was born. Where would they keep all the stuff a baby would need? The flat was so tiny. There was no storage whatsoever, they had no bedroom for themselves let alone for a baby. Jane was not in the least concerned about any of the details surrounding becoming a mother and how it would change their lives. Before living with her he had never noticed that she only wore three outfits on a rotation and only washed her hair once a week. Anna had washed her hair every day and wore a fresh outfit daily. Why had he never fully appreciated how beautifully groomed she was? She always smelled so wonderful. Her bedding was crisp and clean and smelled of flowers. He had never told her but when he thought about her, he always conjured up her smell, a fragrance he suddenly missed very much.

He shook these thoughts away and tried to focus on the fact that he was now with another woman and he had promised to make a life with her. He was going to be a father in a few months so issues like moving to a bigger flat or a house with a garden would have to be addressed at some point, but not right now. With a heavy heart he cleared away the dishes from the previous night and got out the spray bleach to clean the surfaces. The sofa bed was covered with a crumpled duvet that looked shabby and grubby. 'He allowed himself momentarily to think of his beautiful bedroom back at home with its Egyptian cotton sheets and pale oak flooring. He also imagined soaking in the huge white tub in their en suite and he could have wept. Home seemed far away in a past he suddenly realised he wanted back.

'What about scans, getting you booked into the hospital … a birth plan?' he would ask Jane, but she would wave him away.

'There is no rush, stop stressing. We can sort that out later,' she would tell him. But Piers wanted to get things organised; it was how he and Anna had always worked. They liked being organised. If Anna had been having a baby, she would have sorted out the nursery by now and would have made numerous lists of what they needed to do. She would have put together a wardrobe of classy maternity outfits that showed off her long slim legs. Then it hit him with a tidal wave of emotion!

'Oh my god, I miss Anna, I miss her being a clean freak, I miss her wanting to be in charge and organised … I even miss her bossing me around and telling me what to wear on a night out. What the hell have I done? I want the two of us to be having a baby, me and Anna. I even miss her bloody lists.'

He tried to reassure himself by remembering Anna had never wanted babies or the accompanying clutter, but then he countered maybe she had been right all along. Right now, he was not feeling certain about the idea of becoming a father himself. If it was with Anna, he knew he would have been over the moon at the prospect of being a dad. He felt strangely tearful and very lonely.

Piers looked ahead and saw a future full of chaotic rooms, dirty dishes, mountains of laundry, filthy toilets and dirty sinks. He thought wistfully of the uber clean kitchen he and Anna had created and the pristine marble bathroom with its huge slipper bath and the antique oak console that Anna polished so lovingly. Anna loved the smell of bleach. She also insisted on lots of scented candles on the sill adjoining the bath. She was also obsessed about laundering the towels every day and filled a willow basket with a mountain of fragrant bath towels. He thought about the Jo Malone candles in his old bathroom and the colourful woven rag rugs alongside the slipper bath. Jane didn't bother with candles, bleach or even fabric conditioner to ensure the towels were sweet smelling.

Jane's towels were an awful grubby grey and were scratchy to the touch. She was useless at cleaning the kitchen or the living room and the small, terraced garden resembled a tip. It could have been a pretty outside space but Jane threw cardboard boxes and refuse sacks out there. She hated fresh air and never allowed him to open the windows. The small flat had French doors opening out onto the terrace but Jane refused to open them. Piers had bought a pretty cream wrought iron table and chair set and suggested they clear the terrace. Maybe fill a few pots with plants and enjoy meals outside.

He had cleared away the debris and pressure washed the paving stones but Jane had laughed scornfully and accused him of being a snob. 'What's wrong with eating on our laps. Don't go bringing your poncey ideas here,' she had retorted. Piers realised with a shock that shy little Jane was not all she had appeared to be. In fact, he was finding out a lot of things about Jane that were so far removed from the person he thought she was. She was not simply sloppy and dirty in the house; she was also selfish and only thought about herself. He decided that there was a lot about Jane he did not find attractive. At dinner last night he had noticed her nails were bitten and dirty and there were food stains on her shirt. He had expected her to shower and get changed before they sat down for the evening but Jane had simply placed a pizza and oven chips in the oven and had gone to lie down on the sofa. Without a word to him, or even a glance in his direction, she had picked up the remote control and put on a seriously tacky reality show that made Piers wince.

He could not understand why he had been so blind. He had been so lonely that he had failed to see what she really was. He knew deep down that Jane was not too bothered about making him happy. He could see clearly that all Jane had been set on was getting Piers to leave Anna. He was the prize in some sick competition she had invented to get one over on the boss she hated. She had succeeded and fooled him into thinking they were meant to be together. Now all he could think about was how clean and fresh his home with Anna had been and how she had always filled the fridge with fresh fruit and salads. Their home had always been filled with flowers and fragrant candles.

He sighed as he looked at the cheap artificial roses Jane had stuffed into an old jam jar. With a jolt he also realised that most importantly he missed talking to Anna; just being her friend and sharing her life.

With mounting misery, he started to wash the mound of dishes piled in the sink. He tried not to lose his temper when he opened the fridge to discover a pile of rotting vegetables, food that was way past its sell by date, and curled up, green ham. The milk was off and the cheese they had shared the night before had not been covered so looked hard and waxy. Life seemed very bleak. As he cleared out the rotten food, he decided to take control and suggest they move house very soon. He couldn't cope with living like some ageing student, and he certainly was not going to bring a baby into this tip. He didn't care what Jane said, he was not going to stay in her awful bedsit a moment longer than he needed to. He picked up the *Evening Standard* and headed out to the small terrace where he had cleared enough space for the table and chairs. There were no pretty pots and trailing plants, but at least he didn't have to watch the trash Jane had on the TV. He tried in vain to ignore the stench of rubbish bins spiralling up from the courtyard below. Piers felt he was in hell, and it was a hell of his own making.

RICHARD

RICHARD HAD TRAVELLED BACK from his conference in Edinburgh fully prepared for a big row with Claire. He had felt shocked when she had walked in on him and Martha, but he knew he could fix things. Claire was sweet but she was weak and loved him unconditionally. From the moment he had met her that fateful first day and had managed to sort out her flat tyre he knew he had her hooked. She was a pretty young thing and he had meant to simply have a meaningless fling, but somehow things had developed further than he had planned. At the time he had found himself with nowhere to live when his previous girlfriend found out he was cheating on her once again. The prospect of moving into Claire's beautiful cottage was an inviting one. She treated him like a king and in bed she was willing and eager to please. He had her wrapped around his little finger in no time. She was like all the women he had met before. Flatter them and tell them what they want to hear and they will do anything for you. Claire was naïve and trusting and refused to see anything wrong with him.

He had an easy life and getting married seemed like the answer. She made no demands upon him and for a while he played the part of a perfect new husband until he became bored of her adoration. Then along came her sexy best friend, Martha. She was another story. He knew she didn't like him at first and he had seen this as a challenge. Bit by bit he wooed her and made her think he was the kindest, gentlest man alive. He played on the fact that Martha was ever so slightly jealous of Claire, of her home and her daughter. The rest was easy.

His fling with Martha had been fun, but she had become a bit clingy and had started to make noises about him coming clean with Claire about their love affair. She had also insisted he think about moving out of their home. He had no intention of doing either of those things. Life with Claire was ordered and calm, she adored him and let him do pretty much what he wanted. There were no dramas or rows and while Claire could be a bit dull at times, she was attractive and attentive. She kept the house clean and tidy, always made sure his laundry was done to perfection and was a fantastic cook. She was the perfect wife in so many ways; though he admitted he had become a bit bored with her. She had always been curvy and in the early days he had loved that, but he had felt lately that she had let herself go a bit. Claire had started looking mumsy and matronly. and he had struggled to find her physically appealing. Martha was vivacious and sexy. In fact she was almost too demanding in the bedroom at times. She was not wife material. He enjoyed long afternoons in her bed where she was wild and very body confident. She always wore amazing underwear and didn't balk at anything he asked her to do to please him.

Martha was 38 and had been hinting about her biological clock lately. He was beginning to think it was time to cool things. He had no wish to have any children with her, or anyone for that matter. Claire had a daughter and seemed happy to stick with one child. Financially she made no demands on him either. Leaving Claire would be foolhardy. He just had to break up with Martha, then go home and make things right with Claire. He was confident she would be glad to have him home. He wouldn't make waves with Martha during their weekend away, and there was no denying the sex was fantastic, but it had to stop. This affair had got a bit out of control. Once he got home, he planned to tell Claire how Martha had made all the running, maybe hint at feeling a bit neglected. That always seemed to work with Claire; he had used it in the past several times to get his way. He would do it again. He would miss the fun and sex with Martha, but he had a few women friends at work that had shown more than a passing interest in him so there was always the prospect of some no strings sex with one of them. He had done this before. This time with Martha, he had made the mistake of choosing someone too close to home and she had fallen in love with him. He had allowed it to go too far and agreeing to meet up for those three days in Edinburgh had been a big mistake. Martha said she had been mortified when Claire had walked in on them but she had reasoned it was probably for the best. In fact, looking back, she had seemed delighted and was smiling as Claire ran out of the hotel bar. Martha had often said she would happily talk to Claire and tell her that they had fallen in love, but he had managed to stop her.

He realised he should probably have tried to run after his wife when she had left the hotel in Edinburgh. But Martha was insatiable, and he was looking forward to three days of pure pleasure. Martha knew how to turn him on and now that their affair had come out into the open, he had never known her so wild.

In the past he had told Martha he would tell Claire when the time was right, but he had never intended for it to be the right time. As he left Martha at the station car park, he gave her a long, lingering kiss but was non-committal when she asked when they would be meeting up again.

'Surely now is the time to sort things out once and for all. Claire will be upset but it's out in the open and we can be together properly,' she purred, as Richard unlocked the boot of his car and put his suitcase away.

'Look, let's just give her a bit of time for this to blow over and leave me to sort it out calmly. I don't want her kicking off and getting nasty. Financially we need to have enough money to make a proper start together.' He knew that would keep Martha quiet for a while; at least long enough for him to get Claire back on side. He had noticed Martha looking at property details and she had also taken to leaving her laptop with properties featured for sale in her area. It had all become too heavy and he wanted out.

Richard gave Martha a final hug and smiled secretly into her hair. Yes, he decided, this affair had run its course. It was time to go home and face the music and try to rescue his marriage. On the way home he pulled into the local M&S store and bought Claire a £12 bunch of mixed tulips, her favourites. 'This will do it,' he thought, heading to the check out. In the past a £3 bunch of daffodils from Tesco's could make Claire smile again. However his affair with Martha was a different matter and he thought that he might have to push the boat out, maybe even take Claire to her favourite local pub for a drink on Friday. It was months since he had bothered to do that.

As he turned into the driveway at the cottage he wondered if it would be pushing his luck to suggest she made him a shepherd's pie for dinner. He was expecting her to be a bit put out on seeing him at first. But she would forgive him. She was crazy about him and in the past he had known exactly how to get around her.

He suddenly felt very tired and was looking forward to a relaxing night at home. All that fancy hotel food was all well and good but he had missed Claire's plain home cooking. All that athletic sex had left him feeling exhausted.

Hopefully Claire wouldn't mind if he suggested they talk things through in the morning. He turned the key and stepped into the small lobby to be met by an unusual silence. Claire normally had Radio 4 on in the kitchen, she loved *Gardeners' Question Time* and the afternoon drama and news programmes, but today all he could hear was the ticking of the grandmother clock just inside the front door.

He moved through the hallway to the large, farmhouse kitchen and found it empty. The surfaces were clean and shiny, the sink was clear and there was no sign of any domestic activity whatsoever. Usually, the washing machine was churning and the oven was alight and full of scones or a casserole. The French doors which led out to the garden were usually thrown open and Claire would be outside in her gardening clothes with her silly straw hat on, or pruning, weeding or running around with Harriet. But this afternoon the only activity he could see was a few birds pecking on an empty bird table. He headed upstairs and found the bedroom tidy, but devoid of any clothes on the chair at Claire's side of the bed. It drove him insane when she had a morning try-on session of would-be outfits, then simply threw the discarded items on the chair. Her favourite lotions and creams were also missing from the dressing table.

Her wardrobe door was ajar and he noticed quite a few hangers were thrown on the bed. He decided Claire must have decamped home to her parents and he frowned at the prospect of having to face them too. But face them he would because Claire was his wife and her place was home with him. She was coming back home and that was final. He knew that there would have to be a confrontation with her parents, but he was confident that he could smooth things over with them all. Claire was a push over. She was obviously going to be angry with him about his lapse with Martha, but he had sorted that out and he could easily convince Claire it had all been a mistake. In fact, he knew he could make her feel almost responsible. Martha had a great figure and was sexy and fun. Claire felt overweight and vulnerable, and it was possible that he had done her a favour even, given her a wake-up call.

She was always going on some stupid diet or exercise regime that never worked. Maybe she would sort herself out and stop eating herself into oblivion. Was it any wonder that he had strayed? Yes, she had to take some responsibility for the affair.

Smiling to himself, Richard put his case on the bed and headed off for a shower. He would change and have a shave and perhaps put on his new pink shirt which Claire had bought him. She had told him that he looked irresistible when tried it on. She would be putty in his hands, though getting past that witch of a mother of hers might be tricky. He would buy the old boy a bottle of malt whisky and get him on side. The rest should be easy. Claire had never been able to say no to him and though he had to admit that embarking on an affair with her best friend was a bitter pill for Claire to swallow, he knew she would forgive him. She had told him more than once that he was her life and she couldn't imagine living without him.

Holding that thought he slipped into the shower and put his phone on charge. He would need it later to ring his friend Phil. They had planned a night out at the pub at the weekend and Phil was very friendly with the new barmaid there. Richard had already decided that she was young and flighty enough to agree to some harmless fun. Claire would never know. Maybe he would not take Claire to that pub after all; the local pizza joint would do. Claire was usually happy for any attention he directed her way. No point letting the barmaid see that he was married. He felt the stir of an erection as he thought of the perky young girl who had flirted with him when he had popped in for a pint last week. He had been heading off to see Martha so he had not had time to chat with her. Stopping to glance in the mirror to check his reflection for a final time, he decided that he looked pretty good. He rubbed on some of his new moisturiser and squirted some Bleu on his neck and his hair. Claire was a sucker for that fragrance. She had bought him a bottle for his birthday and he wore it when he wanted to get his own way with her. She was such a pushover. He hoped they could get back on track pretty quickly as he wanted an early night and he was hungry. He was sure Claire would have something in the freezer for them. She was a good girl; shame she was so boring. He had fallen for the whole Nigella lookalike thing in the early days, and he enjoyed being looked after and adored, but he had become bored. But not bored enough to leave. He was comfortable and as long as he could live his life on his terms and have fun on the side then nobody needed to get hurt. He had learned his lesson with Martha; he would not let that happen again.

As he drove to Claire's family home, he rehearsed his concerned, serious face. He kept practising the look he would give her parents. He almost laughed out loud. The whole family were suckers, he had taken them in hook, line and sinker when he married Claire. They had no idea who he was or where he had come from. Claire had just assumed he was a kind, helpful stranger who had come to her rescue. How wrong could she be? When he met Claire, he had been driving away from the home he had shared with his long-term partner. She had just found him in bed with his latest girlfriend. The stupid woman had messed things up by arriving home a few hours early. He had had a great set up there. It ended as his partner, a successful businesswoman, ordered him out on the spot and unceremoniously threw his clothes out of the bedroom window, much to the amusement of the neighbours who were having a family barbeque at the time. He had not meant it to end so soon, he had loved his life with her.

He had a great home, a car she had given him, sex on tap and four foreign holidays a year. He always got bored once he had won and bedded a woman. But she had surprised him by reacting as she did. He had thought she was smitten and would forgive him anything. He had been so wrong. She was incensed and had retorted she had been about to finish with him anyway. She had the nerve to call him a useless sponger. She told him that she was bored with him and his inability to do anything but watch TV and that his affair had done her a favour. Bitch. He knew she was just saving her face, but it was embarrassing to have to skulk away with his clothes thrown over his arm.

He was driving to Phil's house to sofa surf for a few nights when he had spotted a young woman with a flat tyre on the side of the road. She had proved an easy target and within weeks he had moved in. Claire had never been a match for him and he was confident that she would take him back without putting up a fight. He just had to look sorry and sad and make all the right promises. He could manage that!

Richard arrived at Claire's family home and pulled into the driveway. He got out of the car and slowly but purposely made his way to the front door where he rang the bell. He thought it was a respectful touch. Normally, he would have simply opened the door and made his way to the kitchen where Claire's mother and father were usually to be found. He knew he had to play the game and act the part of the remorseful son-in-law who had come to make his peace.

After a few minutes Claire's mother, Joan, opened the door and his heart sank a little, she was not a walkover and he knew she had never truly approved of him. Once she saw Richard, she closed the door slightly. He had to stop himself from pushing it open and kicking it. He could feel a red haze of temper flooding through him. How dare she treat him like this! He knew better than to lose it at this moment in time. He needed to wheel out the cool calm and charming Richard; the apologetic son-in-law who wished to be welcomed back into the fold.

'I am sorry to trouble you Joan, but I really need to see Claire and have a talk.' He used his penitent look, but Joan was not falling for it. She looked past him as if she were bored, then fixed him with a dark glare and asked him to leave.

'Claire is not here but even if she was, she certainly has nothing to say to you. Best you just leave Richard, there is nothing for you here, I would appreciate it if you would leave and never come back. Thank God our daughter has finally seen you for what you are.'

Richard felt his anger build even more. How dare this ugly old woman order him about? 'I would rather hear that from my wife, I really don't want to talk to you Joan. You have never approved of me and now if you don't mind, I would like to speak to my wife and take her home where she belongs. I will go and wait in the car and I would appreciate it if you told Claire to get a move on. The traffic will be heavy on the way back and I think it best we get away from here as soon as we can.'

Joan laughed softly and shook her head.

'Richard, sit in your car for as long as you like, but believe me you are in for quite a wait.' Joan fixed him with a cold smile he had never seen before, and it unnerved him. 'Claire has gone to stay with a friend for a while and she plans to be away for a few weeks. I happen to know that she has nothing to say to you – or ever will for that matter. I can safely say that my daughter has finally come to her senses. Incidentally, she would like you to move out of her house before she gets back from her holiday. She has already contacted her solicitor and sorted out a settlement for you. Personally, I think she is a bit mad, I would have made sure you had nothing, given the circumstances. But she told me to assure you that this will be her final offer. She wants nothing from you. I think she said something along the lines of realising you being a shallow shit with no morals. Oh, and she also mentioned that you are not as great in bed as you think you are. I overheard all this in a telephone conversation with her friend, so maybe I should not have repeated it. I can tell you I have never been taken in by you and your stupid vanity. You are a control freak, and a weak and stupid man. Thank God she has finally seen sense. There is nothing for you here, today or ever. Just clear out of Claire's life and stay out, Richard.'

Richard had not been prepared for this. He was expecting Claire to have rushed to the door by now. Surely, she had seen him arrive and would want to talk to him? He was not buying the whole 'Claire has gone away' act.

Suddenly Claire's father John appeared behind his wife and nodded politely at Richard. Sensing he had an ally, Richard stood a bit taller and made to walk through the door into the hall. At last, all this nonsense would stop and he would have some time to talk to Claire and sort this mess out. He may even have time to nip down to the pub a bit later after all. He would make sure Claire knew how angry he was and how badly her parents had behaved towards him.

But it suddenly dawned upon him that Claire had made a stand as her mild-mannered father was now standing firm too.

'Sorry old man, but you are not welcome here. Claire has told us what happened and we really don't want to see you again. Claire has gone away and she has no wish to see you. What you have done is appalling. It's unforgivable – best you leave now. This thing with Martha was the end for Claire, surely you must have known that?'

With these words John closed the door in Richard's face, leaving him dazed.

Richard had certainly *not* known that and he refused to believe it. Claire could not survive without him.

She was a mouse, a mumsy sort with no confidence who had only come to life when she met him. She would come running, he knew she would. Although he was more than a little concerned at the speed at which she had made arrangements. Very formal arrangements if the solicitor thing was true. And she had cut him out of her life so swiftly.

For a moment Richard experienced a chilling feeling that maybe this time he had pushed his luck. The affair with Martha had been a bit close to home, he had known that from the start, but that had made it even more thrilling at the beginning.

He had had to wear down Martha's resolve to get her to fall for him but once he had put on the charm and made her the focus of his full attention, she had succumbed.

He had realised that Martha secretly envied Claire with her beautiful house and settled life. He used this to win her over and offer her a slice of that life by stealing Claire's husband and lobbing a bomb into the calm of her secure married existence.

'I am so bored, Martha, I can't begin to tell you how happy you make me. I realise I have made a huge mistake and you are giving me a reason to leave.'

Martha just jumped on the hook, and he reeled her in. But he hadn't planned for the affair to get so heavy, even though he had promised Martha that she was his dream woman. Once she had fallen for him though she had become clingy and he began to tire of her. It was always the same; the chase and the risky sex behind his wife's back were fun. Now it was all out in the open and Martha was looking at bloody property details, he wanted out.

She had also hinted at wanting babies, which had totally freaked him out.

Angry at himself for getting things so wrong, Richard felt himself get mad at both Martha and at Claire, and even angrier with that old couple who had just thrown him out of their house.

He kicked the front door and started shouting abuse, screaming that their fat, ugly daughter was punching above her weight when she had met and married him. He kicked at the door a final time but he realised it was futile. He walked back to his car, angry and incredulous that his wife had not been there to support him. Typical Claire, never around when she was needed. He would see to it that she regretted this. He would make her pay and wish she had been the loyal wife she was supposed to be. OK, so he had strayed, but he truly believed she had to share some of the blame. He had come back to her, hadn't he?

He threw the bouquet of flowers out of his car and swore as he pulled away. He would find out where Claire was hiding and he would find her, get her back, then punish her. How dare she humiliate him. He would get even and already he was forming a plan on just how he would do that. But tonight he was unexpectedly free, and he had an idea of how he could distract himself for a few hours. Seconds later he was checking out his profile in the car's rear view mirror and wondered if he still had time to pop to the pub on his way home and chat up that barmaid. The thought cheered him up no end.

JAMES

JAMES HAD NOT BEEN shocked when he found Gina had packed up and left him. He knew he had pushed his luck lately and he had lost his temper too often. But actually it was her fault, she was always picking on him and finding fault. She was like every woman he had ever known. They wormed their way into your heart and then they trapped you and let you down. His mother had done so together with every woman he had met after her. When he met Gina, he thought she was different; she was sweet and seemed kind. But she was like the rest, he knew that now. She would push and push until he lost control, she knew what buttons to press. In fact, he believed that some part of her enjoyed the drama.

He regretted hitting her though and knew he had hurt her in the past, but she seemed to thrive on it. She seemed to enjoy the rows and the make-up sex. He thought she got off on him losing his temper with her. Gina used to be so outgoing and fun but gradually she had gone all moody on him giving him the silent treatment. He could hardly believe her disloyalty. He worked so hard to give her a lovely home, a good lifestyle, holidays and meals out. He was a fun husband and he never denied her anything. Since she had left him, he had been so angry he had smashed up the kitchen in a rage. He smiled as he thought of how he was looking forward to her coming back to find her precious kitchen ruined and the oak worktop gouged and burnt. He had enjoyed doing that. She had spent hours in that bloody kitchen creating meals on that flash new range of hers. Well, she wouldn't again. He had smashed that up too and he had also ripped out the Victorian dresser that she had lovingly stripped down and put in pride of place against the breakfast room wall. He had never liked her antique crap.

She had left a lot of her clothes and shoes behind. He could not stop grinning when he imagined her face when she discovered he had put them all in black sacks and dropped them off at the local charity shop. The young assistant could hardly believe her luck when she found piles of Karen Millen dresses and the beautiful Jones shoes Gina loved. It served her right. She was an ungrateful bitch and she deserved to be punished. He knew despite all she had said to him, she would be back. When she came home, he would give her a beating she would never forget. It was her fault; she had brought this upon herself. He suddenly felt much better so decided to go out and buy himself the expensive suit he had seen last week. When she came back and he had finally forgiven her, he would take her out for dinner and would wear the suit. He knew he would look good and she liked him to look smart. Smiling, he headed for the car. Tomorrow was another day. It would all be fine, they were good together. Things had just got a bit tense and difficult lately. She would calm down and realise she needed him. Gina would forgive him; she would be back.

JANE

WHEN SHE HAD FIRST worked for Anna, Jane had loved the pace, the fun and the madness of having to keep ahead of the game. She admired her boss who was gutsy and brave, but, on the flip side, Anna was also prone to throwing a huge workload at Jane and didn't show any appreciation for what she did.

As months went by, Jane found herself beginning to resent the woman. She was never satisfied with what Jane did and was always pushing to get more and more out of her team. She was driven, ambitious and worked long days, and she expected everyone else to do the same. Jane had a life outside the office and felt Anna resented this. She began to hate Anna's bullying ways. She also felt a bit sorry for Anna's partner Piers, who she thought was a wet blanket.

She had thought Piers was a bit of a joke at the beginning. She flirted with him and got a kick out of seeing how pathetically grateful he was when she gave him any attention. Anna seemed to simply walk all over him, and Jane made a point of showing him that she thought this was out of line.

Finally seducing him after she knew Anna was attending an overnight trip to their Manchester office had been a breeze. The guy was so desperate for affection it was easy and Jane enjoyed his obvious growing interest in her. It was a power game and she enjoyed claiming Piers right under Anna's nose. It served her right. She saw it as pay back for Anna's constant put downs. She was a stuck-up bitch. She thought herself better than everyone else and she lived for her work. Anna thought that everyone should live and breathe their job so woe betide anyone who didn't put the paper first. Anna ruled everyone with a rod of iron and though a lot of the men on the team admired her, Jane found her unbearable. But she was smart and played the game; simultaneously getting close to her boss so that she could try to steal her man and put her in her place.

Piers was a lap dog to Anna but even he had got fed up with being side-lined. Getting him to have an affair was so much easier than she had expected. Eventually she encouraged him to believe that Anna was not at all bothered with him. Jane had told him a few things that she claimed Anna had said about him. None of them very complimentary or even remotely true.

But she had never meant for their affair to get as serious as it had and, now she was in a dilemma. A while ago she had missed a period and thought she could be pregnant. She had told Piers who understandably went into shock, however he said he wanted to look after her and the baby. It was a laugh to go along with that at first, but now she had allowed things to go too far and she was in a mess. She was not pregnant after all and now she had Piers pestering her about check-ups and scans. Today he informed her that they were moving!

He said they couldn't bring a baby back to this flat and she had been horrified. She did not want to move. She loved her small bedsit right in the heart of Camden and Piers was beginning to grate on her. He was always cleaning up. She could no longer spend Sundays in the pub with her friends, as he wanted her to trail her around baby shops and estate agents. No, it had all got out of control and she had to do something soon. There was only so much time she could get away with the baby lie. She also wanted to find a job. She had been forced to resign as Anna's assistant, but the money had been brilliant and now she was having to rely upon Piers. He was in the driving seat in their relationship and this was not the way she had planned it. Not the way it was meant to work out at all.

What had started out as a bit of a game to get one over on Anna was now becoming a problem on many fronts. Piers was not her type. They had nothing in common and she wanted out.

Jane had also been back in touch with Marcus, her ex. He had been living in Germany promoting his latest band and was now back in town and he wanted to see her. Jane was sorely tempted. Marcus was exciting and fun and always up for a laugh and a session in the pub. In fact, he was everything Piers was not! She was going to have to decide what to do and soon. Marcus had made some noises about her going with him to Amsterdam where he had been offered a record deal. He had asked her to give their relationship another go. While she wasn't sure Marcus would be a long-term option, right now he seemed like a perfect solution to her problem.

She decided she would let Piers stay in the bedsit until he could sort himself out. She would be free to head off and make a new start with Marcus. Piers was going to be angry, but she reasoned; the longer they left things as they were the worse it would be. She had enjoyed their fling and the satisfaction of him leaving Anna but now she was bored with him and needed to get away. She was also tired of pretending to be pregnant as it meant he watched everything she ate and drank. She could kill for a double Jack Daniels and Coke!

Jane spent the day at home looking at daytime TV, enjoying all the programmes Piers hated. As she ate her lunch consisting of a cold tin of baked beans, she giggled at how Piers was always horrified at the way she lived. It had been fun at first, she enjoyed shocking him with her bohemian ways, but now he was just irritating. He wanted a perfect home with a full fridge and weekends at the garden centre. This was not her style and never would be. There were times when she would catch him looking miserable, idly staring out of the window at the rubbish-strewn terrace.

She wondered if she had been wrong to take him away from his beloved Anna. She had been to their home and everyone knew Anna was a clean freak. They had had the perfect home and the perfect life, but then if that was so, why had he even looked her way?

No, she was not at fault. She had not forced him to leave, though she realised telling him she was pregnant had been a big mistake. It had forced him to tell Anna and move out. Now things had gone too far. Way too far.

She had also tipped off the press about Anna's so called 'flee to the Caribbean', just to rub her nose in it. Anna's career was now on the skids and Jane did feel a tiny bit guilty that she had been instrumental in helping things along. She hated Anna, always had. Piers had been a pawn in her game but now it was time to call a halt. She had called Marcus and agreed to meet him that afternoon in the pub. They could have a good talk about the Amsterdam idea and if he was really as keen as he had said then she would have to talk to Piers. She reasoned that Piers might be OK with it, they were getting on each other's nerves anyway. She knew the baby, or rather the lack of one, was going to hit him hard. He seemed to be looking forward to becoming a father. Dismissing these thoughts, she decided that it was time to face facts and get back on track.

The prospect of an afternoon session in the pub had motivated her to wash her hair and discard her uniform of oversize leggings and baggy sweaters. She had a great figure and she intended to look her best for what was going to be a big date.

Jane scooped up her hair in a quirky multi-coloured bandana, slipped into the tribal print kaftan that Marcus had bought her when they first met and slicked on her brightest red lipstick. Glancing at her reflection she decided she looked the part. All this pretence of being pregnant had lost its charm. She had a long overdue date with a bottle of Jack Daniels in their favourite bar down at the Lock and she hoped maybe Marcus would provide some much-anticipated dessert afterwards. He was the sexiest man she had ever been to bed with. She had to admit, Piers had hardly set her on fire. Poor Piers. No, the time had come to end their relationship; in fact, she had never really felt they had a future anyway. It had been fun, but he was not her type at all.

PIERS

As the morning stretched on Piers looked at his emails and for the fourth time in as many minutes he checked to see if there was a message from Anna. He knew she had flown off to the Caribbean, in fact the whole country knew that story. The front-page picture of her looking so startled still haunted him. She had looked so young and vulnerable and his heart ached that he had not been able to offer his help or his love. He now knew she was the one he loved. He had never stopped loving her but they had got into a rut. Whether by accident or design, Jane had been there to make sure he made a hash of his life and throw what he had away.

Slipping even further into a fog of absolute misery, Piers thought back to last night and how Jane had almost driven him over the edge. She had come home in a bad mood and had refused to speak to him as he made supper and tried to get her to eat it. She had looked scornfully at the salad he had created and grabbed a slab of bread and smothered it in jam. She was still smoking and he was appalled that she could not see how harmful this was to their baby's health.

She had flounced out of the living space, had a shower, and called out that she was going out to meet a friend. She refused to say who the friend was and he was already in bed when she came back.

It was clear they were not happy and he wondered if he should simply offer to give her the money to buy a flat, maybe set up a trust fund for the baby and walk away. But he knew he was not the cut and run type. He was going to be a father so he was stuck with this woman, like it or not.

In the morning he had got up at 5am and was in the office by 6am. He had begun to shower at the office and take most of his meals there too. His staff were beginning to notice and he made lame excuses about a big account needing his attention and not wanting to disturb Jane as she was now tired and needed to rest. Nobody was buying that excuse and everyone tip toed around him knowing that he had dug himself into a big hole.

By lunchtime Piers felt as though the walls were closing in on him and after checking his emails a final time, he headed out to buy some lunch and sit in the park to clear his head.

Once he started walking, he couldn't stop. His office was in a tiny street off Covent Garden but he just kept walking and walking until he found himself sitting in Hyde Park. There were young mothers everywhere pushing buggies and try as he might he could not imagine Jane as one of those young women; cooing over tiny babies and toddlers, feeding the ducks and lazing happily in the sunshine on picnic blankets.

He walked for what seemed like hours, then changed to aimlessly getting on and off buses allowing himself to be ferried around the city. Eventually he arrived outside a pub in a side street in Camden. He had no idea why he had walked into it, but he had always loved the Lock and he and Anna often spent their Sunday afternoons exploring the markets.

He almost wanted to weep as he thought back to that life, a life that had been replaced with a strange and bewildering one he couldn't relate to

Suddenly he wanted a drink, a very long drink.

Pushing open the door into the bar he could have sworn he recognised the animated young woman sitting at a corner table. But she was holding hands with an unruly looking young man with a cascade of bright blue curls. They were smoking and laughing. At one point the man leaned across and pulled her into his arms and gave her a long, lingering kiss.

Piers looked away but heard the woman laugh and he turned back in horror. It was Jane. But not the messy, unhappy Jane he had seen this morning. This version of Jane was dressed like a bohemian princess in a long kaftan, and she was showing off her slim body. He thought back to the frumpy dresses, loose leggings and baggy cardigans she had worn of late. She had claimed that as she got more swollen and bloated, she needed to be comfortable. He realised with a jolt that the figure in front of him was not in the least bit swollen. There was no hint of a bump and it seemed clear that Jane was not carrying his child after all. Her face was flushed and her eyes sparkled and she could hardly tear her eyes away from the gaze of the scruffily dressed man sitting so close to her. They looked almost glued together. As she caught his eye, Jane had the grace to look a little shocked but she quickly composed herself and simply raised her glass at him. There was a half empty bottle of Jack Daniels on the table and it was clear she had consumed most of it. Her look was a mixture of defiance and regret but its message was clear. Jane and Piers had come to the end of the road and while he should have felt something, anything; all he could conjure up were feelings of self-disgust and a deep sense of loss. But the woman he was missing was not Jane, it was Anna, who was now out of his life forever. Anna, the woman he now realised he had treated so badly and who would probably never speak to him again.

Walking towards Jane, Piers took a deep breath and waited for her to explain what he had just witnessed; clearly this was the end of their brief fling. It was all becoming apparent. It had not been real at all. Jane was not his Jane; she had obviously moved on and she was clearly not pregnant. How blind and stupid was he, to have mistaken her game playing with true feelings of love. She had set her sights on him and he had proved such an easy target. But stirring deep in his soul he recognised a new emotion creeping into his psyche. It was called hope. He was not stuck in that tip of a flat with this awful woman after all. He no longer had to come back to a dirty sink, a stinking fridge and an unmade bed. He shuddered to think of how he had ever managed to live in that dump, with its terrible smell of damp and rotting vegetables. Maybe, just maybe there could be a way to go back home to Anna.

What should have been a terrible shock and a crashing blow to him was in fact a huge relief.

'I don't think there is much to say, do you?' he asked Jane as he finally reached the table to find her still hand in hand with the blue haired man. Jane met his gaze, but she failed to look anything other than bored and slightly irritated by his presence.

'I am sorry Piers, but it was never right between us, was it? I suspect you know the baby thing was all a bit of a mix up too.'

'A mix up, a bloody mix up! Is that what we are calling this?!' His temper finally kicked in with the realisation of what this woman had cost him.

'You trap me into leaving Anna with all this talk of loving me and wanting our baby, a baby that never even existed. I was just one of your sick mind games to get me away from the woman I love! You sit there with this freak show of a man and tell me your pregnancy was a mix up! I think we both know what your game was. You are a cheap and nasty tart. A slovenly, lazy excuse for a woman. I wish old Blue Beard here the best of luck because it looks like he is going to need it.'

The blue haired man had the grace to look a bit shocked at this piece of information, but Piers simply nodded and backed away. There was nothing he wanted to hear from her. He had got himself into this mess and now he had to sort it out. He had lost Anna but he was going to try his damnedest to win her back. He knew she was a proud, strong woman, but he hoped that perhaps if he tried hard enough, he could convince her that he had made a terrible mistake. He would do anything if she would just forgive him. He hoped with every fibre in his being that like him, she had had some time alone to think.

He prayed that she had missed him and would at least give some thought to giving him another chance. They were a team, a team that had worked for so long, but one that had withered on the vine. Partly due to her obsession with her career but also because he had never put his foot down enough. The one time he had rebelled he had gone completely over the top and had bedded her office assistant. A tidal wave of shame swept over him and he felt desolate. He was desperate to try to talk to Anna and make her see what was suddenly clear to him.

He had never felt so sure of anything and the conviction made him feel more positive than he had in months. The tiny grain of hope gave him the strength to get back to his office and do what he should have done a lot sooner.

He hailed a cab and during the long ride back to the office he replayed what had just happened. For the first time in a long time he felt that he could breathe.

He entered his office and sent the rest of the team home. He needed to be alone and he needed to think.

He opened his laptop and clicked on to his email account. Sitting back in his chair he realised that this message could be the most important one he had ever written.

Over the years he had concocted thousands of life changing emails for clients. Emails that had saved careers, clinched money-making deals, had kept some clients out of prison, others had saved marriages, others ended bad relationships. But this email was probably the most important one he would ever send. The problem was that he didn't have a clue about what he was going to say.

CLAIRE

IN ANTIGUA THE SUN rose early, and Claire was sitting quietly on the beach watching it climb, as the turquoise surf kissed the shoreline. The beach was empty, the air was already quite warm and there was a gentle breeze coming off the sea. She had thrown a gauzy shirt over her swimsuit and without bothering with flip flops she had stepped out from their terrace onto the sand and walked the length of the bay. At the far side of the beach there was a busy resort but nobody had surfaced yet. Claire took deep breaths and she drank in the view and felt more relaxed than she had in months. She didn't even give her situation any thought. She saw this trip as time out from everything and everyone together with the pain and drama that had occurred in the weeks and months leading up to her Caribbean adventure.

Claire walked back to the deserted end of the bay and slipped into the warm ocean and for a long while she simply floated and looked up into the sky. She was going to get her life on track, she knew that now. She didn't know what the future held but it would not include Richard. She also knew that she had to make some changes in herself that would give her back confidence and allow her to build a new life. More importantly she had to build a safe and happy life for Harriet.

She wanted to be able to run around on the beach, in the park, and be the active mum she used to be. She knew that her weight was holding her back. In recent months as she became heavier and lumpier, she had felt increasingly unhappy and listless. She vowed to start moving more and eating better. It would be easier out here, especially as the other girls seemed to be so slim and fit. Gina had also kindly hinted that she would help Claire with a healthy eating and exercise plan. Claire vaguely recalled pouring her heart out to Gina about her weight problems and how miserable it was making her. Gina was like a goddess, but she said she had not always looked the way she did now. She had managed to lose weight after she finished university where she had piled on the pounds. Discovering the joy of just walking and moving her body had helped her become fitter and she embraced a healthier lifestyle and began to eat much more healthily too. Of late her problems with her ex had made her weight plummet and now she was aiming to gain a few pounds and get her curves back. 'It's all about being healthy and happy in your skin,' she mused and that was Claire's plan.

Claire turned over and swam, kicking her legs hard as she ploughed across the bay. This was an exercise she enjoyed, and she had forgotten how much she loved to be in the sea. The warm, clear, turquoise waters called to her. She vowed to be the first to get up and swim and maybe work up to being able to run onto the sands too. She had read somewhere that even if you walk 10,000 steps a day you start to burn fat more efficiently. Gina had shown her how to download an app onto her phone that told her how many steps she had clocked up. She pledged that today she would try to exceed her 10,000-step goal and start to eat more healthily. It was a start. Literally baby steps, positive ones that would help her become the woman she knew was buried deep inside her.

Claire walked out of the sea, grabbed her shirt and headed back to the house where she planned to make a coffee and sit outside to wait for the others to stir. She was in no rush to do anything much. They had agreed that today would be one to simply relax on the beach or laze around their pool. To tick the activity box they planned to organise a barbeque later that night. Claire vowed to cut back on the alcohol today too.

She headed to her room to change into a dry swimsuit and throw on her new sarong and maybe make a start on reading one of the books she had brought with her. One had caught her eye as she browsed at the bookshop in the airport. It was a gripping tale of a wronged woman who emerged fighting and Claire hoped it would serve to keep her resolve to do the same.

At home there was never time to read. She thought fleetingly of home; of Harriet whom she knew was happily with her grandparents and cousins and then of Richard. She wondered if he had moved out yet and let out a long sad sigh.

Time to let him go, she decided. She was amazed at how quickly she had managed to stop loving him. Some distance had given her the head space to see him for what he was. A user, a cheat and a liar. She almost felt sorry for Martha. Part of her knew that he did not love her. She was just his latest conquest. It was obvious that Richard had simply targeted her and she had fallen under his spell. She wondered how many other women had fallen for his smooth talk and charm? Strangely she didn't feel jealous or angry. What she felt was a calm indifference. He no longer had any power over her and she felt as though a huge weight had lifted. She really was over her sham of a marriage. She felt stronger than she had in years.

One of her friends at home ran a yoga class in the village hall and suddenly one of her favourite mantras came into her head – 'Release what no longer serves you.'

She had mentally released Richard and now looking down at her bulging thighs and lumpy waistline she promised herself that she would be shifting this excess weight too.

Her mother had called Claire as she prepared to board the flight to tell her about how Richard had arrived at their home full of pompous outrage and demanding that Claire come to heel. She almost laughed at his nerve but it was evident that her mother had made it clear that the marriage was over. And Claire knew with a certainty that it really was over. She didn't want to see him again and the thought of Richard living in the home she and Stevie created made her feel sick. How could she have been so blind and been so taken in by a man like that? The brief conversations she had shared with the girls last night had shown her how he had used her and taken advantage of her when she was so vulnerable.

She found it incredible that only weeks ago she had not wanted to live without him. She had put him above everyone – her daughter, her parents, and her friends. She had spent her whole life thinking of ways to get him to notice her. Even the smallest crumb of praise or attention was enough to get her through the day. She felt ashamed of her weakness. Now the scales had fallen from her eyes and she saw him for what he was, she felt so stupid that she had lived for so long in his thrall. What had she been thinking of? She despised him and felt distanced from that emotionally stricken woman who had boarded the flight to Edinburgh. Was it only weeks ago? She shuddered as she recalled the scene at the hotel bar when she had walked in on her husband and his mistress. It was as though a lifetime had passed since then. She knew that she was no longer that sad, isolated woman. She had a future to look forward to which was not going to include Richard or any man who could make her feel so diminished.

Claire had also decided that although Martha had done something terrible and the betrayal was still very raw, she could not really blame her. She knew what Richard was like when he was on a mission. He could turn on the charm and make any woman's head spin. She had been in the spotlight of his attention all those years ago too. Everyone had warned her to give the relationship a bit more time before jumping in so deeply, but she was powerless to resist him. Martha never really stood a chance.

Richard would always have some poor woman in his sights. He could never be faithful and it was as if she was watching her past life through someone else's eyes. He had systematically ground her down, making her feel dowdy and insignificant. She had been so grateful to have him that she had totally lost sight of the woman she was. She realised with a jolt she had to forgive herself first for bringing this man into their lives.

Talking to the other girls she discovered it was classic stuff. He was a narcissist and that would never change. He didn't care how his behaviour impacted those around him and the only person he cared about was himself. He would call her stupid and accuse her of having all manner of terrible character faults, but in truth he was the weak one.

'It's how they operate,' Gina told her quietly. She should know, she had left a similar relationship behind too.

Anna had joined in and was equally supportive as she listened to Claire's account of her awful break up. 'I have met a lot of Richards in my time. They have to beat you down because it is the only way that they can feel better about themselves. He love bombed you then he gas lighted you ...'.

Claire decided she would have to do a bit of homework; the clichés were alien to her but everything Anna described rang true. He wooed her, then beat her down. Nothing she did was good enough; her hair, clothes, her friends. He never acknowledged her achievements or took any interest in the things she enjoyed. It all had to be about him.

Claire knew she needed to shed the old Claire in the same way she had rubbed Richard out of her life. She could tell she was looking more toned already, and simply moving her body for the first time in a long while had already made her feel different. She certainly felt fitter, but she knew she had some work to do rebuilding her self-esteem. Her newly found girlfriends were working their magic on her though and already she felt her head had shifted into a more positive place.

She felt strong and vibrant and could finally see past the gloom. Most importantly she believed there was a whole new life ahead of her. She felt different and she aimed to look different too. In a month she knew she could make some important changes to her mind and her body. She also knew that, unlike the empty promises she had made to herself in the past, this time she would keep to them. She felt empowered and happier than she had in months.

Humming happily to herself Claire went into the kitchen and prepared a fresh fruit salad which she would share with the girls when they finally surfaced. Smiling and feeling strangely at peace, she made a pot of coffee and stretched out on a sunbed to enjoy the view and start on that book. Significantly it was entitled *The Survivor*.

ANNA

ANNA WOKE UP AND groaned as she felt a wave of nausea hit her. With a throbbing head and a dry mouth, she realised that the last few cocktails last night had not been the best idea. They had drunk for England, France and the USA! And as she had not eaten much the effect had been quite acute. At some point during the evening she had come clean with the others about her breakup with Piers, though she hoped she had not dished up all the gory details.

Claire had been so open about Richard and for once Anna felt it was time to start being honest about why she had joined the crew. 'I had my heart broken, plain and simple, so my story about researching a book was a lie and I am sorry to have misled you Jesse,' she told her.

All this girl talk was a first for her but she had surprised herself by enjoying the camaraderie of the others, who it seemed had all been in the wars with relationships too. She had found it easy to share her pain and they had sunk quite a few bottles while the story unfolded.

She just wished she had woken up in paradise not feeling so hungover. Anna was used to drinking, in fact she prided herself on how she could hold her liquor, but for some reason the mix of champagne, cocktails, and the odd beer or two had proved too strong a combination.

Staggering to the bathroom she sank to the floor and threw up. She felt like a silly teenager who had been let off the leash and could not hold her alcohol. Why had she gone so crazy? She lay on the cool tiled floor and the last few weeks flashed before her. She felt overwhelmed, sad and lost. She started to weep and once she started, she found she couldn't stop. A while later she felt a cool cloth on her forehead and Jesse 's soothing voice was telling her she would be fine as she handed her a tumbler of iced water and helped her get off the floor. She gently led her back to bed.

Anna lay with the cloth over her eyes and whimpered like a small child. Once she had allowed the emotional flood gates to open there seemed no way to stem a tide of misery as the tears poured down her cheeks and sobs racked her chest.

'Just let it out, you will feel better if you do.' said Jesse gently.

Jesse stroked Anna's arm and it served to calm her down. Eventually her sobs quietened and she accepted a tissue and rubbed at her eyes.

'I feel so bloody stupid,' Anna said finally. 'I don't do crying like a baby.'

'Well, I think it's time you did.'

Anna allowed a smile to creep over her face as Jesse sat quietly beside her and encouraged her to sip the iced water.

'I don't think it's just about the booze you had. I think you've been bottling up so much pain and you had to let it out. Look, you are in good company. I think you know that all of us are here because we are running from something that has been painful. Everyone is feeling like you do, so just go with it. I know we have only just met but I hope you feel you are amongst friends.'

An hour passed and Jesse simply sat in the armchair beside her bed. Anna finally dozed off and Jesse slipped away, leaving her to rest.

A few hours later Anna emerged looking a bit pale and sheepish, but the girls were kind and supportive and explained that they had decided to relax around the pool, read their books and wait for her to make an appearance. Nobody felt they wanted to leave her alone in the house and she was touched by their kindness.

'I didn't want to hold you guys back, you didn't need to stay here just for me,' she said. But secretly she was happy to see them all sitting around the pool when she finally surfaced.

'Look we are in this together and none of us wanted to leave you,' said Gina.

'Let's face it, it's hardly a chore sitting here looking out at our own personal paradise.'

Anna looked at the group and smiled feeling happy despite the remnants of her hangover leaving her feeling slightly queasy.

'I have never had girlfriends before and I think I like it,' she said. 'But here's the thing I do not want to touch a drop of alcohol tonight so please don't let me.'

Like mother hens the girls fussed over her, settling her onto a sunbed, pouring her iced water and insisting she wear sun cream and a hat. Wordlessly she stretched out and closed her eyes feeling safe and secure. She was surrounded by a fantastic posse of women she had not even known 48 hours ago. Already she knew these girls were friends for life, and within minutes she was dozing with a smile on her face. She had planned to stay aloof, not share her story or get involved in the group dynamic; but she decided, plans can change. These women were a great group who she knew had her back. She had never experienced this sort of friendship group before and it made her sad to think of all the time she had wasted in the past. But she was going to make some changes and that started today. Or maybe tomorrow when she hoped her stomach would have stopped churning.

Later the girls planned a barbeque.

'It's lime and soda for me tonight, but please don't let that spoil the fun,' said Anna, not sure if she was up to eating anything yet.

Gina was in control of the barbeque and Jesse was in the kitchen preparing salads. Their housekeeper had been in earlier with a massive platter of mixed meats and cheeses and as they waited for the barbeque to fire up, they enjoyed the tasty nibbles and reflected on their day.

Suddenly Claire let out a scream as a bright light flashed from one of the nearby palm trees which fringed their terrace.

'There is a man up there and I think he has a camera, I think he just took photos of us,' she screamed.

Gina and Jesse rushed to see but Anna, who had been replenishing the ice bucket, hung back. She was terrified that her worst fears might be about to come true.

Gina ran out onto the sands and started running after a figure who was a few hundred metres ahead of her.

'You bloody pervert,' she yelled, but whoever it was had fled.

Walking back to the terrace she found Jesse already on the phone to the local security team who guarded the entrances to the resort. Part of the villa's appeal had been that it was in a secure, gated community.

Anna walked outside and sheepishly asked if the others would join her.

'Look, I haven't told you everything about me. I suspect that guy is not a random pervert spying on us. I have a strong feeling that he is a photographer who has been sent over from England to find me. I am so sorry. I really didn't think anyone would trace me to here as we are at a private house, and I told nobody where I was going.'

The group turned to stare at Anna their faces said it all.

'So, what is so special about you that a paparazzi guy would climb up into a tree to catch a glimpse of you?' asked Jesse.

Taking a deep breath she grabbed a beer, deciding she could not do this without a drink or two. The group deserved an explanation and taking a huge swig of the local brew she began her story. Anna told them about her job as the managing editor of *The Globe*, then refilled their glasses and motioned them to sit down. Over the next hour she gave them a blow-by-blow account of the story that had broken just as she flew off. She also revealed her pain about Piers, and the fact Jane was about to produce a baby.

'Look, the timing sucked. I was truly just escaping the Piers and Jane nightmare, but the scandal broke on the day I left and they all decided I was running away to escape the heat of the celebrity scandal. I know my team is doing its best to sort it out, but to be honest I haven't dared get hold of anyone to find out how things are. I am a bit scared to hear what they may tell me; I could be out of a job for all I know. When we arrived here, I did spot a photojournalist who has one hell of a reputation for digging the dirt. He thinks he is a sex god and I admit he is drop dead gorgeous but don't be fooled by those bright green eyes. The guy is a ruthless creep. All designer stubble and sexy moves, you know the type.'

Claire nodded but in truth she had never met anyone who fitted that description. However, Gina felt her face flush as she recalled the handsome man who had sat next to her on the flight over.

Gina decided not to mention the fact she had fancied the stranger like mad and had regretted not making more of an effort to talk to him on the flight.

'I think the guy you are talking about was sitting next to me on the way over. He certainly had the most amazing eyes and a great physique. He was sort of rugged and mysterious but he didn't say one word until we were about to get off the plane. Then he started flirting with me, or at least I think he did.'

Anna nodded. 'That's so like him, he is so far up his own arse he thinks he is God's gift to the female population. You should hear about the women he leaves in his wake. Look, he did you a favour. Trust me, you don't want to mess with the likes of Dan Bridges.' But Gina was thinking back to those soulful eyes and the gentle way he had put his hand on the small of her back and escorted her off the plane. Surely if he was a sleaze bag he would have hit on her during the flight?

But she was on Anna's team and resolved that if the opportunity arose, she would give the guy a wide berth. Though deep down she had to admit, he was a real looker. But then she had got it wrong before, she was not about to do so again. Sexy green eyes or not, she decided she was off men and had no wish to start getting involved with another man any time soon. An all-girl trip had been a great idea and during the past couple of days she had allowed herself to relax and simply enjoy the peace and the beach. Above all she loved the feeling that she was among women she could trust.

Jesse was still angry at the guy having stalked them and compromised their privacy.

'They are sending one of the security team over a bit later to get a description of the guy and they want us to make a statement. Jolly Harbour authorities pride themselves on their security so a breach like this is a big deal. They rely so much on tourism and there are lots of millionaire types with homes on the beach they do not want to scare off tourists. There's no need to worry I don't think he will be back at the gates and if he does try, they will turn him away.'

The group was quietly glad that Jesse had seemed to take on the role of group leader. She was the tiniest of them but what she lacked in stature she more than made up for with her feisty nature and her direct no nonsense approach to life. She was like a mini warrior, but she was also a kind soul, and the group knew she was someone you could lean on in a crisis. From what they had seen, and heard, there was certainly a crisis looming for Anna.

An hour later the girls had given their account of the episode to the chief of security who promised them that his men would be patrolling their property hourly and they would be extra vigilant about who was coming and going through the gates. The girls hadn't been able to give an accurate description of the intruder; only that he was tall and could certainly run fast, but they all felt safe once more.

Anna found it impossible to relax. She knew Dan of old and was sure of one thing, he rarely if ever left without getting his picture.

Later after they tucked into delicious portions of coconut prawns and barbequed jerk chicken, the girls decided to have a game of cards and stay around the pool. Nobody was in the market for a night out. Anna was afraid that Dan may be lurking close by; he could be hiding out on one of the super yachts in the marina or in a villa just outside the main gates. She didn't intend to give him a chance to capture her on camera.

The group disbanded early admitting they needed an early night. The next day they had elected to go on a trip to Nelson's Dockyard in English Harbour to enjoy lunch at a smart but relaxed beachside restaurant that Denzil had recommended. For now the drama was over.

SHIRLEY HEIGHTS: GIRLS ON TOUR

THE NEXT MORNING THE sun rose early and the girls emerged refreshed and ready for their adventure. But first they ran into the sea for a long swim followed by a leisurely breakfast and headed off to get ready for their day out.

Once again Claire had risen at dawn and walked for more than an hour across the long bay and back. She had also elongated her walk by taking the steep path over the far ridge. She was enjoying being out in the early morning and was delighted to be clocking up thousands of extra steps on her phone app. Suddenly being active and doing exercise was not the chore it had been at home. She was doing this for herself and was so much happier than she had been in ages. Her self-esteem was at an all-time high and she was becoming the confident woman she knew was lurking inside.

Later the group assembled on the terrace and Jesse agreed that they looked like a stylish bunch.

They were going to enjoy a lovely long lunch then later they planned to take a taxi up to Shirley Heights; a lofty vantage point where bands played and locals danced the night away. They also planned to watch what they were told would be an amazing sunset.

Quietly Anna was worried about heading off to such a tourist trap but she was reluctant to be a party pooper.

'Wear your baseball cap and sunglasses and we will simply lose ourselves in the crowd; we can't let a low life like Dan stop us having fun,' decided Claire.

They had all opted for gauzy tops and shorts except for Claire, who looked a picture in a vibrant, blue silk sarong. The night before Anna had shown the girls how a sarong could be used to create a fantastic cover up. Claire had rushed inside to find a couple she had brought and allowed Anna to create one for her.

The effect was stunning as it showed off Claire's beautifully toned shoulders and the folds camouflaged the rolls around her waist and hips. The style enhanced her curves and for once she felt satisfied with the way she looked. If nothing else this trip was helping build her self-confidence and the other girls were so sweet and supportive. When she was with them, she didn't feel frumpy or boring, just content and happy.

Grabbing a collection of sunhats and sunglasses, the troupe looked like a bunch of schoolgirls going on a summer trip as they bundled into the people carrier. They chatted away excitedly and teased the driver about his bright union jack t-shirt.

'I wore it for you girls as a mark of respect,' he said with a grin. He was Denzil's cousin Seymour – they all seemed to be related to Denzil. He told them his cousin would be joining them later when they headed up to Shirley Heights.

The ride to the dockyard was a long one and they were very quiet as they drove through the ramshackle villages.

Their driver proudly pointed out his village but all the girls could see was a down-at-heel collection of scruffy, wooden shacks with a few roadside food stalls including an outdoor bar where an old woman was selling fruits and what looked like fried bananas.

It was Sunday and each of the villages had immaculately painted churches with colourful gardens packed with people wearing their best clothes and hats. Gospel music belted out of the doors and the group felt humbled to see how people with so little seemed to be enjoying life to the full.

The girls reached the dockyard just before noon and explored the site. They oohed and ahhed at the super yachts moored at the quay whilst enjoying the exhibitions that told of the early settlers and the life of the garrison.

At 1pm their driver reappeared at their agreed meeting point and drove them around to Katherine's, a beautiful top end restaurant right on the edge of Pigeon Point.

They looked out from the dining deck and drank in the view of the bay and the hills which rose above the stretches of sand. They chose a selection of delicious seafood dishes and exotic salads and sipped the most delicious rosé wine which the young bartender had recommended.

After enjoying a long, leisurely lunch they walked the stretch of the bay where the locals were swimming in the sea and lounging near the shoreline. Most of them clutched iced beers, whilst music boomed out from a nearby beach hut.

Children raced in and out of the sea and one by one the girls waded out into the waves to cool down.

'This is one hell of a way to spend a Sunday lunchtime,' Anna decided. Even so her heart ached a little as once again she thought about Piers and how she wished he were here with her now to share it. She knew he would love this laid-back lifestyle and most of all, he would have preferred this laid-back Anna. She was aware that in the past few days she had not acted like the selfish go getter she had been in the past. With time to reflect it was clear that she had pushed him away and delivered him on a plate to the first female who would give him even the smallest bit of attention. She was still mad at him, but she knew Piers was not solely to blame for what had happened between them.

Her work had been everything to her and she had taken him so much for granted. She had pushed him too far, and not for the first time she blamed herself for the mess her life was in.

What would Piers make of this new Anna with her clutch of girlfriends, and a make-up free face wading out into the sea in some cut-off jeans and gauzy top? He would not recognise her, and in many ways, she didn't recognise herself. She liked herself for the first time in years. Just being away from the dynamic of a busy, gossipy newsroom and the dramas and power struggles that went with it had certainly changed her.

Once again, she marvelled at how she was no longer continually checking her phone or logging into her emails, in fact she hadn't looked at either since she had arrived at the villa. She knew she was calmer, quieter and felt so at peace with herself. If she had not been so sad about Piers she would have felt totally happy and fulfilled.

She could not mend the heartbreak, at least not yet; but she knew she could never go back to being that woman she had become back in London.

There would have to be some changes in her life, of that she was certain. But right now, she did not know what they would be. She tried to think about going back to the bitching and scheming world at *The Globe* and the thought appalled her.

No, for now her life was this beautiful Caribbean bubble where the only decisions to be made were what cocktail to choose and which beach to swim on. For today and for the next few weeks that was about all she could manage. Feeling strangely comforted by the thought she headed for the beach and waded out into the warm sea to swim off her lunch – and those early cocktails.

As she slipped effortlessly into the sea she felt so at peace. She knew one thing, and that was this trip had been a brilliant thing to do. This was such an adventure and the girls were such a bonus. She had never had such close girlfriends and while the friendships were very new, she was sure they would be longstanding.

She swam across the bay and shielded her eyes as she walked back up to the beach.

The others were sprawled out on sun beds. At five they gathered up their belongings and made themselves presentable for the drive to Shirley Heights where they were going to watch the sun go down.

Denzil picked them up at the quay at English Harbour and whistled when he saw the quartet looking so pretty. All were decked out with Panama hats, sarongs and jangled with an assortment of bangles.

He thought back to the pale, stressed-out group he had picked up at the airport and marvelled yet again at the power of the Caribbean sun and the laid-back island lifestyle. Each of the girls had seemed so distracted and edgy and not at all like this new group. The girls were laughing together and gently teasing each other with glowing skins and smiling faces.

By the time they arrived the peninsula was crowded with tourists and locals and a variety of food stalls were piled up with burgers and spicy chicken dishes. Other stall holders displayed racks of silk scarves and throws and local craftsmen tempted the crowds with hand-made jewellery.

Anna bought a selection of intricate silver bangles and earrings and brought tears to Jesse's eyes when she handed her a tiny paper bag containing a pair of silver and pearl earrings.

'These will look fabulous. A tiny present for looking after me,' she whispered.

The women linked arms and went to find the others who had found a small space to sit on an outcrop of rock on the headland.

'This is the most amazing spot,' Jesse breathed, as the girls took in the sights and sounds of the point and watched as the sun slid silently into the horizon. It was a beautifully clear evening and the golds and russets of the sun's rays bounced off the glasses and camera lenses all around them.

An hour later the girls had bought beers and were munching their way through burgers and singing along to the steel band which was playing on the raised stage.

The group wandered around the stalls treating themselves to jewellery and vibrant silk scarves and by nine they all decided that their long day was catching up with them. It was time to head back. The steel band was still in full swing but they were aware that they still had an hour-long drive to get back to the house.

As they drove away from English Harbour, Gina decided she would like to return and maybe spend a bit more time exploring the town. She felt tired and happy and was more than ready to just fall into her bed and sleep.

Claire's day had been incredible and she felt more alive than she had in years. She decided that this Caribbean lifestyle suited her and she could only hope to hold on to this 'new woman' who was suddenly driven and fearless when she got home.

Jesse was also in a world of her own marvelling at the amazing time they had enjoyed. She peeked at her silver earrings and smiled at the lovely gesture they represented. Who would have thought that someone like Anna would ever consider me a friend, she thought to herself? They were indeed an unlikely duo, but it was clear they had formed a strong bond and she looked forward to them becoming closer.

Anna was the last out of the taxi and as she approached the villa, she called out to Jesse to wait for a moment. 'This place is magical, and I want to thank you. I feel as though it has brought me back from the edge.'

'We all feel that way,' admitted Jesse as she linked arms and stepped back onto their terrace at the house. 'I don't know what I was expecting, but less than a week in and I feel so very different. I think we all do.'

Her companions agreed. Jesse made coffees and they headed out onto the terrace where the bay lay glittering in the moonlight.

'This must be one of the most perfect places to come to relax, how could you ever tire of living here?' sighed Anna as she sipped her coffee and breathed in the warm night air.

GINA

By ten most of the girls were ready for bed but Gina felt restless and decided she would take a final stroll. She could see that at the far end of the beach there was a live band playing and a group had lit a small fire.

The flames of the fire seemed to call to her and she walked in the shallow surf listening as it hit the sand. She felt so at peace, lighter and happier than she had felt in years. Not for the first time did she thank the angels and the universe for allowing her to come to this special place and meet such an amazing group of friends. She felt part of a sisterhood and knew that they were helping her to heal her emotional wounds. She didn't feel judged or silly, neither was there any pressure to come up with a plan for the future. She could just be.

She found herself laughing out loud and began running across the shoreline kicking at the waves like a small child who has just seen the sea for the first time. She felt so carefree and at peace with herself.

Out of breath and still giggling at how she must look, she was jolted out of her reverie when a voice called out to her.

'Hey lady, you OK out there? Looks like you are having fun.'

She spun around to see a solitary figure sitting a few hundred metres from the beach party. He was holding a beer and waved her over to him.

For a second, she hesitated but something in his voice made her feel it was fine to approach. And as she got closer, she realised with a jolt that it was the stranger from the plane and her heart did a flip.

She shrugged her shoulders back and strode over to him, feeling both brave and angry. She intended to tell him what she thought of him as he was almost certainly the photographer who had tried to take photographs of Anna at the villa.

As she drew nearer, she realised that he was very drunk and he was finding it hard to sit up straight. He lolled to one side and as he steadied himself, he patted the warm sand alongside him, gesturing that she join him.

'You are a very beautiful woman; do you know that?' he slurred at her.

She frowned and was about to lay into him when he looked up at her with those huge green eyes and smiled at her in a way no man had ever done before in her life. Suddenly his being drunk and a potential enemy seemed irrelevant. She basked in that slow smile and felt her insides start to buzz.

She would not fall for this! For one thing she had barely just escaped from a rotten marriage and for another it was him, the man Anna had warned her about. What was it that Anna had said? That he was a predator, that he knew all the moves and the right words and that women fell for it every time? No, she was not like the rest and she would not succumb.

'I have nothing to say to you. You are a snake, the worst sort of snake. You use people, you are ruthless and cruel and just out for what you can get. I don't even know why I am wasting my time telling you.'

He didn't move or take his eyes off hers; he just smiled that slow sexy smile, raised the beer to those full lips and took a long swig.

He patted the sand next to him again and motioned her to sit beside him.

At once she was infuriated with him, angry at her inability to walk away, but also flattered! Why was this man having this crazy effect on her? She was determined to walk away but felt unable to move.

What was it about this man?

'Lady, just chill. Sit down here beside me and let me tell you a story. I liked the look of you on the plane. I like the look of you even more now. You are looking so riled it makes you look even sexier.'

Gina decided that she really was getting into dangerous territory here. She was also worried about what the others would say if they knew she had even given this creep the time of day.

The prospect of their wrath was the incentive she needed to get her back to the shoreline and heading for the house.

She turned on her heel and with an angry wave of her hand she strode away.

'Hey, come back pretty lady. I really would like to talk to you,' he called out as she vanished into the night air.

'I bet you would,' she shouted as she walked away, not bothering to look back. Once she was a safe distance away from him, she let out a long breath of relief. 'Idiotic man.' she muttered under her breath. She sprinted the last few metres back to the terrace trying not to think about how her tummy had flipped when he suggested she sit next to him. Fleetingly she had also wondered how it would be to have those lovely lips press down on hers.

CLAIRE

CLAIRE WAS FIRST TO rise every morning and she would head off for long walks along the shoreline and had started to jog the last few hundred metres.

It wasn't much but it was a start. For once she no longer felt as though her thighs were rubbing at the top as they normally did. Claire had always avoided exercise as it had seemed a chore, but now she loved walking in the outdoors. She was proud that she was able to jog a little too.

She was not concerned about her weight anymore; she no longer thought about it. She was feeling better about herself fitter and she knew the rest would follow. She was just happy to feel more confident and carefree – and not so out of breath. Only a few weeks ago walking had left her wheezing with a tightness across her chest. Now she could happily walk for an hour or two. She was also swimming across the bay two or three times each day and still she had the energy to have fun with the girls in the evenings.

'I just feel so much more alive here,' she confided. 'At home when I was with Richard, I felt so boring. All I felt able to do was to cook him the meals he loved and potter in the garden. I would not have dreamed of heading out for a walk. I feel so guilty that I could have played more with Harriet and gone swimming with her. She was always asking me to go into the pool like the other mummies, and now I will!' She was not the reserved woman who had arrived a few weeks ago.

The other girls were happy that she was finding herself and realising her self-worth. Her confidence had been on the floor when she arrived in Antigua. Gina was the member of the group who was closest to Claire, as she knew only too well what it was like to be under the spell of a control freak.

'Bide your time and before you know it you will be back to being the strong woman you were before "Bloody Richard",' she advised.

'You look incredible. You are getting in shape, laughing, having fun and everyone loves having you around. He just ground you down and we all know how that feels. You were always an attractive woman, he just managed to make you forget who the real Claire was. He was a control freak, and that's what they do.' Claire knew all this was true and she was no longer afraid of the future. She wasn't as bold as Anna or as feisty as Jesse, or as beautiful as Gina, but she knew she was strong, and she was suddenly not fearful of going home to the new life she planned to embrace.

KICKING BACK

Most days the girls headed across the bay and back but occasionally they would walk out of the Jolly Harbour community and trek to Valley Church or Ffryes Beach. This was quite a route march and not one they would attempt in the heat of the day, but as evening fell it became cooler and they loved walking along the deserted, white shoreline with only the waves and the seabirds to keep them company.

Once or twice, they stopped off at Sugar Ridge, a ritzy hotel above the bay to enjoy cocktails before heading back to the villa. Generally, though, they were happy to stay local, with regular visits to Castaways, the bar right on the edge of the beach. Locals and tourists alike flocked there to cool off at the end of the day. The barman always had four sundowners ready for them as they approached the bar.

By the end of the third week the girls felt like a family and none of them could even imagine a future in which the others would not figure in some way.

They enjoyed an alfresco barbeque on their deck that Saturday evening and resolved that the following week would have to include a few trips out to see the sights. 'We have been holed up here pretty much since we got here, and only left the resort once,' said Jesse.

'I am thinking a boat trip on Monday. Or maybe head up to Dickenson Bay? Denzil says we should give it a go. He has offered to drive us to Dickenson's for the day then come back to fetch us later, are you all up for it?'

Everyone agreed it was a plan. Gina had also agreed to join Jesse on a sunset cruise out toward Turner's Beach the next evening.

On the morning of their trip to Dickenson Bay, Gina woke up feeling a bit groggy and decided she would stay by the pool.

She promised the girls that she would cook supper ready for them when they returned.

'Shall I stay and keep you company?' Claire asked kindly, but Gina waved her offer away.

'No, I think I could use a bit of time on my own, I'll just hang around here and read and maybe have a swim later. I really don't feel up to the drive or a boozy lunch because I know Denzil has a pre-lunch cocktail hour planned. Go ahead and have some fun.'

Claire smiled and dashed up to her room. She was excited at the prospect of dressing up a bit and having fun with her newfound friends.

What a difference these few short weeks had made to the way she now felt about herself. Richard was definitely a thing of the past and would never have the power to hurt her again.

She felt a bit wistful at the loss of Martha's friendship, weirdly that loss had been almost harder to accept. But it showed the power of her ex who knew how to put on the charm.

She was a long way from home and all her past troubles. She was determined to make the most of it, so pushing thoughts of home away she prepared for her day out with the gang.

The others whistled as Claire strode out to the car in a psychedelic kimono in shades of vibrant pink and turquoise. Gina had loaned her a pair of huge gold hoops to give her a Caribbean edge and Gina felt a surge of pride at how far her new friend had come in such a short space of time. She looked fabulous and she had an inner glow and an air of confidence that had been so sadly lacking when she had first arrived. The little mouse had turned into a stunning cougar who was happy to strut her stuff and hold her own on nights out.

'Very sexy lady,' cooed Denzil and the others all laughed and clucked around her as Claire blushed, clearly delighted at the compliments. There was no doubt that Claire was in a very good place.

Back at the house Gina found she had got a bit tired of reading by the pool so she went to her room, quickly threw on some shorts, a silk camisole, and a battered straw hat, and set off for a walk across the beach.

As she reached the beach bar, she decided to stop for an iced tea. She froze when she saw Dan sitting at the bar looking at her from behind some sexy designer specs. He was stripped to the waist and peering over his glasses he gestured her over.

'I am not the devil you think I am,' he drawled. 'Come here and have a drink with me.'

She felt guilt at feeling tempted, but also acknowledged the truth that she would indeed enjoy having a drink with Dan. She allowed herself to weaken and adopted a slightly bored expression as she made her way to the bar.

He had pulled out a stool for her and extended a strong tanned hand. She found herself putting her own in his and sat beside him feeling a delicious tingle surge through her.

She tried not to gaze into his eyes and her mouth suddenly felt strangely dry.

'Shall we start again sexy lady? We got off to a bad start. I have been beating myself up that I never even talked to you on that flight. I was in a bit of a bad place and not feeling very talkative. I was rude and I apologise.'

Gina was taken aback by his words and found herself smiling.

'Look, it's OK. What worries me even more and makes me feel guilty is that I am even here with you. It appears you are out to get photographs of one of my friends. I really can't live with that if it is true, and I certainly should not be sitting here with you. I feel so disloyal.'

Her words did not have the reaction she expected. Dan seemed to choke on the iced beer he was swigging and he started laughing so hard he was literally rocking on his stool.

'Is that what you girlies are thinking?' he asked, giving her the whitest, broadest smile she had ever seen.

'Well, if that's all that's stopping us from getting it on then you can rest easy beautiful lady. I am certainly not here to work or take photographs of anyone. To be honest I think my days as a photographer may well be well and truly over so whoever was trying to take photographs of you and your group is not me. Climbing trees, playing peekaboo, and perving at women is not my style.'

Gina looked at him and narrowed her eyes as she tried to let the words sink in.

'Well, you are a pap photographer after all. Anna saw you at the airport and freaked. She told us that you would do anything to get photographs and right now she does not need that. She is going through a tough time and she just wants peace that's what we are all here for.'

Dan seemed to soften and he eased back in his stool his eyes not leaving hers. He then leaned slightly forward. She could feel his cool breath on her face and she felt strangely dizzy.

With a swift movement he had pulled Gina to him and covered her lips with his, sending sensational flashes to a part of her she had forgotten existed.

He kissed her long and hard and she found herself sinking into him like some lovestruck teenager.

'Whoa cowboy, where did that come from?' she said laughing, but it was clear she had enjoyed the moment. For a few seconds they looked at each other wordlessly; knowing a line had been well and truly crossed.

'Lady it's called chemistry. Have you never just kissed someone because right that second that's all you can think of doing? From the moment I saw you on the beach the other night I knew this was going to happen, I just had to figure out the how and where.'

He gave her a boyish grin that made her heart turn over. What was she thinking, making out with a virtual stranger at a beach bar? The Caribbean sun had got to her and she had lost her senses.

In truth she had never felt such an animal attraction. Her past boyfriends had been outgoing and fun, but this encounter with a stranger was like no other she had ever had. It was certainly not the intense or rather tense exchanges she had experienced with James. Lately, the last thing she had wanted was to kiss him, let alone have sex with him. The few physical exchanges between them had left her cold.

Latterly she had always responded to his advances because she had been terrified of the consequences if she dared to reject him. Now the prospect of getting up close and personal with a man who only hours ago she thought she would detest was all she could think about.

Sensing the moment was right, Dan took her hand and led her to the car park at the back of the beach. He gestured for her to jump in his jeep.

'We are going for a drive; I want to show you something.'

He drove at speed allowing the warm air to hit them as he sped along the coastal road. Soon he was heading down a deserted track and pulled into a clearing where ahead of them was an empty white stretch of sand and a clear slash of turquoise sea.

'I found this place yesterday when I went hiking. It's not somewhere many people come as it is so off the beaten track, but it's a stunning bay and the water is so warm.'

Gina stood in the surf and admired the shoreline where weathered old tree trunks were being buffeted by the sea. The trunks were rubbed smooth, and Gina ran her hands along them enjoying the knowledge that she was alone with this beautiful man.

It seemed the most natural thing in the world when Dan stripped off his clothes and run into the sea whooping and laughing and daring her to join him.

Gina had her bikini bottoms on under her shorts and she felt completely liberated as she threw off her top and ran into the sea to join him.

Within seconds he had swum to join her and instantly the pair were entwined, tasting the salty sea on each other's lips and faces. They tumbled and rolled in the waves like children, laughing and splashing each other, lost in the craziness of it all.

The two swam far out into the bay, then stopped to tread water and look back to the tiny beach with its powdery, white sand and stark black tree trunks jutting out of the surf.

Eventually they made their way back to the shore and wordlessly dressed, before walking hand in hand back to the jeep.

'I am thinking lunch?' he smiled shyly at her.

She nodded and he turned the car towards the main road. Minutes later he took a turn into a side road, and it wound back down to the coast, and they pulled up outside a wooden beach bar which was perched above Ffryes Beach.

'This is Dennis's joint; he's a mate of a mate. You must sample his seafood stew. I always come here when I visit the island. It's a bit of a hidden secret, a real local haunt; but believe me you are going to love it.'

They chose one of the rustic tables set out on the open veranda which jutted out over the beach. There was a cool sea breeze and the pair marvelled at the armada of tiny boats that cruised past the bay. At times a motorized dinghy would head into the beach and deposit its crew to set up barbeques or head to the bar for much needed beers.

The pair were happy to just sit and take in the view and marvel at what was clearly a newfound attraction.

Almost by magic Dennis himself appeared with two huge glasses of Long Island iced tea and gestured for them to look at the menus he placed in front of them.

The pair lingered for hours over chilled rosé wine and endless plates of delicious seafood stew, cold platters of lobster and prawns and rice dishes that just kept appearing at their table.

Gina tried to get Dan to tell her the story he had been so keen to share that evening on the beach. He implicated that his life was a bit complicated however he assured her he would tell her the story at some point.

'It's a long and unhappy story and I don't want to spoil the mood. We are having fun, so let's take a rain check on that subject, OK?

'Things are up in the air right now and I would rather not dwell on it and spoil the mood. I was drunk the other night on the beach and feeling a bit sorry for myself but I think I have made some good decisions since then.

'Something major happened to some people I care about and I am still processing it. A few things happened this week that mean I have to make some pretty big changes to my life. And I realise that getting wasted at beach bars late at night won't solve anything!

'I just want to hear what brought you and that crazy gang of girls all the way out here?'

Gina took a long sip of her wine and decided to answer as she wanted him to just keep talking.

'From the moment I watched you walk off that aircraft I regretted not getting to know you. I knew I had lost out. When I saw you on the beach that night it felt like fate had given me another shot. Just a pity I was so wasted, sorry. I was a mess and you were right to walk away from me.'

Gina felt flattered and not a little turned on. As the day wore on, she found herself warming to this man more and more.

After a lot of prompting, he persuaded her to recount the story of her difficult marriage and the final assault that gave her the courage to move on.

At one point Gina saw Dan's eyes fill up and she stopped talking and reached across and held his hand.

'Hey, I am sorry, it doesn't make for easy listening does it? I didn't want to put you off, I hear myself talking about what went on and feel so silly and such a victim. I know I should have walked away before.

'I felt so ashamed and diminished by what happened to me. I always prided myself on being self-reliant and independent. I was so afraid and miserable with no clear way out. I couldn't tell anyone what was happening. Then eventually I realised if I didn't leave him, he would end up hurting me badly. That's the reason I finally escaped and the reason I came here. I needed to get away, find some head space and discover what the next step was for me. Life has been so confusing. For now, I have walked away from everything and being suspended in time works for me at the moment.

'It really is not the right time for me to get involved with anyone so can we be friends? I can't offer anyone more right now. Does it all sound ridiculous?'

Dan fixed her with those almond shaped green eyes which seemed to blaze into her soul.

'I would describe you as many things, but ridiculous is certainly not one of them. Your husband was a violent bastard and I just wish I could lay my hands on him for what he did to you.'

Dan gestured for her to walk with him and wordlessly they fell into step and walked across the breadth of the bay in the shallows enjoying their surroundings of rolling surf and endless blue seas and skies.

They didn't speak for a long time and Gina was touched when he scooped up a heart shaped shell and handed it to her.

'It has a tiny hole big enough for a chain. Wear it for me one day.'

He gave her a shy smile and she closed her hand around the pearly shell and decided she would treasure it forever. How could a simple conch shell suddenly seem so significant to her?

They climbed back into the jeep and Gina was sorry when they arrived back at Jolly Beach and he gently led her back to the bar.

'I guess it would not be the best idea to walk you all the way back to the house? I suspect your house mates would not be too keen to see me?'

Gina smiled at him, shaking her head.

'I would imagine you are the last person anyone back there would like to see. At some point I will tell them that we have met and talked and I promise I will explain you are not the man they think you are. But for now, can we keep this between us? Not that there is an "us" or anything.'

She found herself stumbling over her words and blushing as she had assumed there would be other times like this.

He pulled her to him and seemed to consume her with his eyes.

'You can tell them about me. I am going to give you a day or so to have that conversation, then I am going to call for you.'

She swallowed a huge lump that had formed in her throat and felt her heart race. It was all happening so fast and she had certainly not planned on a summer fling if that was what this was shaping up to be. She couldn't deny the chemistry between them, though she knew she would be foolish to rush headlong into anything with a man she barely knew. Particularly a man that none of the girls trusted.

Pulling back from him she fixed him with a look that she hoped showed she was stronger than she felt.

'OK, I will talk to them later or maybe tomorrow. I am sure I will see you around when I have straightened things out? They are a great bunch but they don't take prisoners, so let me smooth things out first, OK?'

He pulled her to him one last time and kissed her before pulling away. Without a backward glance he headed back to his jeep and drove off.

It was only then she realised that she didn't have his number or the first idea of where he was staying. She had been so caught up in the moment that she hadn't a clue where he lived or how to get hold of him.

All she knew was that he obviously came to the island a lot as he knew local people and places and he claimed he wanted to see her again. Just how that was going to happen was now a bit of a mystery.

Feeling like a silly teenager she headed to the house, realising that the girls would be back soon. Now she had to somehow come up with the meal she had promised them!

An hour later the group arrived at the villa, bursting through the door and full of stories about their day.

Claire shyly held out a small brown paper parcel. Inside was a pair of long silver earrings inlaid with a tiny pearl nestling inside a shell.

'We all thought you would love these,' she said. Gina found her eyes misting over.

'You girls really are the best. Thank you they are so beautiful; I promise I will treasure them always.'

She also had a fleeting thought that the tiny shell Dan had given her would make a great necklace, as it replicated the delicate silver shell of the earrings.

'I feel this has been one of my best days yet,' she told them, smiling broadly.

'Sorry supper is a very simple one. Just seafood and salad and some pastries. I'm afraid I went to the beach and got a bit carried away and forgot that the clock was ticking.'

Gina felt awful not telling the whole truth, but at this point she had no intention of sharing the details of what she had been up to.

The girls said they were grateful not to have to cook and they all busied themselves making cocktails and setting the outdoor table.

Gina placed the salad platters on the terrace and marvelled at the amazing views over the bay. She let her gaze wander across to the far end of the beach where she knew people were gathering for sundowners.

She felt instinctively that Dan was probably there with them. Part of her yearned to wander along the beach and join him. But she had promised the girls she would be the hostess and she turned on her heels and announced she planned a swim before supper.

Claire and Jesse appeared with swimsuits and towels and the threesome waded into the warm ocean and swam far out, chatting about the day they had had and how lucky they felt to be there.

The evening passed in a blur of laughter and jokes, together with anecdotes about Denzil and his outrageous stories.

Gina secretly stroked the shell Dan had given her and wondered when the time would be right to mention him to the girls.

'Not tonight, but maybe in the morning,' she promised herself.

They all drifted off to bed as the day had been full on for them all, though Gina could not help but feel guilty that she had not spent it in quite the way she had told the group.

THE ST JOHN ENCOUNTER

THE NEXT MORNING THEY woke to driving rain and dark grey clouds hanging over Jolly Beach like a drab cloak.

They had planned to laze on the beach but everyone agreed this was not going to be a day for sunbathing or swimming.

Jesse, who had taken on the mantle of team leader, announced that she had a plan.

'I think this may be the perfect day to explore St John. We can jump on the local bus, get off in the marketplace and head down to the boutiques near the Quay. Denzil said there are some great shops there so we could do some shopping, get a few gifts and maybe find somewhere nice to have lunch?'

Claire and Anna agreed that it would beat looking out over the rain swept beach though. Secretly Gina hoped to be able to escape for an hour to find Dan.

The girls trooped to the bus stop just outside the gates leading to the resort and found themselves squashed into a bus packed with locals who were heading to the market.

They were carrying bags and boxes filled with crafts and fruit and vegetables and everyone exchanged polite hellos.

The bus took them through a succession of villages, where increasing numbers of people piled onto the bus.

At the bus station everyone scrambled to get off and the girls stopped to get their bearings, before heading toward the quayside where Denzil had suggested they begin their shopping.

Gina found herself being bombarded by taxi drivers asking to take her for an island tour her silky blonde hair and stylish clothes marking her out as the wealthy tourist she was. But Gina was in no mood to be pestered. Her head was too full of all that had happened in the last few days. She felt she needed some time and space to process it all and decide on the way ahead.

She good naturedly waved them away and the girls headed into the tempting row of duty-free designer stores with their amazing window displays.

They agreed looked very at odds with the ramshackle local shops just a street or two away. The shops were a Mecca for wealthy tourists from the cruise ships moored nearby.

The girls soon tired of the bustle and noise of the quay and found a small café where they enjoyed frothy coffees and plates of fruit while idly watching the world go by.

Gina decided it might be the time to broach the subject of Dan. She was about to launch into her story of the chance meeting on the beach the previous day, when Claire grabbed Anna and gestured wildly at a man further down the street.

'It's him, it's him, he's right there!' she hissed, indicating a good-looking middle-aged man who was sauntering along on the other side of the street.

'Who and what are you talking about?' asked Anna. She had also noticed the black-haired Adonis who was more than aware he was attracting a fair amount of female attention.

The man was very tall, held himself very straight and was dressed head to toe in Ralph Lauren. He had on beige, knee length shorts teamed with a pale blue casual shirt and leather loafers. His fringe flopped sexily over one eye and he kept brushing his hair back as if he knew he was being watched. He had slung a cotton sweater over one shoulder and kept stopping to gaze into shop windows, clearly checking out his own reflection.

'It's bloody Richard! What the hell is he doing here? I can't believe he is here, but he is.'

Claire looked flustered and wore the haunted expression that she had arrived with.

As usual it was Jesse who was the first to react. She stood up and prepared to square up to the man she knew had almost destroyed her new friend.

'Don't worry, if he comes within a metre of you, he will get both barrels! It can't be a coincidence that he has found himself here. It's obvious he has come to find you Claire. Let's just get out of here quickly and get back to Jolly Harbour and think this through.'

Gina and Jesse walked either side of Claire and almost frog-marched her in the opposite direction to Richard to the nearby taxi rank alongside the quay.

'We don't want to risk seeing him again. It may be that he doesn't know where Claire is and is just snooping around, but best not take any chances.'

The girls bundled a bewildered Claire into the back seat of the cab and Anna hopped in the front seat and told the driver to get them back to the resort as fast as possible!

Back at the house Claire walked to the back terrace and sat down quietly, not wanting to speak to anyone.

The three other girls hastily made some sandwiches and Gina made them all laugh when she pulled out a bottle of brandy and four large glasses.

'Hold fire on the tea, this is a conversation that needs alcohol!' she announced.

Anna had gone to her room when they got back and sat quietly thinking over the past couple of hours. She appeared a little later looking steely eyed and driven.

'I have been giving this whole thing a lot of thought and the best thing we can all do right now is nothing. The guy is a creep but what can he do? None of us is going to let him near Claire. He can't get to her here and if he tries, we will get security to boot him out. The worst thing we can do is hole up here like a gang of fugitives. He can't have that effect on you again Claire.'

She sat by Claire who was now weeping and put her arm around her.

'He spent years controlling you. It says it all that just by seeing him you felt you had to run and hide, but with our help that is stopping right now.'

Claire stopped crying and raised her eyes to the three women who were now surrounding her.

'I just got freaked out at the sight of him. He thinks he can manipulate me. For just a moment back there I thought that maybe I wasn't strong enough to keep him at bay. But you are right. I am over him and he has no place in my life. I'm just not that sure I am up to seeing him or talking to him. He always knew me as a pushover and I suppose he thought that making the grand gesture and turning up here would be his way back.'

In the next couple of hours, the girls demolished the bottle of brandy. Anna opened another one and popped open a bottle of champagne to make a brandy-based cocktail Piers always made when she had been feeling low.

Even a sip of the sweet drink brought tears to her eyes as she recalled how Piers was always so good in a crisis. He always knew what to say to make her feel better when the chips were down. She bit down hard on her lip to try to stave off the image of lovely Piers with his kind, soft voice and natural ability to make her feel safe. Anna wished she could have just five minutes with him so she could tell him this and many other surprising things that she had discovered about herself in the past few days.

Jesse ordered in massive pepperoni pizzas and the four talked for hours about how the day had once again shown them how they had bonded as a group. Claire was now lying across one of the outdoor sofas and the others were fussing around her making her feel safe and cosseted.

'I have decided that if I do bump into Richard, I will be fine. It was just such a shock to see him. He always had such a physical impact on me and that may take time to go away, but I do know that I don't love him anymore. We're done. I just can't work out how he knew I was here. My parents certainly would not have told him.'

The girls finally went to bed, having tucked Claire up with assurances that she should call them if she needed them.

As Anna drifted into a fitful sleep, she wished that she could get to a place where she could honestly say that she no longer loved Piers. Despite his recent betrayal she knew that deep down she still loved him and part of her blamed herself for not realising what she had had when they were together.

If the chance ever came her way, she would happily trade in her Jimmy Choos for a pair of trainers and would play bloody rounders for as long as he wanted her to! The idea of an afternoon with his friends and their assorted offspring now sounded lovely.

She even allowed herself a vision of a chubby baby lolling on a soft picnic blanket enjoying the late summer sun. She felt her heart flip at the thought of a tiny child who would be a curious combination of Piers with his loving ways, and perhaps a hint of her spirit and drive. He would naturally have his mother's bright auburn hair. The thought of this dream baby somehow soothed her, and she decided it was time to call it a night.

'What has happened to me, who am I?'

She finally fell into a restless sleep and dreamed she was racing around a muddy field playing games with a group of small children who all looked like Piers.

ANNA and GINA

When she woke up Anna half expected to see Piers' handsome face alongside hers on the pillow, but then the reality of her situation kicked in.

Even the beautiful turquoise seas outside washing onto the powdery white shoreline did not help one bit. She got up, threw on a swimsuit and headed out to the beach for an early morning swim in a bid to clear her head.

As she reached the water's edge she realised that she was not alone. Gina was swimming back to the shoreline and waved as she saw Anna sitting on the sand just above the tideline.

'Couldn't you sleep either?' Gina shook the water out of her hair and joined Anna.

'I suppose I just have a lot on my mind.'

Sensing that she had an ally, Gina decided that she had to tell someone about her time with Dan. As Anna was the person who may be opposed most to the man, she felt it may as well be her!

'Look, I haven't been as straight with you all as I should have been. I feel terrible about it but something happened the other day when you all went off and I feel so bad about it. I have to tell someone ...'.

She took a long, deep breath then poured out the tale of bumping into Dan that night on the beach. She recounted their chat and how she had run away, only to see him the following day.

Anna's eyes widened as Gina spoke about how they had spent an amazing day together, first enjoying a drive, then a lunch before heading back to Jolly Beach and having a final drink at the bar.

'He says that he is going to call for me and he gave me until tomorrow to tell you all about us meeting. He insists he is not here on some witch hunt for you and though I know you are not going to believe him. I really think he is telling the truth.

'As much as I am afraid of your reaction at seeing him and as much as I am terrified of him just turning up here out of the blue, I am more worried that he won't. There is something between us and I just want you to give him the chance to come here and explain himself. I have been thinking a lot about it. Why would he come clean and want to turn up here if he wasn't on the level?'

Anna took a deep breath and was about to point out that he was a chancer and a charmer and that he was just using Gina when she suddenly stopped and thought better of it. Who was she to judge Dan? She had got her own life very wrong.

'Look, he may be all he says he is. What do I know? You are looking at a woman who had it all and basically threw it all away. I was so blind, right now I don't trust my judgement about anything, particularly where men are concerned. I am certainly not going to judge you, so go right ahead and spend time with him.

'Just do me a huge favour and at least be careful. You are not exactly in the best place emotionally either so it's wise to hold something back. At least you have all of us as backup.'

Gina had not been expecting such an easy time of it and threw her arms around her new friend and hugged her tight.

'You have no idea how happy you have just made me and what a star you are. You were the one person I thought would be angry with me, so thank you for being so kind and understanding. I promise I will watch out for myself. But he really was a sweetheart and he made me feel things I had not expected to feel ever again. I know this is all a bit sudden and maybe I should give myself a break from men, but this guy is not like James. I know that much, anyway a fling may be just what I need. I have not given my ex one single thought since meeting Dan.'

Smiling, Gina walked back to the house determined to talk to the other girls and let them know about a certain male visitor they could expect to see on the doorstep later that day.

She wondered how she would be able to make contact but if not she felt confident that Dan would be in touch with her very soon.

As she expected, the rest of her group were happy and were supportive of her decision to give the young photographer a chance. Privately though, they did wonder how he was going to convince Anna that he was not on a mission to dish the dirt on her – and get a photo into the bargain.

'We've had plenty girly time so why not?' was Jesse's reaction, while Claire was a little more sombre. This was no surprise given what had happened in St John's the previous day.

For the rest of the day Anna, Jesse and Claire lazed around the pool while Gina felt restless. She decided she would go to the supermarket to stock up on some fresh fruit and goodies for later.

They all agreed on a cocktail hour at sunset and if Dan made an appearance, he could simply join in.

Gina took one of the golf buggies and headed off to the small shopping centre humming happily as the warm breeze whipped through her hair.

Her mind wandered back to the past few weeks and the strange turn of events that had led her to this incredible place and the three strangers who had very quickly become very close and firm friends. She felt at peace and happy at the prospect of what might lie ahead in the future. She realised and not for the first time this trip, that her past was well and truly behind her. She had no hang ups about what had happened with James and she realised that she would not simply walk back to that life.

She had just parked up and was making her way through the supermarket doors when she was stopped in her tracks by the sound of someone shouting out her name, followed by an ear shattering wolf whistle.

She turned slowly and found herself staring at Dan who was grinning at her from across the street.

'Just the girl I need to see. What time am I coming to call later?' A slow smile spread across his rugged jaw and she found herself holding her breath.

She managed to compose herself enough to make her way over the road and stand inches from him, feeling that familiar tug. 'The girls are fine about you coming by later, in fact I am here to buy a few provisions.' She felt like some star struck teenager about to go on her first date.

'Make it about six thirty. Then maybe we could head off and grab a pizza or something? Everyone has agreed they need to meet you properly and ensure that your intentions are as honourable as I've said they are!'

She hated that she acted so flustered and breathy around him and she struggled to compose herself. She could tell that Dan knew the effect he was having on her. Fixing her with his eyes he pulled her to him and brushed his lips against her cheek.

'Lady why do you always smell so good? Yep, it's a date, but I can do a bit better than a pizza. I want to show you where I live. So, I'll cook for you but it will be good to meet your girls first. And without a backward glance she watched as he jumped into his jeep and headed off out of the compound.

As she walked back toward the supermarket Gina found herself trying to remember what she had come to buy and tried to focus her mind on what had just happened. This guy had the ability to make everything else fly out of her head! She couldn't help smiling as she found herself in front of the chilled drinks cabinet where she reached for a bottle of champagne, it seemed to be calling to her. As an afterthought she also purchased a pack of beers in case he was not a champagne sort of guy.

She almost skipped back to the golf buggy as she was desperate to get back to the villa so she could sift through her capsule wardrobe. She aimed to look stunning for the night that lay ahead.

What had happened to the haunted, buttoned up girl who had arrived in Antigua only a few weeks ago? A tiny voice was trying to make itself heard reminding her that she should be careful about not getting hurt. But right now, the prospect of a night being wooed by a green-eyed hunk was all she could focus on.

'What is the worst thing that can happen?' she wondered.

Smiling broadly, she reversed the buggy and headed back to the villa, eager to choose what she would wear and share the latest interlude with the girls who she knew were now on side.

SAM

SAM STRUGGLED TO OPEN his eyes and he groaned as he heard the rain beating down on the windowpane. It was the weekend and while he didn't have to go into the office, a real bonus as he was not coping too well at work, two long bleak days rolled ahead of him.

He had no plans to go and see friends, had no food in the fridge and his flat looked dismal and dirty. In fact, it seemed to reflect his life and his mood. There was dust on every surface. He was surviving on cereal and beer and the sink was piled high with dishes. The worktops were cluttered with empty bottles. He had no milk or bread in the house and he had no energy or desire to cook, clean or even eat for that matter.

Every morning when he woke up the realisation of what he had done, and more importantly the woman he had lost, hit him anew.

At work his boss had taken him aside and asked him why his work had dipped so badly. 'We have noticed that your time keeping is just off the radar Sam. You are sullen and quiet, it's so not like you. Surely you must realise that your targets have been way off too. You can talk to me about it, my door is always open to you, but whatever it is you have to get your head around it because we can't keep carrying a passenger. We are a small team and we all rely on each other, you know that.'

The words stung but Sam felt unable to share his story. He felt ridiculous and anyway, nothing anyone could say would make a difference right now. His life was a mess and he felt as though everything was caving in on him. It didn't matter how much he told himself he had to pull himself together, he just couldn't do it. He had no energy to go to the gym or meet his friends. Going to work was a chore and he had stopped bothering about how he looked. He knew he was not looking his best.

He had always prided himself on being fit and groomed but these days he simply put on the first thing he found in the wardrobe. He had not had his hair cut or shaved properly for weeks and he knew that he looked as bad as he felt.

Zoe had made his life hell too. She had bombarded him with threatening texts and telephoned him at all hours of the day and night screaming at him that she wished him dead. Going to sleep and not waking up had seemed a good idea to him a lot of the time. Thankfully his sister Jen arrived one Sunday afternoon and found him in bed with his curtains shut.

She refused to leave his room until he had taken a shower and she had laid out some clean clothes. She then went into the kitchen to make them both beans on toast. Thankfully she had brought provisions with her, as all he had in the fridge was beer and a couple of eggs.

'Mum always says that when the going gets tough, eat beans on toast,' she trilled. Something in her tone set him off and he struggled to hold back the tears. He wanted to be that small boy again when his mum always had the right words, rustling up beans on toast and let him stay home from school. They would watch his favourite television programmes and Mum would somehow magically make all his problems just disappear.

Oh how he wished that a can of Heinz Baked Beans and a runny egg could solve his current dilemma!

Taking a deep breath, he realised he had to talk to someone. He poured it all out to Jen, filling her in about his misery, describing how he felt he had messed up his life and how he didn't know how to get out of the big black hole he had dug himself.

He told her all about Jesse and how even though he had tried to walk away from her and go ahead with the wedding to Zoe, his feelings had proved too strong. Most of all he was ashamed of how weak and stupid he had been not to have realised he was pushing away the woman he knew he wanted to be with.

Jen was silent and he sat waiting for her to berate him and agree that yes, he had been a complete fuck up. Instead she smiled kindly at him and stroked his arm.

'Look Sam, these sorts of messes happen. You fell for someone at the worst possible time and it's no wonder that you felt torn and confused. Who wouldn't?

'I think you need to look at it in a different way. You are slipping into a depression and that's not a surprise given all the drama you have been through, but it is time to get your head straight. Right now, it all seems a mess but things will slowly become clearer and the solution will present itself. Nobody died! You fell out of love with the woman you thought you wanted to marry and you fell in love with someone you did!'

She also made him feel 100 per cent better when she confided that secretly she had been relieved when he had broken it off with Zoe.

'I would never have said anything to you but she was a nightmare. To be brutally honest none of our family liked her. Mum was certainly over the moon when you called it off. She was always talking down to you, she was never very nice to mum and always seemed to have a bad smell under her nose. I know you left it to the final hour to come to your senses, but at least you did! Imagine if you had gone through with the wedding and THEN told her she was not for you! Now that would have been a disaster. In my opinion, you had a lucky escape. At least you realised before you made it official, and I for one am so relieved. I hope that one day I get to meet the lovely, mysterious Jesse because I think she saved you. There, I have said it, someone had to. I think you will find your friends all feel the same. You should be celebrating because, let's face it, you dodged the proverbial bullet!'

Sam began to feel a cloud lift. He agreed with his sister and resolved that he would go back to the gym, eat better, stop drinking himself into a stupor at weekends and get back on track at work.

His main problem was Jesse, he couldn't get her out of his head.

'Jen, I want to be with her more than anything but she has just disappeared. I can't get hold of her and I am not even sure that she would speak to me if I did. I blew it because I was such a coward and I couldn't be honest with Zoe.'

Jen listened and simply rubbed his back. She told him that she understood and reminded him that Jesse had obviously loved him deeply. Her running away had not changed that. Nor could she forget him or get over him that quickly.

'Women mourn a lost love, I will bet my house on the fact that she is somewhere feeling utterly miserable right now and wishing she was with you. Don't forget, she still believes that you got married; she has no idea that you backed out of the wedding and left Zoe. As far as she is concerned you went ahead with it and abandoned her. It's simple really, you just have to either bide your time and wait for her to come back so you can set the record straight, or you go all out to track her down now. Why sit here waiting though? Go out there and find her, tell her how you feel, let her know you walked away from Zoe because you didn't love her. You really don't have anything to lose, do you?'

Suddenly Sam shook himself out of his malaise and a huge smile spread across his face.

'Jen you are incredible! You are a genius, why hadn't I thought of all that? I have been stupid but that's what got me in this mess in the first place, being an idiot who couldn't see the wood for the trees.

His sister looked at her handsome younger brother with his tousled hair and dreamy eyes and thought he looked just like he did when they were children and he'd fallen over in the playground.

She always ran to him and sorted him out. She was always able to soothe him and dry his tears because for all his intelligence and kindness he was so dumb when it came to emotions. But she could see that he had resolved to sort himself out and maybe this Jesse girl was 'the one'. It was obvious that he had deep feelings for this girl and Jen so wanted things to work out for Sam. At least he had begun to start thinking a little more clearly.

'Look Jen, I am going to sort myself out and try to find her. You don't need to worry about me.'

With those words he walked Jen to her car, went back to the flat, cleared the debris from his kitchen worktops and made himself an omelette. While he ate he made a list of the things he had to address and first on the list was sorting out his tip of a flat.

Getting back on track at work was a biggie too but at the top of the list was trying to find Jesse and begging her to see him. It would not be easy, but he knew that first thing tomorrow the search would begin.

The following evening he called up his best friend Ben and asked for a summit meeting in the Fox and Grapes in Wimbledon Village. It seemed fitting that it was the last place he had met up with Jesse and he had bittersweet memories of that fateful day.

Ben listened as Sam told him about Jen's visit and how he had resolved to sort out his life once and for all.

'She didn't die mate; she ran away and who can blame her?'

Ben had tried several times to drag Sam out of his stupor and he was relieved that his friend was finally showing signs of rallying around and getting on with his life.

'Stop moping about. So, you messed up, we all do that. Just go out there and find her and make things right. She obviously thinks you are the one otherwise she wouldn't have done a runner. I agree with Jen. If you want her, get out there and beg her to give you another chance.'

Although he had told himself those same things, hearing Ben say the words somehow galvanised a resolve to do just as he had said. Feeling more positive than he had in a long time

Sam grabbed his coat and punched Ben on the shoulder. 'We have some thinking to do so let's head to the Indian. Tonight it's on me.'

PIERS

PIERS STARED AT A blank screen for more than an hour trying to find the words to email Anna and tell her how much he regretted cheating on her and how he knew he had been the worst sort of a fool. But nothing he wrote seemed good or honest enough. Time after time he hit the delete button to be faced once more with an empty screen.

How the hell did you even begin to justify being unfaithful to the woman you loved, someone who had also been your best friend? Worst of all to have done so with Anna's PA who, he now realised, had only been interested in getting one over on her boss. Jane had never intended to get serious about Piers, it was all a big joke and now that joke was on him.

He had betrayed the woman who had been his world. Yes, at times Anna could be difficult, but she had always been true and kind and loyal.

They had a beautiful home and enjoyed an easy life with few dramas. OK, so she didn't always fall in with his plans, but generally they were on the same page. He missed living with her, hearing her key in the door, and sharing a bottle of wine and gossiping about their days. He missed the smell of her; a fresh fragrance that was a mix of tuberoses and the ocean. He loved it that she could rustle a meal up out of nothing. Even after a long tiring day in the office she would breeze into their flat and light it up with that huge smile. She was never untidy. The flat was spotless and each week she filled it with bowls of roses and tulips. In the early spring she loved placing vases of vibrant gold daffodils everywhere. She said it cheered her up.

'It's like letting the sunshine in,' she would tell him. He hadn't realised, until his nightmare living with Jane, how much it meant to live with someone that shared his values, someone who loved a clean, beautiful home and who enjoyed living a healthy lifestyle.

Piers cast his eyes around the junior suite he had rented in the hotel next to his office and inwardly groaned. The walls, floors and bedding were beige, as were the lamps and bathroom tiles and towels. Everything was beige, including his life he decided. Life with Anna had been like vibrant hues of bright fuchsia, emerald green and gold, his life now was dull, boring and lonely.

And he was to blame for it all. What had he been thinking of? Why did he have an affair with awful Jane? Jane who dressed so badly and who barely showered. Jane with bitten nails and a dreary, dirty flat.

She didn't bother with fluffy white towels and bowls of flowers. She had scratchy grey bath sheets that had seen better days. When Piers had once bought her a bouquet of roses, she hadn't even bothered to put them into a vase. They were left in the wrapper flung on the draining board. In the end Piers had put them in a large glass jar but they had stayed on the draining board until they went brown and crisp.

Jane was slovenly and unkempt. Worst of all she had just played games with him in a bid to take him from Anna. Fool that he was, he had gone along with it. The prospect of a baby had turned his head and made him someone he didn't recognise at all.

He reasoned that he had felt obliged to stick it out because of the baby. But there were many times he had begun to question her pregnancy. The smoking, her refusal to go to doctors' appointments ... he had been an idiot.

Worst of all, he had stupidly believed that Anna would not be upset about losing him. The moment he told her about Jane the stricken look on her face had told him a very different story. 'You bloody fool,' he told the reflection in his bathroom mirror. 'How the hell do I attempt to get Anna to forgive me for any of it?' The face staring back at him had no answer. He had blown it and lost the woman he loved. He felt lonely and devastated but he knew he deserved it.

For the umpteenth time he went to his laptop and re-read the email he had been composing earlier.

> My dear Anna, how do I begin to ask your forgiveness, how can I ever make up for all the pain I have caused? ...

Looking at the words he decided yet again they were not right. They were not enough, he figured, but what words would ever be enough? He had hurt her more than he could bear and he kept thinking of the look of shock and horror on her face when he had confessed his affair with Jane.

Anna had looked so crestfallen and sick and it made him want to weep. What had he been thinking? Where was she? And would she even want to hear from him? He very much doubted it, but something deep inside him felt that she deserved to know he realised he had been a fool. He wanted Anna to know he had got what he deserved. He owed her that much.

Piers knew Jane was now living with the blue-haired musician. All he felt was relief that he was out of it. At least those days of living in her grubby flat were over. He shivered at the thought of that dirty kitchen and the lingering smell of rotten food and unemptied bins. He felt so embarrassed.

It was a long shot, but maybe Anna could find it in her heart to hear him out. Perhaps it would give her some satisfaction he had been repaid for all the pain he had caused her. Once 'Blue Hair' arrived on the scene he had seen Jane for what she really was. He also wanted Anna to know that there was no baby, and most importantly there never had been. It would not make a difference to the betrayal; the affair had happened and everyone in their circle now knew about it, but it might help if Anna realised that he had felt obliged to stand by Jane. Once the baby had come into the equation, he had not been able to see a way out even if he had wanted one.

He had known for some time that Jane was not the woman

for him but he had gone along with it all as he couldn't see an alternative.

The only positive thing was that Jane was out of his life for good and her mess was not his problem anymore.

Piers was free of her and her chaotic lifestyle but he didn't want to be a single man, he wanted to be with Anna. They couldn't pick up exactly where they left off, but maybe they could make a new life and start again.

He decided that he would be happy to live on any terms she might lay down. The million-dollar question was would she give him the chance to prove himself to her?

He deleted the email he had been working on. It was too long and rambling and he sounded pathetic. Anna despised weakness. A blank screen stared back at him, mocking him and his inability to convey anything that would even begin to make sense.

'Just remember the advice of all good PRs,' he told himself. 'If you fuck up then say so and be as sorry and sincere about it as you can be.'

That was what he had always told his clients. Now it was time to take that advice himself, so, taking a deep breath he set about making a start.

Dear Anna,

I keep writing emails then deleting them as nothing I write is ever enough. I am a mess. Without you in my life I don't make sense, nothing makes sense.

Words are usually my thing but there are no words for what I did. I can't justify any of it. I just need to see you face to face and tell you that. I am deeply ashamed of what I have done to you, and of the pain I have caused. If I could change what I did I would. You know how much I have always loved you – I still do. You may find that hard to believe, but despite all that has happened I never stopped loving you.

I can't expect you to forgive me but I need you to know that I

cannot stop thinking about you. I have been an idiot and I miss
you, and us, more than I can ever say.

Jane and I are no longer together. There never was a baby. I was
a fool and I have nobody to blame but myself. I want you to know
that I have never felt as sad and disgusted with myself as I do now.

I have no way of knowing if this email will reach you. I have called
your office several times and nobody is willing to tell me where
you are or how long you intend staying away. I just pray that you
are picking up emails and that you will see this.

I hope you feel able to reply to me. Any sort of contact with
you will be better than the misery I am feeling now. I know I am
rambling on but I MUST keep saying it. I love you; I miss you and I
am the worst fuck up in creation because I lost you.

Piers

He didn't bother to re-read the email he simply hit send and
snapped shut the laptop. He would just have to sit it out and
see if she replied. He felt a bit better because at least he had
made a move. It wasn't the best thing he had ever written but
it was certainly the most raw and honest. So much rested upon
her getting this email. He just had to hope that she would find
it in her heart to reply to him. He figured he may have to wait
quite some time. Anna was not a girl to rush into anything.
She owed him nothing.

Holding that thought Piers looked around him and
decided it was time to sort out his living situation. He could
not assume that Anna would take him back so he needed to
find somewhere to live and make a home again. Maybe being
positive would help heal him a bit. Living as a gypsy, albeit in
a beige, hotel room, was not helping.

He picked up the property paper that had arrived with the
local rag and started flicking through the pages. On a whim
he found himself logging onto an agent's site that offered
country hideaways to city dwellers looking for weekend
retreats.

He had often dreamed of living in a village somewhere rural. He and Anna had joked about him retiring early and finally writing that book he had spoken about for the past few years.

Maybe it was the time to do just that? Feeling more energised than he had in weeks he went into his bedroom and threw a few things into a bag. He scooped up his coat and his keys and headed out the door.

He was going to drive out into the country and find a house. No, not a house, a home, and he would make it beautiful. He would start to write that book. He wanted to believe that one day Anna might forgive him and maybe, just maybe, join him.

BLOODY RICHARD

Richard returned to the cottage to find a solicitor's letter addressed to himself on the kitchen table. In his haste to get to Claire's parents he had failed to notice that it was propped up against a vase of flowers which were now dead.

He ripped it open and slammed his fist in frustration as he read the settlement she had offered him. He was to move out immediately and she would pay him a lump sum in recognition of the time they had spent together. She made it clear that should he try to contest this he would get nothing. The house had been put in her parents' names when Stevie died. While her parents had been against the idea of the lump sum, they had agreed to release funds from a trust they held for Harriet to pay him off. In law, Claire was not obliged to give him anything, but her parents had accepted that it meant getting him off her back forever. They reasoned he was greedy and selfish enough to leave if he was given a financial cushion.

Claire's advice that he take the money angered Richard but he was inclined to take it and run. He had no money for lawyers and maybe £50,000 was enough for him to put a deposit down on a flat. Every fibre in his being was screaming out for him to fight Claire or at least mess up her dream home. But he knew that he needed the cash and if he lashed out, he would not get a penny.

He headed up to the bedroom and started pulling his clothes out of the wardrobe. He was searching for a holdall in the bottom of the dresser when he saw a page ripped out from a magazine. Claire had ringed an advertisement with a red pen and he saw a telephone number scribbled alongside the ad.

Reading the advertisement, he suddenly realised where Claire had run to. She had gone to bloody Antigua with whoever had placed this ad. He ripped it out and stuffing the last of his belongings into plastic bags, he slammed out of the house and threw them into his car.

Phil had agreed to let him sleep on his sofa for a few nights and Richard knew that he could probably persuade him to let him stay a bit longer. He didn't have a long-term plan; he just wanted to clear his head.

He had struggled when Claire had acted all weird on discovering his fling with Martha. Why couldn't she just leave well alone? Just put up and shut up? He had come back to her, hadn't he?

Reversing his car out of the drive he headed to the local pub and decided to follow up on the flirtation he had started with the flighty little barmaid.

Phil had given him a key but he was in no rush to get to the house and the sofa bed. Maybe he could persuade the little barmaid to take him home with her.

As he drove towards the village, he began to think about the life he had had with Claire and it hit him that he had been a fool. He had an easy ride at home. She made no demands on him. She looked after him, worshipped the ground he walked on and best of all, with Claire he had no money worries. She gave him an allowance, paid all the bills and on the whole, she turned a blind eye to his little dalliances.

He had really made a big mistake with Martha. It was all meant to be a bit of fun and the fact she was Claire's best friend had made her a real challenge. But it had gone too far and he had got in too deep. Martha had started talking about setting up home together and maybe thinking about babies and this had really freaked him out. Claire was quite happy with Harriet and didn't want any more children which suited him just fine.

He was Claire's world and now he realised with a jolt that he had blown it big time. He had made a big mistake when Claire had walked in on him and Martha in Edinburgh. He should have run after Claire and begged her to forgive him. He could have easily found a way to push the blame onto Martha, who had quickly lost all loyalty where Claire was concerned.

When he had finally finished with Martha, she had been a clingy nightmare, crying and begging for him to see her. When he refused, she had turned into a psycho bitch, accusing him of using her and leading her on. He made it clear he was not interested in her and blamed her for the breakdown of his marriage. He had also cleverly turned the tables on her, saying she had been the one to seduce him. He told her he realised that she had been jealous of his relationship with his wife and had been hell bent on wrecking their marriage.

He said she should be ashamed of the way she had betrayed her so-called best friend. Martha had been shocked at first then horrified as it dawned on her that she really had wronged Claire and taken advantage of her good nature.

Martha had started to sob over the phone and had agreed that yes, she had been jealous of Claire's life with him. She had been very wrong to try to take Richard away from her friend. He laughed at how pathetic she had sounded and how easy it had been to make her take the lion's share of the blame. He could easily make up a story of how Martha envied Claire and had begrudged her happiness. He knew he could come out of this as the duped husband who had fallen for flattery. He would rehearse his sad stricken face. He knew Claire would fall for it.

Now he just had to find Claire and repair the damage his stupid dalliance had caused. He could then get back on track. It would take a month or two of eating humble pie and treating Claire like a princess but he could do that. If he could just find Claire and talk to her face to face it would be fine. She had never been able to resist him. That couldn't have changed in such a short time.

JAMES

It took James just a few weeks to realise that Gina was not going to walk back into his life. He deeply regretted smashing up the kitchen and he had been devastated when he had received a letter from Gina's solicitors saying that she intended to file for a legal separation. They had invited him to come up with a proposal about the house. They said that their client had no intention of returning and suggested that he consider buying her share of the house or it would be put up for sale.

He was beyond rage. As the days went on, he realised how much he missed his easy-going wife. For the first time he was forced to stand back and look at the part he had played in the breakdown of their relationship.

James had never had real friends, only work colleagues and a few guys he knew through playing squash. He didn't have family or anyone else he could confide in. So, at night and the weekends he would sit and drink beers, trawl the internet and feel sorry for himself. He knew he had a temper. He also knew he had made a lot of unreasonable demands on Gina and realised deep down it had been wrong to hurt her. But he felt compelled to punish her. His own mother had loved him but she had often hit him and abandoned him for hours at a time when he was small. He told nobody. His Mum said that he would be taken away from her if he ever told anyone that she regularly left him on his own. She would take his baby sister to a friend, but she said he was old enough to look after himself.

He remembered one weekend she had gone away and left him for a whole two days. She had left cereal and chocolate and locked the door, but it didn't stop him from being frightened. He had been about 10 and even now he could still recall how terribly alone he had felt. He had turned every light on in the house because he was terrified of going to sleep in the dark. Eventually he had cried himself to sleep. When he woke he was convinced people were outside the house looking in at him through the windows. Two days later his mother arrived home to find him hiding in a den he had made under the stairs and she had mocked him and shouted at him for being such a baby. He was also ashamed that he had soiled his clothes as he was too scared to go upstairs in the dark and use the bathroom. He felt dirty and lonely and made himself a promise that he would never rely on his mother again. He couldn't trust her even though she said she loved him. He wondered what love was if that was what you did to people who you were supposed to love.

Women he decided, were strange creatures. They said things they didn't mean. They were cruel; they made you love them and rely upon them and then they lied and hurt you. He was never ever going to let anyone hurt him again. They got you to care for them and then they let you down, again and again. You tried to be strong; you tried to stay kind and positive but they always hurt you. He made a promise to himself that he would never trust a woman. He began to hate the mother he had so loved. He would fantasise about how he would one day make his mother pay for the hurt and humiliation she had piled upon him. Though still a very young boy he pledged to become strong and build a wall around him; a steel boundary that nobody would ever penetrate.

His mother noticed a huge change in her sensitive son. Almost overnight he grew loud and aggressive and became a real problem child at school. She was constantly being asked to come in as James was disruptive and surly, hitting out at his classmates. He would often hurt the girls, lashing out and spitting at them as they played at lunchtimes.

When he went to the local Grammar School, he seemed to control his temper and he found a way to charm the staff and duck under their radar. His way of coping was to study hard and become very adept at passing exams. He was the golden boy, always top of his class in every subject.

Nobody realised that at the same time he was storing up a huge amount of anger and resentment. His mother was a drinker and chain smoker and over the years she had not aged well.

She had been a good-looking woman who attracted men, lots of men. After his father left, James lost count of the number of uncles who entered both his life and his mother's bedroom. As her lifestyle took its toll, her constant stream of boyfriends began to dwindle and one day it ceased completely. Along the way she had met a couple of down beat men who had stolen money from her. One had also assaulted her and left her bruised and broken. After that she stayed home and refused to clean the house or cook for herself or for James.

He took on the role of housekeeper and became compulsive in his need for cleanliness and order. He bleached floors and sinks, made sure his room was immaculate and his clothes were always freshly laundered. Nobody realised that he was looking after both himself and his mother. She stayed in bed most days and rarely ventured down into the kitchen. James accepted that there was only one person that he could rely upon and that was himself.

When he reached 16, James decided not to take his A levels. His teachers pleaded with him to change his mind. He was a bright boy and they had visions of him going on to university. He was such a talented student and argued that he was throwing away his future. But James was not in the least bit interested. He just wanted a way out. His sister had left long ago to stay with a cousin who had been happy to take her in.

James was left to fend for himself and he liked it that way. He was eager to get a job and get away.

'Sorry, but I need to earn some money and leave home,' he told his favourite tutor. It was the most he had ever admitted to anyone about his private life. James was a loner. He never bothered with friends and despite being very handsome, never showed any interest in girls. He found a live-in job working in a pub kitchen so left home and cut all ties with his mother without even a backward glance.

Years later he refused to acknowledge his lack of respect for women. Yes, he liked women, enjoyed their company, loved to bed them, but above all he enjoyed controlling them. He became expert at wooing girls, then dumping them when they got clingy. He liked smart women, but also hated that they enjoyed interfering in his life. When he met Gina, he knew he had met his match. She was bright, beautiful, kind and caring, but she was also fiercely independent.

He knew he could win her over by playing the silent, brooding man who needed a strong woman. Once she was in his thrall, he would bore of her and discard her as he had done countless times. But something about Gina kept him coming back for more. She was such fun to be with, she was neither clingy nor dependent on him. No, Gina could stay in his life a little longer. She had got under his skin. The realisation frightened him a bit. He would have to be careful; he was in danger of getting in deep. He might even marry this woman and make her his own. She was a good fit and he knew she loved him so much he could mould her. They had a whirlwind engagement and married very quickly. They had secretly run off to do so with only her parents there. She had agreed to a wedding without her many friends there but had drawn the line at leaving her mum and dad out of the ceremony.

For a while James played the dutiful, adoring husband and made sure Gina was entirely hooked before he began to systematically take control of their lives. He disliked her friends with a fervour and made every excuse not to see them or allow her to see them. Her family were the sort of middle-class snobs who irritated the life out of him. He couldn't hide the fact that he despised them and he found ways to make sure they knew this.

Gina had climbed quite high up her career ladder and if she had to, she could easily live without him. Financially she was more secure than he was. This made him feel out of control and threatened. He couldn't allow a woman to have that much say in his life. His mother had shown him that women could not be relied upon, even those who said they loved you.

The day she came home happy and excited following a works' party to celebrate her promotion was the day he knew it was time to take her down a peg or two.

It was the first time he threw his dinner plate at the wall and called her a whore. It was not the last. The next day he was contrite and she fell for it, but the path was clear; he knew what he had to do.

Gina tried to talk to him about his outbursts but he would always fob her off and try to turn the tables on her. It seemed to work for a while. Then one weekend he knew he had gone too far. He had thrown her mobile phone on the floor and stamped on it because he had got sick of one of her friends texting her.

She had tried reasoning with him, explaining that Carl was going through a terrible time after losing his mum to cancer, but he became incensed about the time and attention Gina was giving him.

'Look, if you were more easy-going with my friends I could have them here and you could become part of my group,' she argued. He simply swore at her and slammed out of the house, saying she was pathetic and he was getting tired of her. He realised that she was now afraid of him and he was anxious about that but he knew deep down she was going nowhere.

When he arrived home late one evening to find Gina gone, he realised he had finally gone too far. He had not meant to hit her so hard ... he knew he had hurt her very badly. He understood why she had left but he hadn't expected it to be permanent. As he looked at the letter telling him it was over, he felt a red mist come down over his eyes.

He had spent a few days feeling confident that she would come back. When he received the solicitor's letter he was overwhelmed with a feeling of pure hatred. He lashed out systematically going from room to room, destroying the home they had built together.

There was nothing left for him here, he planned to leave and start over somewhere else. He also knew that should she ever come back here seeing this would destroy her once and for all. He was not sure if he wanted that or not. He felt confused but decided she had brought this upon herself and it was time for him to move on. He knew he could not trust a woman and he had been foolish to have ever thought he could.

CLAIRE

As the days rolled into weeks Claire fell into a comfortable routine of getting up early for a swim, then going on increasingly long hikes. In the past few days, she had also managed to run half the length of the bay and back.

She was the most relaxed she could ever remember and was looking as good as she felt. Her skin glowed, her limbs felt toned and her eyes shone with health and the newly found self-confidence which had come from being in a safe supported space.

Claire was looking forward to a late breakfast with the girls and was making her way back to the villa when she heard a loud scream. Turning on her heel in alarm she saw a tiny boy was sitting on the shoreline holding his foot and weeping loudly. Claire's maternal instinct went into overdrive and she ran to the child and scooped him up to see what was wrong.

There was a tiny cut on his ankle and she looked around her looking for something to stop the flow of blood. Out of nowhere a tall figure approached and held out a small towel and a bottle of water.

'Here, rinse the cut with this and dry the little chap off and we can go into the house where I am sure I can find a plaster. I was watching him play and saw that he had hurt himself.'

Claire looked up and struggled to make out the man's features as the sun was dazzling her. 'You are very kind, thank you.'

'It's not a problem, I can carry your son over the sand, the house is just there.'

Claire didn't have time to point out that the little boy was not her son as she was distracted by the incredible villa the figure was striding towards. It was painted a pale blue and as she approached the huge, paved terrace she glimpsed a massive glass fronted living room overlooking an incredible turquoise infinity pool.

'Set him down on the sofa over here,' the man pointed to a long pale blue chaise.

She took a moment to take in his height, and broad shoulders and handsome tanned face. He broke into a huge white smile as he gently tended to the little child.

His hair was almost snow white but was thick and curled over the collar of his tee-shirt. What struck her the most was his calm aura.

'Don't worry little chap, we can clean you up in no time.'

The boy seemed to respond immediately to this kind stranger and his whimpering stopped. He even managed a shy smile as his rescuer cleaned him up and put a plaster gently on the cut.

'Thank you so much,' said Claire, as she stroked the child's hair and softly asked him for his name. Her rescuer looked puzzled and she felt compelled to explain that she had been an onlooker too.

'This young man is not my son and I am sure he has a mum and dad anxious to know where he is right now. My name is Claire and this young man is ...' she looked at the child and he beamed and answered, 'I am Sonny, my mum is at the beach café over there.'

'Well, I am Glen and it has been a pleasure to meet you guys. Stay as long as you wish and if you like I will go over to the café and fetch your mother young man. She may be getting a little worried about you.'

Claire noted the Southern American drawl and found herself mesmerised by this man and his soothing manner. She suggested that they go to find his mother all together.

Sonny decided that he felt well enough to accompany Glen and Claire and he fell into step with them as if it were the most natural thing to do. Glen smiled at her as he helped her down the wooden steps from the paved deck and the three of them made their way along the shoreline.

'Your home is so beautiful,' she said, her eyes drawn back to the beachside mansion. 'Why, thank you, young lady. I built it for my wife, she always loved the beach here and when a plot came up for sale, I snapped it up as a bit of a surprise for her.'

Claire felt a twist in her stomach at the mention of a wife. Of course, this attractive silver fox was not going to be single.

She was still in a bit of a reverie and thinking how his wife was such a lucky lady, and how he must love her very much, so his next words came out of the blue.

'Sadly, she didn't live long enough to see the house finished. It has always been one of my biggest regrets that she didn't get to enjoy some time here as we had planned.'

Claire felt sad for him but also slightly embarrassed to admit that someone had suddenly given her a precious gift, an opportunity, maybe?

What am I like? she berated herself. Why am I being such a fool? I hardly even know this man.

'Oh, I am so sorry to hear that. It's tragic that you missed out on sharing this amazing place,' she said, only half meaning the words she was saying.

Shaking herself back to reality she smiled broadly as the little boy's mother started running up the beach towards them, shouting his name and opening her arms wide for the child to run into them.

'I was so worried,' she said, 'I could see Sonny on the shore and suddenly he was gone.'

The small boy started crying loudly as he showed his mother his cut foot.

As she soothed him, Claire and Glen smiled at the pair and made their excuses.

'So now what young lady? How about I take you on a tour of the house, that is if you would like that?'

Claire fixed him with her widest happiest smile and announced that she would love to see it.

'Lead the way, I know that I am going to love it.'

Two hours later and with three cups of coffee consumed on the upper terrace, Claire knew she did indeed love this beautiful house. She also had to admit she felt like a giddy teenager on a first date. She wasn't even that keen on coffee but just kept accepting cup after cup as she didn't want the afternoon to end.

The conversation flowed easily and she felt as though she had known this man for a very long time. He had walked her through the deck area to the expansive glass-fronted living room which was a vision of painted walls, cream distressed furniture, pale blue cotton rugs and cashmere throws.

It was incredibly expensive and stylish and the soft sofas screamed comfort.

They wandered through to the huge kitchen dining space which had the most exquisite pale aqua painted units and led to yet another living space.

The tones were white and stone with touches of pale turquoise and Claire could just imagine curling up with a book or simply gazing out onto the blue sea which seemed to meet the terrace.

'How on earth do you ever tear yourself away from here?' she asked him.

'Truth is that I seldom do! I live here for most of the year. I go back to the States very occasionally when my business partner insists, but apart from that I prefer staying here. My late wife loved Antigua so much and, in many ways, I feel closer to her here than in our home back in Boston.

'I swim every morning at six, head into my study which overlooks the bay and work until about 10; then I just kick back and do very little. It's good to be able to do what I want when I want. Though I would be lying if I told you I don't get lonely at times; even living in an amazing place like this can't protect you from that.'

Claire spent the next hour or so telling Glen about her life back in England. It seemed the most natural thing in the world to spill out her sad tale about life with Bloody Richard and recount the affair he had with her best friend.

'The best thing I ever did was to leave him and to head out here to heal.'

Glen was sitting alongside her and suddenly she felt a charge between them as he fixed her with those kind eyes and told her that her husband was a fool.

'Any man who let you go is just plain nuts. You are a beautiful woman, a kind one too and if you had been mine, I would never have let you go.'

His words filled her with something she didn't recognise, not the same sexual buzz she had felt when she first met Richard, but something deeper, warmer. This was something else, something almost comforting and for the first time in a long while she felt safe and content to just be with a man. She stopped her reverie and decided it was ridiculous to be feeling like this given that she had only just met him.

A silence hung in the air between them. Claire felt herself blush; suddenly aware this beautiful man was gazing at her as if she were the most important thing ever.

'Look Claire, I know I may seem like a lonely old guy – you are so much younger and so very beautiful – but I really would be honoured if you would allow me to take you out for dinner. I know we only met a couple of hours ago but I have so enjoyed your company and our talk. I don't want this afternoon to be the first and the last time I see you so can I call for you later or tomorrow maybe? If dinner is a bit too much too soon, would you meet for a coffee or even an ice-cream on the beach sometime?

'One thing I have learned the hard way is that life is too precious to not make the most of something or someone when it feels right. So, if this is not scaring you too much how about a date? You will make an old guy's day.'

Claire beamed and nodded, adding 'I can't think of anything I would rather do than spend some time with you. I have loved talking to you so tonight is a date! Do you want me to come to call for you?'

'Hey, in my country we call on our ladies and treat them like the princesses they are. Call me old fashioned but I can see you need some spoiling. It's been a while since I had a beautiful woman on my arm, so the pleasure is going to be all mine.'

Claire felt herself blossom in the glow of this man's attention.

'We will have a few cocktails at a place I know nearby. It's going to be fun. I will be around to pick you up at seven. I am looking forward to meeting those friends of yours too.'

Claire smiled and had to stop herself from doing a little dance as she made her way out onto the terrace and strode across the white sand, waving at her new friend. She was already trying to decide what she would wear on what was her first date in quite some time.

GINA

GINA PRIDED HERSELF ON being able to get ready for a night out in minutes but in the run up to her date with Dan, she found herself in a bit of tizz not knowing what to wear. Should she go all out glam or opt for the natural look?

She looked back at her room and was astounded to find that she had emptied almost the entire contents of her wardrobe onto the bed and floor. She had intended to go for the casual look but jeans and a basic cotton top did not quite hit the mark. But her sexy tribal maxi dress seemed as though she was trying too hard.

Eventually Anna had come to her rescue by walking in with a jewelled halter neck top, which she insisted was just the thing to wear.

'Team this with your jeans and silver flip flops. It is just the right side of sexy but it doesn't look as if you have tried too hard. You are going to knock him sideways.'

Gina took the peacock blue top and brushed her palms over the silky sheath. It had tiny crystal beads along the seams and they glistened in the sunshine. It set off her lightly tanned skin and she agreed that it would look incredible.

'Are you sure don't mind me wearing this, it looks new?'

Anna brushed her away and insisted she take it.

'Look this top has never been out on a date and I think it's high time it did. I bought it as a confidence booster because how can you not feel fabulous in it? So please, take it as a gift from me. You have been so kind.'

Gina did a giddy little dance and hugged her friend.

'You are so lovely! And thank you so much, it's just what I needed.'

She headed off to shower and got herself ready while Anna walked out onto the sunlit terrace and once again the sight of that beautiful turquoise sea glittering back at her made her feel very sad.

'I just wish you were here to share this, Piers,' she whispered to herself, then shook her head and decided to head out for a swim.

Claire had just arrived back at the villa, and from her wide smile, was in good spirits.

'Hey, I have a date! A lovely guy who lives along the beach has asked me out and actually wants to go out to dinner,' she gushed, her eyes shining.

She grabbed Anna and swung her around and the pair started laughing like schoolgirls.

'My God what is it about this place? Everyone is getting fixed up!' cried Anna, but she was smiling and felt so happy for her friend.

'Enjoy it, you deserve some fun ... and if I can help with hair or make up then give me a shout as I don't seem to be busy tonight! Claire shyly agreed that she wouldn't mind a bit of help on that front and they agreed to meet later to decide on an outfit and fine tune her hair and make-up choices.

An hour later, Gina emerged looking effortlessly beautiful in her jewelled top and jeans and Claire floated in wearing a deep red off the shoulder dress with a gossamer wrap tied around her toned shoulders.

Her beautiful brown eyes shone, and her tan was set off by silver wrist cuffs and exquisite pearl and silver drop earrings.

'Wow, you girls look stunning!' said Anna, who had walked onto the terrace with a tray of cold fizzy wine in crystal flutes.

'I thought we should make a toast. Let's drink to girl power, friendship and amazing times ahead!' Jesse joined in, having just come off the beach in her bikini and she draped herself on one of the outdoor sofas and smiled happily at the group.

'Girls, I can't tell you how happy I am to see us all here tonight just having fun. And the two of you are going out on the town! Who would have thought it!'

As if on cue, the doorbell chimed and Anna ran to open the door to find a very suave Glen standing at the door smiling broadly. He was dressed in a loose-fitting linen suit and beautiful navy loafers. The neutral colour set off his amazing tan, and with his silver hair and white smile he looked distinguished and dishy.

'I have come to collect the lovely Claire,' he announced, brandishing not just one bottle of champagne, but two, along with the biggest bouquet of orchids the girls had ever seen.

Claire blushed and stepped forward to greet him and he surprised her by pulling her to him and planting a very firm kiss on her cheek.

Claire just smiled and didn't make any attempt to pull away as he led her to another sofa on the terrace where they joined Jesse. Nobody could quite believe how Claire's eyes shone as she took in the sight of her sophisticated date.

She felt like pinching herself, could this really be happening to her? Glen looked even more handsome than he had on the beach and he was wearing the most wonderfully subtle cologne, a mix of lemons and sandalwood.

Jesse and Anna were busying themselves getting drinks organised when suddenly Dan appeared on the sand in front of the beach in cut off shorts and a white t-shirt. His tanned feet were bare and his bleached blonde hair and white teeth made him look every inch the surfer dude. He could not have looked more different from the suave silver fox who was now holding Claire's hand. The pair were openly gazing into each other's eyes.

Dan jumped onto the deck with a casual wave to the group.

'Hey girls, sorry I am not exactly dressed for dinner, but I am going to treat this little lady to some home cooking and it's going to involve wading through some surf.'

He nodded respectfully at Glen and the pair exchanged a handshake.

'Hey Dan, it's been a while since I last saw you ... I can see things are finally looking up for you, my friend.'

For a split second a shadow seemed to cross the younger man's face but he quickly regained his composure and punched the older man's shoulder playfully. 'Looks like things are looking up for you too!'

The group spent the next half hour sipping champagne and making small talk until it became clear that Dan was getting twitchy and was keen to leave.

The girls watched with a mix of shock and intrigue as he scooped Gina into his arms and carried her down to the shoreline, where a small motorboat was bobbing on a bright red buoy.

'You said dinner at yours!' said Gina, laughing as he swept her up and waded out to the boat. 'Yes, that is exactly where we are going.' He started the engine and the boat roared off out of the bay as the onlookers at the villa just stared with their jaws dropping.

Claire and Glen headed off for their dinner date shortly afterwards, while the others looked on, beaming at what they had just witnessed.

'Well, I guess it's dinner for two,' said Anna as Jesse poured the remainder of the champagne between them.

'Hey, why don't we just throw some steaks on the outside grill and make up a salad? It's so beautiful out here I may even have a swim before we have dinner.'

The girls spent a relaxed evening together occasionally wondering how the others were faring on their dates.

Anna yawned and decided it was time for bed. 'I am betting that we won't be seeing Gina later ... though I suspect that Glen will get Claire back home at a reasonable hour. I wonder when it will be our turn for some fun?'

Jesse laughed as she too decided to turn in for the night. She went around the house switching off most of the lights, apart from a few discreet lamps in the entrance hall and on the terrace.

Anna allowed herself to take in a last look at the bay and wondered again just what Piers would make of her all-girl jaunt to the Caribbean.

GINA

AFTER RECOVERING FROM THE shock of being scooped up and carried out to a motorboat, Gina found herself sitting alongside Dan as he steered them out of Jolly Beach to a headland adjacent to North Finger.

Amid the trees she saw a wooden bungalow with a wraparound deck facing the mouth of the harbour. Dan carefully tied up to a mooring at what she discovered was his private jetty alongside the house. Gina could see twinkly lights strung out across the bay.

'Welcome to my very humble abode,' he said, as he gently helped her out of the boat and led her inside the sprawling wooden house.

'It doesn't look so humble from where I am standing!'

She felt instantly at home in what was a very masculine, yet uber stylish living space. The huge lounge area was filled with pale oatmeal sofas, lots of white wooden lanterns and colourful Caribbean wall hangings and rugs.

She sank down into one of the sofas and watched as Dan lit a selection of giant candles in glass domes on the large rustic coffee table.

'Well, I was not expecting this!' she said, smiling shyly.

He produced a couple of cold beers and taking her hand pulled her up so she was suddenly face-to-face with the handsome man whose green eyes were now blazing into hers.

Without thinking they just seemed to melt into one another's arms and she felt suddenly giddy with longing. Minutes later they were sprawled on his beautiful wooden bed with its cloud-soft quilt and blue voile panels, which were dancing seductively in the Trade Winds' breeze.

Without her realising he had slipped swiftly out of his jeans. Gina's own jeans were flung on the floor too and her top was now a jewelled panel on the nightstand.

They kissed each other deeply, his tongue searching her mouth, his hands tracing her back, then tantalizingly he brushed her now erect nipples with his fingertips.

She felt powerless to resist the tidal wave of longing and when he stopped briefly to look at her, she simply nodded. 'You have no idea how much I want you right now,' he said and she smiled, knowing that he was making sure that this was what she wanted too. In that moment she had never wanted anyone more in her life!

When he finally entered her, she groaned with pleasure as he moved within her rhythmically. She couldn't hold back any longer and grabbed at him, biting his lips and clawing at his buttocks in a bid to have him enter her even more deeply.

Her orgasm when it came was one of the most extreme she had ever experienced and Dan held her gaze as she climaxed in a way she didn't think possible. 'Wow!' was all she could say when he decided that she was totally satisfied.

'I wasn't intending to do this yet,' he admitted to her when they had both got their breathing and heart rates under control.

'Well, I hadn't planned a one-night stand either,' said Gina.

'My beautiful little lady, this is not a one-night stand ... and I think I can do a bit better this time if you don't mind a playback.'

At the end of the evening Gina had never felt so sated with lust. He had proved to be an affectionate and considerate lover and she struggled to move out of the bedroom.

'We have to eat,' Dan had insisted. 'I spent hours sorting out this food and you are not leaving here until you have eaten it all!'

The wooden kitchen island was piled with a delicious spread.

There were king prawns marinated in lime juice and sticky coconut rice, served alongside a platter of salad and chunks of fresh pineapple and mango.

He had roasted sweet potatoes and plantain and there were jugs of fruity rum punch to wash it all down.

As the night wore on Gina realised there would be no boat trip back to the villa. She was happy when Dan gave her one of his soft cotton t-shirts and invited her to join him and sleep.

They opened the sliding doors and lay side by side watching the stars. Gina did not know exactly where this was leading but she knew something significant had changed between them. She knew she had jumped in soon after leaving her marriage, but she didn't care. She was taking this for what it was, casual and fun. She hadn't had fun in a very long time. They had made love; this was more than just sex and they both knew it. She felt his body wrapped gently around hers and she listened as his breath deepened and sleep finally claimed him.

She smiled to herself in the darkness and wondered how this had all happened so fast. There was so much she didn't yet know about this beautiful man but she knew that this was something very important. She was in no hurry to run away and she had the distinct feeling that he wouldn't let her go anyway.

Just as he fell into a deep sleep, he hugged her even closer to him. He said goodnight and though she could have been mistaken, she was convinced he had also murmured that he was falling in love with her ... wishful thinking? Perhaps, but he was definitely the sort of man who just might convince her to give this whole love thing another go. Love aside, she had never felt so desirable and for her, that was a real first. She refused to think about her ex, but it was hard to not compare this amazing, caring soul with the man who had made her his victim. She allowed herself just a few moments to remember the old Gina in her sensible grey dresses and buttoned up cardigans. She couldn't believe how far she had come. As she glanced over at her lover with his tousled locks and ripped abs, she couldn't help but feel a bit smug – and extremely turned on!

In the morning as the sun appeared through the voile blinds Gina awoke to find Dan already up and outside on the deck.

She was momentarily disappointed as she had planned to seduce him all over again! Who was she suddenly?! But she loved hearing him pottering around in the room next door. She had glimpses of his beautiful physique as he ran bare chested to the pontoon where he was piling towels and provisions onto the deck of the boat.

She stretched out in the comfy wooden bed with its gauzy cotton panels which just fluttered in the early morning breeze. A smile spread across her face as Dan walked into the room and joined her on the bed. He had showered and smelt delicious, a mix of fresh cotton and the ocean. She ran her fingers through his sun-kissed locks and smiled happily up at him.

Brushing her lips with a kiss he pulled her off the bed and pushed her toward his shower room, with a gentle order to get ready as they had a breakfast date somewhere rather special.

'Don't worry, I plan to get you back in my lair later young lady, but we really do have to get going.'

His words made her tingle all over as she realised that he was as keen as she was to repeat the delicious love making of last night. She was in no doubt that it had not been purely sex, even though she was more turned on by this man than she had been by anyone in her whole life. There was a deep connection of that she was certain. If he was a player and had been pretending then he had certainly fooled her! Quietly though she recalled all the things Anna had warned her about, but she still felt that she could trust him.

He threw her some jeans and a cotton sweater, along with some rope soled flip flops which had seen much better days.

'The jeans and top may be a bit big but I can see you would look good in anything ... I know these are not cutting-edge fashion young lady but they will be perfect for where we are about to go. You'll see.'

He headed into the kitchen, promising eggs and coffee would be served before she knew it. He asked her to be quick, he wanted to be on the boat and gone within the hour.

Fifteen minutes later he whistled as she emerged onto the deck with the jeans pulled in tight using a makeshift belt to show off her trim waist. She had also tied a knot in his cotton t-shirt so that it looked like a trendy cropped top. Gina had piled her hair up into a loose ponytail and with just a slick of lip gloss she looked like a fresh-faced teenager.

'At least the flip flops fit,' she said, raising her eyebrows at him. 'Left by another overnight guest?'

'Actually yes, they were, but it was my sister ... I never bring women here so this is a real first for me.'

Gina glowed at his words and felt her tummy do a silly flip as he put his hands on her waist, helping her to clamber onto the boat.

Dan deftly took the boat off its mooring and the engine revved into life taking them out of the main pool of the bay and into the ocean.

'Relax, this won't be a long voyage but I can guarantee you are going to have fun.'

Gina sat back and put her face up to the sun, breathing in the sea air and enjoying the feeling of tiny splashes of foamy surf on her skin. She didn't know how long this would last or even what it meant but for now the torment of her former life felt a million miles away.

She told herself that for once in her life she should live in the moment and just enjoy herself. There was no script for this, and she had no idea what was going to happen next, but she didn't care. Today she was just a girl out on a boat with the prospect of a wonderful day ahead accompanied by a good-looking man, who it seems was smitten with her too.

As if on cue he pulled her to him and gently placed her hands on the wheel. He wrapped his arms around her waist and she lost herself in the thrill of this new and exciting experience.

'I feel truly happy for the first time in so long,' she told herself and without warning she just began to laugh out loud.

'I am loving this!' she shouted. Her outburst was rewarded with a gentle kiss on her neck which sent a shiver down her spine.

'Please,' she asked the universe, 'please can this last a tiny bit longer?'

As they rounded the point and headed into Ffryes Beach, Dan took the wheel and told her to take the boat hook as he wanted to see if she could grab the buoy.

Gamely she kicked off her shoes and clambered onto the deck. She squinted into the sun looking for the buoy and the tell-tale piece of chain that she had to somehow hook and pull aboard.

'Hey, Gina, how are you at rounders?' he shouted while rewarding her successful attempt at hooking the buoy with a dazzling smile.

'Why do you ask?' she shouted back, the sound of the surf hitting the shore drowning out her reply.

'You'll see very soon.'

Back at the villa the other girls were on the terrace after an early morning swim. They were placing bets on when Gina may or may not make an appearance.

'She's in safe hands I don't think we need to worry about her too much,' offered Claire. She reminded them how Glen had known Dan when they met the night before. While he had not revealed too much about the young man's history, over dinner he had hinted that Dan had been through some tough times lately. But he assured Claire the man was good-hearted and could be trusted. 'He isn't what I think you women class as a "player"; he is kind and has a lot of soul. But I think you have to let your friend find that out for herself.'

Claire had arrived home late, sparkly-eyed and glowing after having one of the nicest nights she could recall.

She had never felt so relaxed and at ease and, as the evening wore on, she found herself becoming more attracted to this attentive older man who just seemed to want to make her happy.

'All this attention is very new to me,' she admitted.

Glen gently picked up her hand and kissed it.

'Well, it's time you were treated like the princess you are. I suggest while you are with me, you get used to being spoilt.'

Claire beamed and not for the first time she thanked her lucky stars that she had come on this trip. She knew that the woman going home was not the one who had left a few weeks earlier.

Jesse had found the past few days tough as she realised that while it was easy to put her heartache on hold while they were in this idyllic bubble, she would at some point have to go home and take up her life again.

She confided this to Anna who said that she felt the same way.

'We are here for a while yet. You have this place for 8 weeks if you want it and the way things are, I think I will be in it for the long haul with you. I am in no rush to hurtle back to the mess that is my life right now. I can't bear to even think about trying to get my job situation sorted when the Piers thing is still so raw. OK, Jane has left the office but it doesn't change the fact we have a flat to sort out and the idea of seeing Piers with his pregnant girlfriend kills me ...'.

Jesse put her arm around her friend and smiled.

'You and I seem to be in a bit of a pickle. You are so right, why rush back?' She raised her glass and suggested they toast to keeping their heads down, at least for as long as they were in paradise.

PIERS

As HE PARKED HIS car near the village green in the tiny hamlet of Great Whittingham, Piers took in the sight of the incredible property he had come to view.

He felt as though he had driven into another universe as the city streets disappeared. They were replaced by endless fields filled with sheep and cows and fragrant hedgerows, heavy with early autumn blackberries. As he left the main roads he drove through a succession of villages, each one prettier than the one before. The pale yellow stone houses were draped in wisteria and rambling rose bushes. He was hoping that the house the estate agent had picked out for him would be as beautiful.

He need not have worried because *The Folly* was a rambling stone house with a quirky front door surrounded by pale cream roses. A magnificent wisteria tree filled the whole of the gable of the house and crept over onto the porch.

He couldn't wait to get inside and clutching a large metal key he walked towards the huge grey painted door which was flanked either side by impressive bay trees. Above the door a stone plinth revealed the date 1822.

When he stepped through the front door and saw the flagstoned hall Piers knew this was the house for him. The hallway let into a huge, vaulted kitchen diner where the flagstones complimented an uber modern kitchen. A vast island took centre stage and alongside the far wall a massive inglenook fireplace housed a cream-coloured wood burner where a log fire was ablaze. Somehow the fit of old and new just worked.

A knock at the door startled him and the young estate agent breezed in apologising for being late.

'I had meant to meet you outside to let you in but I can see you made yourself at home,' he said, laughing.

Piers said that he certainly felt like he had come home. Once he had toured the rest of the house with its vast, light filled bedrooms and sumptuous bathrooms with quirky beamed ceilings, Piers knew he had to have it.

The garden was also a dream and he could envisage hosting some wonderful alfresco parties outside on the sprawling stone terrace.

'The owner is a landscape gardener and his Canadian wife is an architect with a flair for combining old and new,' said the agent, who realised his job was done.

Piers was smiling broadly as he confirmed they had a deal. He knew that if he could ever get Anna to see this house she would be smitten too. It was the sort of place she would love. It was the sort of house they had often talked about buying if ever they got tired of the pace of London life.

They would spend hours looking at properties online and she subscribed to *Country Life*. She dreamed of having a kitchen with a fireplace and squashy sofas. *The Folly* was everything and more. This was a house for a family and if Piers had anything to do with it, he intended to raise one here. He just had to win his lady back but, for now, he was keen to get the wheels in motion and make *The Folly* his own. Who would have thought it?

As he finished viewing the first-floor bedrooms, he found a tiny anteroom alongside the master suite. When he pushed open the door, he realised it was a nursery. His heart twisted at the thought that not so long ago, he had thought he was going to be a father. But there was an outside chance, at least he hoped, that he would have a child with the woman he loved. This was just the sort of nursery Anna would choose. The walls were painted in a soft shade of blue and the room was furnished with a mix of antique wooden furniture with white wooden blinds at the window. On the wall was an amazing mural depicting a fairy castle with a tall white tower. A princess with long, red hair was waving happily down to a handsome prince sitting astride a white stallion.

There were soft fairy lights threaded around a tall white wicker lamp next to the crib and he noticed on the wall the artist had written '*Anna's Room*'. He wondered if it was a sign.

Later that evening Piers was sitting in the local pub sipping a beer when the phone rang and the agent confirmed that his offer on *The Folly* had been accepted. 'We can probably wrap this up in six weeks,' said the agent.

He explained that the owners were relocating back to Toronto and needed to sort everything out quickly. 'They also asked if you wanted any of the furniture'.

Piers did not miss a beat and agreed that he was happy to move as quickly as they needed him to. He added there were quite a few pieces of furniture he was interested in.

He had loved the feeling of this home and most importantly he knew that it was decorated and furnished in the same style that Anna loved. Lots of soft sofas, beautiful dressers, white walls with accent colours in shades of powder blue and grey. These were complemented by areas of exposed stonework. She would love the flagged floors in the hall and the kitchen too. He realised the kitchen was very similar to a magazine image she had ripped out of *House Beautiful*.

'Now this is what I call a dream kitchen,' she had said. And while he tried not to be too optimistic, he hoped to get the chance to show her his new home. Imagining that it would become hers too was perhaps a step too far but why not?

The owners were keen to sell their beautiful oak four-poster, the oversized sofas in the family room and the three dressers that were dotted around the kitchen and the dining room. They had also decided that their oversized refectory dining table which weighed a ton would cost them a small fortune to ship over to Canada. So, all the key pieces Piers had earmarked were up for grabs!

As he ordered himself another pint of real ale in celebration of his good fortune, he mused that in a single day he had bought a stunning house which came almost fully furnished. For the first time in a long time, he could see a way out of his gloom.

He was finding it hard not to think of how so many of the beautiful things in Anna's flat would sit very well in the house. Her collection of wooden lanterns and candlesticks would look great in the spacious timber clad extension.

Piers knew that Anna had always dreamed of having a whole wall of glass doors that rolled back to open out onto a garden, and *The Folly*'s kitchen diner did just that.

He flicked through the details once again and admired the images of the beautiful wooden staircase that led up to an open plan mezzanine study.

It had its own wood burner and he could visualise himself on cold days writing his book, the fire ablaze and the woman he loved curled up on the pale turquoise chaise sofa in front of it. After all the heartache he had put them through could he hope to make this happen?

As he imagined roaming through the light-filled house he felt his spirits lift. Was it possible that life could begin again? He was not a fool; he knew it was a long shot that Anna would forgive him. But if they were to have a fresh start, he could not think of anywhere else he would rather do that.

But he was running way ahead of himself. As far as he knew, Anna still thought he was shacked up with Jane with a baby on the way. He had looked at his emails and there was nothing to indicate she had received his message. He had also tried to call her several times but his calls went straight to her voicemail. Piers didn't think it was appropriate to leave her a garbled phone apology so he left a pathetic 'it's me, please call me' style message and hung up.

No, he had to be pragmatic. He was buying this house to make a fresh start for himself. From the moment he had walked through that massive front door he felt like he had literally come home. The house had wrapped around him like a warm blanket.

There was a small orchard to the west side of the property with apple and pear trees that were dripping with fruit. There were also raised beds made of old railway sleepers filled with herbs and vegetables. He discovered an orangery accessed through a glazed walkway attached to the kitchen which had grapevines and lemon and lime trees growing in massive pots. The owners had paved the floors and built a wooden tiki bar. It was clear they enjoyed entertaining and the house had a wonderfully warm feeling about it.

People have been happy here he told himself and he wondered how on earth the family who had created this beautiful home could bear to leave it.

He had also spied a goalpost at one end of the lawned garden. He hoped that would be staying. You never knew, if he ever had a son, that could come in handy one day too. Smiling, he ordered yet another pint to go with his steak pie. He was staying at the pub overnight and he was in the mood to celebrate.

RICHARD

RICHARD HAD ENJOYED HIS journey to Antigua. He had travelled business class. He never missed a chance to talk to women who might have money and what better opportunity than on a long-haul flight to the Caribbean.

The gods as usual had shone down on him and, within a few minutes of taking his seat, a well-groomed American woman slipped into the seat alongside him.

He smiled warmly, offered to put her tote bag in the overhead locker and gamely offered her his window seat. But she brushed the offer aside and revealed that she did this trip all the time.

'I am Laura by the way. I suggest we get acquainted as it is going to be a long day. It's great if you find a fun travelling companion. So, I hope you are fun.'

He struggled to decide how old she was. She had a svelte figure, her designer clothes screamed style and wealth, and he thought he recognised a waft of Tom Ford Santal Blush when she brushed past him.

He checked out her watch – top end Rolex. Her fingers dazzled with diamonds, though he noted the third finger on her left hand did not sport a wedding ring. It was time to bring on his A game.

'I am Richard and if the champagne was not complimentary anyway then I would be ordering us some,' he said smoothly, fixing her with his widest smile.

He took her hand and squeezed it gently.

'So nice to meet you Richard,' she breathed and lowered her long, false lashes. She then looked up at him seductively, leaving him in no doubt that the lady liked the idea of sharing this flight with him.

They spent the first two hours talking about their lives – she was an art director at a swanky creative agency in New York. She regaled him with stories of ritzy launches at the

Guggenheim and Macey's and celebrity filled lunches at the Plaza. She boasted of a loft style apartment on 6th Avenue. It was clear she was well connected and seemed to know everyone who was anyone in the city. She didn't have a problem with name dropping a few movie stars who, she added, often graced her dinner table.

'I love having brunch with Catherine (Zeta-Jones) and Steph ... Lady Gaga to you. We girls have such a blast. Often Micky pops by too for a coffee and catch up. He sometimes brings Al along as he is often in town and likes to catch up with all the gossip. And one thing I know about is all the gossip.'

Micky, if he was to believe her, was Michael Douglas; and Al was none other than Al Pacino (one of his movie heroes), Richard felt his interest piqued. To think he had come on this flight in a bid to win back little 'Miss Mousey' Claire.

He realised that he had to step up to the mark a bit but thankfully he was a master at reinventing himself. He could spin the facts to fit any situation. In fact, he was adept at telling lies; it was how he had managed to come as far as he had. Of late though he seemed to be losing his touch, so maybe if he could woo the lovely Laura, he would find himself a new niche and taste a bit of the high life into the bargain.

So, carefully, he began to reinvent himself as an investor in works of art. He knew this had impressed her no end. He kept it low key, not acting over the top but imparting just enough knowledge to show he knew a thing or two.

In his last job selling insurance, one of his clients had had a modest art collection and he had been forced to do a little research to offer a quote for insuring their house. He hoped he could distract Laura with his charms enough that she didn't dig too deep into what he did know about art.

He knew a little about the impressionists and spoke about his favourite artist of all time, Renoir. It was the only artist he knew anything about, and that was only because when he and

Claire had gone on a mini break to Guernsey, in the Channel Islands, he had bought her a guidebook as a present. He had flicked through it and learned how Renoir had painted lots of scenes on the island's south coast. Richard was so glad that he had forked out £5.99 as it was now paying dividends. He also waxed lyrical about the 'Bathing Belles' a group of nude swimmers by Renoir. He cheekily suggested that Laura would make a fantastic life model.

She blushed and snuggled up a bit closer just as he hoped she would. Give a woman of a certain age a bit of flattery and she is putty in your hands, he decided.

As they enjoyed a second bottle of French champagne Richard piled on the charm even more. He tried to think of a way to make sure that when they landed the lovely Laura would want the fun to continue.

Richard had booked a very modest room in a basic hotel in central St John. He had only booked it for a few days because he intended scouring the island for Claire. He planned on wooing her back and then moving into her villa. From the information he had seen in the ad, it was quite a place.

Suddenly his game plan had changed. When he asked Laura where she was staying, he was stunned and delighted to hear that although she and her ex-husband owned a boutique hotel on the tip of Nelson's Dockyard, she had opted to stay in their modest four-bedroom villa.

She has told him it was on a hill overlooking Ffryes Beach in a relatively new development with the most amazing contemporary finishes and the kind of sea view that you only read about in high class lifestyle magazines.

Laura had been given the villa as part of her recent divorce settlement. She said she had only been there once for a few days and was looking forward to spending a couple of weeks or more there. She explained she needed to buy some swish furniture and she was also keen to host a few parties for her friends who lived there.

'My best friend has the most divine restaurant on Turners Beach, they call it "Jackie O" because it was one of Jackie Kennedy's favourite haunts on the island.'

He sipped champagne and simply nodded, not wanting to come over as impressed and unsophisticated. My God, he knew nothing about Antigua or the Kennedys but he realised he had to get up to speed if he was going to close this deal. And close it he must, for the prospect of a future camping on sofas and relying on Phil to bail him out was wearing thin.

He decided that Laura could be a game changer who would finally allow him to live the life he felt he deserved. He pretended that he knew the terrain of the island and made a few noises about the amazing views. As soon as he could though he studied the Antigua guidebook in the seat pocket and started memorizing pages and pages about the beaches and local hot spots. He also memorized some historical facts and figures and was keen to read about the famous people who had houses there.

He was delighted to see that Eric Clapton had a holiday home on the island, a remote mansion perched on a cliffside. He intended to trot that little nugget out when the in-flight meal arrived. He would not be surprised if Laura didn't have him on speed dial.

As the hours ticked by, they flirted and made idle chit-chat about where they had travelled and what they planned to do in Antigua. Richard found himself inventing a whole new persona.

Laura was interested to know why he had elected to come to Antigua alone and he said he had just negotiated a huge deal with a gallery in Amsterdam and had rewarded himself with a holiday.

He smiled as he wondered how his new lady friend would react if she knew that the meagre belongings he possessed following his exit from Claire's house were stored in a damp lockup in Shoreditch. Phil had a mate who made a bit of extra cash renting out the space.

He had had to loan the storage fee from Phil and had also borrowed the money for this flight and holiday. Richard had promised him that he would pay him back once Claire's cash went into his bank account.

Richard had in fact already received the money but as he had intended to win her back, he hadn't touched it yet. He planned to play the 'I need and want you more than any money so please forgive me, let me make it up to you, and get back together' card.

Now he wished he had cashed in a bit of his pay out so he could at least splash out and maybe spoil his new love interest – at least to begin with. He had his credit card with him and judging by the speed at which Laura was sinking the Laurent Perrier he thought he might need it. But he looked upon this as an investment in his future.

He might well be living on his mates' handouts and was worried about blowing any of his pay out from Claire; but as far as Laura was concerned, he was a successful and solvent go-getter. She seemed to accept that intellectually and financially he was her equal.

He reasoned that he would not give her any information that would allow her to track him down back in England if their holiday fling came to nothing.

So, he painted a picture of a corporate go-getter with a loft style apartment near The Barbican and a season ticket to Lord's Cricket Ground and the Covent Garden Opera House. He said he was a patron of the arts and claimed that he was a philanthropist by nature and enjoyed supporting the young.

Laura's eyes never left his face. At one point she put her hand on his arm saying she had never met a man quite like him.

Six hours into the flight, after they had watched a movie and enjoyed a sumptuous dinner and yet another bottle of wine; this time a spicy Malbec, she gave him the much-anticipated invitation for him to join her at her villa.

'There is so much we haven't yet discussed and it would be great to have such charming company.'

She smiled at him and gave him a smouldering look that left him in no doubt that she was expecting more than sun cream rubbed on her back!

He pretended to struggle with the decision, claiming that he hated to let his friends down (he had lied that some of his arty crowd had insisted he make up their annual summer party). But after a lot of fake soul searching, he said he would love to join her. Laura promised that she would have his friends around for a party to make up for them losing out on his company,

'They are planning a ski trip to Chamonix soon, so I will catch up with them then. It was a very casual arrangement and I don't think they will worry too much. They know I am a bit of a maverick and given to spontaneity, so it won't come as a shock that I have taken up another offer and a much more attractive one.' The lies just flowed and he was enjoying watching her lap them up.

Laura seemed over the moon with the idea of having him to stay for a couple of weeks. She even hinted that if he was up for it, he could extend his stay a little.

By this time, he was massaging her wrist and stroking her forearm and he could tell it was having quite an effect on her.

OK, Laura must be in her 50's but she was a good-looking woman and she certainly knew how to look after herself. In many ways she had reminded him of the woman who had thrown him out before he had met Claire. She was a lawyer in her early 50's and he had loved her energy – and her salary. He found older, worldly women attractive, especially wealthy women!

They were financially independent, dressed well, liked to eat out at good restaurants and always enjoyed lovely holidays in far flung places. He also liked the fact that they kept him on his toes and he had to raise his game.

They didn't put up with him watching mindless TV or eating meals on his lap glued to a game of football. He couldn't get away with treating them to a night at the local pub and a quick bite at Pizza Express. Poor Claire, he realised she really had settled for so much less than most women demanded.

He felt she was to blame for that and he despised her for being such a doormat. In fact, he put their breakup down to her. She had got complacent and had pushed him towards lithe, sexy Martha.

For a few moments he allowed himself to think of that last fling in Edinburgh with Martha and the sort of wanton and downright dirty sex that had him screaming out for more. As he felt his erection grow, he noticed that Laura had become aware of it too and she smiled seductively. He realised she thought she had caused this sudden and obvious reaction and he pulled her to him and kissed her softly.

He became a bit bolder and tried to put her hand onto his crotch but she sat back and said quietly, 'Let's not do that here. I have plans for you later.'

He smiled, acquiesced, and took his hands away. He picked up his glass of red wine, closed his eyes and remembered the downright blatant look Martha had given him as she knelt in front of him, taking the whole of his erect penis in her mouth.

It was all he could do not to release a groan of pleasure, but instead he stood up and took his Antigua guide with him to the bathroom.

He used it to hide his erection from the rest of the passengers in Business Class. In the bathroom once he had sorted out his uncomfortable predicament he brushed up on a few more facts about Antigua, to impress Laura with later.

He hoped Laura was good in bed. Martha had been a mistake, but she looked good and was as sexy as hell and a real wild cat in the bedroom.

He could not face sleeping with Claire once he had experienced a night with Martha. He had crossed a line.

Suddenly he could see a way ahead and the lovely lady back in Business Class could present him with an opportunity to gain some ground.

By the time he returned to his seat, there was hardly any time to talk before the seat belt sign was illuminated and they were told to prepare for landing.

Once disembarked they queued at passport control then claimed their luggage. He wished he had not just brought a canvas holdall that had seen better days when he saw Laura's matching set of Louis Vuitton bags.

He trotted after her as she headed off to find the chauffeur driven limousine, she had arranged to take them to her house. He tried not to get irritated when she hurried him along when he stopped to admire some designer sunglasses in one of the glass showcases.

'Richard do hurry up!' she had snapped. Then realising she had been a bit sharp she rubbed his back in an almost motherly way that made him feel slightly uncomfortable.

The old Richard would have told her that he did not like to be treated like a child, but he knew he had to bite his tongue and let things go. He had hoped she might have offered to buy him the glasses as a little 'Welcome to Antigua' gift. He hurried to catch her up and with a smug smile, decided that once again it appeared that he had fallen on his feet. Once he had turned on the charm, she would be all over him and those slightly sharp edges would be rubbed smooth.

As they arrived at the house, he decided he would have forgiven her anything just to stay in such a beautiful home. It was a two-storey villa on a new complex high above the beach. The slightly tinted glass walls which opened onto the view prevented people from seeing inside. He spied a horizon pool and a mini waterfall which flowed onto a magnificent lower outdoor terrace.

The terrace overlooked the most beautiful powdery white beach he had ever seen.

Laura took him on a tour and he marvelled at the sumptuous lounge with a bar and a massive contemporary kitchen. The furnishings were chic and expensive and as he walked into the dining area he gasped at the expansive outdoor living space that took in the views of the whole bay. On the lower floor the master suite and guest suites all had their own adjoining lounges and alfresco terraces with hot tubs.

'It's like something out of a movie,' said Richard as he struggled to take in the size of the place and the great luck that had led him here.

Laura simply thanked him and said that it was modest compared to the home she had shared with her husband above Nelson's Dockyard; but she felt it was big enough for her needs as she rarely spent much time here.

Richard had already decided that if he had anything to do with it, they would be spending a lot more time here. It was stunning, luxurious and he had never felt more at home.

'I do like to entertain when I am here. We usually have about twenty of us here at Christmas so I had to think big,' she said laughing.

Richard decided that he was going to be one of that number at Christmas. He could not imagine living in a more beautiful villa and while he could see that Laura was going to be a bit of a challenge, he felt it was worth holding out to see if he could get her in his thrall.

He was sick of working at second rate jobs and putting up with mumsy types like Claire and bunny boilers like Martha. If he played his cards right, and he had a fair idea of how he could do that, he reckoned he could find a way to ease himself into this nice little number.

Laura had gone to unpack a few things in the master suite and he swung around as she reappeared in a tiny sheath of black chiffon with spaghetti straps and sheer panels that left nothing to the imagination.

'Darling, why don't you fix us a drink and join me in the bedroom? I take it you don't have a problem with sharing, do you?'

He took a deep breath and fell in step behind her as she sashayed into the master suite. The bed was enormous and was positioned so that all you could see was sky and sea.

Stripping off his shirt Richard prayed that the long flight, jet lag and all that champagne was not going to let him down. He had a feeling Laura was going to be demanding. And this was not a time to fail to rise to the occasion!

SAM

SAM'S ATTEMPT TO TRACK down Jesse had hit a bit of a wall. Things had turned a corner though, and he had made some changes following his epiphany after the pep talk from Jen. He was no longer staying in bed for hours on end at weekends. He had made his peace with his boss and was performing better and acting more upbeat. He was also working out in the gym regularly and had caught up with the friends he had lost when he was with Zoe.

But he had failed to make any progress to contact Jesse. He was still desperate to know what her feelings would be if he suddenly rocked up out of the blue.

He knew that Jesse had flown off to the Caribbean. After going back to talk to her friend and beg for more information, he knew that Jesse had not seen his texts. They had gone to her business mobile and Milly was monitoring those. He had never been given her personal number and Milly was not going to reveal it to him. 'The thing is, Sam, Jesse is a friend and a promise is a promise' she said.

It was not a surprise that Milly seemed to be in the know about the recent break up – and why he was now so desperate to get hold of Jesse.

Milly was sympathetic though and he believed her when she said that if she could have given him the number she would.

Milly had revealed that she was only able to give Jesse back up for eight weeks as she had a trip planned to visit her brother in New Zealand. But eight weeks was a lifetime away. He wanted to talk to her right now, to beg her to forgive him and give her another chance. But he had hoped to see her face to face, look into those beautiful eyes so she could see how much she meant to him.

Above all he kept berating himself for being such an idiot and such a coward. He really didn't deserve her. He left the shop feeling downbeat with those empty weeks stretching out miserably in front of him.

At weekends he would mope around his flat constantly checking his phone and email account in case, by some miracle, Jesse had been in touch. But he knew she wouldn't be in contact. As far as she knew he was only just back from his honeymoon in Mauritius.

The thought depressed him and he resigned himself to just getting through the next few weeks. He would then camp on her shop doorstep until she agreed to talk to him. He also knew that he would marry her in a heartbeat. And it would not be at some fancy mansion in front of 400 strangers. He was getting ahead of himself, getting her to talk to him would be tough enough. But still, he would daydream about an outdoor ceremony on a Cornish headland overlooking the sea with just a handful of friends looking on. She would look beautiful and of course she would have flowers in her hair. Stop! What was he thinking?

Once again it was his sassy sister who put him straight.

They were walking on Wimbledon Common on a blustery early autumn morning and once again Sam was feeling sorry for himself and was driving Jen mad with his negativity. They abandoned their walk as Sam decided he just wasn't feeling it that day. He had hoped they would pop in for a swift pint in the Fox and Grapes. But Jen had other ideas and almost frog marched him into a cosy little coffee shop tucked into a corner of a bakery on the High Street. It was a popular haunt with the locals and it was Jen's favourite place to linger over a coffee when she wandered through the village.

'We need to talk Sam. You are not being very smart about this, are you? I mean, I know men can be a bit clueless about this sort of stuff but don't you think you are missing something here?'

He didn't have the first idea what Jen was talking about. He followed her into the café and didn't have to wait too long before she said her piece. It was the thing he loved about his sister. He was the emotional one who missed the big picture; she was Miss Practical who always knew what to do. She never held back and would always get straight to the point. Right now, he needed all the help he could get.

As they sipped their cappuccinos, Jen said she hated to be hard on him but she couldn't stand another minute listening to him bleating on about how bad and sad he felt.

'Are you really as dumb as you are acting? So, her friend can't give you Jesse's number but it's obvious she touches base with her. She told you that herself. Go back to her shop, dazzle her with that beautiful smile, fix her with those puppy dog eyes and beg her to pass on YOUR number! You don't have to mention the whole Zoe drama. Just say that you need to talk to Jesse urgently. She can see you are head over heels in love with the woman and if she is the friend I think she is she will bend the rules. You said yourself more than once you think she may have already seen those texts you sent to Jesse's mobile. I think she might be convinced to send her an email or a text, however they keep in touch, to let her know that you have been looking for her.'

Sam grabbed his sister and hugged her.

'I hadn't even thought about that. You are a genius!'

Jen rolled her eyes at him and punched him affectionately on the shoulder.

'Little brother, it isn't that I am a genius, it's not exactly rocket science. You just never think of the obvious. Since the day you met the mysterious Jesse – whom I may add – I can't wait to meet should you ever get your act together, that head of yours has been in the clouds. You just need to come back down to earth with the rest of us mere mortals.'

He smiled sheepishly and not for the first time his sister wondered how he could have such beautiful long black lashes. What a waste on a boy!

'Jesse was insistent that she wanted no contact with anyone so I just thought that I should honour that.'

'Sam, the last thing Jesse wanted you to do was to leave her alone. My God you are a plonker! Just go back to that Milly woman and be your charming self and make sure you don't leave until she agrees to tell Jesse you need to talk. Now go!'

Sam drove at breakneck speed to Milly's tiny little flower shop.

He waited until the shop was empty before he summoned the courage to approach Milly, who initially looked a little startled.

'I know you must think I am being a pest, and you can't give me Jesse's number, but will you at least consider sending her a message? Please tell her that I have been asking for her number because I so need to speak to her! Jesse has my number, she may have deleted it for all I know, but I am desperate to talk to her! So please will you forward it to her and put it in your phone just in case you need to send me a message. It really means a lot to me Milly. I suspect you know that I am the reason she left so suddenly.'

Milly sighed and nodded her head.

'Sam, I don't know you but I do have a vague idea of what went down. Jesse was in such a bad way. She is a great girl and I saw her really struggling. She needed some space. I will think about it, but no promises. Although she does pick up messages and we do exchange the odd email about clients, I can't guarantee that, even if I do as you ask, she will call you, OK?'

Sam smiled broadly and wanted to hug her. He felt so relieved that at last he might finally be getting somewhere.

'I completely screwed up, but Milly you have to know that I love this girl and if I don't talk to her and explain how I feel I will never be able to forgive myself. She may have moved on, she may not even want to speak to me or see me, but I promise you all I am asking for is a chance to find out.'

Milly decided that she could afford to give him a little hope because it was clear that this guy was genuine. She had not been completely truthful with him. Jesse was not as far off the radar as she had made out.

'All I can say Sam, is that from what I can tell your girl has not moved on, well at least not yet. So, what do you want me to say exactly?'

'Well Milly, that is something I thought you could help me with?'

CLAIRE

Claire caught a glimpse of her reflection in the hall mirror and did a double take. Was this really her? All those hours spent swimming and those long hikes along the shoreline and up onto the 'Sleeping Indian' had paid dividends. She had never felt so alive and so fit. Her toned legs, firm thighs and smooth tummy were rewards for her newly found healthy lifestyle. Each day she felt better about herself.

Her clothes now skimmed smoothly over her body and gone were the days when her skirt and jeans cut into her waistline leaving her itchy and miserable. When she was getting ready for this trip, she had realised she didn't even possess a swimsuit. She had been forced to buy a 'hold-it-all-in' granny style one piece, but this no longer fitted her. Her waistline had shrunk, the cups of the bras she had brought with her were gaping and the loose fitting harem pants were way too big for her now.

Anna had gone shopping with her to an outlet outside of the resort and when Claire had started looking at hideous floral swimwear, Anna had steered her away to another rail that catered for the younger set. She picked out a sexy black one piece with a gold buckled belt, and an animal print number with a low back and a keyhole cut out front. Claire had looked momentarily shocked and had started to protest that the swimwear was far too showy. She was secretly mortified. But Anna was having none of it and she pushed Claire into the changing room where, to her surprise, she had easily managed to slip into a size 14! Unheard of! She looked over her shoulder and just stared at the curvaceous yet toned figure looking back at her. How had that happened?

She had to admit the swimsuits Anna picked out looked amazing and they did show off her figure. She would never be skinny, but then she didn't want to be. She was happy with her new-found shape and her newly discovered love of moving her body every day. She didn't need to get on the scales to learn that she had dropped at least a stone, she felt fitter and healthier and that was the greatest gift of all.

Walking arm in arm across Jolly Beach with Anna, Claire admitted that she had never felt so happy and so at peace with herself.

'I still have moments when I feel guilty about leaving Harriet, but my Mum says she is loving her time with them at the caravan and she is going on holiday with the cousins next week. I don't know if this is true, but Mum says she is not missing me at all.'

Anna squeezed her arm, genuinely happy for her friend.

'After all you have been through you deserve some "you" time and I envy you that feeling of being at peace with yourself. I am loving my time out here, but sometimes all I can think about is how much Piers would love it too. He would not recognise this laid back, chilled Anna. I think it's who he always wanted me to be. I couldn't be that woman when I was working at the pace I did. I was so driven and there were always people and things that demanded my attention more than he did. This trip has shown me how I wasn't really there for him. I was never present in the moment. I always expected him to support me and go along with my life, but I never thought about what he wanted. I brushed him aside so many times, and now just feel so sad and stupid. I had to lose him to bloody Jane for it all to become clear.'

'Stop beating yourself up? Stop it! You are a great woman, and I bet there were times you were there for him too. OK, so you lost your way for a while but it happens. I love being around you, you have this amazing energy and when I am with you, I feel anything is possible. I bet Piers felt the same. I can't tell you how much you have helped me. Deep down I bet Piers is sorry and is missing you too. Women like you don't come along very often; Piers knows that.'

'If that were true then why did he leave me for that awful Jane woman? And let's not forget they are expecting a child. He had some great friends but I never bothered to get to know any of them. The women had careers, well at least some of them did, but I couldn't relate to them. I thought their lives were a bit dull; I couldn't see the point of the weekend barbeques and big group holidays. Now after coming out here with you guys, I can't think of anything I would rather do!

'The worst thing is that just before we split up, I was feeling a bit restless. I thought it was my job and I felt maybe the time had come to move on. But just as he dropped the bomb about Jane, I realised that I was feeling broody. That's why I had been out of sorts at work and probably why I took my eye off the ball and also why all that celebrity scandal rubbish went so far.

'Now I can't think of anything worse than going back to that office and all the politics and knives coming at you from all angles. After he left me, it hit me hard because I knew I was finally ready to have a baby with Piers.

'At the time he was running into the distance with awful Jane, who just happened to be pregnant. How ironic is that?

'Now I dream about babies who look like Piers but with my red hair. For the first time I look at couples with babies wishing it was me!'

Claire looked at her friend and saw her eyes were brimming with tears. She squeezed Anna's arm tight and for a while the pair continued their walk, not needing to talk.

'You are being too hard on yourself, you have had some pretty shitty stuff thrown at you. Deep down you are a real softie. You are kind and generous so don't beat yourself up. I don't know this Piers guy but I think he loved you and had your back. He was proud of what you did and I think from the things you have said, this Jane woman was on a mission to take him from you. I am not making excuses for him, it was wrong; but from the things you say about him, I think he felt obliged to stay with this awful woman because of the baby.'

Anna nodded. 'Maybe, but any way I look at it, I have lost him. You may be right about Jane, but I drove him away and she couldn't wait to snap him up. I delivered him to her gift wrapped and ready to be a daddy because I was a blind, stupid cow.'

Silently they headed towards Castaways and though it was only midday they both decided a pre-lunch cocktail was in order.

'We can head back and maybe get the girls to join us for a swim. And am I right in thinking you are having another date night with the lovely Glen later?'

At the mention of his name Claire blushed like a teenager.

Things had moved on quite a pace since that first night out. They had spent lots of time together driving around the island. They had loved discovering some of the more out-of-the-way bays, heading out on his day boat to enjoy picnics and swims in more secluded coves and dining alfresco on his stunning terrace.

Glen had made his feelings very clear after their first few dates. He told her that he had never thought he would find someone to love again and while he knew he was older than her, he admitted he had fallen for her.

'I don't know how you feel or if we could possibly make this work, but I really hope we can. I am an older man but I promise you for the time we have left together I will do everything I can to make you happy. You make me feel alive again and I can't lose you.'

She pulled him to her and kissed him gently, enjoying the taste and smell of him. He always made her feel so loved, safe and desired.

She knew that tonight was going to be special because last night over dinner, he had asked if she would go on a little staycation to the other side of the island. It would mean spending the night with him and she had agreed. Both knew that they were about to take things to the next level.

Claire was 15 years younger than Glen but she didn't care about the age difference. He was handsome and kind and he had an amazing body. He was super fit; he still ran five kilometres a day, swam and enjoyed keeping trim.

They had not made love yet, but she was in no rush. Bloody Richard had rocked her confidence so she was content to take it slow. On the other hand, Glen seemed very anxious about the whole thing. They had started getting very passionate lately and while Claire felt OK about it, Glen admitted he was a bit nervous.

'I have not made love to anyone for so long Claire; I really am worried that I won't make the grade. I feel like a nervous teenager again.'

She put her finger to his lips and said that she was sure things were going to be just fine. For once she felt in control and explained that in her book, they should just let things happen naturally. But secretly she was a bit worried too. How would he feel seeing her naked in his bed? Yes, her confidence had grown, and she no longer felt so bloated. But she was no supermodel and there were tell-tale stretch marks across her belly and cellulite on her thighs. She reasoned that if he was sincere about how he felt about her that should not matter but she was still anxious about it.

She was a mature woman and her body showed signs of motherhood and maturity. When she thought of spending the night with this beautiful man, her tummy did a little flip. Who would have known that this could happen at her age? Just weeks ago, she had arrived here feeling unhealthy and unattractive and now a whole new life had presented itself to her. But she did wonder how they could make this work. Her home was back in England with Harriet. His life was worlds away. For now, all she could about was the amazing night ahead of her.

Claire admitted that despite all her assurances to Glen she wasn't feeling entirely confident about sleeping with him for the first time either.

'I really don't know what to do Anna. I mean, I am not exactly in my first flush of youth, am I? I never stripped off in front of Richard. He was a 'lights off at the end of a night out' man. I am not sure I can be seductive. I think I will just feel stupid.

'When it comes to the crunch, what if he doesn't fancy me? I have stretch marks and though I am getting trimmer I still have cellulite, lots of it and ...'.

Anna cut her off and stood facing her, wearing a stern expression that Claire had not seen before. Though she suspected in Anna's old life, her employees would have seen it a lot!

'Now you listen to me. You are one of the sexiest women I know and Glen is totally besotted with you. Believe me, once you two get it together you won't need to worry about a thing. There is so much chemistry between you, it's written all over your faces that you two fancy each other like mad! Jesse and I are green with envy. It will feel natural to take it to the next step. Look how smoothly things have gone so far. Glen is a gem. He's sexy and he's a real gentleman who can't believe his luck that someone like you has come into his life.

'He is such a silver fox. And let's not forget the little matter about him being fabulously wealthy, with a dream house in a dream location. I would say that your life is looking up! Just go out tonight looking amazing and let the rest just happen.'

Claire giggled and said that she hoped that she wouldn't disappoint him. 'What if ...'.

'Enough! Let's get you back to the villa and get you looking smoking hot!'

The girls strolled back to the villa and the others joined them for a leisurely swim. That afternoon Claire was happy to lay by the pool reading as she wanted to take her time getting ready as she had some packing to do for the overnight date!

A few hours later she had packed a small bag with toiletries and a floaty slip that doubled as a nightie. She had a chiffon wrap around cerise top and cropped jeans for the following morning as Glen said they would be doing a little sightseeing. But despite trying on the entire contents of her somewhat limited holiday wardrobe, her date night outfit was proving a problem.

The red off-the-shoulder satin number seemed too over the top and her maxi beach dresses were not right either. She wanted to wear a smart dress as the restaurant he had booked was going to be a bit special. She wanted to show him that she had made an effort.

A discreet knock on her bedroom door woke her from her reverie and she turned to see Anna holding out a pink carrier bag.

'I thought it might be the right time to give you this.'

Claire took the bag and lifted out the most beautiful emerald midi dress which she knew would show off her newly toned figure. She held it up and did a little dance.

'There is a wrap that goes with it too, it would have been a pity not to buy it as they look so perfect together. I saw the dress in the store when you were trying on swimsuits and I knew you had to have it.'

Claire felt overwhelmed by her friend's kindness and knew that the dress would be a perfect fit. The colour would set off her bronzed skin and her cascading chocolate coloured hair which was now threaded with sun bleached highlights.

'This is such an expensive outfit, why would you buy it for me? It's so generous of you I hardly know what to say.'

'Why not? I saw it and I wanted you to have it. I have never had a friend to treat so it was fun for me too. Just go and try it on.'

By the time Glen arrived to pick Claire up she was a vision having danced around the terrace showing off her new outfit to the delight of the girls.

Glen whistled softly as she approached him. He took her arm and pulled her to him whispering how beautiful she looked. As they set off for their romantic date the three girls watched them and decided that they needed a sundowner!

Anna had got used to rounding the gang up and suggested a visit to Castaways. 'Watching those two has given me a thirst. They almost had steam coming out of their ears!'

But they were happy for Claire and realised that they had all played some small part in helping her get her confidence back. The woman who had just danced off into the sunset was not the same one who had arrived here just weeks before and each of her friends was happy for her.

The trio ambled along the shoreline watching the last of the sun's rays and the few tourists who had come out to enjoy a sunset swim.

Anna was strangely quiet and Gina seemed lost in thought too. Jesse walked to the table they frequented as it had the best view of the bay. Everyone gathered to see the sun slip into the sea and sometimes they were rewarded with a stunning emerald flash on the horizon as it hit the sea.

This evening the bar was packed with locals and residents from the nearby South Finger villas, a mix of American, Canadian, German, Dutch and British. They were called the Snowbirds as they tended to head out to the sun in November sit out the winter and head home in late spring.

Jesse decided to break the silence. Sipping her cocktail, she looked at the group and admitted that she didn't want this trip to end.

'It is going to be so hard to leave here and go back to real life. I am not sure I am ready to face it to be honest.' Anna agreed and had come to enjoy this laid-back lifestyle.

'There is nothing much waiting for me at home; just the prospect of being sued, an empty flat and ready meals for one!'

They nodded in agreement and looked to Gina to find out her take on heading home.

Gina realised that the time had come to be honest and own up to how things had been developing between her and Dan.

'Girls, I have been waiting for the right time to tell you this. I would rather have told you when Claire was here too, but I don't think I can keep this to myself any longer. When you all fly home I don't think I will be coming with you.'

The girls gave a collective gasp and turned to look at Gina. She gave them a wide smile and threw up her hands as if surrendering her past life for a new one.

'I know, it seems to have happened so fast. But I have fallen in love with Dan and he feels the same about me. Dan knows that eventually I will have to head back to London to sort things out, but there is nothing that requires rushing back any time soon. I have arranged to sign over the house to an agent to sell and there is no need for me to be there. The legal stuff with James is a bit more complicated but I am going to sign over the power of attorney to my solicitor who is more than happy to help me out. My family know too and are happy for me. They are relieved that I am not going back to James.'

Gina told them she had done a lot of soul searching but she knew what she was doing.

'We are not rushing into anything heavy too soon, I just want to give life out here a try. Although there are one or two things which are making things happen a bit speedier than I may have wanted.'

'My God, you aren't pregnant, are you?' Jesse squealed.

'No, nothing like that. But Dan's life is a bit more complex than I realised and I need to stay on and see if we can make things work between us. I have been trying to get my head around things before I told you the story. It was all a bit overwhelming at first. I didn't tell you what happened following our first date. That's when things changed for me. I so wanted to tell you then, but it was just all a bit much and I didn't know how I felt about it all. Now I do.'

Anna couldn't stand the mystery any longer.

'Stop talking in riddles and just tell us what the hell happened!'

'Well, as you know I stayed at his villa on the harbour side that night, I was with him all the next day and he said he had something special planned for me. It was an amazing day because I got to meet his children.'

Jesse's eyes almost popped out of her head. 'What? Dan has kids. Hey, that is not what I thought you were going to say!'

'Well not exactly, but yes, in a way he does. He has taken some on ...'.

Gina suggested that they get more drinks as the tale was a long one. She and Dan had made some very important decisions in the past few days and she was relieved that she could finally be up front and share her plans with the girls. She hoped that they would not think she had lost her mind, though she couldn't deny it had all been a bit of a whirlwind.

She had not intended looking for a new man, let alone a man who had taken on two children. And if things worked out between her and Dan, they would become part of her life too. It seemed very surreal but she was totally at peace with the idea of it.

'Dan knows how much your opinions mean to me. I really want you to know who the real Dan is and why I want to do this. Yes, he was a pap photographer, and he admits that he has not always been the kindest guy when it came to selling on images that earned him money.

'He has wanted out for a long time and it's not who he is deep inside. When he started doing the job, he was young and it was a bit of a laugh – racing after celebrities, flying off at a minute's notice to beautiful locations to get a snap of royals or politicians often holidaying with risqué partners. Eventually he began to hate the lifestyle as it had no value or true meaning and he knew he was hurting people. Dan was looking for a new direction. Suddenly his sister and her husband both died and he knew he had to keep making money to support his family. Sorry girls, I am jumping ahead here.

'His sister came out here six years ago with her husband and they ran a dive school at a resort over at Carlisle Bay. He says they were literally living the dream. They had two children, Reece who is now eight and Lola who is five. Dan loved coming out to visit them, and they would sail off for days at a time exploring the coast. He became quite an experienced sailor himself. He talked to them about maybe investing in the business, buying another boat, and starting a day charter to enhance what they were offering at the dive school.

'Then just over a year ago Dan had to step up big time after his sister Julia and her husband Owen were involved in a car accident. They were driving back on the coast road after a night out at Shirley Heights and the police think they were run off the road. There were no witnesses. The car was a write-off and Owen was killed outright, Julia died two days later.'

Dan told Gina he had gone into a deep depression for a few months. He then made the decision to go ahead with his plans to come to Antigua – it turned out to be on a permanent basis.

'So, Dan is financially responsible for the children, though right now they live full time with Owen and Julia's best friends, a couple called Iris and Winston who have a home near Valley Church. The children go to a local school nearby.

'They have young children too and the families were such good friends. After the accident it was a given that Lola and Reece went to stay with Iris and Winston. Dan said his sister had no other relatives who could take the children on apart from him and he was in no fit state to do that back then. Dan knew that Julia would want Iris and Winston to care for them. They are an amazing couple, but Dan feels now that he is ready to be there for the children on a more permanent basis. So, he has given up his job and is going to relocate out here full time. He inherited his sister's villa along with the boat as she made it a proviso that if he became the children's guardian the whole of her and Owen's estate would go to him.

'There was an option for him to sell on the boat and the business but he has decided to ahead with the charter business. And ... well, this is the scary part; he wants to see if we can be a family. I can't think of anything I would like to do more than make a life with him out here. Wow, there it is, I have said it, quite a turn of events!'

The girls were mute as she looked to each of them for a reaction.

'I will have to go back home to tie up a few loose ends eventually but I plan to stay here a while longer. I can't leave Antigua. I love it here and even before the Dan thing got so serious, I had been giving some thought to maybe finding work and staying out here. There are some great estate agencies and Jolly Harbour is a fantastic spot for sales and rentals as there are hundreds of villas on South and North Finger. I love the more remote ones too and lots of new developments are being built, so the potential is huge.

'I went into the two main agents here as I wanted to see what sort of rental I could afford. I got on well with one of the girls I met she is Irish and came out here five years ago. She now runs the rental side of one of the agencies and she says the boss is always looking out for experienced staff. Dan has asked me if I would also think about doing the charter side of things with him.'

'Crickey you have been busy!' said Jesse, but she was smiling broadly and raising her glass.

The group were transfixed as Gina filled them in on all the research she had done even before her romance had taken off and became something big.

'I have a lot of possessions at my house back at home but to be honest, I don't need any of them. I have a feeling that business suits and heels won't be much use out here on the boat!

'And Dan is incredible, honestly he is so kind ...' her eyes glazed a little and a smile played on her face at the mere mention of his name.

'Every chance he gets he flies out here to see the children. Lately he realised he really wants to be more involved in their lives. Iris and Winston are great, but the children love being with Dan and he wants to give them the sort of life he knows his sister would want for them. The morning after I stayed with him, he took me out on his boat and sailed to Ffryes Beach. There was a crowd of schoolchildren having a picnic on the headland and that is when he introduced me to Lola and Reece.

'He told me the whole horrible, sad story. He was worried about asking me to even consider taking on so much, but I knew the moment I met him and got to know him that somehow my life was about to change.

'He didn't ask me to live with him then, but over the past couple of weeks it has felt more and more natural to be with him and to share time with the children too. I realised how huge it is for him to take them on, and he knows it's a hell of a big ask for me too, especially as we have only just met. We both know what a change it will make to our lives, but I think we can make it work. That day on the headland we all played rounders on the grass alongside the beach and he was just so amazing, not only with his niece and nephew, but with the other children too. They all love him. He goes into the school and works with them when he is here and he has done so much. He has helped them build new classrooms and set up a new fundraising scheme to pay for new teachers as the school is growing. He's persuaded quite a few businesses to get involved and the fund is growing ... Yes, I know I am gabbling on, but I love it that he is so passionate about life out here!

'Julia and Owen wanted the children to be educated at the local school so Dan wants to make sure it is the best it can be. They were very hands on at the school and Dan wants to take that on too. We both think that we can make a life out here. The children are happy to stay with Iris and Winston during the week but at weekends they will live in the villa with us. We will take them out on his boat and get used to being a family. They love the sea because their parents were always out on their boat. It's what they love too. The idea of making a life out here seems like a big ask but the more time I spend with Dan and Lola and Reece it just feels right. It was certainly a shock to me, but a lovely one. I feel I belong with them and that means living here!'

The group let out a collective gasp at this twist in the story and Gina scanned the faces of her friends as she wanted their support. The deathly silence hinted at the fact that maybe it was not forthcoming.

'Wow ... that is a lot of news to take in. But I for one think it's great,' said Anna. 'You look so happy. Why not give it a go? I only hope that you take things a bit slowly though, after all you have gone through. This is one hell of a leap.' Gina beamed at her and enveloped her in a hug.

Jesse didn't seem to know what to say then came around the table, planted a kiss on her cheek and gave her blessing too.

'Hey, it looks as though you are jumping in fast, but if in your heart it feels right and you can see a future, then why not?'

Jesse also admitted that she was just a little bit envious. As usual she found the right words.

'You have had so much hurt and unhappiness with your ex. I know you were not looking for love when you came out here, but sometimes you have to just go with it. I think it's a great idea, who would have thought? It's like something out of a movie!'

Gina let out a huge sigh. She had been afraid to tell them her plans, and Anna, more than any of the group, had reason not to trust Dan.

'Anna, that means so much coming from you because I know you had such misgivings about Dan. But he really is a kind, caring man and I have never felt so safe, loved and happy.'

ANNA

WHEN THEY GOT BACK from their sunset cocktail hour the girls threw a salad together and sat on the terrace just staring at the incredible view, all lost in their own thoughts. They had made a heartfelt toast to Gina's new future and wished her well. Each of them seemed to be thinking of what the future may have lined up for them. The weeks had flown by and for Claire, Jesse and Anna, the departure date was looming.

Anna had been very quiet after Gina had revealed her plans for a new life with Dan. Not for the first time that day, she began to wonder what it was that she wanted out of life. She had run away from her problems and she had enjoyed being with the girls in their cocoon living a life that seemed almost suspended in time. But she could not ignore what she had left behind forever, and while her head had often been filled with regret and misgivings about how she and Piers had ended, she was equally troubled about how she felt about her job. Did she even want to fight for it?

She had always been driven and ambitious. As a young news reporter, she had set her sights on working for the nationals. She had climbed the career ladder and held her own in the cut and thrust of a male dominated world, Although, women like her were now coming up through the ranks and making their voices heard in top roles in the media, and in other industries and key organisations everywhere. But she had lost her fire and the fight had gone out of her. She wondered if it was the effect this place was having on her, or if more importantly, the way her new friendships had made her rethink her priorities.

She knew her life needed a reset; she just didn't have the first idea how that was going to happen.

Anna had not bothered looking at her emails since she had been in Antigua as she had no wish to hear what was going on at *The Globe*. She may or may not still have a job, but she felt strangely distanced from it all. She also had no wish to receive any emails telling her the latest gossip about her ex and Jane.

The last time she had logged onto her personal account was the night before she flew out to Antigua.

As she was putting her 'I am out of the country and can't be contacted' message on, an email had dropped into her inbox from Jen, her PR agent.

She had forwarded an email request from the executive producer of ITV's *Loose Women* asking her to go along for a chat about the possibility of joining the team.

She had read the chatty exchange with interest because Jen had always had her back and her emails were always chatty and fun. She always cut to the chase and never wasted Anna's time with projects that she didn't think were in her best interests.

She was probably the only woman in her working life that Anna had grown to trust over the years. She was down to earth and Anna had always enjoyed their email exchanges. It struck her that she had never invited Jen out for a drink or a meal. Once again, she realised, she had never truly allowed herself to bother with girlfriends.

At the time the email had arrived she had not been in a good place and had neither the will nor the energy to do more than say she would be in touch when she got back from her trip. Now, with her life so up in the air on so many fronts, she felt it might be the time to give this TV opportunity some consideration.

Opening her laptop, she re-read Jen's message which seemed to have been sent a lifetime ago:

Hi Anna.

I have had a call from my friend Rosa. She is on the production team of Loose Women and they have had their eye on you for a while. They love how outspoken you are, you don't take prisoners and it helps that you have so many famous friends. It's always a bonus if you have good connections – and you do! And my friend, you scrub up a treat!

They are suggesting you do a couple of guest spots when Jane Moore goes on hols later this summer. If it goes well there may be a regular spot for you. You also get on so well with that Nolan woman, and you told me yourself that she says she has so much fun on that show. I bumped into Andrea McClean at a dinner do at The Ivy and she said she'd love it if you joined the team. I know you hate the whole girlie gossipy thing, but you would bring something different to the show. Rosa said you are a lot like that Carol McGiffin – ballsy is how I think she described you. They believe with all your news experience you have a great take on things and you are not scared to call a spade a shovel. Basically, you would sit there, wear something amazing and just be you! So, how about it? The money is good, the exposure is great and with so much uncertainty surrounding your current situation I would strongly recommend you give it some thought.'

Anna had never thought about a career in TV, though surely it couldn't be as tough as her role at *The Globe*? Maybe the time had come to look at other jobs. Her agent had promised to forward the contract details to her should her initial try out be successful.

'And there is no reason why you wouldn't smash it'

Jen had said as she added a sign off.

Deciding that as she had nothing much to occupy her for the next hour or so, as the others had gone for a late dip which had not appealed, she would email Jen to say she'd give it a go.

Which is how she came to be on her laptop, her eyes wide with shock, at the sight of another email which had been waiting in her inbox for the past few weeks.

When she saw it was from piersistheman@icloud.com she nearly screamed out loud!

It was his personal email and it had been a bit of an in-joke between them. When she had been introduced to Piers at a gala night at the Odeon, Leicester Square, there had been an instant connection between them.

One of her associate editors had pulled her over and said there was someone she had to meet. 'Anna, you have to come and say hi to Piers because Piersistheman!'

Her initial thought was 'what a load of pretentious crap.'

She was transported back to that first meeting when she had felt flushed and breathless when he fixed her with those beautiful eyes and held her hand for a few seconds longer than he should. He told her that he had admired her for so long from afar and was delighted to have finally met her. Bloody hell. This man was like a magnet, she felt so instantly drawn to him.

'So, why is Pierstheman?' she kidded.

He had the good grace to laugh out loud and agree that the label was a stupid one – and not one he had given himself!

'Look, it's a very long story and if you have had enough of this awful cheap white fizz, I suggest we head over to Joe Allen's for a late dinner and I can tell you all about it.'

It wasn't so much an invite as an order, and although she was not used to taking orders and doing as she was told she allowed herself to follow him out into the street and into a cab. Minutes later he had led her to the bar and she realised with a jolt that this tall, handsome man had held onto her hand all the way there. She hadn't minded a bit!

A whole host of famous faces shouted hello and waved over at them but everyone was someone in this place so nobody ever made a fuss.

Anna had felt herself relax and enjoy herself for the first time in ages.

The rest, as they say, was indeed history. She never discovered the whole back story to the 'piersistheman' handle.

He explained that when he was at boarding school, he had earned some money for being known as a fixer. He found ways to smuggle in cigarettes, beers and vodka under the noses of the caretaker whose job it was to ensure that no alcohol, cigarettes or illegal substances found their way through the porter's lodge entrance into the school.

He said that his natural ability to fix things and act as a catalyst to get things done had led to a life in PR and event management.

'I promise you I never hurt anyone or broke the law, we just had fun. I realised I had a knack for bringing people together. I also had a way of keeping people out of trouble! Two very useful attributes that helped me to get my business started. So, that's my story. Now, let's talk about you. I need to know who you are young lady.'

He was quite old school, so comfortable in his skin, and yet not showy or boastful. He was genuinely interested in her life, and that had never changed in all their years together. He was fun and easy to be around and that first dinner had led to a whole host of very unusual dates. Piers knew everyone and their lives melded quite naturally.

Within weeks they were an item and by the end of the year Piers had moved into her beautiful apartment in Wimbledon Village. They had carved out a happy, privileged life together with no money worries or rows to speak of. They were both career driven and they seemed content to support one another and give each other space. He had a host of very famous clients but he kept them at a professional distance. He preferred his mates from the local rowing team and a scattering of old school friends who still loved to be around him.

They had never discussed getting married and naively she had thought Piers was happy for life to go on as it had. How blind had she been? What an amazing man she had let fall through her fingers.

So how, she wondered, had it all gone so very wrong? Deep down she knew the answer to that. What she didn't know was why Piers had sent her this email with its cryptic subject matter.

He had walked out telling her that he had fallen for Jane and that was that. Apart from a few brief exchanges arranging to have his belongings packed up, a process that had nearly killed her, there had been no word from him. But she hadn't expected there to be. He was building a life with Jane now and preparing to become a father, so why would he want to contact her?

As she stared at the screen part of her was tempted to simply hit delete. But her curiosity got the better of her and, she decided there was only one way to find out why he had contacted her out of the blue. She hesitated momentarily before she clicked on open.

The subject box had read simply:

'ANNA! PLEASE READ THIS!'

Piers had a rule; he never used capital letters in his emails. He said that to him it smacked of a desperation to be noticed. She poured herself a large glass of cold white wine and made her way to her room. Whatever he had to say she needed to be alone when she read it. She tried to decide how she felt about hearing from him and realised she just felt numb. The worst had happened, he had left her broken. What more was there to throw at her?

An hour later when Jesse came to check on her, she found Anna lying on her bed staring up at the ceiling. She was very still, not appearing to be focusing on anything.

'Are you OK? We were a bit worried.'

'I am not sure if I know the answer to that. Piers has emailed me and says he wants us to talk. In a nutshell ... and this is tough to say ... he isn't with Jane. She isn't pregnant after all and he's asking for a chance to meet to see if I can find a way to forgive him and start again.'

'And can you?'

'That's the trouble, Jesse. I have been thinking about him a lot and missing him, and at times wishing he were here, but

I am not sure I can do it. The trust is gone, he left me for someone else and he told me he loved her for God's sake! How can you come back from that?'

'Well, only you know the answer to that one, People make mistakes and learn from them. You said yourself you drove him away.'

'Yes but ... I don't know how I feel about anything anymore, I need to think about this. It's all been a bit of a bombshell; this is the last thing I expected to happen. Can I just put it all behind me, do as he says and move forward?'

But Jesse noticed that the ghost of a smile was playing on her lips as she said it.

'From where I am standing, I think you both got it wrong. You admitted that you pushed him away and you have changed so much in the short time you have been here. Maybe the guy deserves a chance. What harm can come from at least talking to him? You don't want to make another mistake and years later look back and think "What if?" – do you?

'I don't know Piers, or anything about your life together, but I do know you came here looking like a ghost, a very spiky one! I think you need to think long and hard before you make any decisions. I agree he needs to sweat a bit more, but I think you owe it to yourself to at least have that talk. This time be real and tell him what you want. I don't doubt that you need to give him a hard time, but maybe it's worth a shot?'

The pair went downstairs and headed out onto the terrace. On the way through Jesse scooped up a bottle of brandy and three very large brandy bowl glasses from the outside bar.

'I have the feeling we have a long night ahead, and this may just help us get through it!'

RICHARD

RICHARD WOKE UP AND for a while he had to dig deep to remember where he was. The past 24 hours had been a bit of a blur. He had flown over to Antigua on a mission to find Claire and talk some sense into her. But then he had met the lovely Laura and found himself ensconced in her rather beautiful beachside mansion. She was a far better option, though he could tell she was going to prove a bit of a challenge. But he had met women like Laura before and he knew how to smooth out those rough edges and get them in his thrall.

The flight had been flirty and fun, and he knew at the end of it she was hooked. They had arrived at the house, drunk champagne on the terrace and Laura then led him to the bedroom. He believed he had performed to her satisfaction and now it seemed a replay was about to happen.

She had indicated a door that led to one of the biggest and most luxurious bathrooms he had ever seen, suggesting that he should join her in the shower.

He had learned from his previous experience in the bedroom this was not so much a suggestion, more of a directive. But he was more than happy to do as he was told.

She was a demanding lover and he had felt like a sex slave, trying to fulfil her fantasies and satisfy what was clearly a huge sexual appetite. He had never met or bedded a woman like her; she was insatiable.

'Richard, you are quite the stud,' she purred, as he rolled over to find her leaning over him giving him a look that he recognised from the previous evening.

This woman was really something. He thought that he had earned a rest this morning after putting on his A game the night before.

But Laura had other plans and slipping under the silk duvet cover she ordered him to kneel above her. As he fought every fibre in his being not to come in her mouth, he had to admit, he had never had a blow job like this. She was doing things with her tongue that he had only read about in the porn magazines he had hidden in the closet at home. This woman was like an absolute tiger in bed. He pushed her head into his groin and moaned as she caressed his balls with her long talons making him scream out. As she somehow managed to take him even deeper into her mouth he knew that he was about to lose control.

This woman was incredible and he couldn't hold back any longer. He climaxed for what seemed like forever and she simply licked him dry and climbed on top of him.

'Now my darling boy, I am going to ask you to repay the compliment ...'. Cat-like she arched her back and pushed her body forward so that her ample chest was right in his face.

'Now, please suck these rather magnificent nipples for me and here is a little toy which might get the party started again.'

Laura leaned across him and reached into her glass mirrored bedside cabinet and pulled out the biggest vibrator he had ever seen. It was silver with glass panels filled with lurid purple stones that rotated when she turned it on and made a faint buzzing sound.

Laura could see that he looked uncomfortable but it seemed to turn her on even more.

'It's called the Purple Pearl and it's incredible, when you have finished sorting me out my sweet boy, I will use it on your butt and I guarantee you will want to buy one.'

Richard very much doubted that! It looked bloody terrifying, but he thought that at least it might give him some time to recover because he had a feeling he was not going to get much rest until Laura had decided she had had enough.

Wow, what a woman! He had never met anyone quite like her and she put Claire and naughty, sexy Martha in the shade.

The sound of the Purple Pearl interrupted his thoughts as Laura straddled him and showed him exactly what her coveted toy could do.

Richard had never heard such primal screams. In equal measures of amazement and delight he felt his erection grow and he decided to take control. He felt, somehow, she was testing him and this was one test he was determined to pass with flying colours.

Taking the vibrator from Laura, Richard threw it onto the bed and lowered her to the floor. He made sure her screams continued long and loud and it was all down to him.

They spent a lazy morning by the pool – he needed the rest – then Laura suggested they go down to the mall alongside the quay at St John.

She had a few errands to run and she suggested they treat themselves to a few goodies.

'I may just have to buy you something special after this morning my darling, you were quite the caveman.'

Richard felt a little patronized but let it go. He was trying to guess what she might buy him. He had hinted about how he loved her diamond encrusted Rolex and had also mentioned in passing that he had recently lost his Hublot and felt lost without it.

'Well, we shall have to see what we can do about that my sweet boy.'

The pair left for St John and Richard allowed himself to relax in the back of the limo feeling like he was finally living the sort of life that he was meant to.

There was champagne on tap, the house was incredible and as for the sex, well she was a nymphomaniac. She was so demanding and he had never experienced anything like it. God, she was the best! In fact, men would pay for some of the tricks that she pulled out of the hat. No wonder she had ended up living the high life. He wondered who the ex was and how he had made his millions, but for now he was happy to be living the dream. He decided that he had better splash a bit of cash and maybe buy her something nice.

He knew his £50,000 pay out from Claire was not going to last long if he tried to keep up with Laura and her crew, but he looked upon it as an investment.

They arrived at the quay and decided to go their separate ways for an hour or so. Laura said she had some banking to do. There was a boutique she wanted to check out too as they were dining out later and she wanted to buy something new.

Richard was at a loss to know what to buy her. He had seen her admire a sapphire silk kimono at one of the designer outlets and he doubled back to buy it for her. But he wanted to impress her and that meant spending a bit more.

He was drawn to a white gold bracelet adorned with rows of sapphires and diamond chips. It was over the top and he knew it would impress Laura. It would quash any misgivings that she may have that he was not in her league. This was the sort of store that didn't put price tags in the window so he had to go inside to find out the cost of it.

The people who shopped here didn't need to worry if they could afford to buy these baubles. He wanted to be one of them and he decided if he played his cards right, he could soon be in the big league.

He even allowed himself to contemplate getting engaged. Of course, it would mean getting divorced from Claire, but she was ancient history now. Laura was a whole new beginning for him. While he hadn't intended to get married to Claire back then it had given him a leg up when he needed it. He reckoned he would soon be living the high life and once Laura was well and truly into him, he would make sure she picked up the tab.

He was not surprised to find out that the bracelet was £8,000 but what the hell? If it bought him a life out here and perhaps another six months in her loft in NYC then why not? He had always imagined himself in a brownstone house in the West Village. Claire was a *Sex and The City* devotee and he had watched it because he had fancied Samantha. She too was a cougar who knew how to enjoy sex. Now he had his very own Samantha and he intended keeping on her right side.

On a whim he had the sales assistant gift wrap a pair of sapphire stud earrings – a steal at £2,500. They matched the bracelet and he knew he was going a bit OTT but he felt it was time to invest in his new future. He hoped these gifts would seal the deal. He had always fancied taking a bite out of The Big Apple and it looked as though it might happen.

He allowed his mind to wander back to last night and he had to admit he was looking forward to the next instalment.

He had thought Martha was the best but Laura could show her a thing or two. He decided that all things considered he had landed on his feet and for the time being at least, he was going nowhere.

Two hours later they arrived back at the house and though the sun was blazing and the cool turquoise sea below was beckoning, they headed straight to the bedroom as he had predicted.

As they lay exhausted and dripping with sweat, Laura revealed that they had house guests arriving later, which was news to him! Putting on a breathy voice which irritated him no end, she asked him if he would be a darling and pop to the supermarket for a few essentials. Could he also head back to a marvellous local deli in St John which was the only place to sell a few must have goodies.

Richard was not happy to be told to go grocery shopping. He was also a bit put out that their intimate dinner for two at Katherines on Pigeon Point would now include another couple. His plan to surprise her with the gifts he had bought earlier would have to wait. But he was not going to lose his cool and he managed to mask his irritation. As she instructed, he showered and dressed and waited while Laura put a shopping list together.

Since when had a crate of vintage Krug been classed as essential provisions? She hadn't told him that she had also factored in a stop at a wine merchant nearby. As well as the champagne she wanted a case of her favourite French red wine and a few extra bottles of New Zealand Sauvignon. 'Darling, they only sell that cheap Chilean stuff at the local store.' He gamely agreed that of course it wasn't a problem. He didn't mix in the circles Laura obviously did and his days of getting away with a cheap glass of plonk at the pub and garage flowers were a thing of the past.

The supermarket list seemed endless and he gasped out loud on the way home when he checked his credit card receipt and saw he had blown over £2,000 on wine and mountains of food. What the hell, he had the money in the bank hadn't he? It wasn't as if it was costing him to stay with Laura. He reasoned that he would reap the rewards of his investment once he had wormed his way into her life. When she flew back to the US he intended to be at her side.

He sat in the back of the air-conditioned car feeling very smug, if a little dazed, at blowing so much money on booze and food.

He had enjoyed the athletic sex that morning and once again Laura had proved herself to be an amazing lover.

There was no 'lie back and lights out' for her. She was a demanding cougar who knew what turned her on and insisted on it – more than once – he remembered. A smile playing on his lips.

She had also surprised him with a beautiful cashmere sweater and some Ralph Lauren loafers.

'I like my men to look the part,' she explained, caressing the sweater, and allowing her long painted fingernails to trail down his chest and linger over his belt loops.

He felt an erection build but she laughed and pushed him away.

'Later darling, we have guests arriving and I want to make sure we are ready for them.'

At one point while he was out shopping, he spied a curvy woman on the street near the Quay and for a moment, he thought it could be Claire. But this woman looked more toned and was wearing an amazing outfit. Her face and hair were hidden by huge sunglasses and a black straw hat. She looked chic and expensive and he quickly dismissed the idea that it could possibly be the pathetic mouse who was now firmly in his past.

This woman carried herself with confidence and was strutting down the street. He noted she was attracting quite a lot of male attention.

That was not Claire's style. When he looked back to double check she had disappeared. He dismissed the idea as ludicrous. Since when did Claire dress like that – or appear so sophisticated. Pity really, had she been that girl he may have hung around a little longer.

He was in a hurry to get back to Laura and get ready for what the night may bring. He had meant to ask more about the people who were joining them but Laura had seemed a bit mysterious and guarded about them.

He hadn't wanted to push it. Women like Laura didn't come along very often so he was on his best behaviour. At least for now. He couldn't wait to tell Phil all about her and the amazing life she led. Phil would be impressed and no doubt a bit envious. But hopefully he wouldn't be seeing Phil for a very long time.

JESSE

THE SUN WAS RISING on yet another spectacular morning at Jolly Beach when Jesse awoke from a restless sleep needing to get up and jump into the sea. She had felt restless for the past few days; trying to digest both Gina's new plans for a future with Dan and Claire's burgeoning romance with the lovely Glen, who clearly wanted to make her happy.

She and Anna had discussed staying on for the next three weeks after Gina moved into Dan's beachside villa. Claire was going home to work out how she and Glen were going to progress what was clearly a very promising beginning.

As she headed out to the far side of the bay where she found solace and peace in the early mornings, she wondered what the future had in store for her.

Only yesterday Milly had sent her a text saying that she needed her to give her a call. It appeared that something important had cropped up that Milly had not felt able to share in a text. Jesse wondered what that could be. A bridezilla maybe, or perhaps a problem with the shop? She hadn't allowed herself to think about going back to her old life which had been fraught with despair and misery. Even the prospect of returning to her beautiful home in Putney did not excite her in the least. In fact, she had seriously considered selling it. There were far too many painful memories there now. Here she felt safe and she had no wish to return to the emotional mess she had left behind. As she gazed out at the impossibly turquoise sea and the deserted early morning powdery beach, she couldn't imagine her life back in the grimy grey city.

Part of her wanted to stay here in this idyllic bubble forever, but the other pragmatic Jesse knew that at some point soon she had to go home and try to re-establish her life and get her business back on track. Walking away from the shop just after she had managed to get such a publicity boost was stupid. But she knew her work would not have been her creative best. Her phone had been ringing off the hook just before she had headed out here, and she had been able to cherry pick some high profile and lucrative contracts. It was great that Milly had stepped up but clients wanted Jesse and sooner or later she would have to come up with the goods.

She had agreed to be the wedding florist for a budding soap star, and a Premier League football manager and his model bride (who had hammered out a very attractive deal with *OK!* magazine). One of the finalists from *Strictly* had also booked her for a surprise, swanky 40th birthday bash. They had hinted that Claudia and Tess were expected to be there alongside Bruno and annoying Craig Revel wotisname, but she could not summon up any enthusiasm. She knew this sort of exposure was priceless but she no longer had the heart. Try as she might she had not managed to come up with any innovative ideas for any of these contracts and her heart sank. Had this stupid affair really impacted so heavily that she had given up? Unfortunately, she thought she had lost her creative spark alongside her heart.

Walking along the shoreline, watching the tiny boats heading out for a day snorkelling and diving, she wondered how she was going to slip back into her old life. This one seemed so much simpler. But it was not reality and she had to take back control. Her heart had ruled her head causing her to have a major meltdown, resulting in this impulsive rental. But she would never regret coming out here, or for choosing to share this special time with her three new friends.

Jesse sat on the sand at the far end of the bay and allowed her mind to wander back to Sam. She replayed the conversations she had had with him, remembering his haunted eyes when he admitted that Zoe was his fiancée. Worst of all was recalling that last cold hearted phone call exchange. Far from being concerned about how she felt he had simply wanted to ensure that she saved his sorry arse.

But she had loved him, hadn't she? She was beginning to wonder if those iconic words uttered by Prince Charles hit the mark. What was it that he had uttered during that awkward engagement interview with Princess Di when he had been asked if they were in love. 'Oh yes!' she said, then Prince Charles had countered 'Whatever that means.' She was suddenly much more on his team about this love stuff. It just got you hurt.

She tried not to think of what Sam was doing now. She had to believe that it had all been a huge mistake and that she had read him completely wrong.

Suddenly she felt angry with him and decided that instead of moping about here, she would go back to the villa and do something constructive. It was time to get her head back on straight. She had seen some birds-of-paradise blooms in a neighbour's beautifully planted out courtyard and they had given her the germ of a theme for that *Strictly* woman's party. She had brought a sketch book with her so she decided to go back and put a few ideas onto paper. Even that thought made her feel a bit brighter.

She knew she should ring Milly; she had seemed insistent that she speak to her but, as this was the first time in weeks that she had felt even remotely interested in work, the call could wait a while.

She quickened her step as she was keen to get back and find the sketch book. She was sure she had seen some Sharpies in one of the drawers in the study. They would do nicely.

SAM

IT HAD BEEN AGES since he had begged Milly to get in touch with Jesse and pass on his number and he had heard nothing. He longed to pop in again and speak to her but he suspected that if he did this, he would be pushing his luck. Milly hadn't promised him anything but she had said she would be in touch if Jesse responded. Part of him was afraid that she had received the message to call him but she had not wanted to … and who could blame her?

The thought depressed him but he decided there was not much time before she came back. He was still hoping to turn up and camp out on her doorstep if he had to. This woman was worth the wait.

JAMES

IN THE WEEKS SINCE Gina had left him James had done a lot of thinking and had finally accepted that his marriage was over. He realised that he hadn't been the easiest man to live with. He had very high standards and he knew he could be demanding and at times bad-tempered. He refused to think about the times he had lashed out and physically hurt Gina. Once he started to see that red mist descend it was as if he had no power to stop his actions. But his wife's treachery, in leaving him the way she had and cutting him out of her life had been a cruel blow. He had thrown himself into his job and a new training opportunity had presented itself in the office in Bruges.

Within his first week he had taken a shine to an accountant called Marissa. She was a beautiful brunette who was younger than Gina, and a lot more responsive to his whims. She seemed very keen to please him and didn't have a large family or a close circle of friends which suited him down to the ground. She was also more than happy to fit around his busy schedule of working and obsessive visits to the gym. He had decided to draw a line under his first marriage and when she asked him about his past, he insisted that he had never married. He had rubbed Gina out of his life as if she had never existed.

She had let him down just like his mother had done. In time he might let the lovely Marissa into his bed – but nobody was ever going to get under his skin again or into his heart. He would see to that.

RICHARD

RICHARD WOKE UP IN Laura's bed and groaned. Recollections of the previous evening floated into his head and none of them were good.

Things had started off perfectly well the night before. Laura's friends, Amy and Pete, had arrived as planned and the four of them had spent hours drinking cocktails and chatting. He found them a bit aloof and they were not forthcoming about where they lived and what they did. He decided to just play along with it, they would be gone in a few days. Dinner was booked that night at Sugar Ridge in the roof top restaurant and that's when the trouble started. Laura became quite irritated with the staff, at one point demanded to see the manager as she thought the waiter had been offensive. Then she became angry with Richard for not being attentive enough and for not fighting her corner. The meal was a strained experience and it was a relief to leave. They had headed to West Point, a relaxed open-air bar alongside the marina where Laura started downing shots as though they were going out of fashion. By the time the bar closed she was hammered. He had never seen her so drunk or so aggressive, though the other couple seemed to take it in their stride. They piled into a taxi and returned to the villa where Laura crashed out but not before she and Pete had gone out to chat on the terrace.

Again, things got heated.

She came back to the room to inform Richard that she wanted to sleep alone. She said she wasn't feeling well and needed the space. His plan was to give her the bracelet and earrings and broach the subject of him returning to New York with her but he decided it was best to wait until Laura was in a better mood.

Pete and Amy didn't seem to care about how sour the night had turned and Petey made some comment that suggested this behaviour was par for the course. It didn't help that the waiter had presented Richard with the bill at the end of the evening and Laura was too drunk to notice.

Pete had made no attempt to cough up his share of the bill and he didn't pick up their drinks tab at West Point either.

Once again Richard winced at how much he had spent. He didn't like the other couple and begrudged spending his time and his money on them. They were very furtive about their connection with Laura and had managed to spend the whole evening without divulging anything about what they were doing in Antigua. The foursome had planned to charter a boat to explore the coastline and snorkel on some coral reefs, but Richard was not feeling in the mood. He also suspected that Laura would be too hungover to go anywhere today.

He was right on that count. She finally emerged from one of the guest rooms at noon wearing sunglasses and demanding he find her an icepack.

He spent the afternoon fussing over her as she languished by the pool with a massive headache, demanding that he make lunch for everyone as though he was on her staff. The fact that he was the one currently paying for everyone and everything seemed to have escaped her!

By the end of the afternoon, they had all recovered enough to start drinking again and Richard found himself on bar duty; making cocktails and rustling up a few snacks.

This was not how he had imagined things were going to play out and he couldn't hide his irritation. Laura simply ignored him and treated him like a petulant child. It was only as they prepared to have an early night that she began to revert to the wanton cougar he had encountered that first evening.

He made sure he met her needs in the bedroom but this time there was no enjoyment; in fact, he felt used and he quickly showered afterwards and fell asleep. The other couple didn't stick around the next day, which surprised him as Laura had told him they were due to be at the villa for a week.

'Pete has been called away on business sweetie. There is some trouble with one of his deals that only he can handle. They may come back in a few days depending on how things work out.'

Richard felt relieved. He was glad they had gone, there was something sinister about the way the man had acted around Laura.

She seemed on edge and, from what he had seen, nobody messed with Laura. The next few days passed in a blur of trips to the coast and expensive alfresco lunches and dinners at ritzy restaurants. They enjoyed a great night at the open-air restaurant at Dickenson Bay and Richard finally had the chance to surprise Laura with the gifts he had bought her. But while she had seemed pleased, her reaction was not the one he expected. She seemed to inspect the stones closely before slipping the boxes into her handbag. He had thought she would at least indulge him by putting the bracelet on and admiring it a bit more but, he reasoned, she was used to being treated. It was the norm in her world.

They often popped to the Quay at St John where Laura enjoyed indulging in some pricey retail therapy. She had charge accounts at a couple of the stores and Richard marvelled at how much she could spend in one hit.

It was clear that money was no object to her. But he loved it that she dressed so well and very often she would indulge him with designer shirts and shorts, a new fragrance or silver cufflinks. She told him she liked him to look good. She had also given him an engraved 'man bangle', not something he would usually wear but it looked expensive and it showed off his tan to perfection. 'You are such a beautiful man Richard you deserve the very best.' Catching sight of his reflection in a shop window he had to agree with her. He could hardly believe his luck.

They had been at the villa for just over three weeks when Laura took a call on her phone and indicated that she needed to talk in private. She went out to the terrace and he watched as Laura paced up and down, gesturing with her hands, obviously not happy with the news she was receiving.

When she came back to speak to him, she seemed agitated. She composed herself and came to sit with him wearing an expression that he faintly recognised but could not quite put a name to.

'I am sorry Richard my darling, but I have to go back to the States to sort out something urgent that has cropped up. My assistant back home is booking a flight for later today. It's short notice I know but it can't be helped. I am so sorry to be cutting our holiday together so short.'

He smiled as this was his chance to see New York. He started to say how he could be packed and ready to go as soon as she liked and was happy to go with her. But she stopped him in his tracks, again her eyes not quite meeting his.

'Ah honey I am so sorry, but I think it's best if I head back on my own this time. You can stay here and hold the fort for me, OK? I promise to get back as soon as I can. Why not just make yourself at home, enjoy the luxury and have some you time and some fun? The wine rack is full, there is plenty of food and our driver will take you anywhere you need to go.'

Fixing him with a sultry look she stroked his thighs and purred that he should rest up while she was away. When she got back, he had some hot action coming his way.

He wondered fleetingly if she was not the divorcee she had claimed to be. Maybe Laura had a husband waiting back home and that was why she was refusing to let him tag along? He found the idea strangely exciting.

'Hey, why don't I give you something for you to remember me by?' he said, turning on the charm and pulling her to him. He gestured that they continue this chat in the bedroom. The housekeeper had arrived and was making a bad job of pretending not to eavesdrop.

'Sorry kiddo, but I am in a real rush. The limousine is coming very soon and I have lots to do before it arrives. Let's take a rain check huh?' For a moment he was disappointed and a bit taken aback as he wasn't used to being rejected. But then he remembered that beautiful waitress who always made a fuss of him at the quay. She was young, pretty and toned with the most beautiful butt he had ever seen. He had been transfixed. She had seemed happy to flirt with him when he popped over there yesterday. He hadn't intended pushing his luck and ruining his new lucky streak with a mindless shag. But what the hell? Now that Laura was leaving him to his own devices, he felt it would not do any harm to have some fun, and if he was lucky, some no strings sex.

CLAIRE

CLAIRE HAD JUST COME back from her morning swim and was sitting on their terrace drying off. She waved to some early morning joggers, who like her had taken advantage of the deserted beach.

Last night had been magical. Glen knew that her time in Antigua was ending and while he was not pressuring her to commit, he was seeking some form of reassurance that she felt the same as he did.

And she did on so many levels.

The problem was that her time out here with the girls had shown her that for her to enjoy life and embrace this newfound confidence, she had to acknowledge that she could be alone. She had learned to like herself again. She felt strong and independent for the first time in forever, and she had no wish to lose that feeling again. As wonderful as Glen was, Claire knew it was a mistake to give her independence away as she had with Richard. She realised that having a man in your life is not the answer. Women don't need saving, they needed to be recognised for who they were, accepted, appreciated but most of all, respected. Being loved is just the icing on the cake. She had learned the hard way that you had to love yourself before you could have healthy relationships with a partner, your family or your friends.

Glen had come into her life by accident and she had grown to care for him very deeply. They laughed and had fun together and he had begun to make her believe she could trust again. But she knew she needed time.

He was not at all like her ex. She knew he wanted to take care of her and treat her like a princess. Enticing as it was to know he wanted to protect her, she was not ready for that level of commitment.

Quite how she was going to tell him this without him feeling rejected was a worry. But she knew she had to take her time and really enjoy being the newly confident Claire for a while longer.

She had so much she wanted to do and discover about herself and she had her girls to thank for that. She had always known she had an inner strength; she had drawn on that when Stevie was killed. But she had been dazzled by Richard and for so long she had lived life his way. It was her time now. She wanted to see what the new Claire could achieve. As much as she enjoyed her time with Glen, the answer was not to run from one man to another. Even if the new man was an incredible one.

This new-found independence had left her eager to go home and show Harriet that her mother was ready to do so many things she had never done before.

Harriet had been so young when Stevie had died, barely a baby, and she had only ever seen her mother as a grieving widow and latterly a downtrodden wife. The more she thought about it she couldn't recall a time when she had been really present with her daughter since Richard had come into her life.

Looking back Richard had barely tolerated his stepdaughter and as time went on, he had insisted she spent more and more time with her grandparents. Until his affair with Martha had begun. Then he made any excuse possible to be rid of Claire too. So now she intended to be the sort of mother she had always wanted to be, active and fun. At least she now had the energy to be both. In some ways, she could not wait to get home to show Harriet that she could do better as a Mum. She needed time and space to be herself, but when she got home Harriet was in for a lively time with a Mum who now loved life and was going to make sure they both had fun.

Although her time out here had been magical, the girls had become like family and Glen was the attractive, attentive icing on the cake, it was just too soon to jump into anything serious without truly finding out who she was.

They had planned a night at his house and Claire had already decided that it was time to tell him how she felt.

She went into their villa in search of Anna; she would help her find the words to tell him. Words were her thing, and she was kind. She had understood how damaged Claire had been when she arrived and had encouraged her relationship with Glen from the start.

Anna had also made her realise that just being herself was enough and had encouraged her to throw caution to the wind and just have fun.

It was time to face the next chapter of her life. This bit was totally unscripted.

GINA

Now THAT SHE HAD made her decision to stay in Antigua, Gina had allowed herself to get excited about her new life in the sun. Dan laughed as he watched her dance around the outside deck as she began to move her few possessions into his house.

He had cleared out the closet in the guest room and they had decided to paint the whole of the inside of the villa a soft powder blue.

'It's a house on the sea; I really think blue walls would be lovely.' Dan didn't care what she did, he was just happy she was going to be with him.

'You go ahead honey; it's going to be your home too.'

She had taken him at his word and had asked if he minded her adding a few touches to the interior styling too.

Dan had agreed, saying he wanted her to be happy. He had inherited the furniture with the house and he was cool about her doing as she wished.

He had driven her to a designer outlet where she splashed out on some amazing pale blue cashmere throws, turquoise cushions, and a set of beautiful white bedding. She also picked out a huge coir rug. She was sure her new purchases would transform the space.

She could not resist buying a few oversized white wooden lanterns which would look great lit up at night. She could hardly wait to get back to play house!

They had got into an easy routine of meeting up most days, sometimes heading out in the boat for a lazy day at sea, sometimes staying local. They walked on the beach, swam and enjoyed spending the odd meal or two with the girls on their beachside terrace.

One night she had insisted Dan leave her to spend time with her friends and they had enjoyed an alfresco barbeque on the beach.

'I have to pinch myself; this is so amazing. I can't believe that I am going to be living here. It's just too good to be true.'

Deep down Anna could not help but think back to her early days as a journalist when one of her mentors had said that if something seems too good to be true, chances are it is.

But she stayed silent. Her friend was so happy and she wasn't going to burst that bubble. And she had her own life to sort out. She still hadn't responded to the email from Piers because for once she didn't have a clue what to say to him.

Making her excuses, Anna said she needed an early night. In truth she hadn't been able to settle since his email had popped into her inbox. Every day she changed her mind about what she wanted to say. Her emotions were all over the place, but Jesse's words had made an impact. Maybe it was worth giving him the chance to talk at least.

RICHARD

RICHARD HAD MOPED ABOUT the villa for an hour or so after Laura had made her speedy exit. He had poured himself a beer and sat by the pool but he was restless and bored. He decided that maybe it was time to pay a visit to the quay and see if his little waitress was up for some fun.

He showered and changed into his cream linen shorts and a pale blue shirt and was about to ring for the car when the doorbell rang. It was an insistent buzz and he felt irritated by it.

When he answered the door, he recognised it was their limousine driver Kenton, but for once he was not smiling broadly as he normally did when he called to pick them up.

'Hi Kenton, I was just about to call you I need a lift to St John ... you have saved me the call.'

'Sir, I would like to say this is a social call. But I am afraid I need you to settle this before I can take you anywhere.'

He held out a buff envelope and Richard felt slightly uneasy as he opened it. It was a bill, a very large bill.

'What is this, Kenton? I thought Laura was sorting this out, she told me she had an account with your company?'

'Well yes Sir, she does, but she called earlier to say that you were settling this for her.' Richard could only stare in horror at the statement that showed they owed more than £10,000 for Kenton's services over the past few weeks.

'But this is not right, Laura is due back in a week or two so can we sort this all out when she gets back?'

'I'm afraid the account has been closed. From what I can tell she has no intention of coming back next week, or ever for that matter.'

Richard was visibly shocked and he was struggling to process exactly what was happening.

'This invoice includes a number of things I am not responsible for, Kenton. There are invoices for beauty salons and a long list of boutique purchases that had nothing to do with me.'

But Kenton just shrugged. 'We often pick up items for Laura and usually she settles her account on her departure, this time she told us that you had kindly agreed to pick up the tab for her.' Richard looked at the list and noted that all the clothes and jewellery gifts to him were included alongside the many goodies Laura had treated herself to.

Had he been such a good liar she had been taken in and thought he could foot this bill for her?

Kenton refused to budge and just fixed Richard with a cold stare. He added, using a menacing tone, 'Richard my boss does not take kindly to people who do not pay their bills.'

'But the house, she lives here half the year. And what about her staff? I don't understand. I was her house guest, no more. I really don't think this is right.'

He was bewildered. Then a terrible cold fear gripped his insides as Kenton opened the door to point out an elderly couple waiting in the limousine.

'This is Esther and Frank Carr; they own this place and Laura had a rental on it. They had to come back a few days early which is why I called Laura, to give her some notice. The housekeeping crew are due in shortly so once you have settled my bill – oh and the rental account, she said you would pay for that too – you can make your exit. Laura said you would be moving on once she had left.'

A second invoice was thrust into his hand and he slumped into the nearest chair. This bill was for £25,000. If he paid this it would clean him out!

'Can you just give me a moment to call Laura? I think there has been a mistake, Kenton. I am sure she can sort this out very quickly.'

He made his voice sound calmer than he felt because inside he was seething. It was all beginning to make sense, the way she had him picking up the tab for everything, a bloody limousine on tap. Running up massive food and booze bills. What a bloody idiot he had been! He thought he was playing her along but she had been playing him!

Kenton had the good grace to look down and walk back to the car. For the next few minutes Richard tried to call Laura.

It came as no surprise to him when the mobile number Laura had given him to call her when she got back to the States was unavailable.

'You bitch! I will find you, don't think you can make a fool out of me!' he screamed down the phone despite knowing that it was certainly not connecting to Laura.

Laura had really stitched him up and if he did have to pick up the tab for the last month, he was broke.

There was nothing for it but to go to the bank and see what was left of the money Claire had deposited in his account.

Two hours later he was in a bar in St John with exactly £200 to his name; not even enough to get him onto a plane home. Taking a deep breath, he took out his phone and dialled Phil's number. He hoped that Phil would forget that last meeting when they had argued and he had said that he'd had enough.

'Phil it's me, it's Richard. Look I know we had a fall out but I am in a real mess and I promise you this is the last time I will ask you to bail me out. I am in Antigua and ...'.

He didn't get a chance to say another word. The phone suddenly went dead. He was on his own.

A couple of hours and a few beers later Richard found himself sitting at the bar staring at the pretty young waitress who he decided might just be the one to help him.

She did just that as it turned out, but not in the way he was expecting.

'Hey mister, good to see you again.' Richard smiled thinking things might be OK after all. But after a few moments a young, muscle-bound hunk bounded into the bar and swept her up, covering her with kisses.

He suddenly felt very old and tired and the enormity of his stupidity enveloped him. He looked up and saw a sign asking for casual bar help.

Well, if that was the only way home, bring it on.

'Excuse me miss, I would like to apply for the bar tender's job. I make pretty good cocktails and I am quite experienced.'

In fact, until he had met Laura, he had never made a cocktail in his life and the only bar experience he had was propping one up every weekend at his local!

A tall, slightly menacing man came out from the back room and sized him up.

'OK mister, you look the part but how about we start you off in the back, there's a heap of dishes and our usual guy didn't turn up.'

He thought of his plans to live in a brownstone in New York. How had this gone so badly wrong?

There was no time to think as he was ushered into the grimy kitchen, and a grubby apron was thrust upon him. He looked miserably at the mountain of greasy plates all caked in stale leftovers. He wanted to cry. He wondered how many dishes he was going to have to wash before he could afford a one-way ticket home.

'Hey man, you gonna just stare at them, do you want the job or not?'

He looked down at his linen shorts which were now smeared with streaks of guacamole and dark soy sauce and for a moment he longed to be back home. He fleetingly wondered if later he could call Martha. Maybe she would give him a second chance.

LAURA

As she prepared to land in London, Laura De Lisle smiled secretly to herself. She applied her lipstick and started collecting her belongings from the seat pocket in First Class.

She had received a call at the airport from Kenton telling her that the plan had worked perfectly. They had pocketed more than £40,000. Not a bad return for just three weeks putting up with Richard's vain bullshit.

All she had to do now was pay the old couple a few hundred dollars for pretending to be the owners of the villa. They often stepped in and helped her. And of course, she had to pay her contact at the estate agency. The girl had given her the heads up that the villa was free for a couple of months and she was keen to keep her happy. Kenton also took a large cut but he was an integral part of the scam. She could not do it without him. The girl in the agency often helped Laura out but this villa had surpassed all expectations – and she thought smiling to herself, so had Richard.

She and Kenton were in a partnership and she made the trip out there a few times a year. It depended on what scams she had going on at home and which villas she could get hold of. But this time she had really hit the jackpot. The sex was incredible too which had been a bonus. Usually, her stings involved elderly Americans with fat wallets and limp dicks so Richard was a first.

She normally picked her men up on the beach or in resort bars but Richard had jumped on the hook as soon as they had taken off from Gatwick. She had occasionally made a connection mid-air, but never like this. He was sexy, he was loaded and he took the bait so fast.

It was a pity she had to cut things short. Pete had a big sting he needed her for in London. While she had tried to buy more time in Antigua, he said she had to come back. He was her husband after all.

She also had the bracelet and earrings to sell on, so if she was lucky this trip would prove to be her most successful so far. She had not meant to pick up a punter on the plane, but had thought 'why not?' Richard was attractive enough and with all his talk of his job and what he owned she had felt it might be worth her while buttering him up a bit. He was so vain and gullible.

He had forked out for so much she could hardly believe her luck. When she landed Laura (aka Sandra Lewis, mother of two from Woking) smiled and thought how she could afford to leave it a few months before her next trip out there. She had enjoyed playing the role of a rich NYC cougar, but it was tough keeping up the accent and she couldn't wait to get home, see the kids, and buy everyone some fish and chips. All that fancy food and fizzy champagne was OK for a while but she longed for a chippie tea and a mug of PG Tips. As for Richard, he only had himself to blame. He thought she was an ageing, desperate New Yorker. Idiot! Maybe she had taught him a life lesson.

ANNA

AFTER READING AND RE-READING the email from Piers, Anna thought it was now or never to attempt a reply.

She hadn't written anything for nearly two months. Back at home she wrote daily leader columns for the paper, fired off hundreds of emails and created complex strategic policies for all her department heads without giving it a thought. Now a blank email stared back at her. So, let the fingers do the talking ...

Hi Piers,

I hadn't expected to hear from you and even now I really don't know how I feel about anything. My time away has given me some head space and I feel very different about a lot of things. I know I have changes to make. But I have no idea about my next move and seeing you might just complicate things even further. As you know, my work life is not exactly settled either.

But I agree that we should talk if nothing else to draw a line. I will email you my return flight details and if you wish, you can meet me. I don't feel able to see you at home, so maybe the airport is as good a place as anywhere. I have no plans and no real place to be. I travel very light these days. That's all I have to say.

Anna

CLAIRE

CLAIRE HAD AGREED TO meet Glen at his house as she always loved to walk along the beach to his mansion. It was a beautiful evening and he had asked her to make sure she made it to the house in time to see the sunset.

She lingered on the shoreline breathing in the smell of the sea, enjoying the peace. She had grown to love this place and though she missed Harriet and her house, she hated the thought of leaving Jolly Beach. As she reached the house Glen greeted her on the terrace. She smiled as she took in his handsome face and toned physique.

'Hi, my beautiful girl. Come here and sit with me for a while and watch the sun go down.' He had a table laid out with a silver champagne bucket and two crystal flutes. There was an impressive seafood platter with an array of side dishes and soft warm rolls with curls of golden butter. He had also made a fresh fruit salad with heaps of mango and pineapple which he knew she loved.

'You said keep it simple so I just rustled up a few things, I hope it's OK.'

'Where I come from this is anything but simple! You have gone to so much trouble and you really shouldn't have.'

Claire looked into his kind eyes and then she looked away, dreading what she was about to say next. Instead, he made it very easy for her.

'Let's take a stroll across the bay, it makes it easier to talk – at least that's what my late wife always said. I hope you don't mind me mentioning her but she was a lot like you, so very kind. I know what you have come to say. You can't be with me. You are a young mother, and a very beautiful one I might add, and you have a whole different life back at home.

I realise that. I am too old for you. Why would you want an old beat-up crate like me? But Claire you know I love you and all I want to do is make you happy.'

'Oh Glen, you have it so wrong. I would love to be able to stay here with you, I have never felt happier or more content about everything but I do have to go home and find out who I am. When I was home, I was so lost, sad and so depressed. I was not a good mother or a good daughter and I hate who I was. I need to make up for all that lost time and decide who I am now, and what I need to be happy in future.

'I don't know what will happen between us, but I don't regret one moment with you. Who knows, maybe in time we can work something out? The world is a much smaller place these days and, if it's meant to be … I just want to thank you, that's all. I owe you so much for reminding me about what it's like to feel cared for and appreciated. I think I am in love with you, but out here it is so easy to just fall into this amazing, beautiful life. I must go home and see what is real. Does that sound crazy?'

She pulled him to her and she kissed him long and hard.

Glen took her hand and kissed it.

'You owe me nothing. You are such a special girl; I don't want you to ever forget that OK? Until you came into my life, I had given up without even realising it. Promise me that one day you will at least ask yourself if I could fit into your world or you could consider fitting into mine. I am going nowhere; you know where I am. I would do anything to make it work, and I want to look after you and Harriet. I think she might enjoy life out here. I have even thought about maybe buying one of the villas near here as a guest bungalow for your folks when they visit, a sort of second home for them. But I figure it's all a bit too soon to be talking like that and I get it. The last thing I want to do is frighten you off. There, I have said, it that's all I want to say.'

Silently they fell in step and headed back to the house.

Glen finally broke the silence as they arrived back on the terrace.

'I realise you are leaving but hey, you won't be going home tonight my darling. So, let's make the most of the time we have together and not waste any more of it sitting out here.'

He led her inside not trusting himself to stay out on the terrace because in the champagne bucket he had concealed a black velvet box with the largest emerald and diamond ring he could find. He had intended proposing and giving her the ring at sunset in the hope that the emerald flash made an appearance. But the look on her face as she had walked along the beach toward him was enough for him to know this was not the time or the place. He had to hope that someday there would be a time and a place.

PIERS

FOR THE PAST FEW weeks Piers had kept himself busy organising the purchase of *The Folly* and finally he had the key. He had stayed in the nearby pub which was a four-minute walk from the house which had allowed him to meet lots of locals and make some new friends already.

He felt very at home there and he was on first name terms with Ged the publican and his straight-talking wife Pam. Once he had their approval the whole community seemed to take him into their fold.

This evening he was having supper with Frank and Moira. They owned a garden centre nearby and they had promised to help him sort his new garden, not that it needed much TLC. But they were so friendly he didn't want to refuse.

His new drinking partner was Barney, the local farrier. He was newly divorced so the pair had bonded over a few pints. They met regularly and he already trusted this tall, strong, ox of a man who thought the best of everyone.

Piers was also a hit with Frances who ran the Post Office which doubled as a general store and she enjoyed filling him in on all the gossip. It might have seemed a sleepy hamlet but he was fast learning that there was an undercurrent of sexual tension between quite a few of the pub regulars. Frances did not hold back. She enjoyed regaling him with some of the antics she had witnessed in the pub snug.

'It's not as if there is any wife swapping going on or anything Piers, but let's just say there are a lot of partners turning a blind eye.'

Piers wasn't sure how he felt about that. He kept thinking of the mess he had created by dipping his toes into the pool of infidelity and he had no wish to repeat the experience.

He cut Frances short and quickly changed the subject by saying that he was sure it was all just harmless fun. He decided he would rethink her offer of sending her daughter Mary in each week to do a bit of cleaning.

Frances had been insistent: 'She doesn't drive but I can drop her off and we can have a catch up while she does her bit for a couple of hours.'

The thought of having to put up with her prattle each week was not one he felt he could cope with, and what if Anna ...

Frances was the sort of person who would drive her up the wall too. Anna didn't do gossip and he knew what she would say to Frances if she tried to bend her ear.

He had been careful not to tell anyone too much about his past. For now, they were happy to know that he was some kind of writer and that he planned to live in the village for most of the year. Everyone knew *The Folly* and they seemed happy that Piers had bought it.

Frances confided that the previous owners had not been popular.

'Proper stuck up she was, thought she was above the rest of us, and as for him, well he never had a word for anyone. Rumour is they are selling up because she's made him go back to Canada, she never really settled in.'

Holding that thought Piers said he really had to get back as he had emails to check. He didn't but he wondered if he should check just in case Anna had replied. It had been a couple of weeks or more since he had sent his email and he was beginning to wonder if he would ever hear from her.

He walked slowly across the village green, once again struck by how beautiful the village was.

Arriving at his front door he smiled when he pulled out the oversized door key. Every time he walked into the house, he marvelled at how at home he felt. The pale flagged flooring, the cosy sofa in front of the fire in the snug, it was all beyond anything he could have ever imagined buying.

The previous owners had left behind enough furniture for him to be able to move in with just a few essentials. He had bought some beautiful white bedding and towels, a few kitchen appliances, pots, pans and masses of cream church candles, Anna's favourite. Well, you never knew.

He had seen some of the colourful rag rugs that Anna had so loved in the local haberdashery store and he had invested in a few to scatter over the flagstones. They looked incredible.

The village had a popular second-hand shop too and he had surprised himself by buying an old pine rocking chair, an ornate over mantle mirror and a goldfish bowl style vase.

He had lots of flowers in his garden and as soon as he got home, he headed out and picked some late blooming blue hydrangeas to fill it. Suddenly he enjoyed being a home maker.

There was a beautiful rocking horse at the back of the shop that was crying out to be renovated but he stopped himself from buying it, even though he kept imagining a tiny red-haired toddler playing on it.

'Am I losing the plot?' Yes, he was!

He had also enjoyed filling the fridge and the pantry. In the past couple of months since he cut his ties with Jane, he had rediscovered the joy of cooking.

He would put *The Great British Bake Off* on TV and make a few mental notes of things he would try out at the weekend. Who was he suddenly? But he loved his new home and he was desperate for Anna to see it. He could only pray that one day she would.

He had intended rustling up a stir fry for his supper but when he opened his laptop, he saw that there was a message flashing in his inbox. He had marked Anna's email address so that should she reply there was a red light flashing on his desktop. She had replied!

He was half afraid to open it up. What if she refused to meet? Fool he thought, just bloody open it!

Moments later he was beaming. She wasn't exactly enthusiastic about seeing him, and it looked as though she was only going to give him a brief audience on her way through the airport, but at least she had agreed to talk.

His heart lifted and he let out a huge breath that he hadn't realised he was holding while he had read her reply.

So, he was going to meet Anna. She was sending her flight details, and by his reckoning that must be quite soon. At this point he was smiling broadly.

He had some thinking to do and he had to make some plans. But first he needed to talk to Barney. Picking up his mobile he sent a very short text.

Meet me in the pub in 10? Pie and pint on me!

JESSE

WHEN SHE LOOKED AT the time Jesse could not believe that she had been sketching for three hours. It seemed like only minutes had passed since she sat at the kitchen island and started putting her ideas on paper.

She spread out the sheets of paper and her colourful drawings made her heart soar.

She had created a Caribbean style 40th birthday party for the *Strictly* lady and she had also come up with a fantastic 50's retro wedding theme for the footballer and his soon to be model wife.

She felt stiff and tired from sitting for too long, with her head bent over her designs, but it felt good to be working on ideas again and she felt the clouds in her head were clearing. She had decided it was time to head back. Her business needed her and at least she would have some control over her financial future.

She would talk to Anna later and see what she thought about flying home in a week or so. She knew she was ready.

She let her mind drift to how things had worked out for each of the group. Every one of them in their way had grown, had processed what they had been through and had healed or at least started to heal.

Gina was like a different woman, so happy and excited to be moving in with the gorgeous Dan. He had literally turned her world upside down and Jesse was glad that for once feisty Anna had been wrong about him.

Gina was moving into the harbourside villa at the weekend, although she spent most of her time there already. The girls didn't mind though. They knew Gina could hardly bear to have him out of her sight and who could blame her?

Claire had surprised them all when she returned early this morning to say that she had decided it was time to fly back. She and Glen had talked it over and he realised she needed to be her own person.

'Maybe he was just meant to be my transition man, you know, the one that gets you over the heartbreak.'

But neither Jesse nor Anna who were having a coffee on the terrace when she arrived, were buying that. They seemed such a great couple and secretly Anna thought that Glen might have planned to formalise things before Claire headed off.

But they knew Claire had finally found herself and was at peace with who she was. So, who could blame her for wanting to embrace this newfound feeling of self-worth?

'I like the idea of being on my own. I no longer need a man to complete me. Richard had me thinking that I couldn't be without a man, but he was wrong, I know I am very happy being just me,' she told them.

'Glen is wonderful but I am not just jumping into his life. I want to go home to Harriet and just enjoy being a family. I relied on Stevie, then I fell into my marriage with Bloody Richard. I am in no hurry to be in another serious relationship any time soon.'

She insisted they leave it at that and she hurried off to start sorting out her laundry as she planned to do some packing.

'I seem to have so many more clothes than when I arrived, but that's down to you Anna!' They all laughed as Claire headed off. Anna, Jesse decided, was harder to figure out.

They all knew that Piers had been in touch and that he wanted to talk, but she had been very closed about how she was going to play that one.

'I will wait and see and how I feel when we meet,' is all she would say. But her friends knew she was a woman who always had a plan. She was usually so organised, but maybe this time she was simply going with the flow.

Anna and Jesse decided they would fly back together. Claire was heading off on Sunday so the girls opted for the Tuesday afternoon flight.

'Once Gina has moved out, we can organise the cleaners to come in then we can finalise things,' said Jesse, who was now in full organisation mode.

She went to her room to fetch her laptop so she could email the letting agents and give them their departure details.

She noted that Milly had sent her an email and she felt guilty that she had never called her back.

She opened the email, expecting to see a rant about tricky brides or problems at the shop but her eyes almost popped out of her head when she saw the subject matter.

SAM WANTS TO SEE YOU

She sat down and read the email over and over again.

She headed back to the kitchen where Anna was doing her morning barre workout with her online community back in London.

Her toned back, legs and incredible bum were a testament to her fixation with her 45-minute total body workout. Jesse knew not to interrupt her; she was obsessive about her regime and insisted that it kept her mind clear too.

After she had finished, she joined Jesse on the terrace and instinctively she knew that something was troubling her friend.

'Hi there, you OK?'

Jesse looked up and smiled but said nothing in reply. 'I need a swim after that sweat session, fancy joining me?'

Moments later the pair had walked to their preferred spot at the far right of the bay, where the wind and waves had sculpted out a series of natural lagoons. It was still very early but already the sun was quite strong and the women enjoyed falling into the sea to cool off.

Anna and Jesse swam far out and said nothing to each other for quite a while.

Anna lay back and just floated looking at the cloudless blue sky, happy to enjoy the moment.

Then she flipped over and swam towards Jesse who was heading back to shore.

'OK, so give it to me, what's going on with you?'

Jesse sat on the shoreline letting the waves wash over her feet and Anna sat beside her. They were both a vision. Tanned, toned and in very different ways, striking and beautiful.

The Antiguan sun had dusted both of them with a light tan and they looked healthy and carefree but Anna had a nose for trouble and it was sitting right next to her.

Jesse took a deep breath and said that Anna must be a witch.

'How do you know something is wrong?'

She laughed but Anna was not going to let her off the hook. 'So, tell me, what has suddenly got into you? Yesterday you were buzzing, firing on all cylinders creating story boards for those events you have coming up and now you look like someone who has just lost their last dollar.'

Jesse carried on silently looking out to sea.

Anna refused to break the silence. Her years as a journalist had taught her not to.

Whoever breaks the silence first will dish!

And as if on cue, Jesse turned to her and repeated almost word for word the email she had received from Milly.

'So, that's a good thing surely?'

'But is it? He let me down so badly and I don't know why he wants to talk to me. Maybe he is suggesting I could his bit on the side? He's married now, what on earth have we got to talk about?'

Anna laughed. 'Look it's no different than Piers and me. He hurt me more than anyone will ever know, but despite all that I have to see him. If nothing else to put it to rest.

OK, so this Sam guy hasn't laid it on the line but from what you told me about Milly and how she had your back, I suspect he must have something pretty important to tell you. She wouldn't be setting you up for a fall, would she?'

Jesse agreed, she hadn't really thought of that. Milly had seen the state she had been in when she had begged her to help her out so that she could come out here.

'Maybe you are right, perhaps I should call him.'

'I am often right, that's been my problem!' But pride was stopping Jesse from taking that leap of faith. He had hurt her; she would not be weak. She was not going to call him.

GINA

IT TOOK GINA BARELY an hour to move into Dan's villa. He said she should now consider it her home too. She pulled the voile panels open so that she could look out to the sea and the entrance to the marina. It was such an amazing view. All day long there was a flotilla of motor cruisers and sailing boats gliding past and she felt like she was in a dream.

How lucky was she? Dan said he had some photographs to file for a freelance job he had taken on, so he suggested she took the time to unpack and make herself comfortable in her new home.

The new purchases she had made at the designer store had helped her put her stamp on the place too. They were eating with the girls tonight as it was Claire's last evening and Glen was joining them. It was going to be a bittersweet occasion, but she hoped that it wasn't the last time they would meet up as a group.

When Dan finally made it back, they sat on the deck for a while and watched as the light faded before they jumped into the jeep and drove to South Finger.

Dan was unusually quiet but Gina figured that he had been up since 6am. He had also been super busy working hard to file his pictures at an office he used in St John.

They arrived at the house to be greeted by the whole gang who were in high spirits and already sipping champagne cocktails.

Claire looked amazing and had decided to go all out glam with her off-the-shoulder red satin dress. A clearly besotted Glen could hardly take his eyes off her.

'Glen insists that dinner is on him tonight and he's booked a table for us at Miracles for about eight if that suits you?'

Everyone was happy to go with the flow and the night seemed to fly by. The evening was relaxed and fun and none of the girls wanted it to end. As Dan headed for the jeep at midnight Claire followed Gina out. She pulled her into her arms and hugged her. 'I am going to miss you so much; promise you will call and text. The girls are sorting out a WhatsApp group and we can do some Zoom meetings when you are all settled in.' Claire had tears in her eyes as she waved goodbye but not before she made Gina promise to come and stay with her when she came back to England.

'I have to come back in a month or so as there are some legal things to tie up with the divorce and the house sale. I won't make this a long-drawn-out goodbye and I will most definitely stay with you. I want to meet Harriet and check out that beautiful house of yours.'

Dan said very little on the drive back and he wrapped her in his arms when they went to bed. She had been a bit teary and said it was going to be even harder when Anna and Jesse left in a few days' time.

'These women have been like family to me, I am going to miss them all so much.' He stroked her hair and said he understood.

'But you have me now pretty lady, so get some sleep as we have a busy day tomorrow.' Much later she woke up to find the bed empty and she could just make out the silhouette of Dan sitting out on the deck. He was swigging a beer and smoking, something she had not seen him do before. Dan had seemed troubled earlier and she stopped herself from going out to him. He looked like he needed some space; she would just have to wait until he felt ready to tell her what was worrying him.

CLAIRE

CLAIRE HAD INSISTED SHE didn't want or need anyone to go to the airport with her, but Glen said she could not stop him.

'If you don't let me drive you, I will just follow your taxi, so what's the point?!'

She laughed and conceded but was insistent that they did not have emotional goodbyes.

'We are going to Facetime each other a lot. Let's just see how things go, OK?' He agreed and squeezed her hand all the way to the airport. He helped with her luggage and stayed with her until she had to go through to departures. They both had tears in their eyes as he gave her a final kiss. He then handed her two red velvet boxes, one slightly larger than the other.

'Please just put these in your purse and open them when you are on the plane.'

Even if she had known what to say, at this point she couldn't trust herself to speak. She just held him tight again and drank in the sight of this broad, handsome man who had come to mean so much to her.

Silently she walked away and raised her hand in a final wave until the escalator took her up to the next floor and out of sight. Later as she counted down the hours before she would arrive back to reality, she took out the velvet boxes and looked inside them. In the smaller box there was a tiny silver shell bracelet for Harriet and in the larger box a slim gold bangle with a single emerald clasp.

On the inside of the bangle, he had had the words inscribed 'Always know I love you'. There was a tiny card inside the box and he had written that she was incredible, had brought him back to life and no matter what happened he would always be happy to have known her.

'You are an exotic creature, so know your worth and don't ever settle for less again.'

Only then did she allow her tears to fall.

ANNA

AFTER GIVING JESSE A firm talking to, Anna decided that she would text Piers her arrival time. They would be arriving in Gatwick at 10am and Anna had not made any firm plans. She intended talking with Piers then maybe getting hold of Frank to see how things had panned out in her absence.

She could order the work taxi to pick her up but she had felt almost detached from that part of her life. She would see how the chat with Piers went, then she would get the train and go home. After that, well she didn't have a clue. She still had the option of the *Loose Women* try out but she didn't know how she felt about that. Everything was up in the air and, for once, she didn't care.

JESSE

Since she had received the email from Milly, Jesse had found it hard to think about anything other than whether she should call Sam.

She was annoyed with herself for letting him occupy so much head space.

As much as she was still angry with him part of her was desperate to know why he wanted to talk to her so urgently. She decided that as she was due to go back home soon, she would leave it until she could have a proper talk with Milly.

Her message had been a little cryptic and she didn't really have a clue as to what was going on. There was packing to do and Anna had suggested a few drinks at the beach bar later so they could say their goodbyes to Gina. It felt weird leaving her behind but they knew she was happy with Dan, and you couldn't blame her for giving it a try. It wasn't too hard a life out here! She had a hot man, and she was living harbourside in a beautiful quirky villa with the sea literally on her doorstep. Gina had also made contacts with a view to a job with one of the local realtors. It was all falling into place for her and Jesse felt happy for her friend. Sometimes you can have a happy ending.

Later as the group assembled at Castaways, Glen arrived and insisted on buying everyone cocktails. Gina was looking incredible. She had adopted a hippie beach look and had taken to wearing flowing cotton skirts, braids in her sun kissed hair and was usually barefoot. Her new life didn't even call for flip flops!

Gina looked down at her outfit and laughed. 'I know I look like a beach bum, but I love it. I live in shorts and bikinis, but I promise when I get my job sorted, I will sort my wardrobe out. I might even wear shoes!'

Everyone laughed. Dan, she said, was running late.

He told her he was on an important job today. Lately he had been spending more and more time in the office in St

John, but he promised her that when the girls left, he would be around more. 'We are now promoting the new daily charters, so we expect to be busy soon. I have been spending some time with Bonnie, the chef from Miracles. Dan got her to agree to give me a crash course on some simple Antiguan dishes that I can prepare ahead of the charters. I am quite the domestic goddess these days.'

Dan finally joined them at 11pm, apologising for being so late; but he seemed ill at ease to be there and was eager to take Gina home. By that time the party was beginning to break up anyway as the girls had an early start the next day. Gina joined in a group hug, finding it hard to let go. 'I am going to miss you guys so much. You are like sisters to me. I had no idea how hard saying goodbye was going to be.' They both hugged her back and said that they were only a phone call away. Jesse looked in the direction of Dan who was revving up the Jeep and Gina realised it was time to go.

'Look, let's say our goodbyes now. I can't face another emotional session in the morning, can you?' Jesse agreed. 'Anyhow, depending on how things go with the handsome hunk over there who knows? You may need my services for a wedding bouquet sometime soon, so I will be back!'

They laughed and reluctantly Gina walked away from them towards the man who had opened a whole new life for her.

That night Anna found it impossible to sleep and she stayed out on the terrace for hours, wondering what she was going to find when she got home. She had felt so safe here, but life had to go on. Dawn was almost breaking over the beach when she finally went to her room, where she lay on her bed replaying so many things that had happened during their stay.

She was going home a happier, more relaxed woman. Her priorities had totally changed. She realised it had taken her nearly 35 years to be open to the joys of having a girl gang in her life. Who would have thought it?

She realised that she had a lot to tell Piers. Most of all she wanted him to know that she was no longer someone who wanted to be a tough talking iceberg, with no need of friends. She hated leaving Jolly Beach but most of all she was dreading not seeing the girls.

Two hours later Denzil turned up, insisting that it was his goodbye gift to take to them to the airport and see them safely on the plane.

They sat quietly as the people carrier left the beach and headed out toward the airport.

Denzil tried to engage them with his friendly banter but after a few minutes he gave up. He had seen this countless times. People arrived in Antigua stressed out but very quickly they switched into Caribbean mode and became laidback, stress-free versions of themselves. He could tell that neither of his passengers was happy to be leaving this easy way of living behind.

When they arrived at the airport it was a mass of new arrivals. They were pale and excited, queuing for taxis and desperate to get out of their travelling gear and hit the beach.

As a surprise, Anna had upgraded Jesse's return flight home. They were delighted to find themselves whisked through departures and into a small select gang of VIP First Class passengers who were boarded ahead of everyone else.

'Wow, it's a full flight. I am so grateful for the upgrade Anna. I don't think I could have coped with cattle class I feel so bloody miserable.'

Anna didn't reply but she felt the same.

On the aircraft they turned left to the oversized leather seats with cellophane wrapped cashmere blankets and a zipped silk goodie bag containing complimentary toiletries and chocolates.

They both busied themselves settling into their seats, happily accepting the welcome glass of French champagne and briefly checking out their travelling companions.

There were only about ten people in their section so they knew they could relax and spread out.

The Virgin Cabin Services Director came over to introduce herself and told them that she would be looking after them for the duration of the flight.

They each accepted another glass of champagne and looked at the leather-bound menu card which promised a delicious brunch, followed not too many hours later by a fabulous four course dinner. There was also a large selection of the latest movies and they both agreed that they would check one out to pass the time. As the aircraft took off Anna raised her glass to Jesse and suggested they make a toast. Anna had always loved the experience of being suspended between two worlds. Who knew what the future held for all of them? These three strangers, whom she had not known two months ago, now meant the world to her and she really cared about what happened to each of them. The island started to fall back into the distance and Anna decided there was only one toast she could make. 'To new beginnings for all of us.'

PIERS

Piers woke up with a start. It felt like the middle of the night and it almost was. He knew he had a long drive ahead of him and this was one appointment he did not want to be late for.

Anna had texted him her arrival time and suggested they meet in the coffee spot to the right of the arrivals gate. There would be crowds of people so it was a no-frills venue for people simply passing through. He knew it was going to be a difficult meeting and no venue would have made it easier.

He hoped he would find the right words and at least claim enough of her time for her to see how very sorry he was, and how much he still loved her. It was a bleak reunion but it was better than nothing.

The day before he had been wracked with nerves. How did he play it? Should he take flowers? Was a welcome banner too much? Of course, it bloody well was! Should he look pained or hold out his arms and stand there looking at her adoringly? Both felt like scenes from the worst rom-com and she hated rom-coms!

He decided to get there very early, find a corner table and be in a spot that allowed him to see her come through Arrivals. It was an emotional minefield. He hadn't seen Anna in almost three months. So much had changed for him. He knew a little of what had changed for Anna, but he prayed she had not hooked up with some amazing guy in Antigua. His worst nightmare was for her to walk through Arrivals on the arm of some muscly Adonis.

Now on the motorway heading for Gatwick, his thoughts were whirring around like a washing machine.

'Just stop this! I am driving myself mad!' he said out loud, realising how close to the edge of sanity he really was. This meeting was so important to him and he was at a loss to guess how it would go.

He put on Radio 4 in a bid to distract himself. Unfortunately, it was a *Women's Hour* special on life after infidelity. He decided it wasn't what he needed to listen to, and neither was *The Archers*. Since when had there been so many people having affairs in Ambridge? *Gardeners' Question Time* also failed to distract him. Who bloody cared if your dahlias had earwigs and your mulch was too smelly?

He finally tuned into Radio 1 where his senses were bombarded by some head-banging garage music, performed by a multi-millionaire moron who had a name that sounded like a root vegetable.

He turned off the radio. He knew he was getting older when he found Radio 1 a challenge! It was a sign; he'd read that in *GQ* magazine.

He put his foot on the accelerator so he would get to the airport early. He had to plan what he was going to say, and this was a pitch he had to get right. His future pretty much depended upon it.

As he took the Gatwick turn off his stomach was doing cartwheels but at least he would soon know where he stood. He shuddered when he thought back to those final days living with Jane, in what was only one level above a squat. He thought of *The Folly*; his forever home which cried out for a family to live in it and make it a happy place.

Silently he prayed that when he drove back up to it later today, he would not be alone.

JESSE

THE FLIGHT HAD STARTED off well and the girls enjoyed unwrapping their goodies in the complimentary travel bag. There was even a mini Jo Malone candle. Who would give something like that away for free?

Jesse had drunk too many freebie glasses of champagne ahead of dinner, but she managed a power nap and sobered up when the cabin services director placed a sumptuous feast in front of her. There was silver cutlery and linen napkins and a comprehensive wine list to accompany the four-course dinner.

Jesse ordered a delicious avocado and crab cocktail, followed by beef medallions with side orders of fresh green beans and sauté potatoes. Anna had opted for salmon fillets with a side salad. She had managed a sorbet but cried off a pudding, admitting that she felt too nervous to eat much.

Jesse went full pelt and ordered an Eton Mess, the most delicious combination of chewy, toffee flavoured meringue, ice-cream and chocolate fudge sauce topped with candied nuts. Amazing!

Although she was full to bursting, she was then offered a large cheese platter, along with a carafe of the most incredible port wine. At least Anna grudgingly agreed to share this – and finished off most of the port.

It was no surprise that Jesse nodded off almost immediately after coffee was served. She had intended starting the box set of *The Crown*. Everyone had raved over the mini-series, but she had lost interest in TV and not seen it. But the combination of a full tummy and too much alcohol had proved too much. When she awoke, she realised four hours had passed and Anna had left her seat.

Moments later she saw her striding through the cabin and the look on her face clearly indicated something was very wrong.

Anna was holding a national newspaper and there on the front cover was a full colour photograph of herself walking out of the sea 'à la Halle Berry' under the banner headline:

ANNA'S SAD SECRET

The strapline revealed:

'Globe boss flying home to face the music after love life and career plummet.'

The writer claimed to have tracked her down to a mystery address in Antigua, where Anna had talked about her heartache and how the sun and sea had helped her heal.

'What a load of bullshit! That snake, why would he do this?'

Jesse could only gawp as Anna threw the trashy tabloid onto her lap to reveal a four-page colour spread. It featured photographs of Anna on their private terrace, in a variety of swimsuits on the beach and a montage of shots of the girls having a barbeque and enjoying cocktails at Castaways. Worst of all, enjoying a last goodbye dinner with Glen and the girls.

The article included amazingly accurate details about the two-month sojourn, together with information about all of Anna's travelling companions. There were a few juicy snippets about nights out at Jolly's bars and hints of romance being on the cards. It concluded that Anna had 'healed her heartache in the warm waters of the Caribbean but was now flying home to sort out her career and a very tangled love life.'

The journalist spoke of how the girls had all found excitement in the resort and revealed that Anna planned a make-or-break talk with her ex-lover on her return.

For good measure there was an inset photograph of Piers and a brief description of his affair with bloody Jane.

Jesse looked from the newspaper to Anna and she groaned out loud.

'Oh my God, those photographs! We both know who took most of those, don't we? How on earth would that journo know all those stories about us? They are things we have discussed as a group, but nobody else would know this stuff.'

Suddenly a lot of small things added up and made sense at last. Jesse thought of the night they saw a photographer staking out the house. Of how distracted Dan had been during the last couple of days. She also remembered how Gina had said he had been working on a project with one of his colleagues in St John. It suddenly all fell into place and Jesse felt sick.

He had sold them out, hadn't he!

Slowly Jesse raised her eyes to Anna, who was wearing a thunderous expression. It hadn't taken her long to work out who was responsible for this betrayal. As much as she was angry to see her face plastered all over a newspaper, she was even angrier about the impact this would have on Gina.

That bastard had timed it just right, it had hit the news on the day Anna flew back. They would have to tell Gina and she had already been through so much.

'Anna, how do we handle this? If what we think is true, how is Gina going to cope?'

Anna said she needed time to think, but they both accepted that once they landed, they were going to have to make a very difficult phone call to their friend in Antigua. The conversation was not going to be an easy one.

As things turned out they had their own problems awaiting them. As they walked into Arrivals, they were unprepared for the crush of photographers waiting to pounce on them. The cacophony of sound as they shouted out their names was deafening, and camera flashes blinded them as they tried to get through the crush. Anna was so mad that for a moment she had forgotten that Piers was somewhere in this circus.

'Dan really has done a job on us. He must have tipped them off about us flying in today.'

Suddenly Piers appeared out of nowhere, put his arm around both women and pushed the crowds aside as he ushered them to the nearest exit. Excitedly photographers ran after them. Piers had seen the headlines when he arrived at the airport, saw the posse of tabloid media camped out in arrivals and realised his summit talk was going to have to wait. The pair allowed him to take control as he summoned up all his PR swagger to shout for a path to be cleared as he made it to the exit, dragging his two freaked out companions in his wake. They ran to his car and minutes later, still in a daze, they found themselves hunched down in the back seat whizzing toward London.

They pulled into the first service station they came across and sat sipping bland coffee trying to get their heads around what had just happened.

'I am Piers by the way in case you hadn't already guessed.' He put out his hand and put it on Jesse's arm in a gesture of support; she was still visibly shaking. Anna had barely had time to look at him. Now she took in his kind face, his strong physique and felt an overwhelming feeling of gratitude.

He had been there when they needed rescuing and their talk would have to wait. Anna felt strangely shy as she told him how grateful they were.

'Imagine if you hadn't come to the airport, they would have eaten us alive!'

Piers allowed his eyes to meet Anna's and he smiled at her.

'I am just happy that I could help you both. By the way Anna you look great. I love the new look, it suits you.'

He began to relax a little as having his meeting ambushed by the airport fiasco seemed to have broken the ice. 'I am so sorry Anna this is not the way I had hoped things would go. I know you must be angry and upset about all this so I will understand if you are not in the mood to talk. But I can at least try to make sure that you both get where you need to go.'

Jesse suggested he drop her off at home. 'I hope that's OK, but I think I should leave you to it.'

Piers said he was more than happy to take Jesse anywhere she wished.

'If it's OK with you I would like to head to my shop first, there are a few things I need to check.' She intended to see Milly too. There were a few questions she needed to ask about the Sam situation, and she hoped she could manage that before her jet lag kicked in.

Piers then turned to Anna and asked her where she would like to be dropped off. His heart was hammering in his chest, afraid that she would want to get rid of him as soon as she could. 'Do you know something Piers? Right now I have nowhere I need to go. I suspect that my place is currently under siege. So, if you still want that talk and you can think of somewhere a bit more private than the airport coffee shop, then I would be happy to go anywhere.'

His heart did a leap and he smiled at her.

'Strangely, I do have somewhere in mind, though it's a bit of a long drive. Is that OK?'

'Right now, Piers a bit of a drive sounds like heaven.'

Before they dropped Jesse at her shop, they agreed she would be the one to place the call to Gina. Anna couldn't imagine the fallout from the bomb that was about to be thrown into Gina's life out there. Bloody men!

Jesse said that she would let her know how things went later, though she was not looking forward to making the call. Hugging Anna very tight, she skipped out of the car at the top of the main road. She fixed her friend with a look that she hoped conveyed her wish that things could work out for them. Then she turned the corner to find Sam sitting forlornly on the doorstep of her shop. She had to stop herself from letting out a huge yelp.

'Welcome home Jesse! Wow I hoped today might be the day. I checked Arrivals and saw your flight got in this morning.'

As she struggled to cope with yet another unexpected turn of events, Sam jumped up and took her case. He took the keys out of her hand before guiding her through the door as if it was the most natural thing in the world for him to do.

'So, how long have you been sitting on my step?'

'Four or five days give or take. Milly wasn't too specific, but I knew you were due back sometime this week ... I just gambled you would come to the shop as soon as you could.'

'But what if I hadn't come back to the shop?'

'Then I would have stayed here until you did. You must be tired. I have some milk with me I brought it just in case, because I knew you would be gasping for a cuppa. Whenever I come back home from abroad it's the first thing I look forward to.'

Her head completely scrambled, Jesse watched as he filled the kettle and presented her with a cup of PG Tips. It felt as if she was having an out of body experience, but it was not altogether an unpleasant one.

GINA

GINA FOUND IT STRANGE to see strangers sunning themselves on the terrace of the villa where she and the girls had made their home for the past few weeks. She had walked past earlier that day and seen a large group of Americans moving in. She missed the girls already and Dan remarked how quiet and withdrawn she had been since they had left the day before. 'Let's go to the pizza place tonight, it will cheer you up.'

But Gina said she was happy to stay in; she had some preparation to do for the next day's charter and she didn't want a late night. She also couldn't afford even a tiny hangover as they had two honeymoon couples booked in the next day. They had planned a full day of activities, snorkelling, and sunbathing around Green Island. During the cruise she was serving canapés, then a swanky champagne lunch. The day was ending at sunset with cocktails and even more fancy snacks. Gina had shopped and cooked and filled the fridge. She was now making lots of ice to keep everything chilled during the voyage. She was nervous but excited because this was, by far the most adventurous and lucrative charter they had taken on. Dan had seemed more upbeat after the girls left for England, but he was still aloof at times. Though Gina tried to find out what was bothering him he refused to be drawn. As she prepared for an early night, her mobile started ringing. Noting that it was Jesse calling, she grabbed the phone and smiled, excited to be talking to her friend again.

'Hi Jesse, hey I miss you guys so much ...'.

She stopped mid-sentence, vaguely registering that Dan had walked into the bedroom as she took the call. She sat in stunned silence as her friend in London filled her in on the tabloid article and the reception awaiting her and Anna when they arrived at Gatwick airport. She looked up at Dan and his expression told her all she needed to know. She said a hurried goodbye to Jesse, promising to call back later and fixed the man she thought she had loved with the coldest glare she could muster. Her heart was hammering and she felt sick. 'What the hell have you done Dan?' He looked shaken and came towards her.

'I don't know what to say to you. Honestly Gina I never meant to hurt you or your girls but ...'.

She exploded with anger and rushed at him, pushing him to the door.

'You don't know what to say? You total shit. How about "I am sorry for being such a fucking moron, for shopping your friends for a few bucks?" How can you stand there and say nothing? You have betrayed me, betrayed all of us, and for what? You know how close we are, how bad it has been for Anna, why would you do such a terrible thing?'

He looked at her, still not saying a word.

'For Christ's sake, say something. Don't just stand there, talk to me. Aren't you even going to try to explain why you would throw everything we have away for what? Money? Getting a kick from putting one over on Anna? I know there has been some tension between you in the past, but she was the one who encouraged me to trust you. Don't you realise how much she was in your corner? How she fought to get all the girls on our side, even though she knew your track record? She came to admire you and said that what she loved and envied most, was how special you made me feel. How could you betray us all?'

She couldn't help the tears that streamed down her face and she stuck her hand out and gestured to him to keep away.

'Was any of this real? Did you even mean for us to be together? Was it some sort of sick game, to see if you could get me to trust you, have a little fling and then what?'

Gina ran out of words and pushing past Dan she went out to the deck and sat on the rocking chair. She felt completely numb as she looked out over the bay. Suddenly she was that powerless woman back at home who had felt stupid and worthless. She thought she knew this man, she had fallen for him and trusted him. Now all she saw was a liar who had traded her trust for a cheap headline story in a lowly tabloid. Worst of all, he had betrayed the girls whom she had come to love and trust. There was no way back from this. A fire started in her soul and she felt a flicker of empowerment ignite deep within her. She was not the girl who had arrived here! She was strong and she knew what she had to do.

She walked back into the villa and pulled out her case which only days ago, they had stowed in one of the guest room closets. Dan came into the room, flailing his arms around and pleading with her to stop what she was doing.

'Where are you going? Look this is not worth us breaking up over. It's nothing. It's just a stupid spread, a few innocent pictures of Anna and you guys looking great incidentally. There was nothing negative said about any of you, I didn't bad mouth Anna, Jesse, anyone! I do love you and I do want us to be together, all of that is true. It's just I was offered a huge amount of money for those photographs and I didn't think it would matter.'

His words only fuelled her growing anger.

'What? Are you crazy? Don't you see? It matters to me and to them. Have you lived so long in the gutter that you don't care about what you do to other people, how you hurt them? Mister, you got it so wrong this time, you told me you had changed. You said you wanted to be better, but the truth is you don't know how to be different, do you?'

For the first time she really looked at Dan and saw him for what he was. Yes, he was a good-looking guy with a six pack, he had all the right words and yes, he had made love to her like no other man ever had. But he was shallow and he had no scruples or values – at least not where she and her friends were concerned.

'It was a no brainer Gina. They wanted a few good shots and they promised it was just surface stuff, nothing cruel.'

'You just don't get it Dan do you? If you really care about someone you would never do what you have done, no matter how much money you got paid. Right now, I feel dumb not to have seen through you. I was warned, but you wormed your way into my life and got the girls to think the world of you. You must have known I would find out what you have done.'

His reply was a shrug. 'I thought that yeah, you'd be mad. But I figured we could get past that. It doesn't mean anything.'

'Well, it means something to me and if you can't see that, I am wasting my time here. If I have learned anything on this trip is that I won't settle for less than I deserve.'

It had not taken her long to throw her few belongings into her small case and she pushed past him.

'Where are you going? Don't be so bloody dramatic, we have a big day tomorrow!'

She looked back one final time and took in the sight of him. He was suddenly not looking so self-assured. Her heart ached, but it was bruised, not broken, she knew she was worth more than this.

'Tomorrow is your problem because I am done here.'

She walked the long route around the marina and kept replaying in her head what had just happened. She hadn't known where she was going until she found herself standing outside Glen's villa. She rang his doorbell with tears coursing down her cheeks. He answered the door and taking in the sight of this poor girl, so upset and broken, he scooped her up and pulled her inside. 'Oh, Honey, what's happened?'

'I didn't know where else to go Glen. It's all gone so wrong. Please don't be too kind to me as it will push me over the edge.' He walked with her out onto the terrace, settled her onto one of the loungers and wrapped her in a soft warm blanket as she was shivering.

'Let's grab a couple of brandies and then you must tell me what's gone on. We have all night and, young lady, you are staying here with me until we sort this out.'

He had a sinking feeling that Dan was at the root cause of her pain. He liked the guy but knew that in the past he could be difficult to handle. Glen had hoped that Gina was the woman who could take him on and settle him down. Dan had seemed so smitten with her and had taken so much trouble to win the other girls over. Glen had decided he was an OK guy too. How wrong had he been? Dan was a fool. A few hours later and feeling slightly woozy from a combination of brandy and the most amazing French champagne (he said champagne was meant to be drunk when things went wrong as well as for celebrations), Gina agreed that it was time to go to sleep. In her drunken state she had tried to insist on sleeping on the terrace because she said she wanted to hear the sea and look at the stars, but he was having none of it.

'I have made up the guest suite. You will be safe here and when you feel ready, we will work out a game plan. You are not on your own, just remember that. Would it help if I went to talk to him, see if we can't work this thing out?' Gina shook her head sadly. 'What's the point? He can't take back what he did. He doesn't even seem that sorry.'

Glen sat beside her and promised to help her get through this.

'You girls are like family; you all mean the world to me. It's no trouble, stay as long as you need to. It's good to have company. I haven't been that great since Claire left, I miss her so much 'Gina let him envelope her in a fatherly hug and she felt herself relax a little.

'Now try to get some sleep and I will call Jesse to tell her you are here with me. I know they will be worried.'

Gina sank into the bed and fell into a heavy slumber, but it was filled with dreams of Dan. He had been too good to be true. It had all seemed like a dream. When she woke up, while her heart ached as she thought of what had happened, it was time to remind herself that she had been through much worse.

THREE YEARS LATER

THE FAR SIDE OF Jolly Beach had never looked more beautiful and it was the perfect backdrop for the beachside wedding that was about to happen. A wooden weather-beaten bower had been threaded with white calico together with pale pink and soft green foliage. A makeshift aisle had been fashioned out of stones and conch shells gathered from the beach and there was a trail of hurricane lanterns which later would be lit to guide the guests to the reception. The wedding was being held on the beach just outside the terrace, where all day, caterers had been busy creating the ultimate wedding celebration.

Jesse had arrived the day before full of vigour and excitement albeit grumbling that her entire luggage (apart from a swimsuit and her wedding outfit) had consisted of paraphernalia for the wedding and the subsequent reception.

Once the bower was assembled, she arrived on the beach with a crate full of pastel chiffon, ribbons and mounds of pink bougainvillea and fresh trailing greenery which was as near to ivy she could find locally.

She had wrapped hundreds of tiny white fairy lights on tall bleached out wooden poles, so, that as darkness fell, they would light the way for guests and make the setting look magical.

She had never organised a wedding that started at sunset, but she was determined that this one was going to be beautiful and the talk of Jolly Harbour for years to come.

She had flown over with Anna and they were both excited to be coming back. All their lives had changed considerably in the last few years, but today was about their friend Claire, and Glen.

Against the odds they were finally getting their fairy-tale ending.

The pair had parked their relationship for many months, finding it hard to keep in contact as it was just too painful.

Glen had kept his part of the bargain by leaving her be and simply waited in the wings in the hope that one day she would call.

Claire did as she said she would. She had discovered her true self, forgave herself for the mistakes she had made and moved forward to a new happier life. She had also become the active, assertive mum she had always wanted to be.

Claire was now outgoing, fun, and to everyone's surprise – including her own – she had retrained as a personal trainer.

She would never be skinny, but she embraced her womanly curves. Her love of exercise had been ignited in Antigua. When she got home, she discovered barre: a mix of small movement and high intensity, elongating muscle sculpting which resulted in her having the most toned, healthy body she had ever possessed. She had also launched her own niche business empowering women who, like her, had lacked self-confidence. She helped them find themselves by discovering that beauty and strength lies within.

She was mentally much stronger and had become the very best version of herself. It was who she had always aspired to be. Her self-confidence and self-esteem were at an all-time high.

After a year apart, she and Glen had begun emailing and sending the odd text to one another. She was happy to just touch base but as the weeks went by, he asked if he could fly over to see her for a pre-Christmas break.

'No strings I promise it would just be good to see you.'

The meeting proved to be a watershed.

Glen and Harriet bonded in a way Claire never expected and Claire realised why she had let him into her life after that chance meeting.

As he prepared to back to his home in the States, Glen asked her to think about giving him another chance.

'I know you don't need anyone, but I want you in my life on whatever terms you say.'

The deal was a simple one. They wouldn't do anything formal; she would not wear his ring, but they would still be a couple, albeit an unconventional one. She and Harriet would fly out during the school holidays; Glen would fly to see her regularly in the months in between and they would see how it all worked out.

Three years down the line it was Harriet who had made the call that they live in Antigua.

She loved it there, had made friends with lots of children in the resort and was more than happy to enrol in the local school in St John.

Claire had agreed for Glen to buy a modest villa on South Finger for her parents (and her girlfriends) to stay as and when they could. He was also supportive of her plan to open her own barre studio just outside Valley Church.

So, almost three years to the day since they had met, Gina, Anna and Jesse were staying at Glen's villa and getting ready to watch Claire walk down a powdery white aisle.

As dusk began to fall, they made their way to the shoreline and stood holding hands as they watched Claire solemnly walk from Glen's terrace to the bridal bower.

She was a vision in an off-the-shoulder ivory silk dress and she carried a tiny hand tied bunch of pale pink avranche roses which Jesse had somehow smuggled over in refrigerated carton secreted in her case. Her long glossy hair was threaded with silvery clips adorned with fresh flowers.

An excited Harriet, dressed in the palest aqua chiffon bridesmaid's dress scattered petals as her mother walked down the aisle on the arm of her grandfather.

Handsome in a navy linen suit and crisp white collarless shirt, Glen stood at the shoreline. His eyes never left his new bride as she walked barefoot towards him.

The three friends watched with their eyes glistening.

They each had their own stories to tell as the last three years had brought many changes for all of them. But for now, all eyes were on the bride.

Anna finally broke the spell:

'Who could have ever predicted this when we arrived here back then? Four strangers, so anxious and uncertain?' Gina and Jesse nodded just as the bride prepared to throw her bouquet, and it looked as though it was coming their way.

'Who's next?' she shouted to them. Anna laughed and made a leap. She had a secret to tell them later and catching the bouquet might be the perfect way to begin that conversation. Within seconds they were laughing and leaping in the air to join her.

Out in the bay an impressive motor cruiser had moored up. The captain's attention focused on the proceedings on the beach. He had a date with destiny a bit later and he hoped that his friend Glen would do as he promised and pave the way. Time would tell. He had worked hard on himself to become the man the woman he still loved needed him to be. As the lights on the beach twinkled and guests wandered past the lit lanterns to the reception, he decided the time had come to find out.

He wore an expensive linen suit but his flip flops and tousled hair were a nod to his past life, to the man he used to be. 'Well, here I go' he thought as he jumped into the boat's tender and headed for the beach.

ABOUT THE AUTHOR

JILLY CHADWICK is a former Fleet Street journalist who relocated from London to her Channel Island home where she now lives in a house on the coast.

She launched and edited lifestyle magazines before leaving the corporate world to work for a local mental health charity.

During lockdown she returned to her love of writing and her debut novel is in honour of all women who have ever come back from the brink of heartache and hardship to find the warrior within.

Photo: John de Garis

ACKNOWLEDGEMENTS

So many people have inspired me to put myself out there and write my debut novel. I thought the hard part would be the actual writing, but it turns out that was the easy bit. The road to fine tuning your book and getting it to print is by far the biggest challenge.

So, I owe a huge debt of gratitude to Ali Good, Anna McInnes and Becky Gregson who all kindly ploughed their way through Travelling Light and pushed me onwards to print!

Steve Foote at Blue Ormer Publishing has also been a complete hero and despite TL not being his usual genre he threw himself whole heartedly into supporting me and helping me negotiate the scary maze of the publishing world. Without his enthusiasm and patience, I would never have made it to the finish line.

Finally, thank you to all the inspirational women I have met along the way who have helped me to explore the lives of my characters who over the years have become very real to me. My first book proved to be a four-year marathon, my second is turning out to be a real sprint, so watch this space.

COMING SOON ...

SING OUT!

by Jilly Chadwick

When the chips are down and you feel alone ... the solution is a simple one, join a choir!

In her second novel, Jilly explores the highs and lows of life lived within a community choir in South London.

Each week a diverse group of men and women head into a church hall, and for two hours they leave their problems at the door.

Some find friendship and support, a few discover quite unlikely romances, but they all share a love of singing, and feel a part of something special, lacking in life outside the choir.

While Jilly runs a choir in her Channel Island home, any resemblance to anyone in the soprano, alto, tenor or bass sections are entirely coincidental.

Due out early 2022

**For more details subscribe to the
Blue Ormer Mailing List at
www.blueormer.co.uk**